TILLY TENNANT

Once Upon A Winter

Bookouture

Published by Bookouture in 2020

An imprint of Storyfire Ltd.
Carmelite House
50 Victoria Embankment
London EC4Y 0DZ

www.bookouture.com

First published by The Soho Agency in 2016

ISBN: 978-1-80019-211-9
eBook ISBN: 978-1-80019-210-2

Part One:
The Accidental Guest

The milkmaid had a bucket missing from her yoke, part of her little nose chipped off and dirt ground into a dress that could have once been blue but was now so filthy it was anyone's guess. It made a pretty dismal sight. Hannah put it on the coffee table and stared at it.

'Well,' Gina said, 'she's given us some corkers over the years but this one really takes the biscuit.'

'This one takes the whole tin,' Hannah said.

'It takes the McVities factory,' Jess put in. She started to giggle, and seconds later, all three were in fits of laughter.

'Good old Aunt Dot,' Hannah said, wiping tears away. 'It's good to know she's still as nutty as ever.'

'Tight as a fish's arse. I think she only pretends to be nutty so she can get away with giving everyone shit.' Jess rattled the box containing her own gift from the great-aunt in question doubtfully. 'It'd be better if she just came clean and stopped giving us stuff. We'll only have to get rid of this crap on Boxing Day.'

'Awww, where's your Christmas spirit, niece of mine?' Hannah picked up the little ornament and grinned at it. There was a faint ping from the kitchen. 'Well, the unpredictable thrill of opening Aunt Dot's presents will have to wait for the time being while I go and pull the turkey out of the oven.' She got up from her knees and brushed her trousers down. 'Bloody pine needles. They get everywhere.'

'I told you to get a Scot's pine, they're far better,' Gina said.

'I told you to get a Scot's pine,' Hannah mouthed, pulling her face into a parody of her sister's.

'Cheeky cow,' Gina laughed. 'Just remember who's peeling your sprouts for you.'

'Won't you be eating the sprouts?'

'Yeah. But that's not the point. Besides, I'm only eating them because you said I had to.'

'Maybe I like pine needles all over my floor,' Hannah said.

'I don't,' Jess said as she pulled one from the sole of her woolly sock.

'Come on…' Hannah said, 'off your bums, you two. I'm not slaving in that kitchen on my own.'

Gina gave an exaggerated pout. 'When you invited us to dinner, I didn't expect to have to cook it as well as eat it.'

'Are you saying that eating my Christmas dinner will be a chore?'

'Depends what you do with it. I still have flashbacks from Christmas 2010.'

'Watch it,' Hannah laughed. 'You'll be down the Spar getting yourself a frozen dinner for one if you don't stop with the insults.'

Gina threw her daughter a huge grin as they followed Hannah into the kitchen. Like the rest of the house, it had been given an extreme Christmas makeover so that red candles, wax fruit, tinsel and fairy lights adorned every surface not already occupied by food.

'You haven't eaten the Christmas Day chocolate,' Jess said, opening the last door of the advent calendar and popping the contents into her mouth with a smirk.

Hannah plopped her hands on her hips. 'How lucky I have my niece to help me out, eh? Whatever would I do without you?'

'I seem to recall that's a trick you would have played when we were kids.' Gina gave Hannah a pointed look.

'Mum would never buy us advent calendars when we were kids,' Hannah fired back, 'because of the year you opened all the windows on the first of December and ate the lot.'

'That was you!' Gina squeaked.

'I think you'll find it was you,' Hannah replied, folding her arms with a defiant look.

Jess giggled. 'Now I know where I get the chocoholic gene from. It's totally your fault and when I get an arse the size of Greater Manchester I'll know where to point the finger of blame.'

'That day's a long way off,' Hannah said, smiling at Jess. 'God, what I wouldn't give to be seventeen again with your figure.'

'I don't think you look so bad,' Jess said. 'In fact, all my mates say you're dead pretty.'

'Thanks.' Hannah beamed, smoothing an unconscious hand over her chestnut hair. 'That's so lovely.'

'For an old lady,' Jess added with a cheeky grin.

'Oi!' Gina cut in. 'If she's old what does that make me?'

'I don't know but there's some archaeologist applying for funding right now to excavate the wrinkles around your eyes.'

'Cheek!' Gina grabbed the nearest tea towel and hurled it at Jess, who was now laughing raucously. 'You're not too old for a smacked bottom!'

Jess pulled the tea towel from her face. 'I'm not too old to call Childline either.'

Hannah took the towel from Jess and put it to one side. 'Come on, we'll never get any dinner at this rate.'

'You're not seriously putting us to work now?' Gina asked.

'Of course. You want to eat, don't you?'

'What about my snowball? You can't cook Christmas dinner without a snowball on the go.'

'Ugh!' Jess grimaced. 'You two are the only people in the world who still drink those. The first time I mentioned that drink to my mates they thought I was mental; they'd never heard of a snowball, only the ones you chuck at each other; they had to google it! In fact, people should chuck these rather than drink them… the bin is the best place for them.'

'Yes, but it's tradition,' Gina replied in a slightly offended tone. 'We always cook Christmas dinner with a snowball… at least we used to before your dad.'

'I'd forgotten about that.' Hannah smiled. 'It's actually been years since we did dinner together like this. It's nice, isn't it, to get a chance to do it again.'

'Yeah…' Jess sneered. 'It's just a shame we had to find out my dad was a wanker before we got the excuse to relive it.'

Gina pulled her daughter into a brief hug and kissed her forehead. 'I don't want to dwell on bad stuff like that today. I want us to have fun and forget all the awful things that have happened this year, just for one day. So let's talk about something else, eh?'

'Or how about we don't talk at all?' Hannah skipped over to a CD player perched on a shelf and pressed play. The kitchen was suddenly filled with Abba's *Does Your Mother Know?* Hannah whacked up the volume and began to sing along at the top of her voice. Dancing her way to the fridge, she pulled out a net full of sprouts and tossed them to Gina, who caught them neatly as she joined in the song. Hannah found some carrots next, and threw the bag to Jess, who simply rolled her eyes and pulled a paring knife from the drawer. Then Hannah sashayed to the oven. As she opened the door, the glorious aroma of cooked turkey rose into the air. She smiled to herself as she gave it one last baste and put it back in. Who needs men, she thought as she looked around at the two best companions she could wish for on Christmas Day.

'You surely don't want me to peel all these sprouts?' Gina asked, frowning at the net. 'I'll be here until New Year.'

'Not to mention the pong in here if we eat them all,' Jess said. 'Mum farts for England when she eats green stuff.'

'Oi!' Gina squeaked.

Hannah laughed. 'I'd better keep some back then.'

'Let's not bother at all,' Jess suggested.

'No,' Hannah insisted. 'It's Christmas and we have to have sprouts.'

Gina shook her head wryly as she tipped the net and emptied it onto the worktop.

'Looks like the snow has started again,' Hannah added as her gaze was drawn to the window, where flakes floated like goose down from a white sky, collecting in the cracks and crevices of the frame. 'It's nice to have a bit, but if this carries on we'll be snowed in.'

'Fine by me,' Gina said. 'I can't think of a better place to be stuck.'

'It's a good thing you decided to stay,' Hannah said with a knowing smile. 'Though I'd have made up the spare room even if you said you weren't.'

'You know me so well.'

'I know what you'll be like when we open the Christmas champagne. Lightweight.'

'I am not! It's all those bubbles. Everyone knows bubbly booze makes you drunk quicker.'

'I'd better make your snowball non-alcoholic then, or we'll never get any dinner cooked.'

'I think you'll find the stuff that makes it a snowball is alcoholic, and if you leave that out I'm just drinking pop.'

Hannah reached into a cupboard. Producing a bottle of radioactive looking yellow liquid, she blew the dust from the lid and opened it, sniffing at the contents. 'How many years can you keep advocaat before it goes off?'

'I don't know,' Gina said, eyeing the bottle doubtfully. 'Are you actually going to drink that?'

'It'll be fine…' Hannah held up two fingers and crossed them with a grin. 'I think A&E is keeping usual hours today, and I'll keep my phone close as we drink it.'

'Ugh!' Jess screwed up her nose. 'Don't think for a minute that I'm having one.'

'Don't be such a girl,' Hannah said.

'It might have escaped your notice but I *am* a girl,' Jess said.

Hannah got three tall glasses out of the cupboard and poured a measure of advocaat into each one. Jess leaned against the kitchen counter mock-pouting at them, but then suddenly stood tall, her face serious.

'What was that?'

Hannah licked a stray drop of advocaat from her finger. 'What?

'Turn the music down a sec,' Jess said.

Hannah went over to the CD player and did as Jess asked. They paused for a moment. 'There… nothing. Happy now?'

'I heard a knock, I'm sure I did. '

'I didn't hear anything.' Hannah looked at Gina.

'Me neither,' Gina said.

'There it is again!' Jess said. There was no mistaking it this time, though it was less of a knock this time and more of a dull thud that echoed through the house. All three stood in silence.

'You're not expecting anyone, are you, Han?' Gina asked after a moment.

Hannah shook her head. 'Brian and Cynthia from the next house are away in Greece for Christmas, so it can't be them.'

'Brian and Cynthia… aren't they the old duffers who are always coming to check on you because they think you're a brothel madam?' Jess asked, grinning at Hannah.

Hannah's mouth fell open. 'I've never said that!'

'You'd be surprised what I hear you tell my mum when you think I'm not listening.'

'Well, I'm sure they're actually just concerned about a woman living alone, which is quite sweet really. I suppose we are quite cut off from town here.'

'I know, I don't know how you live here; it's creepy,' Jess said.

'Never mind that,' Gina cut in, 'I think we might have forgotten that there seems to be someone at the door.'

'It was probably a pigeon on the roof or something,' Hannah said, though she didn't look very convinced. Even as she spoke, another knock sounded through the house.

'Okay, *that* was the front door,' Jess said.

Gina frowned. 'Who on earth would turn up unannounced on Christmas Day?'

'Carol singers?' suggested Jess helpfully.

'They wouldn't make much money out here,' Hannah replied, 'there's only a handful of houses along this stretch and then nothing for miles.'

'Better hope it's not an axe-wielding maniac then,' Jess said. 'Bags I don't open the front door.'

'Bags none of us opens the door,' said Gina, who, despite being much older, often slipped easily into her daughter's mode of speech, much to Jess's chagrin.

Hannah looked towards the window. 'We can't leave them out there in the snow.'

'Why not? They're either scrounging or up to no good. Either way they can try their luck with some other mug.'

'Have you *seen* the snow?' Hannah gestured to the window.

'All the more reason not to answer the door. Nobody with good intent would be out there. Let's stay quiet in here and they'll bugger off in a minute.'

Hannah rolled her eyes. 'You're all heart, you.'

'I'm sensible. One of us has to be.'

'I'm not the one who married a complete dick.'

'Ouch! Below the belt, Han.'

'You're right, sorry. Look, I'm going to see who it is. They might need some help.'

'Hannah, no…' Gina put a hand on her arm. 'Please…'

Hannah paused. And then she let out a sigh of defeat. 'Okay. But I'm not happy about it.'

'Seriously, you can't be too careful.'

They waited. A few moments passed and all was quiet.

'Do you think they've gone?' Gina whispered.

'Why are you whispering?' Jess asked. 'It's not like they can hear you through the walls.'

'You never know,' Gina began, but then a muffled voice called through the letterbox.

'Is anyone home? Please…'

'That's it!' Hannah grabbed a tea towel and wiped her hands. 'I'm going to see who it is.'

'It's a man!' Gina squeaked.

'And he sounds pretty desperate,' Hannah replied. 'What if he's in real trouble? Where's your milk of human kindness?'

'Gone off.' Jess arched an eyebrow at her mum.

'You'll be sorry if you open that door…' Gina said, ignoring Jess's jibe.

'Too bad.' Hannah marched out of the kitchen. Gina gave chase, with Jess bringing up the rear.

'This is crazy!' Gina hissed.

'Yup!' Hannah replied.

As they reached the front door, Gina reached to cover the lock with her hand. Hannah moved it firmly but gently away. 'I won't let him in,' she whispered. 'I just want to see if he's okay.'

'What if he comes in whether you let him in or not?' Gina whispered back. 'What if he forces his way past you? What if there're about twenty men with him?'

Hannah raised her eyebrows. 'You've been watching too many films. We're on the outskirts of Millrise, not Washington DC.'

'I'll sort him if he tries anything,' Jess interrupted. Hannah turned to see that, on the way through to the front door, she'd picked up one of the soapstone elephants Hannah had brought back from Goa and was wielding it with surprising menace for a teenage girl.

'Did you swipe that from my mantelpiece?' Hannah frowned.

'It'll knock him clean out if he tries anything.'

'The weight of that, you'll kill him! Please be careful with it.'

Jess went to the window and looked out. 'Not that I can see all of the porch from here, but he doesn't look as if he has evil henchmen with him.'

'Does he look dangerous?' Gina asked.

'If you think slumped against the porch wall looking as if he's going to pass out is dangerous, then yeah.'

'This is ridiculous!' Hannah turned the key and yanked the front door open. There was an involuntary gasp at the sight that greeted her. The man had a supporting hand clamped on the frame of the porch door, and he did look distressed. Blood ran from a nasty looking gash that stretched from beneath the thick black hair at his temple and down his forehead, and it was steadily soaking into his powder blue shirt. He was shivering and soaked through, dressed completely inappropriately for the desperate winter weather in well-cut jeans and moccasins that looked like slippers. One thing was for sure, they weren't suited to the four or five inches of snow that lay on the ground. There was no sign that he had a coat with him and no sign of a car that might belong to him parked anywhere nearby. In fact, he didn't appear to have anything with him but the clothes on his back. He looked up and gave a pained smile.

'I'm so sorry to disturb you, but I seem to be in a spot of bother.'

'Oh my God!' Hannah cried. 'Come in out of the snow! What happened?' She opened the door wider and gestured him inside. He stumbled, and she rushed to offer a supporting arm. Gina frowned at her and Hannah shot back a warning look as she led him to a chair.

'Thank you so much,' the man said, lowering his weight onto the seat and instantly looking better, as if the very act of standing up had been an incredible burden. 'I wonder if I could use your phone.'

'Where's yours?' Gina asked, eyeing him warily.

'Gina!' Hannah hissed.

Gina shrugged. 'Everyone's got one.'

'I don't know,' the man said. 'I suppose I must have had one but I don't have it now.'

'Have you been mugged?' Hannah asked him gently. 'Jess, run and put the kettle on, will you?' She turned to the man again as Jess handed her mother the stone elephant with a pointed look and a little mime to indicate that she should clobber him at the first sign of trouble. 'I bet you'd like a drink to warm you up, you look frozen to the bone,' Hannah continued.

'I… I don't know. I think it would be good, yeah.'

'How did you injure your head?' Hannah bent to take a closer look. 'It might need stitches.'

'I don't know,' the man said. It seemed as if the idea pained him more than just the physical injury. Hannah had the sudden, inexplicable feeling that he wasn't even trying to recall the event, like he didn't want to acknowledge it.

'We should call you an ambulance.' Gina looked to Hannah for agreement.

'They won't come out in this weather on Christmas Day for a cut on the head,' Hannah replied.

'Yes they will. Head injuries can be fatal.' Gina glanced at the man. 'Sorry… I didn't mean to freak you out.'

Hannah turned to the man again. 'Is there someone we can call for you? Anyone who can come and get you?'

He screwed up his eyes, as if reaching for a thought that wouldn't quite stick.

They were interrupted by Jess coming back with her mobile phone. She handed it to the man. 'Here,' she said. 'You can use mine.'

He took it from her, and then stared at it.

'Can't you remember the number?' Jess asked.

'I can't even remember who I'm supposed to be ringing,' he said in a dull voice.

'But you must have someone,' Hannah said gently. She gave him another swift appraisal. Apart from his injury, and the fact that he was massively ill-equipped to be wandering around in the snow, he definitely looked as if he had someone. If he didn't, then tramps were a lot more upmarket these days than they used to be. His clothes looked well made – the shirt sporting the little Ralph Lauren logo – his hair was expensively cut and he was well-built, like he was no stranger to the gym. Under different circumstances, he had dark eyes that would have sucked Hannah in like quicksand, the sort of eyes that had often been her undoing over the years. There was no way this man was some directionless hobo. He had a family, or at the very least a partner and a comfortable home somewhere – she was sure of it. 'Where do you live?' she added in an attempt to prompt him.

'I'm not sure.'

'You're not sure?' Gina asked, curiosity now getting the better of her fear and suspicion. The stone elephant that she had been holding in a defensive pose was now hanging at her side. 'Your accent is local.'

'Is it?' he asked, frowning.

Hannah threw a worried glance at her sister. 'Perhaps we'd better call that ambulance.'

'Could I trouble you for some cotton wool or tissue or something?' the man asked. 'I seem to be bleeding all over your sitting room.'

'That's alright, I don't use it very often,' Hannah said cheerfully. 'I'm usually in the little back room or in the kitchen; far cosier in this weather.' She turned to Jess. 'There's a first-aid kit in the bathroom cupboard. Not a lot of first aid in it, to be honest, but there will be some bandages and plasters. Would you pop and get it?'

Jess nodded and ran off.

'I'll call that ambulance,' Gina said, making her way towards the sitting room door. She seemed to have decided that the man was harmless after all, gesturing to Hannah as she did. 'Can I have a quiet word?'

'I'll be back in a second,' Hannah told the man. 'What's up?' she asked her sister as they left him.

'Do you think we ought to call the police too?'

'You're not still convinced he's dodgy are you?'

'No… not that. I think he's lost his memory and there might be a family out there going out of their mind with worry. At least if the police know he's here there's more of a chance they can reunite them.'

Hannah was thoughtful for a second. 'You're right. Ambulance first, police after. I'll go and talk to him some more first, make sure he has actually lost his memory. He could just be confused right now from his clunk on the head, but with a cup of tea and a warm up he might remember it all.'

'And that's another thing… why on earth would he be out in the middle of nowhere in a snowstorm on Christmas Day in just his slippers and a shirt? It's all very weird if you ask me. And he hasn't got a phone. Who goes out without their phone these days?'

'Me.' Hannah smiled.

'Apart from you and we all know you're a bit cuckoo,' Gina said.

'I think you'll find lots of people do. We don't all want to be contactable all the time.'

'Ask him if he has a wallet on him. He may have some ID in there.'

'Good idea,' Hannah agreed. 'You get the ambulance and I'll go and see what I can find out.'

Jess arrived with a green plastic box. 'This gets a lot of use,' she said wryly as she indicated the thick layer of dust.

'As there's just me living here, I try not to get injured if I can help it,' Hannah said. 'It's a bit awkward trying to tourniquet yourself.'

Jess thrust the box at her. 'Go to it, Florence. Go and patch up our random guest who you obviously fancy.'

'How on earth do you come to that conclusion?' Hannah asked, taking the box from her.

'Firstly, you haven't kicked the weirdo back out into the snow where he obviously belongs and secondly, you've been gooey-eyed ever since he arrived.'

'If gooey-eyed means I've been showing concern, then guilty as charged. He clearly has someone out there who's missing him. I only want to help him get back to them.'

'What about our dinner?' Jess said.

Hannah clapped a hand to her head. 'Shit! I forgot about that!'

Jess rolled her eyes. 'I'll go and get the turkey out and I'll turn the veggies off for a while.'

'Be careful!' Gina called after her.

'I'm not ten!' Jess shouted behind her.

'No, but you act like it sometimes,' Gina muttered.

'We'd better get back to our mystery man,' Hannah said. Wiping the dust from the first-aid box with the hem of her apron, she made her way back to the sitting room with Gina following. Hannah turned to her. 'I thought you were going to call the ambulance?'

'I am, just as soon as I check that he's not putting all this on and lying in wait for us with a huge axe.'

'I really don't think so. He's a bloody good actor if he is.'

The man hadn't moved. He looked as if he had spent the whole time staring into space, and he glanced up vaguely at the entrance of the two women.

'Are you feeling sick?' Hannah asked as she opened the box and produced a roll of bandage.

'No,' he replied.

'Dizzy? Like you want to go to sleep?'

'Not really.'

'How many fingers am I holding up?' Hannah asked.

'Three.'

'Why do people do that?' Gina asked.

'What?'

'The finger question.'

Hannah shrugged. 'I have no idea. I just know that you're supposed to ask.'

'Cortical blindness,' the man said.

Hannah and Gina both turned sharply to him.

'What did you say?' Hannah asked.

'Cortical blindness,' he repeated.

'What's that?' Hannah asked.

'The fingers…it's a rudimentary diagnostic test to assess whether someone is suffering from it.'

'How do you know that? Are you a doctor?'

He shrugged.

'You're not a doctor?' Gina asked.

He shrugged again. 'I don't know.'

'What's your name?' Hannah gave him a gauze pad and indicated that he should press it against his head wound.

'I don't know,' he replied simply. He didn't seem distressed about this, just vaguely irritated, as if he had left his umbrella on the bus.

'You don't have any ideas at all?'

'I'm afraid not.'

'Do you have a wallet or something in your pocket?' Gina asked. 'Anything that might have some ID in it?'

While Hannah wrapped a bandage around his head to hold the pad in place, the man felt in his trouser pockets. 'I don't seem to have,' he said apologetically.

'Not even a set of keys?' Gina pressed.

'Sorry…' he said. 'Nothing in my pockets at all.'

'Did you drive here?'

'I don't think so. I feel as if I've been walking for ages.'

Hannah tied a knot in the bandage and studied him thoughtfully. In different circumstances she would have burst out laughing at her nursing handiwork. The man now looked like a war casualty from a black and white film. She was quite sure the professionals would have far more sophisticated methods of treating his wound but hers would have to do for now. 'So you're out in the snow in quite a cut off area – at least, a good hour's walk from the nearest town – and you have no coat, no sensible shoes, no keys, no phone and no wallet. Don't you think that's odd to begin with, even if you didn't have this head injury?'

'I suppose it is,' he said.

'Oh!' Gina squeaked. 'Perhaps you were mugged and dumped out here to die!'

'He was mugged?' Hannah asked with a wry smile. 'So that means he must have been out in the snow in his slippers in the first place for a mugger to find him.'

'Maybe they broke into his house and dragged him out. Maybe they're holding the rest of the family hostage!'

At this, the man looked properly alarmed for the first time.

'I don't think you need to worry,' Hannah said, doing her best to reassure him and shooting her sister a warning look. 'It might happen to Liam Neeson or Tom Cruise, but those sorts of things usually only happen in films. I've never heard of it on Holly Way.'

'Holly Way?' the man asked. 'Is that where I am?'

'Yes. Does it ring a bell with you?' Hannah asked.

'I'm not sure… yes, maybe.'

'It could be because it's Christmas,' Gina said. 'Holly and mistletoe and all that.'

'Oh… probably,' the man said, the hope wiped from his expression again. 'It's Christmas, then?'

'Christmas Day. We did just say that,' Gina replied.

'So you did,' the man said quietly. 'Sorry.'

'Stop being sorry,' Hannah said. 'You're sure you don't have a clue about your name?'

'Tom!' Everyone turned to see that Jess had returned.

'Tom?' Gina asked. 'How do you know that?'

'I don't,' Jess said. 'But he looks like a Tom to me and we have to call him something.'

'He *is* here, you know,' Hannah said, frowning.

'Sorry, Tom,' Jess said with a sheepish grin.

The man smiled. It was a lot brighter than it had been. 'That's alright. I don't mind if you call me Tom.'

Hannah began to pack away the first-aid kit. 'I'll make you something to drink and my sister is going to call an ambulance to have a look at that head injury. I have some dry clothes you can borrow. I can't promise they'll be to your taste and they might not fit brilliantly but at least you'll be drier and warmer in them.'

Gina raised her eyebrows. 'You have men's clothes?'

'Jason left them behind.'

'And you didn't have a sacrificial bonfire with them?'

Hannah clicked the lid of the first-aid box back into place. 'He wasn't *that* bad.'

'Why did you kick him out then?'

Hannah glanced at the newly-christened Tom, and then back at her sister. 'I don't think this is the time,' she said. 'How about you go and see to that ambulance before…' Her sentence trailed off. They had no idea how bad this man's head injury was but it was bad enough to cause amnesia. The last thing she wanted was for him to start being seriously ill, fall into a coma, or worse. The sooner they got help the better.

'Okay.' Gina disappeared to make the call.

'You're cooking,' Tom said. 'I can smell turkey.'

'Christmas dinner,' Hannah replied.

'I've ruined it. I'm sorry about that.'

'No you haven't. We can make it Christmas tea, so it doesn't really matter. Unless you're hungry, of course, in which case we can eat now and you could join us.'

'I don't think I am hungry,' he said. 'But thank you for the offer.'

'Right… I'll get you that drink then. What would you like? I can do tea, hot chocolate, coffee? I even have green tea if you're that way inclined.'

'She means she has green tea if you're a crazy hippy lady,' Jess put in with a grin.

'Thank you,' Hannah said briskly.

'Green tea actually sounds good,' Tom said.

'Hmmmm,' Hannah said. 'So you remember that you like green tea?'

'I don't know. It just sounds good.'

'Jess…' Hannah asked, 'do you think you can look after Tom for a moment while I get those dry clothes and a cup of green tea?'

'No problem.' Jess reclaimed the stone elephant that her mum had discarded on the windowsill. Hannah was about to tell her she didn't need it but checked herself. She had a strong feeling that this man was genuine, but none of them really knew for sure. Perhaps it was a good idea not to let their guard down completely.

'I won't be a minute,' Hannah called as she hurried off.

After flicking the kettle on and being informed by Gina that the ambulance service were having problems with the snow but, given the details of Tom's injury, would be out as soon as possible, Hannah rushed upstairs to find some clothes.

In the spare bedroom, she opened the door of the wardrobe. In between layers of clothes that had long been out of style but she couldn't quite part with, were a handful of trousers and sweatshirts belonging to the man she *had* parted company with the previous year.

When Jason first left she had cried, despite the decision having been hers. It seemed like she was destined to remain alone, as failed relationship after failed relationship left her convinced that the man for her simply wasn't out there. Was she that difficult and awkward? Had she been that awful to live with? Did she have some dreadful social inadequacy that meant she couldn't communicate fully with the rest of the world? She didn't think so, but it seemed that every relationship was doomed to disaster. She didn't get out enough – at least not to the traditional places where women might meet men, like pubs and nightclubs and painting classes – and she wasn't one for internet dating. Somehow, the idea that a soulless computer programme could find your soulmate wasn't one that appealed, no matter how effective it might be. Hannah wanted to discover that person for herself.

So she had begun to travel. And then she had stopped seeing the travelling as a search for her soulmate, and had begun to see it as a search for herself, and the travelling itself had become her love. Gina had frowned and told Hannah that she was running away because she couldn't face the idea that she was incapable of keeping a relationship going. But when her own marriage had gone to the dogs, Hannah had kept the smug lectures at bay, and decided that she would simply be there for her sister. These days they were closer than ever, much closer than they'd been growing up. Perhaps there was something to be said for being single after all.

As she rifled through Jason's clothes, looking for something that might fit their strange Christmas guest, Hannah couldn't help but reflect on the reasons she still had these clothes at all. She had messaged Jason to tell him she was leaving them on the front lawn and he could pick them up or she'd burn them. But when she'd returned home that evening and found them where she'd left them, instead of starting the bonfire there and then, she had gathered them up and packed them away. Every so often she had passed the spare room and had the urge to go in and smell them. Then, as the months went by, and the pain of the split faded, so did his scent, until she could barely recognise him at all over the smell of moth balls and damp. For a while she had barely recognised herself; this last break up had shaken her life around more than she cared to admit. But it had also been a good thing, leading to her quitting her job and setting up a thriving online business designing book covers, business cards and promotional merchandise. She loved her life now more than ever. Perhaps that was why she had kept Jason's clothes – to remind her not to go back to where she'd been before. And perhaps now, the arrival of this stranger in need was a sign that she didn't need that prop anymore; either way, it didn't seem so hard to give them up now.

'Does this guy have sugar in his tea?' Gina called up the stairs, interrupting Hannah's musings.

'Why can't you ask him?' Hannah called back, gathering up the clothes she had chosen and letting the wardrobe door bang shut again.

'I don't know,' Gina said as Hannah made her way back downstairs. 'I just don't want to.'

'You're not still scared of him, are you?'

'I wasn't scared before, I just didn't know if we could trust him.'

'He's harmless; just confused.'

'Yeah, I know. You've got to admit it's all pretty weird though.'

'I suppose so. We're stuck with him now, though, at least until the ambulance gets here. Did you call the police?'

'The emergency operator said the ambulance guys could inform the police when they came to pick him up. Are we supposed to go in the ambulance with him?'

Hannah was thoughtful for a moment. 'I don't know,' she said. 'We hardly know him, but as he doesn't even know himself right now I suppose we're the closest he's got. I wouldn't like to be taken to hospital on my own if I didn't have a clue who I or anyone else was.'

'Me neither. I'd be terrified. It's funny though,' Gina added, 'he doesn't seem that fazed by it.'

'Maybe he's just so confused it hasn't really sunk in yet. And I guess if you can't remember what you've lost you can't be scared by it.'

The kettle shrilled its readiness and Hannah handed the bundle of clothes to Gina. 'Go and take those in to him and I'll make the tea,' she said.

'What about our dinner?' Gina asked.

'We'll have to have it for tea now.'

'But the telly… We can't eat while the best telly is on!'

Hannah frowned. 'Are we seriously having this conversation?'

'You know how much I love my Christmas Day *East Enders*.'

Hannah swung an arm towards the front sitting room. 'We've got our very own drama happening right in front of our noses. Think of it that way and maybe you'll get over missing it one year. Besides, you can watch it on catch-up.'

'It's not the same…' Gina mumbled as she took the clothes through. Hannah smiled to herself. It *was* like a mini-drama. A very attractive mini-drama, now that she thought about it. But they knew nothing about this man and it would be silly to think of him as anything but a poor unfortunate soul who had, by a random quirk of fate, ended up knocking at their door.

So her reaction was so strange and so powerful once he returned from the bathroom, where he had done his best to clean up and change his clothes, that it took Hannah completely by surprise. Her heart did a little skip – that same little skip it always did when she was about to fall for someone. He was wearing one of Jason's soft sweaters – a bottle green one that Hannah had always loved him in – and the sand-coloured chinos she had teamed it with actually fit Tom pretty well. He had been very pale when he first arrived, but now some colour had returned to his complexion and the green of Jason's sweater against his dark eyes and olive skin made him look startlingly handsome. Hannah shook herself as he sat back down on his chair and cupped the mug of hot tea gratefully in his hands.

'I can't thank you enough for your kindness,' he said. 'I'd probably be frozen half to death by now if I was still out in the snow.'

Wow. She hadn't really acknowledged it before, but he was eloquent too. Well spoken, good vocabulary, polite and courteous. She wondered what he did for a living. Was the recollection of cortical blindness a clue? Was he a doctor? He had a fairly local accent but she hadn't seen him around her neck of the woods before. She'd definitely have noticed him if she had.

'We still need to work out how you ended up wandering around in the snow,' Gina said.

'I think we've established that it will have to remain a mystery for now,' Hannah replied. 'As Tom can't remember.'

Gina looked at him. 'You can't remember *anything* at all about why you were out? What you were doing this morning? Nothing?'

Tom shook his head slowly. 'Honestly, I wish I could.'

'Try to think back,' Gina said. 'Try to concentrate on waking up this morning.'

'Gina…' Hannah warned. 'I don't think this is helping. It must be really stressful.'

'It's not,' Tom said. 'It's fine. I'll give it a go.'

Hannah and Gina exchanged looks as he closed his eyes and became silent. The crappy bandaging only added to the air of vulnerability about him that was all at once worrying and inappropriately sexy. As he sat and concentrated, Hannah found herself wondering what he would do if she kissed him now. *You've been on your own too long, Han*, she thought, and quickly shook the idea away.

They waited that way for a good minute, until Jess broke the silence. 'What are you all doing?' she asked.

Hannah whipped around and gave an indignant squeak. 'What are *you* doing? Is that my turkey you're eating?'

'I was starving and mum said we weren't having dinner for ages.'

'That didn't mean you could *steal* our dinner!'

'Chill, there's loads. And I'm not really stealing it if I was always going to be eating it in the first place, I'm just getting my share early.'

Hannah looked so genuinely appalled by Jess's crime against the Christmas dinner rules that Gina broke into a fit of giggles. 'That turkey *is* big,' she laughed. 'I think they might have got the labels mixed up in the shop. What you actually have out there is an emu.'

'You'd be moaning about my stinginess if there wasn't enough,' Hannah said in a defensive tone.

'There's enough for everyone on Holly Way out there.'

Tom cleared his throat politely. 'If you want to eat, please don't put it off on my account.'

'We're fine,' Hannah said, looking pointedly at Jess. 'At least most of us are.'

'What!' Jess cried. 'I'm growing!'

'I wonder if I'm supposed to be having Christmas dinner now,' Tom mused, and Hannah realised that he suddenly looked very melancholy.

'God, I'm so sorry. We're being really insensitive.'

'No, of course not. You've been kinder than I deserve.'

'What does that mean?' Gina asked sharply. 'Don't you deserve kindness? What have you done?'

Tom shrugged. He looked confused. 'I don't know… it's just something I said, it didn't mean anything… at least, I don't think it did.'

'Of course it didn't,' Hannah said. She patted his arm. It was a rather ineffectual thing to do but she couldn't think of any other way of soothing him. 'Did you manage to remember anything just now?' she asked.

'No.' He shook his head. 'And I really tried.'

'It's okay. When the ambulance gets here the paramedics may have some ideas about how to jog your memory for you.'

Tom nodded.

'They really ought to be here by now,' Gina said, going to the window to check.

'Give them time,' Hannah said. 'The snow will be holding things up. We're lucky we've got anyone coming out at all.'

'I suppose so.' Gina left the window and flopped into a chair. She glanced at Jess, who was licking her fingers. 'Can I have some turkey if Jess is?' she asked, looking at Hannah.

'Seriously it's like having a couple of kids,' Hannah said.

'Please…' Tom said. 'Make your dinner. You mustn't put your day on hold for me.'

'We can't just leave you alone,' Hannah replied doubtfully.

'Then… let me help,' he said. 'Until the ambulance comes, anyway. It's the least I can do.'

'Great idea,' Jess said.

'Tom helping doesn't get you out of doing anything,' Gina said, raising her eyebrows at her daughter.

'Bugger,' Jess grinned.

Hannah turned to Tom. 'Are you sure you're up to it?'

'I feel much better now I'm warmed up. Apart from my head being sore I feel completely fine.'

'I suppose it would be nice to eat soon. You could join us.'

'I'll probably be on my way to the hospital by the time everything is ready. But I can make myself useful until then.'

It was selfish and stupid, but Hannah was beginning to wish they hadn't called an ambulance. She was starting to like the idea of him staying for dinner. But then, she supposed that his family would rather like the idea of having him around at dinner too, whoever and wherever they were. Someone would be worried sick about him right now, and sending him to the hospital was the right thing to do, if only to help them find him as soon as possible. 'We'd appreciate the help,' Hannah smiled. 'I suppose it might do you good to be active, jog your memory a bit.'

'It can't do any harm,' Tom said. 'It would take my mind off things too.'

'Are you sure about that?' Gina asked. 'Aren't you better off resting?'

'I don't think I'm able to rest, even if I sit still and quiet for the rest of the day, my mind is still going round and round trying to piece things together. And as I'm not supposed to fall asleep it's probably better to be doing something.'

'I suppose it must be quite traumatic, the idea that you don't know who you are and where you belong,' Hannah said.

'It is. I keep imagining all sorts of disasters that I'm not there to avert and the pain my disappearance might be causing. It's Christmas Day and someone is missing me. I know I'd be beside myself if someone I cared about was missing like that.'

'Come on then,' Hannah said gently, 'if it helps to take your mind off things then we'd love your help in the kitchen.'

She led the way, Gina throwing her a doubtful look as she did so. Hannah tried to return it with one that was encouraging and confident, but that wasn't how she felt. She didn't really know what she felt, but her thoughts were in a strange kind of turmoil, the likes of which she'd never experienced before. Whatever her doubts about who this man was, whether they were doing the right things to keep him safe – whether they were doing the right things to keep *themselves* safe – there was an emotional pull towards him that she was now desperately trying to keep under control. Hannah didn't believe in love at first sight, but the confusion in her head felt like the start of something a lot like it. In the strangest of circumstances this man had been dropped into their lives, as if some higher power had brought them together, and Hannah felt like it meant something. But that would be stupid, wouldn't it? Who believed in fate and destiny? Not Hannah, whose life had been struggle after struggle to make it on her own, despite what fate or destiny, or whatever power ruled the universe, wanted for her.

'Wow… this is very festive,' Tom said with a smile as he stepped into Hannah's kitchen. 'I like your taste in décor too.'

Hannah beamed. It had taken a lot of work to get the room perfect, a project that had been ongoing, along with the rest of the house renovations, for the last five years. Jason had been very little help, disinterested, she supposed, because the house belonged to her alone. But independence was the way she liked it and she was not about to risk it all on anyone. As it turned out, she had made a wise decision where Jason was concerned. But the kitchen had been particularly troublesome, because the house had belonged to an old lady who hadn't modernised since the early seventies. Now it had a rustic country charm about it – handmade wooden units painted in a delicate sage green with butcher block worktops, shelves and a reclaimed dresser filled with an eclectic collection of pots and crockery collected from antique shops and flea markets and sometimes from her travels abroad – but it also featured the best of modern technology, including a sleek fridge and spot lighting. To Hannah, it was the showpiece of the house, and suited the feel of the place perfectly. It was a bright little suntrap too, so she often found herself forsaking her office upstairs to work at the kitchen table, especially on chilly days. Nothing made her happier than feeling the winter sun on her back, sitting in blissful silence with her laptop and a mug of sweet hot chocolate at hand. On those days, she couldn't imagine how she ever kept up with her hectic former life as a sales manager.

However, since Jess had been at work in the kitchen turning various things off and snaffling her own private turkey starter, the pride and joy that were Hannah's kitchen worktops now also displayed the strange, disorganised logic of your average teenager.

'Hmmm,' Gina said, looking at her daughter. 'I see you helped yourself to a bit more turkey than you were letting on.' She angled her head at the glistening roast, which now had a cavernous chunk missing from the left breast.

'I was hungry,' Jess pouted.

'It doesn't matter,' Hannah cut in, 'there's plenty. Enough for you, Tom, if you feel up to it. I could do you a turkey sandwich. You might not be able to eat for ages once you get to the accident and emergency department.'

'Turkey sandwich?' Gina said, 'He'll probably have his fill of them tomorrow.' As soon as she said it she looked as if she wished she could take it back.

'It's alright,' Tom said, clearly understanding Gina's discomfort. 'I don't know where I'll be tomorrow but I'm hopeful that this memory loss is only short term and I *will* be eating turkey sandwiches with my family like everyone else come Boxing Day. If I hold onto that thought and stay positive, that can only be a good thing for my emotional well-being, can't it?'

'Of course,' Hannah said. 'Would you like me to fix you something?'

'I'm sorry; it's kind of you but I really don't think I could eat right now. Why don't we concentrate on getting your lunch ready and, maybe, if I'm still here, I might feel like something then.'

'Where do you think the ambulance is?' Jess asked. 'They've been a long time. It's a good job he's not dying.'

'They'll probably concentrate on the actual life and death cases before they come to us,' Gina said. 'After all, they'll be on skeleton staff and it's turning into a blizzard out there.'

'They don't know he's not dying,' Jess said stubbornly.

Gina glanced at Tom with an apologetic shrug. 'I gave them all the details and they didn't seem overly worried.'

'Not even about the fact that he doesn't know who he is?' Jess returned.

'Apparently there can be lots of reasons people lose their memory and if he's not dizzy or throwing up or anything, then there shouldn't be an immediate danger. They said we could call them again if anything deteriorated.'

'Do you think I actually need an ambulance?' Tom asked. 'I would hate to be using a stretched service if I didn't have a medical need.' All three looked at him. 'I mean, I feel fine… apart from the obvious.'

'I'd say that's pretty big, though,' Gina said.

'It is, but not life threatening. I know how up against it the emergency services are. Maybe I can get myself to A&E later on.'

Hannah glanced at the window. 'Not in my little car, not in this.'

'No… I didn't mean you had to take me,' Tom said quickly, a slight blush rising to his cheeks. The sight of it made Hannah want to throw her arms around him.

'I know you didn't,' she said, 'but it's either us or the ambulance, I'm afraid, as you have no keys, no phone and no memory of who else to contact to take you. Can you even remember how to drive? Could you drive before?'

'Yes. At least I think I could. I'm pretty sure I could drive now if you asked me.'

'I don't think that's a good idea,' Gina said.

'Neither do I,' Hannah said. 'We wouldn't dream of sending you out alone into the snow in your condition.'

'Sounds like I'm pregnant,' Tom smiled. But then a shadow suddenly crossed his features and the smile disappeared. He stared into the distance, as if his mind was reaching for something. Hannah watched, and it was almost as if the thing he wanted to remember was more painful than forgetting it. The episode was fleeting, and then the darkness cleared from his expression and he was back again.

'Well…' Hannah began, feeling unsettled and uncertain after what she had just witnessed. 'If you want to, we can phone again for advice. They might be able to suggest some alternative.'

'They might just tell us to sort it ourselves.'

'But we'd have to get help somewhere,' Hannah replied.

Gina shrugged. 'I suppose they'd send the police.'

Hannah mused on that. She didn't like the idea, and she couldn't say why. Perhaps it was because it made it feel as if Tom, or whoever he was, had committed some kind of crime by being confused. He seemed like the sort of man who had never been in trouble, and sending him off to the police station on Christmas Day to sit with all the drunks and scum felt like a humiliation he didn't deserve, whatever the circumstances. The hospital was a much kinder option. And as Hannah had already made up her mind to go with him, even though she knew Gina would be angry about it, it was a kinder option for her too.

'We should wait for the ambulance,' Hannah said in a voice that suggested there would be no further discussion. 'So, let's get this dinner on while we have time.'

'I don't suppose you need me,' Jess said. 'There're so many of you in the kitchen now.'

'Yes, we do,' Gina said sternly. 'You still have sprouts to peel, remember?' She pulled Jess by the arm to the pile she had been working on earlier.

'I have no idea why we're forced to eat sprouts,' Jess said, wrinkling her nose. 'I mean, does anyone actually like them? Why celebrate the most important day of the year by making us eat the shittest vegetable there is? Nobody eats sprouts at any other time; that tells you a lot about how much people like them.'

'Sprouts can be good,' Tom said. 'You just have to know how to cook them.'

'And you do?' Jess asked.

'I lightly boil them, then fry them with butter, bacon lardons and pine nuts. They're delicious that way. But you can roast them with balsamic vinegar and honey too and they're just as good.'

'You remembered!' Hannah squeaked.

Tom was silent for a moment. And then a small smile appeared on his face. 'I did, didn't I?'

'Can you remember any more?'

'Recipes?'

'No, silly! About your life.'

'I don't know. I don't even know where the sprout thing came from. It just popped into my head. I don't know if I can cook or not.'

'It sounds like you can. And pretty well too.'

'But that might not be my memory. I might have read it somewhere and think it was part of my past.'

'Is it upsetting you?' Jess asked.

Gina gave her a warning look, and Hannah was about to speak when Tom beat her to it.

'It's okay,' he said. 'I'm not upset. I mean, I'm worried, of course, because I don't know what I've left behind. But there's something curiously liberating about the whole thing.'

'Really?' Hannah asked.

'Well, it's odd, but I feel more like myself right now than ever, even though I don't know what that is.'

Gina frowned as she bit into a carrot stick. 'That does sound odd.'

'I wish I could explain it better. Say I was a policeman, and in my everyday dealings with people I always remembered that I was a policeman and had to act in a way that was fitting to my station in life. Perhaps I wouldn't do and say some of the things that I'd want to, because I'd think that police officers weren't supposed to do and say those things.'

'Are you a policeman?' Jess asked.

'I don't think so.'

Jess seemed to breathe a small sigh of relief. Hannah made a note to herself to ask her about it later. She turned her attention back to Tom. 'So what you're saying is that if you don't remember what you are, you don't know how to act?'

'Yes. But that's good, because however I'm acting now is exactly who I *really* am. Do you see?'

'Sort of,' Hannah said thoughtfully. She wondered whether a bump on the head might be something to see about getting herself later. It might wipe away some emotional baggage of her own.

'Do you like Abba?' Gina asked, moving towards the CD player.

'Please say no,' Jess said, rolling her eyes.

'Abba?' Tom blinked at her. 'I have no idea.'

'Yeah,' Jess said, 'right answer. If I had to lose my memory, I'd wipe Abba from it too.'

'You have no taste,' Gina said, sticking her tongue out at Jess, who returned it with her own.

'I'm with Gina on this one,' Hannah said. 'One day you'll have your own Abba epiphany, and you'll wonder why you ever thought they were crap.' She glanced at Tom. 'However, I do think we ought to keep the place quiet for now.'

'Please don't on my account,' Tom said.

'It's best,' Hannah insisted. 'You've got a nasty head injury there and I don't know what a lot of loud music will do. At the very least I'm sure you'll end up with a banging headache.'

'You'd end up with that anyway,' Jess said.

'He would if you put your music on,' Gina fired back.

'Oi!' Jess huffed. 'It's a lot better than the crap you listen to!'

'At least my music has an actual melody.'

'People have to be woken from comas after listening to that middle of the road rubbish.'

'Okay, okay…' Hannah grinned. 'Maybe we should save the big music debate for another time. Right now we have cooking to do.'

Hannah took it upon herself to appoint tasks, which everyone – even Jess – cheerfully undertook. While the veg was being prepared she wrapped the turkey in foil and set about making fresh drinks for everyone. Bearing in mind some old advice she thought she knew about alcohol and head injuries, she made fruit juice cocktails for everyone, tactfully handing them around without saying anything to Tom lest she alarmed him.

'So… let me get this right…' Tom began as he took a break to sip his drink. 'You two are sisters?' He nodded at Gina and Hannah, 'And you're Gina's daughter?' he asked Jess.

'Got it,' Hannah said.

'Do you all live nearby?'

'I actually live just outside Birmingham,' Gina said. 'Though we're hoping to move back soon.'

'Oh. Don't you like it there?' Tom asked.

'We like it well enough. It just feels like the right time to come home.'

Tom nodded. 'Are you going to move close to your sister?'

'I ruddy hope not!' Hannah laughed.

'Thank you for that,' Gina grinned.

'We're only coming back because Mum found out that Dad was shagging his secretary,' Jess said.

'Jess!' Gina yelped. 'TMI!'

'Oh Mum, please do not say TMI again. Nobody's said that for about fifty years.'

'Shagging his secretary. Classy…' Tom said.

Gina smiled thinly. 'I know. He could have been a bit more creative.'

Tom turned to Hannah. 'And is there a Mr Hannah?'

She felt the blush rise to her cheeks. Damn it, why did she have to do that? He was making polite conversation, not asking her to go to bed. Stupid brain. The problem was that she was beginning to think she'd rather like it if he asked her to bed. What the hell was wrong with her? Hadn't she already learned her lessons about men a thousand times over? 'No Mr Hannah,' she replied, trying desperately to think about sprouts and carrots and not forgetting to put the bins out after Boxing Day instead of Tom's dark eyes now regarding her quizzically, and his full lips, and the dimple in his chin that was really only noticeable when he smiled. 'Not now.'

'Not the secretary?' he asked, a trace of humour in his expression.

'Fitness trainer,' Hannah said.

Tom's eyes became wide. 'Seriously? Oh God, I am so sorry! What an insensitive joke!'

Hannah smiled. And then she grinned as she looked across at Gina, and then they both burst out laughing. 'What a pair of sad walking clichés we are!' Hannah cried.

'The secretary and the fitness instructor,' Gina giggled. 'Jeez, all we need is to put curlers in the front of our hair and wield rolling pins at the front door and we'd be characters out of a seventies' sitcom.'

Tom looked confused about whether he was supposed to be laughing along, or had in fact induced some hysterical breakdown in the two women.

'Don't worry, Tom,' Gina said, wiping her eyes, 'it's not your fault. I think we were both so busy feeling sorry for ourselves that we never quite realised how funny it is.'

'I am so sorry,' Tom replied, 'I'm always getting told to think before I say things.'

'You are?' Gina asked. 'Who tells you that?'

Tom screwed up his face for a moment. 'I don't know. I just seem to recall that I put my foot in it a lot.'

'I can't imagine that,' Hannah said. 'You seem considerate and thoughtful to me.'

Tom shrugged, as if he couldn't offer any more explanation than that and it was pointless trying to. Hannah's heart went out to him. His situation must be torture, and he was putting such a brave face on things. She was sure she'd be going crazy with worry had she been in his shoes, but he was keeping a lid on it, only seeming to be concerned with not distressing those around him. He quietly went back to chopping a pile of freshly-washed carrots, while Gina shot Hannah a pained look.

'You really haven't upset us,' Hannah said.

'It's just…' Tom's sentence faded to nothing.

'I think it's only natural that you feel a little at sea right now,' Hannah added. 'Perhaps you ought to rest after all?'

'No…' He looked up and forced a smile for her. 'Please… let me help. I'll go out of my mind if I sit dwelling on things.' He let out a sigh. 'I can't tell you how stupid I feel. I mean, more than anything else I just feel like a complete muppet. Who the hell goes out with no wallet, no phone, no ID of any kind? People don't do that nowadays, do they? I've made a nuisance of myself to everyone – to you, to whoever is looking for me, to the emergency services…'

'Not the last one.' Gina folded her arms. 'They've not exactly rushed out, have they?'

'Maybe there's a problem on the roads,' Hannah replied.

'Yeah, a bit of snow,' Gina said. 'This country is ridiculous. A cloud containing a snowflake floats over and we're shutting schools and businesses all over the place.'

'It's Christmas Day too, don't forget,' Hannah said. 'I'm sure they're coming as quickly as they can.'

Tom finished chopping his carrots and added them to a pan of boiling water. 'We could have roasted these,' he said, nodding his head at them.

'Boiling is quicker and easier,' Hannah said, 'they'll do just fine as they are for today.'

'See…' Tom said with a sad smile, 'that's what I mean. You're rushing everything now because I've upset your schedule.'

'We never had a schedule,' Hannah said.

'We were just going to cook to the pissed up schedule,' Gina added.

Tom shook his head and glanced between the two sisters.

'While we're still sober we cook all the complicated stuff. But the more pissed we get as we go along, the more likely we are to sling a tin of peas into a bowl to microwave and whack some powdered gravy in a boat. By the time we're finished we're usually so drunk we don't care what it tastes like anyway.'

'Sounds like fun,' Tom smiled. 'Maybe I'll try that approach one day. I have the vaguest feeling that Christmas Day in my house is a lot more structured.'

Hannah got the feeling he was probably right. She wasn't sure what it was, but perhaps it was something in his grooming, or the way he spoke. He wasn't likely to be spending his Christmas morning down the pub like her dad used to while her mum cooked. He was more likely to be cooking dinner himself.

'That's everything on now,' Hannah said, glancing around the kitchen as it rapidly filled with steam. 'I reckon we should be done in half an hour.'

'You can guarantee as soon as we all sit down the paramedics will arrive,' Gina said.

Hannah shrugged. 'It can't be helped. If they come, they come. We can always warm the dinner up again.'

'Gorgeous,' Jess pouted. 'Salmonella and sprouts. Merry Christmas.'

'Hardly,' Hannah laughed. 'If we blitz everything in the microwave it should be fine.'

'Even better, nuked salmonella and concrete sprouts. Aunt Hannah, with this lunch you are really spoiling us…'

Hannah glanced up at the clock. 'Maybe I'll go and take a look down the lane while the veggies are cooking. They might be driving around, having trouble finding the house or something. I can show them where we are if I see them pass along Holly Way.'

'It's their job to know where to find people, isn't it?' Jess said. 'If someone's having a heart attack, they're hardly going to be messing about trying to find the gaff on Google Maps.'

'They probably have satnav installed,' Gina agreed.

'But satnav isn't always reliable, is it?' Hannah said. 'Remember when you first tried to find this place? It kept telling you to turn left no matter where you went.'

'Oh yes,' Gina laughed. 'I ended up making my own crop circle and freaking out the farmer who lives up the hill. Maybe you've got a point.'

'So, if you all keep an eye on the food, I'll just go and take a quick look.'

She left them, and returned a few minutes later wearing a heavy blue duffle coat. Jess let out a giggle.

'You look like Paddington Bear in that!'

'Maybe I like Paddington Bear,' Hannah said. 'I know it's not full-on glamour but it does the job.'

'It's no kind of glamour,' Jess fired back.

'It does remind me of Paddington,' Gina said. 'But it's very you.'

Hannah frowned. 'Are you saying I look like a tubby bear who spends the day eating marmalade sandwiches?'

Gina held out her hands in a gesture of surrender. 'You said it, sis!'

'It suits you and you don't look a bit like a bear,' Tom said.

Hannah felt herself flush, and she quickly turned her back and pulled her hood up, pretending to be in a hurry to leave.

*

Outside, Hannah folded her arms tight across her chest to keep the warmth in. The snow was coming down steadily – huge, fat flakes that seemed to be plumping the snowbanks and drifts by inches even as she watched. It was impossible to see where the roadside ended and the pavement began, apart from a few tyre tracks from earlier in the day, now filling rapidly. It was no wonder the paramedic crew was struggling to find them – assuming they'd even started out at all. Hannah's little front garden was barely recognisable, and the road had that eerie smothered stillness that deep snow always brought. Still, the falling flakes against the black trees and peach sky looked postcard pretty, and Hannah half thought about going back into the house to fetch her camera. She had to remind herself that she had a job to do and more important things to worry about. Although… while she was at it she could get a sneaky photo of Tom…

Stupid cow! I sound like a crazed bunny boiler...

Then she heard Tom's voice behind her, and for a moment thought she had imagined it. She span around with a guilty look.

'It looks lovely, doesn't it?' he said. 'I've never seen a more Christmassy Christmas Day.'

'Are you sure about that?' Hannah smiled.

The smile he returned was a rueful one. 'I suppose not.'

'You should go in,' Hannah said. 'You'll catch your death.'

Tom looked as though he might argue, but then he gave a brief nod. 'You shouldn't be long. I think dinner is almost ready.'

'I won't. Gina can get the plates warmed while I'm out here. Are you sure you won't eat with us?'

'Ordinarily I'd love to, but I just don't seem to have an appetite.'

'Hmmmm.' Hannah gazed at him thoughtfully. 'I still don't like the sound of that.'

'You think it's down to concussion? Something to do with my head injury?'

'Maybe.'

'Or perhaps I'm not hungry now because I ate before all this happened.'

'Are you picking mystery bits of meat from your teeth and do you have the desperate urge to fall asleep in front of a James Bond film?'

'No,' he laughed.

'I don't think you've already eaten then.' She was thoughtful for a moment, and the smile faded from her face. 'I wonder what did send you out into the snow like that. It's weird to go out so unprepared and to wander so apparently far from home.' Hannah felt a shiver that had nothing to do with the snow. Put that simply, it sounded like something very bad had forced him out into the snow. But she didn't want to say it out loud, knowing that he must be worried and stressed enough already, despite how calm he was trying to stay. She saw it in his face when he thought no one was looking.

'How do we know I'm far from home? I have no idea.'

'You don't live on Holly Way; I know that much. I'd say anywhere further than here is far enough on foot in this weather to be considered far from home. Can you remember anything of today before you arrived at our house?'

'It's all a bit of a blur. I remember walking and walking and not really knowing why or where to go. But then I saw the lights on in your house and…' He shook his head and smiled.

'What?'

'It sounds silly now.'

'Come on, you can tell me.'

'Well… it just seemed like the right place to go. Like something was telling me I ought to head for it.'

Hannah smiled. 'I like that idea.'

'Me too. Whatever it was, I'm glad. Chances are I'd never have found anyone half as kind as you anywhere else, even if I'd walked a hundred miles.'

Hannah waved away the compliment, feeling the heat rush to her face and a flush of pride fill her chest. 'Anyone would have done the same. So…' she added, trying to steer the conversation back to its original track, 'that's all you know? You don't have any recollection of events leading up to you being outside? A starting point?'

'I can't even remember hitting my head.'

Hannah studied him for a moment. 'Sorry; I'm rambling and you're cold. Go and get warm and I'll be back shortly.'

'I hope so,' Tom said.

He turned to go. As Hannah crunched down the garden path and out through the gate, she tried not to dwell too much on the peculiar sense of elation that his last comment had drawn from her.

Holly Way was still deserted as she emerged out on the road – at least, she could only guess she was on the road. Checking in both directions, she decided to turn right and began making her way towards a tunnel of trees heavy with snow. The air was surprisingly mild and she began to sweat in her heavy coat as she trudged down the lane. The going was tough. Some snow had compacted beneath the top layer, but some gave way easily and she was never quite certain of the depth and what she might find until she put her foot down. After a ten-minute walk, she turned with a sigh and began to retrace her steps to check in the other direction.

It was strange, what Tom had said about being drawn to her house, because that was how she had felt about his arrival. But she supposed it was arrogant on her part to think that the universe worked like that – exclusively for her – and even if it did, who was to say that Hannah herself was Tom's ultimate destiny? She felt like they had somehow connected, like there was a chemistry there, but he was an injured and confused man and she was probably mistaking his gratitude for something more. Maybe Gina was feeling it too, and what made Hannah more deserving than Gina? That was always assuming that he was free and single, which he almost certainly wasn't. Hannah's thoughts went back to Gina. Did he find her prettier than Hannah? She had always been the more glamorous sister, more outgoing and more popular. Hannah hated comparing herself to her sister in such a distasteful way, but there were days when the worm of insecurity took tiny bites of her soul and she just couldn't help it. Today hadn't started out as one of those days, but an hour or so ago an unexpected arrival had tipped everything upside down.

These thoughts raced around her head and her emotions tied her up in knots, and it was because of all this that she didn't hear the stop-start of an engine through the stillness. It was the sound of wheels spinning on ice, of a vehicle getting away from its driver's control, of sometimes making headway and sometimes not but its progress erratic and dangerous. Hannah had walked this lane a hundred times before today and never had cause for fear from the occasional passing car. Today, when her mind was elsewhere, was the one day it needed to be on the road.

It was too late by the time Hannah turned to see the car skid towards her, the terrified face of its driver looming from the shadows of the interior as he struggled with the wheel. Hannah froze, unable to move and bogged down by the snow even if she could. She heard a shout, and it wasn't until afterwards that she realised it was Tom calling her name. She turned to see him race through the snow like a superhero, and in a scene that felt utterly surreal when she recalled it afterwards, he hurled himself at her and knocked her into the grass verge, the impetus taking both of them out of the path of the oncoming car. Hannah was jolted into a snowbank, and he landed with a thud on top of her.

'Are you okay?' he asked, genuine fear in his eyes.

Hannah didn't answer. She couldn't form the words, but could only look up as he rolled his weight off her to see that the car was still skidding and sliding on the lane.

'He can't stop,' Hannah managed to squeak in a panicked voice. 'He can't stop!'

Tom glanced from her to the car and back again, before he pushed himself up and gave chase.

'Off the brakes!' he yelled after the car. 'You're making it worse! Steer into the skid!'

After a few breathless moments, the car slowly came to a halt. Hannah watched as Tom made his way to the driver's door and knocked on the window. 'What the hell…?'

Hannah got clumsily to her feet and rushed over as fast as the snow and her shaking legs would allow. She was dimly aware that Gina and Jess had now come out, but she was too dazed and worried about the drama that was still unfolding to respond to their concern.

'I'm so sorry…' The man opened the door, grabbing onto the frame for support as he emerged from the car. He looked as shaken up as Hannah felt.

'It's alright, George!' Hannah managed to call. 'I'm fine.'

The old man looked at her, his eyes full of shame. 'I could have killed you!'

'You didn't and there's no harm done.'

'What on earth were you doing out?' Tom cut in, his voice terse. 'Especially as you have absolutely no idea how to drive in this weather!'

'I'm sorry –' George began.

'It's fine,' Hannah interrupted, throwing a pleading look at Tom. 'Please don't make a big deal of it.'

'It's not fine; he almost killed you!'

'But he didn't.' She turned to her elderly neighbour. 'Perhaps we'd better give you a hot drink before we do anything else; you look white as a sheet.'

'I'm so sorry, Hannah,' George began as she gently took his arm. 'I had to go to Hilda's grave. I always go, every Christmas, and I couldn't leave her alone today even though the weather was bad. But then the snow kept coming and the light was failing –'

'George,' Hannah said, 'please don't apologise. Of course you must go to Hilda's grave, today of all days. How many years has it been now?'

'Ten,' he said, wiping a coat sleeve under his nose.

'Ten, wow… it must be hard for you.'

'It is, but I manage. And I still have Trixie for company, dear little thing.'

'Is she at home?'

'I have to get back to her,' George began, rubbing his hands over and over as he seemed to recall a new thing to worry about.

'You can, but first I want to make sure you're alright. You're no good to Trixie if you don't make it home in one piece.'

'He can't drive home, that's for sure,' Gina said as Hannah, George and Tom made their way back to where she was standing. She turned to Hannah and lowered her voice to a tense whisper. 'What happened? I heard shouting and skidding and I run out to see you at the side of the road with Tom on top of you!'

'A bit of trouble with George's steering… nothing to worry about. I'll tell you more later. First things first, we seem to have collected another stray.'

'It's like a regular cottage hospital today,' Gina said wryly.

George's plaintive voice interrupted them. 'How am I going to get home without the car?'

'Don't worry about the car,' Hannah said. 'We'll park it safely and you can leave it here tonight. When the snow ploughs have been through tomorrow it'll be safe to drive it home. I doubt much traffic will be coming down here tonight.'

'Apart from the ambulance,' Jess put in.

'Oh, yes, the ambulance,' Gina nodded.

George looked at them all in turn. 'Ambulance?'

It was then that Hannah noticed the bandage she had so painstakingly wrapped around Tom's wound had fallen off. 'Your head…' She unconsciously reached for him, checking herself as she realised. He put a vague hand to his injury.

'It doesn't seem to be bleeding anymore,' he said.

'Is it for you then?' George asked him brightly. 'I can run you to the hospital if you like.'

Hannah resisted the urge to laugh. Tom was in far more danger hitching a lift with George than waiting for the paramedics, with all the unknown risks that might involve.

'Don't worry, George, the ambulance is on the way,' Gina said.

'Come on,' Hannah said, 'we need to get Tom inside and find yet more dry clothes for him. And while we're at it, George can come and have a cup of tea to calm down before we get him home… is that alright, George?'

'Me calm down?' George asked in disbelief as they began the short walk back to the house, 'what about you? It wasn't me staring death in the face a minute ago.'

'Oh… I'm alright,' Hannah said cheerfully. A bit too cheerfully. She only hoped nobody could see that her legs were still shaking. She needed a cup of tea too, but with a bit of something stronger to go with it.

*

Hannah's legs finally buckled as she reached the kitchen, and Gina, with that silent understanding that only sisters possess, gently manoeuvred her to a chair without a word.

'Tea…' Gina murmured as she opened and shut cupboards searching for more cups, while everyone else filed in behind them. Hannah watched, the sudden dissipation of adrenaline from her system making her feel weak and useless.

'That cupboard… On the left,' she said quietly.

'Would you like some help?' Tom asked.

Gina cocked an eyebrow at him. 'I think you ought to get some dry clothes on first.'

George was already peeling his coat and boots off, and looked around the kitchen for somewhere to hang them.

'The peg by the back door will be fine,' Gina told him. Her attention turned back to Tom, who was now looking down at himself and seemed to be surprised that he was, once again, soaked to the skin.

'I don't think my own clothes will be dry just yet,' he said apologetically.

'There are some more in the spare bedroom,' Hannah began, and she made to get up but Gina laid a hand on her shoulder and pushed her back into her chair.

'You sit down. And take that coat off so Jess can hang it up.' She turned to Tom. 'Up the stairs, first bedroom you come to is the spare one. You'll find a hideous antique wardrobe in there.'

'It is *not* hideous!' Hannah squeaked.

'You keep telling yourself that,' Gina said mildly. 'Hotel for woodworm is what it is.'

Tom went off to find himself some clothes. Hannah frowned at Gina. 'Did you have to send him upstairs?'

'Are you worried he'll find something he shouldn't?'

'Of course not. It's just weird, that's all.'

'The amount of Jason's clothes you still have; is that the weird thing you mean?'

'How do you know how much I have up there?'

'I don't. But that you have any at all is weird. I binned everything Howard didn't collect.'

'I was going to get around to it… I just kept forgetting.'

'Of course you did. I suppose it's lucky really that you didn't throw them out or Tom would have been walking around in that silk kimono you brought back from Tokyo.'

George joined Hannah at the table, lowering himself into a chair. She could almost hear his old bones crack as he settled. She wasn't sure how old he was – pushing ninety, at least, she suspected – but she'd always liked him. He was one of her most helpful and cheery neighbours, although his house was a good walk from hers.

'How are you feeling?' Hannah asked.

'I might ask you the same thing,' George replied.

'Oh, I'm fine, don't you worry. A lovely cup of tea and I'll be right as rain.'

Gina placed a shot glass in front of her, and then one in front of George, before bustling off to the boiling kettle.

'What's this?' Hannah asked, eyeing it doubtfully.

'Brandy,' Gina replied. 'Drink up.'

'I don't want one.'

'Sure you do. It'll calm your nerves,' Gina said.

George held his up to the light, inspecting it with a look of approval. 'As I won't be driving today, I suppose it couldn't hurt to warm me up.'

'That's the spirit,' Gina laughed as she poured boiling water into the teapot.

'Can I have one?' Jess asked.

'A cup of tea?' Gina turned to her.

'A brandy…'

Gina planted her hands on her hips. 'What do you think?'

'I'm nearly eighteen.'

'Not near enough,' Gina replied, before returning to her task.

Jess wrinkled her nose, and glowered at no one in particular, while Hannah gave her an apologetic smile. She would probably have said yes, but then she wasn't Jess's mother and that always made things different, didn't it? She had often found herself wondering what kind of mother she'd be, but as the years clocked on and the right father never seemed to present himself, she was beginning to think she'd never find out. She wasn't bitter about it, but faced the fact with a quiet acceptance and a vow to fill her life with other things instead.

Tom returned just as Gina was refilling George's shot glass. She raised her eyes as Tom made his way to the table. 'Did you find what you needed?'

'I think so,' Tom said. He now sported a pair of fashionably faded jeans and a navy brushed cotton shirt. He looked just as good in these as he had done in the green sweater of earlier, and the sight elicited such conflicting emotions in her that Hannah almost felt she couldn't bear to look. Instead, she took a gulp of her brandy and winced as it hit the back of her throat.

'I bet the dinner will be ruined now,' Jess announced in an accusing voice, as if everyone in the room was to blame. 'Mum made me turn everything off before we came outside to look for you so it'll be cold mush.'

'Oh, we can salvage it,' Gina said brightly. 'What do you think, Han? Are you up to eating just yet?'

Hannah couldn't really say that she was. Up until the argument with George's car, she had been ravenous, but not anymore. However, she didn't want to completely ruin what was already hurtling towards a disaster of a Christmas, and she thought refusing dinner might just do that.

'I could eat a little,' she said.

Gina seemed satisfied by her answer. She turned to George. 'How about you? We have tons to spare.'

George looked doubtful. 'I don't know… Trixie will be dancing by the back door if I don't get home soon…'

'His dog,' Hannah said to help clarify the situation for Jess and Gina, who both looked confused. 'She is a gorgeous thing, isn't she, your little Yorkie?' Hannah added.

George suddenly seemed to fill with an aura of immense pride. 'Oh, she is! Sharp as a tack too! Hilda, God rest her soul, picked her out from the litter and she said straight away she'd be the cleverest of the lot and she is… it was just before my Hilda passed on…' Then his face dropped, and he seemed to deflate like someone had sucked all the life out of him. Hannah sensed the mood of the room shift, and as she tried to find something to say that would lighten things, Gina anticipated it and came to her rescue with perfect timing.

'How far away is your house, George?'

The old man looked as though someone had just asked him the meaning of life. He scratched his whiskered chin as he screwed up his face in concentration. 'About ten minutes on foot. Perhaps more in this weather.'

'So if we eat now, you could be home in an hour or so. Why don't you join us? I'm sure Trixie will be fine for a little while longer and then Jess and I can walk you home.'

George shook his head. 'I can't leave her. She's been alone for hours as it is.'

'I'll take George home and you can all eat,' Tom said.

'You can't go,' Jess replied. 'Aren't you supposed to be here when the ambulance arrives, as it's you they're coming for?'

'I'll go,' Hannah said.

'You're not going anywhere,' Gina cut in, frowning at Hannah. 'You're going to sit right there and pull yourself together. And George, I can't let you go alone. Nobody should be walking alone in this weather.'

'I don't need fussing over,' Hannah said, taking another glug of her brandy and proving her sister's point. 'But I do agree that no one should go out alone in this awful weather.' She seemed to have conveniently forgotten that she had done just that herself, and that was why she was now sitting at her table drinking brandy and uncertain of how her legs worked.

'Jess and I will go now then,' Gina said.

'Why do I have to go?' Jess whined.

'Haven't you been listening?' Gina asked. 'Nobody goes out alone while the snow is still coming down like this.'

George pushed himself up from his chair. 'There's really no need.' He padded over to where his coat dripped on the peg. 'I can easily get back.'

'You can easily get into trouble too,' Gina said. 'Anything can happen in weather like this.'

George let out a sigh of defeat. 'I don't like being a nuisance,' he mumbled as he collected his boots.

Hannah folded her arms on the table and rested her head on them. The conversation was beginning to tire her. Or was that more to do with the near-death experience? Or even just the very weird day? It had started so well, distinctly normal but reassuringly so; now she felt like Alice in the rabbit hole, and everything was spiralling into this surreal universe where neighbours tried to kill her, ambulance crews didn't turn up as promised, dinners got ruined, sisters got bossy, and strange, handsome men fell from the sky like amnesiac angels. Worse still, much worse than being snowed in with all this chaos, was that she was afraid, terribly afraid that she was falling for this man with no name. She couldn't stop replaying the moments in her mind – of Tom throwing himself in the path of George's car to save her, of his weight on her as they lay together in the snow on the lane, the feel of his warm breath on her cheek, the depths of his dark eyes that threatened to pull her in and never let go, the odd tingle in her loins that really shouldn't have been there in the circumstances… She felt like a stupid teenager again, not a mature woman who made her own very sensible way in life. She knew all this, so why couldn't she get the moment out of her head?

She felt a hand on her arm and looked up to see Gina appraising her with a worried expression.

'Are you alright?'

'I'm fine.' Hannah sat up and forced a smile. 'You and Jess take George. Make Jess a sandwich to keep her going and we'll have dinner ready here when you get back. There's no rush really, is there? It's not like we have anywhere to be today.'

'Of course not.' Gina glanced across at Jess as if daring her to argue. But for once there was no argument and after a few moments they were both swaddled up against the weather.

'Ready, George?' Gina asked.

'Aye…' George tipped his cap to Hannah. 'Merry Christmas. I'm sorry, again… about the car and everything. Thank you for being so kind about it.'

Hannah waved him on. 'Don't give it a second thought, George; it wasn't your fault. Merry Christmas to you too. Get yourself home and enjoy your evening with Trixie.'

'Don't eat all the glacé fruits while we're gone, you two,' Gina grinned. She seemed to have quite forgotten that she had been accusing Tom of being a potential axe murdering psycho only a short time before, and was now quite happy to leave her sister in his care. Without another word, the three of them trooped out and the house quickly descended into an odd silence.

Tom broke it first. 'I feel as if this is all my fault.'

Hannah forced another smile. They were getting harder to produce as the day went on. 'Don't think that.'

'But if you hadn't been out looking for the ambulance you wouldn't have been in the path of that car. And as the ambulance was for me in the first place…'

'And George might have spun off the road into a tree, or some other more dangerous place, all alone, and anything could have happened to him. Who would have walked little Trixie then?'

'Stop trying to make me feel better; I don't deserve it.'

'How do you know?' Hannah said. 'How do you know you're not some saintly do-gooder always organising jumble sales for Africa at the local church? In which case, you would totally deserve it.'

'I doubt that,' Tom smiled. 'But thanks. You know…' he added, 'the man these clothes belonged to was mad to mess around behind your back with the fitness instructor. He has no idea what he's thrown away.'

'Oh, I expect I'm a complete pain when you get to know me. Gina always says so.'

'I can't believe that. I don't know you, but I've seen enough today to know that I'd like to.'

Hannah blinked at him. What was that? Was it a come-on? Was he asking her on a date? Or was he simply being kind; a courteous guest in her house? What was she supposed to say? She dropped her head and stared into her drink.

'I didn't mean to offend you,' Tom said.

'Oh, you didn't,' Hannah said quickly, her eyes still on her glass. 'It's just been a bit of a strange day, that's all.'

'You can say that again.'

Hannah looked up to catch him studying her, and she felt the blush she had been fighting rise to her cheeks. The moment was charged, and the room was filled with expectation so real they could almost touch it. She wanted to kiss him… *God* she wanted it so badly… She could reach over… It didn't have to mean anything; just a friendly little kiss … She could blame it on the brandy…

But then a knock boomed through the silent house, and the moment was gone. When she thought about it afterwards, Hannah couldn't honestly say it had even happened. Perhaps it *was* the brandy.

'It can't be Gina already,' Hannah said, trying to shake the intense disappointment that mingled with an almost tangible sense of shame at her lack of control.

'I suppose it's the paramedics,' Tom replied. Was Hannah imagining that he seemed almost as disappointed as her?

'I'd better go then,' she said.

Tom didn't reply, and she left him at the table, hands folded across one another as he watched her go.

The disappointment was cemented as Hannah opened the front door to find two smiling paramedics on the step.

'Someone reported a head injury?' one of them asked. He was very cheery for someone who spent his days patching people up, especially as he was working on Christmas Day. Perhaps it had something to do with the fact that he bore an uncanny resemblance to Santa himself. Hannah found herself hoping he hadn't been called out to any young children today, because that would just be weird.

'I did… well, my sister did… this way…' Hannah gestured for them to follow her.

'Are you alright, love?' the man asked. 'You don't look so perky yourself.'

'Oh, it's not me. I'm fine.'

The paramedics followed her through to the kitchen where Tom waited patiently.

'Got yourself a nasty knock there,' the Santa look-a-like said, nodding at Tom's head. His partner, a man who was as skinny as his colleague was portly and who had been silent up to this point, merely pulled in a sharp breath to indicate his agreement. 'How did you do it?' Santa asked.

Tom shrugged. 'That's really the main problem. My head doesn't feel too bad, but I can't remember anything.'

'Hmmm… well, I'd better take some particulars while Jim here takes a look. What's your name, guvnor?'

Hannah frowned. 'He doesn't know,' she said, wondering at what point the paramedic had stopped listening to his patient.

Santa raised a perfectly white eyebrow and glanced between the two of them. 'Blimey… when control said amnesia they really meant it. Do you have any details I can take at all? ID on you? Something with your address?'

'Nothing,' Tom said.

'Well, that's a new one on me,' Santa said. He looked at his colleague, who gave a silent shrug, presumably his own special sign language indicating that he'd never encountered Tom's problem either. 'I'm not quite sure where we go from here. We need something.'

'But you can treat him?' Hannah asked.

'Oh, we can fix the superficial wound, of course, but we need to be able to log you and for that we need a name and date of birth.'

'Well, what do you do when you find people unconscious in the street and nobody knows who they are?' Tom asked.

'Most people will have something on them to give us a clue. Are you sure you don't have a mobile phone or anything?'

Hannah resisted the urge to screech at this man. How many times did he have to be told?

'Not on me, no,' Tom said with a lot more calm than Hannah felt she possessed at that moment. 'What would you do if you found someone with nothing on them?'

'I suppose we'd cart them in and let the people at A&E sort it. It's not our problem once we drop off.'

'Can't you cart... I mean *take* us in then?' Hannah asked.

'Yes, but he's not unconscious, is he? So we need to find out who he is.'

'But I don't know,' Tom said.

'Can't you pretend he's unconscious?' Hannah asked.

'But he's not...' Santa scratched his head.

'*Us?*' Tom turned sharply to Hannah now, two steps behind in the conversation.

'Of course,' Hannah said. 'I wouldn't dream of letting you go alone.'

'Yes, but...'

'There's no point in arguing, my mind is made up.' Hannah turned to the paramedic. 'That's okay, isn't it?'

'I suppose so. Perhaps it might be helpful seeing as he doesn't know who he is.'

'That's settled then.'

'No…' Tom said, 'I've encroached enough on your day. I'm sure once we get to hospital there will be a record of someone looking for me so I won't be alone for long.'

'But you'll be alone for a bit.' Hannah chewed her lip. Perhaps it would be awkward if she was sitting at the hospital and some distraught wife turned up. She knew how she would feel if the tables were turned. She couldn't leave him to go alone either. Despite what he said, it must be terrifying to be in such a confused state. At least one friendly face close at hand would make it better, even if it was a very new friend. *Friend…* was that what she was to him now? Were they friends? Would she ever see him again when all this was over?

Gina's voice interrupted her thoughts. 'You're here!'

Hannah whipped around to see Gina and Jess at the kitchen door, hair wet and rosy-cheeked.

'The front door was left open,' Gina added, seeing Hannah's look of surprise.

'It's not that…' Hannah said. 'How did you get back so fast?'

'Some dude George knew was randomly out in his tractor,' Jess put in. 'I mean, who drives around in their tractor on Christmas Day? Unless he's actually been given it for Christmas…'

'I think it was the farmer up the hill,' Gina jumped in while Jess's mind wandered off to some strange little world where tractors were the Christmas present norm. 'He offered George a lift home. Saved us a job and got him home in half the time without breaking a sweat.'

'And without Trixie peeing herself,' Jess added.

'Right…' Hannah said, getting more confused by the second. 'As long as he got home okay I suppose that's all that matters.'

'So, what's happening with Tom?' Gina asked.

'Tom?' the Santa paramedic asked.

Gina angled her head at the casualty. 'Humpty Dumpty here…'

'Gina!' Hannah squeaked.

'It's alright,' Tom laughed.

'No offence,' Gina said.

'None taken.'

'So, you're Tom?' the paramedic asked with a frown.

'No… well, yes… Sort of.'

'We named him Tom,' Jess said, as if it was the most natural thing in the world to name a stray man just like you'd name a stray cat.

'Right…' the paramedic said.

'Well, we had to call him something, didn't we?' Jess insisted. 'We couldn't keep referring to him as *him* or *that man*.'

The paramedic shook his head. 'I think we'd better get on with examining the patient or we'll be here all night.' He began by gently moving Tom's hair to examine the wound. 'Is it total memory loss?' he asked as he peered at the cut.

'Pretty much.'

'What did you do when you got up this morning?'

'I don't know.'

'What did you have for dinner yesterday?'

'Don't know that either.'

'How old are you?'

'I hope I'm younger than I feel right now.'

'Well, your sense of humour is still intact,' the paramedic smiled. 'What date is it today?'

'I could hardly fail to notice that it's Christmas Day…'

'True. Who's the prime minister right now?'

'Not a clue.'

'Well…' Jess cut in, 'I don't know that either and there's nothing wrong with me.'

'Debatable,' Gina fired back.

'Rude…' Jess said.

'Like you then,' Gina said.

Hannah sighed as she watched them bicker. Usually she found it funny, but right now her head was spinning.

The paramedic questioned Tom for a few moments longer. 'You need some glue on that cut if nothing else,' he announced finally. 'And I expect you'll need a nut scan too.'

'What's a nut scan?' Hannah asked.

'CT, to rule out brain injury.'

'Do you think there is some?' Tom asked.

'It's hard to say. We only patch you up enough to get you to A&E. It's the doctors' job to find out what's wrong with your bonce.'

'Are we going now?' Tom asked.

'That's the idea,' Santa said cheerfully. 'Can you walk or do you need a wheelchair?'

'I can walk,' Tom said.

It was on the tip of Hannah's tongue to say he could also run, launch himself heroically through the air and be generally pretty bloody marvellous. But she decided that it was asking for too much explanation. She stood up. 'Will you and Jess be okay here if I go?' she asked Gina.

'What!' Gina stared at her.

'I'm going with Tom.'

'Hannah…' Gina angled her head at the doorway. 'Can I have a word? In the other room?'

With a sigh Hannah followed her out of the kitchen. Gina waited until they were alone before she spoke again. 'You can't be serious,' she said in a low voice.

'Why not?'

'You hardly know him! *He* hardly knows him!'

'It doesn't matter. What kind of person would I be if I let him go alone?'

'He's got people. He might not know who they are but he has them, so let them deal with it.'

'Not right away, he won't. What if he's alone for hours? It's Christmas Day. Nobody deserves to be alone in hospital on Christmas Day and not even be able to remember who it is they're missing.'

'What about *your* Christmas Day? Or ours – mine and Jess's? Don't they matter?'

'Of course they matter! And we can still do all that later.'

'You could be gone for the rest of the day. You know how long accident and emergency waits are.'

'I'm sure it will be fine.'

Gina paused. She seemed to be casting around for a solid argument that would persuade Hannah of her folly. And it was folly, even Hannah herself could see that. At least she would, if she could hear the small, sensible voice that was trying to shout louder than the totally irrational one that was yelling in her head right now. 'There's another thing,' Gina finally said, with more than a little triumph in her voice, 'how will you get home? It's still snowing, and you don't have a car that would get you half a mile down the road in this.'

'There'll be some public transport.'

'What's going to be running today, even without the snow?'

'What about the farmer? The tractor would get through…'

'Hannah, that's ridiculous, and if you don't start talking sense I'm going to ask the ambulance men to look at *your* head for damage!'

Hannah pushed a hand through her fringe. 'I know you're right. But it just feels like I should be with him. Does that sound weird?'

'Frankly, yes, it sounds nuts. You've done enough – more than many would. Without you God only knows what kind of mess he would have been in by now. Let the professionals take care of things; you need to think about yourself for once. You've had a bad experience with George and his car and you need to remember that. Relax, let me and Jess take care of you and enjoy the rest of your day. If you're still worried tomorrow we'll call the hospital to see if he's been claimed.'

'You make him sound like a lost puppy.'

'When you think about it, the situation isn't all that different.' Gina gave Hannah an encouraging smile.

Hannah didn't like it. In fact, every ounce of her wanted to argue, but even she could see how much sense Gina was making. She was getting far too involved in this man's life and that would only complicate things in the long run – for her and for him. She already felt a connection, something that could be so right, but could also be very, very wrong. Maybe, much as she hated the idea, her involvement should end right here, with Tom going off to hospital. It was time to let the people who did this for a living take over now.

'You can call the hospital later tonight, get an update,' Gina added, 'if that would make you feel better.'

'It would,' Hannah said. 'Do you think they'll keep him in?'

'I've no idea, but I suppose that's something we'll find out when we call.'

Hannah nodded. 'Okay then. I'll stay here.'

*

It had been a strange sort of goodbye. How do you part from someone who has been thrown into your life and entrenched themselves into it so quickly and completely that you can barely believe they hadn't always been there, someone you hardly know and yet know in a way nobody else ever could, someone you don't know anything about but already feel you know all you would ever need to?

There had been an awkward moment, where Hannah wasn't sure whether she was supposed to kiss or hug or show any kind of affection at all. So as the paramedics looked on with barely disguised looks of amusement, Hannah settled for a very formal handshake and a stiff wave at the door. Then the ambulance was gone, and so was Tom. Perhaps for good, but Hannah couldn't let herself dwell on that possibility.

Gina led her back inside. 'Shall we get that dinner on now?'

'It'll taste disgusting,' Jess said. 'It's been cooked about five million times.'

'I think that might be a slight exaggeration…' Gina cocked an eyebrow at her daughter. 'But it can't be helped. What were we supposed to do? None of today could be helped.'

'I'm sorry,' Hannah said. 'This is not exactly the Christmas Day we'd planned, is it?'

'Well,' Gina replied brightly, 'one day we'll look back on it and laugh. And it's not a complete wash out. We still have the rest of Aunt Dot's presents to open, and I don't know about you, but nothing says Christmas to me quite like a milkmaid figurine with only one bucket on her yoke.'

'Or a half-full tube of dried up hand cream,' Jess chipped in.

'You got one of those?' Hannah asked. 'And you didn't even share with us?'

'That was last year,' Jess laughed, 'and it was too good to share so I gazed lovingly at it in secret in the dead of night when nobody else was there.'

Hannah couldn't help but giggle. Despite all that had happened, she could already feel her spirits lifting. If anyone could salvage the rest of the day and turn it into a proper Christmas celebration, Gina and Jess could.

In the kitchen she stared at the chaos. It looked as though Jamie Oliver had been in and thrown a tantrum.

'To be honest, I don't feel like reheating all this now,' Hannah said.

'If I'm honest, I don't really feel like eating it either,' Gina agreed. 'Sorry…'

'Don't be,' Hannah said. 'I feel exactly the same. It doesn't feel like Christmas dinner with all the trimmings time now. Do you know what I think?'

Gina raised an eyebrow in a silent question.

'I think,' Hannah continued, 'that we should have our Boxing day dinner tonight and then settle down to watch telly.'

'Turkey and oven chips?' Jess grinned.

'Just so.'

'And then we can have Christmas dinner on Boxing Day.' Gina clapped her hands together. 'It's kinda topsy turvy. I like it!'

'Right then…' Hannah began to clear a space to work, transferring the food they weren't eating into pots to store overnight while Gina rooted in the freezer for a bag of oven chips. 'Peas too?' she called as she held the bag up for Hannah to see.

'Let's leave the healthy stuff for tomorrow,' Hannah replied. 'Tonight I want to eat chips and ketchup and maybe even a pickled gherkin.'

'Sounds good to me.' Gina shoved the peas back into a drawer and shut the freezer. After popping a tray of chips into the oven, while Hannah and Jess finished up cleaning the surfaces, Gina flicked the CD player on once again and began to bop around the kitchen. 'Time to get pissed,' she laughed as Hannah gave her head a wry shake.

Hannah reached for their slightly battle-scarred turkey to begin carving off some more. 'I think I've had enough with those two brandies you forced down me earlier.'

'They were medicinal,' Gina said. 'These will be purely recreational.'

'Can I have one now?' Jess asked.

'You can have a snowball.'

'Ugh! Can't I have something a bit less disco?' Jess pouted.

Hannah burst out laughing. 'You certainly inherited your mother's way with words!'

'Can I though?' Jess insisted.

Hannah looked at Gina. 'I don't mind if you don't.'

'Only one,' Gina warned Jess. 'A light beer or something.'

Jess grinned broadly. Hannah knew why she wasn't causing more of a fuss. It wouldn't be long before Gina was plastered and then she wouldn't notice Jess craftily refilling her 'one' glass of beer a few times. But it was Christmas, an odd one, but Christmas nonetheless, and Hannah figured Jess was as entitled to let her hair down as they were. And she was pretty sure that both she and Gina had been sneaking shots from their father's drinks cabinet before they were eighteen too, though Gina was a lot more sensible where her own offspring was concerned. It was just another aspect of being a mother that Hannah had resigned herself to never experiencing.

Hannah fixed more brandy, this time mixed with a generous measure of lemonade to make them last a while, and Jess headed out to help herself to a bottle of Belgian beer from the stock Hannah kept in the outhouse down the garden. She came back into the kitchen some moments later kicking snow from her boots. The day was already turning to dusk, and a blast of cold air roared in through the open back door.

'It's stopped snowing,' Jess announced.

'Bloody typical,' Gina said. 'We could have done with that a few hours ago when we were waiting for an ambulance to get through. I bet it'll be melted tomorrow.'

'I don't think so…' Hannah's gaze went to the darkening skies outside the window. 'It feels like it might freeze over rather than melt.'

'Then the roads will be lovely and slippery to cause more havoc for Boxing Day.'

'That's not good.'

'I suppose it just means we'll have to sit around snuggled in our PJs all day and watch films with all those chocolates we've bought each other,' Gina said cheerfully.

'Sounds good to me.' Hannah sipped her drink. 'I wonder if Tom will have been reunited with his family by then.'

'I expect so.' Gina shot a glance at Jess, who returned it with a little shrug.

'Still,' Hannah continued, 'I wonder if he's okay.'

*

Much later, when they had full bellies and were sitting together on the sofa like cats huddled in a barn, Hannah passed a tray of chocolates to Gina.

'I know it's hard to believe, but I think I have to give in.' Gina pushed the box away. 'I've eaten more chocolate today than I have the rest of the year put together.'

'It's Christmas; you have to do that,' Hannah said. She reached for the remote control as the end credits of the festive edition of *Coronation Street* began to roll.

'I told you someone was going to die,' Jess said, stifling a yawn. 'Someone always dies at Christmas.' She reached across and plucked a coffee cream from the box on Hannah's lap.

'Nothing says peace and goodwill to all men quite like a lethal punch up,' Hannah said.

Gina rolled her eyes. 'Gold star to Jess for guessing the utterly guessable.'

Hannah popped the box onto the floor and stretched. 'Another drink before we set up the movie?'

'Tea,' Gina said. 'I hate to admit defeat on the booze too, but I could go for a lovely cup of tea.'

Hannah uncurled herself from the corner of the sofa and padded through to the kitchen. It was there that her gaze fell upon the clothes she had hung out to dry on the radiator: Jason's clothes, which had now, indelibly in her mind, become Tom's clothes, or whoever he really was. Tom had got back into his own before he left. She wandered over and put her nose to the sweater. It smelt different; no longer the fading scent of her ex, but someone new. She inhaled again, and the smell was so comforting she was half tempted to pull the now dry sweater over her head and wear it for the rest of the evening. But then she imagined the look on Gina's face and checked herself. *Idiot.* What the hell was the matter with her today?

Gina appeared at the doorway and Hannah shoved the sweater back onto the radiator, feeling like a toddler caught with a freshly painted wall and a tub of crayons.

'Want some help?' Gina glanced at the sweater, and then back at Hannah. 'With the tea, I mean.'

Hannah waited a moment for the reprimand but none came. 'I can manage,' she said.

'You know he's probably married…' Gina added, going over to take a closer look at the sweater herself. 'Although I can understand why you're interested.'

'I'm not interested, just concerned.'

'He is extremely attractive,' Gina continued, ignoring Hannah's denial. 'I can't blame you for hoping he's not married.' She shot Hannah a sly grin. 'And he clearly fancied you too.'

'No he didn't.' Hannah gave an awkward laugh. 'He was just being a gentleman.'

'More to you than Jess or me.'

'It's my house; that's probably why. You have to be polite to your host, don't you?'

'Does that go for me and Jess then?'

'No, you're not guests, you're family. So feel free to insult me as much as you like… oh wait… you already do…'

'It's no less than you deserve,' Gina giggled.

No sooner had the laughter died down than there was a faint knocking from the front of the house. Hannah looked at Gina in alarm. 'Was that the front door?' she whispered. Quite why she was whispering she couldn't say. But given the day they'd had, Hannah figured they'd already had their fair share of strangers dropping from the sky.

Jess came into the kitchen. 'Someone just knocked. Want me to go and get it?'

'No… I…' Hannah began.

'I'll go,' Gina cut in.

Hannah reached for her arm to stop her. 'I'd better go; it is my house after all. It's probably just George anyway. Perhaps he forgot something, or he wants to get his car now that it's stopped snowing.'

'I hope not. He can't possibly take it tonight,' Gina said doubtfully.

Hannah's heart was thudding in her chest as she made her way through the house, Gina and Jess following. Why? Was it because, in some dark, deluded corner of her mind she thought it might be Tom, like in one of those romantic films where she'd open the door and he'd be standing there, proudly handsome and yet vulnerable, and he would tell her that he couldn't stop thinking about her and how he might die if she didn't marry him immediately? She'd begin to argue, and he'd hush her with a passionate kiss before sweeping her into his arms and carrying her off into the night while Gina and Jess whooped and clapped and cried tears of joy. *Don't be ridiculous*, she told herself. It would be George, good old George, nice and safe. Things like that didn't happen in real life – at least, not to people like her. But there was a strange sense of déjà vu as Jess reached for the soapstone elephant and, just like before, waited, ready to attack at the first sign of trouble. Hannah opened the door, her heart beating so fiercely she was certain everyone in the room must be able to hear it. Never had she been so nervous about answering a knock before and though she knew how utterly ridiculous it was, there wasn't a thing she could do to stop it.

And then the rush of adrenaline subsided and was replaced by a tidal wave of disappointment as she saw not Tom, not even George, but the snow-haired paramedic from earlier that day standing on the doorstep. He raised an eyebrow as he clocked all three women standing at the door looking as though they were expecting a medieval siege to begin.

'Sorry if I disturbed you.' He gave them an apologetic smile. 'Only I wondered if you'd found a watch. I've lost mine, and I wouldn't fuss ordinarily, but the missus gave it to me for our silver and she'll skin me alive if I don't find it. I was wondering if I'd left it here.'

Hannah shook her head. 'We haven't found anything. But if you want to step in for a moment we can have a proper look around to make sure it's not lying somewhere unnoticed.'

'That would be great, thank you.' He followed Hannah in.

Jess closed the front door after him, before sliding the elephant figure back onto the sideboard as surreptitiously as she could.

'I've been retracing my steps ever since my shift finished,' he said.

'Isn't your wife wondering where you are?' Gina asked.

'I told her we'd had some tricky patients today and the paperwork was taking a bit longer.'

'And she believed you?'

'Probably not,' he sighed.

'Let's just hope she doesn't think you're having an affair and you've gone to give your mistress her Christmas present,' Gina said, the tone in her voice implying that she knew more than a little about that particular scenario.

The paramedic seemed to pale in front of their eyes. 'I hadn't thought of that.'

Hannah stared very deliberately at her sister then turned to the paramedic. 'I'm sure not everyone is as suspicious as that.'

'Sure,' Gina agreed, 'only when they have good cause to be.'

As he waited they went through the kitchen and sitting room, scouring for a glint of metal that would turn out to be the man's watch. It was just another Christmas mercy mission on top of a list that kept getting longer and longer. But after twenty minutes they had to conclude that it wasn't there.

'I'm sorry,' Hannah said. 'Do you have anywhere else to look?'

'There was one more call after yours but I can't go back there now because the police are still in attendance doing forensics and taking statements…' He shrugged. 'If it is there, maybe someone will pick it up and figure out it's not part of the evidence. In a way I hope it's not there, though; I'm not sure I'd want it back if it was.'

Hannah couldn't imagine what sort of incident it could have been and she didn't want to know. If it made him feel that way it must have been traumatic. It seemed that not everyone was about peace and goodwill on Christmas Day, and perhaps the annual carnage that was the staple of the festive soap schedule wasn't a million miles from the truth after all. She suddenly had the deepest respect for this man who must encounter all sorts of harrowing events in his day-to-day life and yet still managed to stay cheerful and good-natured.

'Can I get you a drink?' she asked.

'Thank you, that's kind, but I really should head home.'

'What will you tell your wife about your watch?'

'Perhaps she won't notice tonight and I can have another look around tomorrow.'

'Maybe you dropped it in the snow?' Gina suggested. 'When it melts we can take a look outside for you.'

'I'd appreciate that. Here…' He pulled his mobile phone from his pocket and began to scroll down a list. 'I'll give you my phone number in case it turns up. Is that okay?'

'Of course.' Hannah pulled an envelope from a pile on the shelf and turned it over to write his number on the back. 'I'll let you know if I find anything.'

'Brilliant. Well, I'd better go home and face the music,' he said.

'Good luck,' Gina smiled.

As they saw him to the door, Hannah burned to ask him the question that she knew would draw a disapproving look from Gina. Eventually, she could stand it no longer. Gina could disapprove as much as she wanted, but she had to know.

'The guy you took from here…' she began.

He turned on the front doorstep to face her. 'The man with no name?' He smiled. 'I don't think he was in accident and emergency for long. I think he was taken onto a ward not long after we left him.'

'Do you know which ward?'

'I couldn't tell you. It's likely one of the assessment units. They don't stay long on those, though. After that I don't know which one he'll be moved to; it depends on what they decide is wrong with him, but I expect they'll keep him overnight for observation in light of his injuries.'

'His head wasn't that bad, was it?' Gina asked.

'Not on the outside, but it's not normal to forget who you are, is it?' he said.

'I suppose not,' Gina replied.

'So he didn't manage to remember anything while you were with him?' Hannah put in.

'Not a dickie bird. I'd say he almost wanted to forget. It takes some doing to erase everything from your head so completely.'

Hannah nodded. She was thoughtful for a moment. 'We were going to phone tonight but do you think it's worth me going to visit tomorrow?'

The man gave a faint look of surprise. 'You could, though I'm not quite sure how you'd find him in either case.'

'What do you mean?'

'You don't know his name. If you don't know his name how will you know who to ask for?'

'And I suppose it might confuse him even more if we turn up, mightn't it?' Gina looked carefully at Hannah. 'It might be wise to *leave well alone.*'

'You're probably right,' the paramedic said. 'Although I'm sure he'd appreciate a friendly face in his position. I know I would.'

Hannah realised that she had probably got as much information as she was going to get tonight. She was sure he would help more if he could, but he probably wasn't allowed to. After he had bid them a cheery farewell, Hannah closed the door with a sigh.

Jess grinned as she looked from her to Gina and back again. 'Weirdest. Christmas. Ever.'

*

Hannah rolled over and glared at the clock by her bed. It was just past seven, but she'd already been awake for an hour, annoyed with herself that she couldn't just go back to sleep. She'd had enough brandy the evening before to comfortably floor her – at least, it would have done on a normal night – but something was keeping her awake.

There was no point lying in bed any longer, and knowing that a mountain of unwashed dishes festered in the sink downstairs because she'd been too tired and too drunk to care about them the night before, Hannah threw her legs over the side of the bed and into her slippers. So much for her usual lazy Boxing Day lie-in.

Peering through a crack in the curtains, she inspected the weather as she tied her dressing gown. Yesterday's snow still lay deep, the dents of their footsteps glistening on the path from the light of her garden lamp, and the lane was quiet and still under its muffling blanket. It was so peaceful Hannah realised she was actually quite glad she was up to see it after all. She started to think about transport. She didn't fancy her chances of driving; the snow was still deep despite the fact that the sky looked clear and promised no more. On a normal day the snow ploughs would be out and, failing that, one of the neighbouring farmers would do the job with a tractor. But it was Boxing Day and who cared about ploughing snow today? She could safely assume that buses would have the same problem as her car – and it was a pretty scant service from here on a normal working day – and while there was a little station running the short train route less than a twenty-minute walk from her house, there was never a service on the day after Christmas. Gina would say she was crazy for wanting to get to Millrise today and there was no reason for her even to try. If Hannah tried to explain the reasons why she felt compelled to make the journey, Gina would say she was even crazier. Hannah couldn't explain it, and it *was* crazy, but she needed to go all the same.

It was at times like this when Hannah questioned the wisdom of wanting to live in the country. Letting the curtain fall back into place, she stretched, and decided to go and hunt for the posh hazelnut coffee she kept for special days. She would be drinking it alone for now, but she figured she deserved a little Christmas treat and a quiet hour by herself before Gina and Jess got up and made the place mad again.

*

It was around ten when Gina finally emerged from her bedroom. 'Wow…' she said as she came into the kitchen where Hannah was sweeping the floor. 'What time did you get up? It must have been early to get what we left out last night cleaned up.'

'It wasn't that bad really,' Hannah lied as she leaned the brush up against a unit. 'Do you want some breakfast?'

Gina put a tentative hand to her head. 'Maybe just a coffee for now. And a stomach pump if you have one; my body's protesting my Christmas excesses.'

Hannah laughed. 'Sit down. Is Jess still asleep?'

'She won't be up yet. She sleeps in until midday on a normal weekend, so we probably won't see her today at all.'

Hannah nodded. Gina was probably more right about this than she knew. She had seen Jess down a lot more than the one bottle of beer Gina had allowed. Not that she was going to give the game away. 'Let her sleep. She needs it at her age. I seem to recall you being just the same.'

Gina took a seat at the table. 'I would have been, except that you kept waking me when you got up at stupid o'clock.'

'You were my big sister. That's what little sisters do.'

'Little pain you mean.'

'You should be happy I looked up to you and wanted to spend time with you.'

'Now, maybe. Back then I wanted to strangle you.'

'Was I that bad?' Hannah asked, filling the kettle. Gina grinned.

'I suppose you were okay. For a little pipsqueak.' She propped her head up on a hand and leaned on the table. 'So, what's the plan for today?'

Hannah shrugged. She tried to look casual. She had a plan, but Gina wasn't going to like it. But then Gina didn't have to come if she didn't want to. There was nothing to stop her and Jess staying in the house while Hannah went alone; she wouldn't be more than a few hours and they were perfectly capable of making themselves at home while she was gone. 'It's not snowing and it doesn't look as if there was any more last night.'

'That's good. Not that I plan on going anywhere. I was thinking *The Lord of the Rings*, all three films back to back. That should keep us good until bedtime, and we can slot in our Christmas dinner somewhere in between.'

'We could…' Hannah began.

'What?' Gina looked up sharply. 'I recognise that tone. You're going to say something idiotic, aren't you?'

'I thought I might go out, get some air.'

'A walk down the lane? It might kill me but we could try.'

'A bit further than the lane. I was thinking Millrise.'

'What for? There's nothing to see there on normal days, let alone today.'

'That's harsh. I happen to think it's quite a nice little town.'

'You've just described everything I think is wrong with it in that one sentence.'

'Why are you leaving Birmingham and coming back then?'

Gina frowned, and Hannah knew from her expression it was best not to pursue that thread any further. It had been a low blow really, but sometimes, when Gina criticised her life choices, it made her defensive and say things she wished she hadn't. It had always been the same, even when they were kids. Hannah paused. And then gave up trying to skirt the issue. It wasn't as if Gina couldn't see right through her anyway.

'I want to go and see if Tom's okay.'

Gina groaned. 'Oh, God… I knew this was coming.'

'Yeah, so you're about to tell me what you think.'

'I think you're asking for trouble.'

'Okay. Now I wish I hadn't said anything.'

'So do I.'

'So…?'

Gina shrugged. 'You'll go no matter what I say, so if you're looking for some kind of approval, I don't see the point in this conversation.'

Hannah gave a brief nod. 'I can't rest not knowing what's happened.'

'Even if you go bombing up to the hospital, you heard what that paramedic said last night. The hospital is a big place. How are we going to find a nameless man amongst all those patients?'

'That in itself is unusual enough to make someone remember him,' Hannah insisted. 'Someone will have taken notice enough to know what happened.'

'They might. But they probably wouldn't tell us. I'm pretty sure they have rules about giving information to complete strangers.'

'They don't know we're strangers.'

'Yes they do. If we weren't we'd know his name and be taking him home.'

Hannah bit her lip. That actually sounded like a mad but appealing prospect.

'For that matter,' Gina continued, 'he may well have already been claimed. He could be on his way home as we speak.'

Hannah opened her mouth to argue, but then closed it again. She didn't have an answer, because Gina was right, as she always was. But she still had the irrational urge to drive to the hospital, and she knew that it wouldn't go away until she'd seen for herself that Tom was safe.

'You're still thinking about going, aren't you?' Gina frowned at her over the rim of her cup. Hannah gave a slightly apologetic nod; but because she also felt utterly vindicated she wouldn't apologise, even though she felt the nuisance she was making of herself. Gina sighed. 'Give me time to pull myself together and I'll get dressed.'

'You don't need to come.'

'What? Let you go and make a total tool of yourself with no back up? Not likely. Someone's got to talk some sense into you when you don't get anywhere and it's time to admit defeat. Besides, the roads are still dangerous and I'd rather be with you in case you run into trouble on the way there.'

'What about Jess?'

Gina took a sip of her coffee. 'We'll leave her to rot in bed. We'll be there and back before she's up and I doubt she'll even know we've been anywhere at all.'

*

An hour later, Hannah had checked visiting times at Millrise General (as everyone still called it, though it now had some fancy and longwinded name that defied anyone who wasn't a world memory champion to remember it) on their very useful website. She might not get to visit, and he may not even still be on a ward, but it was worth being prepared just in case. She and Gina were huddled in coats and boots at the front door. Hannah fingered her car keys anxiously. She hated driving in snow, but although she wasn't looking forward to it, there was no way she was backing out now, not while she had Gina onside.

'I still think you're both mad,' Jess said. She stood before them, still in her pyjamas, twirling a tendril of bed-knotted hair around her index finger.

'You could come if you don't want to stay on your own. It would be an adventure,' Gina said with an impish grin that took twenty years off her.

'Not bloody likely,' Jess returned. 'I'll sit by the fire and eat all your chocolates while you're gone.'

'Don't you bloody dare!' Gina shot back. Jess laughed.

'How long will you be?'

'A couple of hours.' Gina glanced at Hannah for confirmation.

'I hope it won't be too much longer than that,' Hannah said. 'As long as we can get through the snow okay.'

'I reckon as soon as we get off the tracks and onto the main roads it will be fine,' Gina said.

'Probably,' Hannah agreed, 'it usually is. We've got to get to them first, though.'

Gina gave Jess a brief kiss on the cheek. 'Be good. And if you must eat chocolate please don't eat them all.'

'Don't worry, I'll leave you the strawberry creams.'

'Oh, you little witch!' Gina squeaked as Jess giggled. And with that, Hannah and Gina stepped out into the still late morning.

The snow had hardened, and it crunched under their boots as they made their way down the drive.

Hannah's little yellow Citroen looked as if it had been iced like a Christmas cake. 'The car will take some clearing,' she said.

'I don't think that's going anywhere,' Gina said, angling her head at the marooned vehicle.

'It's certainly more frozen in than I thought it would be.'

'We could get the kettle; melt the snow?' Gina suggested.

'I don't want to risk it freezing up again even more solid. The damn thing is temperamental enough as it is and I'm half expecting it not to start… I think we'll have to dig it out.'

'God, I wish I'd brought my car now instead of getting the train.'

Hannah gave a rueful smile. 'I don't suppose you were expecting to have to go on a crazy mission.'

'True.'

Hannah planted her hands on her hips and appraised the mound of snow that contained her car. Finally, she let out a sigh. 'I don't suppose it's going to dig itself out; I'd better go and find some kind of implement in the shed.' She was about to make her way around the back when there was a shout from the lane. She turned to see George. 'Good morning!' she called. 'How was Trixie when you got back to her yesterday?'

'Oh, she was just about holding on,' George smiled. 'But she's a good little girl and she'd do her best not to make a mess in the house no matter how long I was gone.'

'Come to get your car?' Hannah asked.

George nodded. 'I'm waiting for Paul Hunter's lad to come down with his tractor from Holly Farm. He said he'd help me dig it out so I could get it back home.'

Hannah and Gina exchanged a grin as they both had the same thought. 'Do you think he'd do one extra?' Hannah asked. 'We're just trying to get mine out.'

'I doubt he'd mind,' George replied cheerfully. 'In fact, I think he's planning to clear the road a bit too. Are you going far? It still won't be the best driving conditions.'

'We're just going into Millrise.'

George was thoughtful for a moment. 'Happen I could take you if you like.'

'That's very kind of you.' Hannah gave him a patient smile, but she was still thinking about how he had panicked at the wheel the previous day and nearly hit her. She didn't fancy being responsible for him having another accident. 'I think I'd rather take my car, though. I really don't know how long we'll be and I would hate you to have to wait around in the cold.'

George's breath curled into the air. 'Righto,' he said. 'But let me know if you change your mind.'

'We will.' Hannah could see a faint smile on Gina's lips and guessed that her sister had similar misgivings about George's offer, however kindly meant it was.

The deep throb of a very large diesel engine reached them, and they turned to see a mighty looking tractor charging down the lane as if there were no snow on the ground at all. It came to a halt next to Hannah's gate, and a young man leapt down from the cab. He looked so much like the archetypal blond surfer that he was completely at odds with his cloth cap, thick fleece, green wellies and rural surroundings. He gave George a nod before turning to greet Hannah. 'Afternoon.'

Hannah smiled. 'Hello, Ross. How are you?' Hannah had seen him around, had even exchanged the odd passing pleasantry with him, but this was the first time she had really been this close. He was a lot handsomer than she had realised before.

'I'm good, thank you,' Ross said. 'I've spent the morning searching for my damn sheep but they're accounted for now so I think I'll call that a good day.'

'I suppose they're hard to find in the snow… being soft and white and everything,' Gina said. Hannah looked askance and cocked an eyebrow at her. Gina's voice had developed a coquettish lilt that Hannah knew well. A rebound relationship was a very bad idea and Hannah hoped that her sister wasn't that stupid. A bit of rebound fun, on the other hand, might be just what Gina needed. Ross was young, realistically too young for Gina, but he was gorgeous, and it looked like there'd be a lot of rebound fun in him. A bit of flirting would cheer Gina up if nothing else.

Ross yanked off his hat and ruffled his hair into an adorably dishevelled quiff. 'Yeah, soft and white can be a problem in this weather.' He grinned. 'Perhaps I ought to paint them pink.'

'They'd certainly be the most chic sheep in the valley,' Gina replied with a breathy laugh.

'So…' Hannah cut in, hoping to put the flirting on hold for one second so they could turn their attention to the task in hand, 'George tells us you're hoping to get him mobile.'

Ross nodded. 'Shouldn't take me long. I'll run Bess up and down the lane as well to clear a track.'

'Who's Bess?' Gina asked.

Ross patted the tractor with a slightly worrying show of affection.

'Right…' Hannah smiled. 'I know it's cheeky but I don't suppose you could give us a hand afterwards? I'm trying to get my car out too and, as you can see, it's snowed in pretty solid.'

'I expect so…' Ross stuck his hands in his pockets and ran his gaze over Hannah's car. 'Shouldn't be too much trouble.'

'Brilliant!' Hannah beamed. Ross climbed back into his tractor, clearly excited about the prospect of driving it. Hannah could just imagine him as a small boy, playing with his toy tractors and dreaming of the day when he would be old enough to drive a real one. There was something rather endearing about the expression of joy on Ross's face as he turned the key and the engine roared into life.

In less than half an hour, he had made an impressive job of clearing a path along the lane for as far as Hannah could see. He did an even more impressive job of shifting the snow from around Hannah's car, and as Gina watched with obvious appreciation, even Hannah had to admit that he was a pretty hot specimen of manhood.

But Ross looked doubtful when Hannah's pride and joy was finally revealed.

'Not exactly the wheels for this sort of weather, even with the path clear.'

Hannah held her hands up. 'I knew the full extent of its crappiness would be discovered once you moved all that snow,' she laughed.

'No...' Ross blushed, and Hannah thought she caught an audible sigh of longing from Gina. 'I didn't mean that... just that...'

'I know,' Hannah smiled. 'Sadly it's the best I can do and I have to get into Millrise today.'

Ross lifted his cap and rubbed a hand through his hair again. 'How about I take you? It might be a slow way to travel but you'd be guaranteed to get through.'

'What about getting back?'

'No problem; I'll bring you back as well.'

'But you don't want to be hanging around for us. I've no idea how long we'll be.'

'Have my phone number then. Call me when you need to come back and I'll drive out for you.'

'Oooh, phone number!' Gina squeaked with such eagerness that everyone turned to stare at her, even George, who had been so quiet they had almost forgotten he was there. 'Sorry...' she added, 'I just meant that your phone number would be a good idea.'

Ross pulled out a battered old mobile phone. He glanced up with a sheepish grin. 'I know it looks like something Indiana Jones might be hunting for, but there's no point in me losing a good one in the silage pit. Trust me, it wouldn't be the first time that's happened.'

'And you had the cheek to poke fun at my car!' Hannah laughed.

Ross grinned.

Hannah and Ross exchanged numbers and then Gina and Ross exchanged numbers (in case Hannah's phone ran out of battery, as Gina had wisely pointed out), and after seeing George off down the lane in his car, Ross helped Hannah and Gina up into his cab.

'It might be a bit of a squash,' he said, 'but if you don't mind then I don't.'

'I don't mind at all,' Gina said, and Hannah had to try very hard not to slap her around the face and tell her to pull herself together. If Gina dared to tell Hannah again that she was acting like a lovestruck teenager over Tom, then she would take great pleasure in reminding her sister of this episode as evidence that she was just as bad. But, as Ross started the engine and it roared into life, Hannah felt it vibrate right through her body, and she couldn't help but reflect that there were less fun ways of getting around. She was on a mission of mercy (or so she kept telling herself) but that didn't mean she couldn't enjoy herself at the same time. Right now, she could see why Ross's face lit up every time he climbed into his big shiny tractor; she almost felt like a kid herself sitting up there with him as he pulled away from the roadside.

*

There were more people than Hannah expected to see around and about when they finally arrived in Millrise, and their unconventional mode of transport drew puzzled looks as they made their way through the town. The roads here were almost clear, and observers probably thought it was a severe case of overkill. Ross dropped Hannah and Gina off as close to the hospital entrance as he could get without causing a problem.

'I hope you find him,' he said.

Hannah threw Gina a sideways glance; she had filled Ross in on the whole story and Hannah wished she hadn't.

'Me too,' Gina said. 'Thanks so much for the lift; it was brilliant.'

Ross gave them a wide grin and tipped his cap in an archaic but endearing gesture. 'I've got my phone at the ready. It's no bother at all for me to come back so let me know when you're ready.'

'We will,' Gina said. She looked at Hannah. 'Are you ready?'

'Not really,' Hannah said with a half-smile. Once again, the inexplicable nerves had kicked in and she wondered what the hell she was doing here. As much as she wanted to find the mysterious man who may or may not be called Tom, she also wanted to run back home and pretend none of this had ever happened.

They watched as Ross swung his tractor around in a giant U-turn and then Gina linked arms with Hannah.

'Come on, let's get this madness over with; let's find your Prince Charming.'

'He's not my Prince Charming.'

'Yup… Whatever you say.'

'You can wipe that smile off your face,' Hannah replied tartly as they began to walk. 'Don't make me say anything about you and Ross.'

'Me and Ross?' Gina laughed.

'You're telling me you don't fancy him?'

'Who wouldn't? I'd totally go there.'

'He's half your age!'

'That's rude. Maybe about two thirds.'

'Definitely more than that.'

'Either way, a bit of flirting is good for the soul, as long as both parties are enjoying it. I'm not asking him to marry me, am I?'

'So there's going to be no more than flirting, even if he was willing to go further?'

'If the definition of flirting can be stretched to being horizontal and naked in bed together, then no, there's going to be no more than flirting.'

Hannah rolled her eyes.

'What?' Gina asked. 'He's single, isn't he? He certainly acts as though he is.'

'I think so.'

'There's no harm in it, then.'

'Hmmm…' Was all that Hannah could think to say in return.

*

The main reception of the accident and emergency unit was a welcome and cosy temperature after the brisk chill of the road outside; perhaps a little too cosy, as Hannah was desperate to peel off her coat as soon as she stepped in. She yanked off her gloves and hat and painted on her brightest smile as she approached the reception desk.

'I was wondering if you could help me.'

The receptionist's expression remained stony and blank. Hannah's spirit sank; she had a feeling this was going to be hard work.

'A friend of ours was brought in by ambulance yesterday,' Hannah continued, 'and we're trying to find out what happened to him.'

The woman raised her eyebrows slightly. 'Are you a relative?'

'Not exactly…' Hannah began, but the woman cut her off.

'I can't give you any information if you're not a relative.'

'What about friends? Friends must be able to visit friends,' Gina said.

The woman looked from Hannah to Gina and back again, as if it was incredibly rude that more than one person should be talking to her at the same time. 'Are you friends?'

'We did just say that,' Hannah replied, biting back a ruder retort which would get her nowhere.

The receptionist let out a bored sigh. 'What's his name?'

Hannah glanced at Gina. 'We… we don't actually know.'

'I can't find him without a name,' the woman snapped.

'Could you try? Were you on duty yesterday?'

'No.'

'He had memory loss. Someone might have mentioned him to you? Are there any records of him arriving yesterday?'

The woman narrowed her eyes. 'You don't even know his name. I can't give you any information.'

'We're the people who called the ambulance for him,' Gina said. 'He'd have been dead without us.'

Hannah wondered if that was a bit of a melodramatic statement but she was willing to let it go if it helped their cause.

'I can't tell you anything,' the woman repeated. 'There are over two thousand patients in this hospital at any one time and I can't be expected to know the particulars of every one… that's what computers and NHS numbers are for.'

'So you won't help?' Gina asked, her voice hardening.

'I can't help,' the woman replied. She began to flick through a pile of papers on her desk to signal that the conversation was at an end.

'That's it?' Gina insisted.

The woman glanced up. 'There's nothing I can do. I'm sorry.'

She didn't sound very sorry, and Hannah wished she could tell her, but there was no point. It had been a silly idea and now she couldn't imagine why she had thought coming here would enable her to see Tom again. And even if she had, what then? She'd have asked him how he was, then the conversation would have petered into awkward silence before she finally left, safe in the knowledge that this would definitely be the last time she saw him. Perhaps it was for the best; this was probably less disappointing, less painful.

Gina pulled a face at the woman, who wasn't looking anyway, before motioning to Hannah that it was time to go.

'We tried,' she said as they walked back out into the snowy grounds, 'and at least we had a bit of fun in the process.'

'I suppose so,' Hannah replied. 'I don't really know what I was expecting, but I should have known it would turn out like this.'

'Shall we call Ross?'

'He'll barely be a mile down the road,' Hannah said. 'At least it won't take him long to come back for us and we can get home to Jess.'

'I'm not sure she'll actually be happy about that,' Gina said. 'I bet she's raiding your liquor cabinet right now.'

'I doubt she'll find much; I think we drank most of it yesterday,' Hannah laughed.

As Gina pulled out her phone, Hannah gazed across the grounds towards the car parks. She listened as Gina flirted with Ross on the phone. At least one of them had been lucky today. But then a figure caught her attention. She shielded her eyes, squinting into a low sun that had finally broken through the clouds to throw sparkles across the white lawns and trees of the hospital gardens. She grabbed Gina's arm.

'Is that… Is that him?'

Gina followed the direction of Hannah's gaze. 'I don't think so…'

'It is!' Hannah cried, 'It is him!'

Gina looked again. 'I'm not sure… if it is, he has someone with him.'

That detail hadn't escaped Hannah's attention, but without conscious thought, she began to track towards him, Gina following.

'What are you doing? He's got someone with him!'

'So?'

'So, leave them be.'

'I want to know. I have to know that it is him.'

'Why? If it is, that's good, right? It means his family have come to collect him.'

'Yes… But I need to be certain.'

Gina let out an impatient sigh. Hannah was just about to call out to him when she checked herself.

'It's not him,' she said, the disappointment and relief flooding through her in such conflicting measures that she couldn't tell which emotion was winning. 'It's not him at all.'

'Hurray for that,' Gina said. 'Can we go and meet Ross now?'

'I suppose we should.'

But then Hannah saw a lone figure pushing through the doors of the main hospital. He was clutching a plastic bag, cautious on the snowy path, but there was no mistaking him this time. Hannah stopped on the path, Gina turning with a questioning look.

'There he is,' Hannah said, in a voice so quiet she wondered why she felt the need to keep it down.

'Here we go again…' Gina said, and she followed in Hannah's footsteps as they made their way back. Tom stopped, and turned back to the hospital doors.

'What's he doing?' Gina asked, and then all became clear. Hannah and Gina paused, and watched as he was joined by a statuesque looking blonde woman. She was dressed simply and elegantly, in a navy, ankle-length tailored coat and suede boots, her hair pinned up in a neat twist. She took the bag from him and then gestured to a car park in the opposite direction to the one he was facing, before taking his hand. She led and he followed.

'Get behind this tree!' Hannah hissed, and yanked Gina by the arm.

'What the hell…?' Gina yelped as Hannah almost pulled her off her feet.

Hannah had suddenly felt guilty and a little bit seedy, like a weird stalker spy, and she didn't want him to see her here – not like this.

'I thought you wanted to see him,' Gina said.

'I did, but he's with someone.'

'So what's different this time? A minute ago when we had the wrong guy you wanted to chase after him.'

'And you said I shouldn't.'

'Well, I've changed my mind. I haven't come all this way for you to hide behind a tree.'

'I just can't… it's probably his wife.'

'Possibly. But unless you're planning to throw your bra at him I don't see what difference it makes.'

'It just doesn't seem right, that's all.'

Gina sighed as Hannah peered around the tree. Tom and the blonde woman were almost out of sight. Gina's phone bleeped.

'Ross is waiting for us,' she said. 'He'll be thrilled to learn that he drove us all the way to Millrise for nothing.'

'He didn't. We came to see whether Tom was alright and it looks as though he is,' Hannah replied, her tone defensive, though she knew what Gina meant. She just didn't want to be reminded of what an idiot she'd been.

*

The journey home had been quieter for Hannah. She listened to Gina and Ross laughing and joking and wished she could join in, but she couldn't. She didn't begrudge them their fun, but her own mind was racing. What the hell had she been thinking chasing after Tom like that? What had she thought was going to happen if she'd found him alone? Why was she behaving so irrationally?

When they arrived back at Hannah's little house, Gina put the kettle on and left Hannah to her thoughts as she made them both hot drinks. A few minutes later Hannah was curled up on the sofa, staring into space. While Jess, it transpired, had taken herself up to the spare bedroom to continue a furtive conversation with a boy she vehemently denied she was dating, Gina handed Hannah a steaming mug of hot chocolate.

'It'll warm you up,' she said as she dropped onto the sofa bedside her with a mug of her own. 'Was it a nice dream?' she asked.

Hannah looked across at her. 'What do you mean?'

'The one where your Prince Charming fell from the sky?'

Hannah gave a rueful smile. 'It was that obvious?'

'Sort of. I can't say I blame you. He was pretty yummy.'

'And he saved my life.'

'You saved his first.'

'I suppose so…'

'Perhaps it wasn't his wife. It could have been his sister… Or a cousin… or –'

'Holding hands?' Hannah cocked an eyebrow at her. 'If they weren't married they were something close to it.'

Gina sipped her chocolate. 'Probably best to let it go then.'

Hannah nodded. 'Yeah, probably.'

There was only one problem with Gina's suggestion… Hannah didn't think she could.

Part Two:
I'm Not in Love

Bloody hell, I'm unfit! Hannah raced down Holly Lane, her quarry getting further and further away. It felt as if her lungs might explode, but she couldn't stop. If only her elderly neighbour George hadn't been outside his cottage. If only her car hadn't stuttered to a halt right by his gate, just at that moment. If only Trixie hadn't been in the garden when Hannah climbed out of her car to ask for help, and if only George hadn't left the gate open as he came to look at her engine. Perhaps then Trixie wouldn't have shot out up the lane like Usain Bolt on a promise when Hannah's car engine backfired. There was no way George could chase her, of course, and no way Hannah could leave her to run even if, as George asserted, she'd come back of her own accord once she had calmed down. Because Hannah could tell by the distress in George's old eyes that he really didn't think that's what would happen. So Hannah gave chase, but it only seemed to make the little dog run faster, no matter how hard she tried to coax her back with pleading cries.

'Trixie!' Hannah panted once more. 'Come on girl!' She didn't really know why she was bothering. George had already called her numerous times, and as she wasn't responding to him, she was probably too spooked to respond to anyone, let alone a virtual stranger. But she had to try something; if she didn't stop running soon Hannah was sure she was going to collapse.

They turned a blind bend and Hannah saw Ross's tractor parked on the side of lane. Ross was nearby, inspecting some fencing. Hannah called out, 'ROSS!' His head flicked up. 'TRIXIE!' It was all she could manage to squeeze out and she only hoped he would be able to interpret what she actually meant. But she needn't have worried. In a matter of seconds he had taken in Hannah, flailing madly, and the little terrier hurtling towards him like a bullet from a gun, and he launched himself into the thankfully deserted lane.

Trixie skidded on the loose surface, her feet scrabbling for purchase as she tried to turn and run in the opposite direction, but Ross was supernaturally fast. She hadn't made it a foot before his hands had closed around her and Trixie was in his arms.

'There now...' he crooned to the little dog as he walked towards Hannah, who was now bent double in the road in a less elegant position than she would have chosen for greeting such a handsome young man. The sky spun above her as she fought for breath, and she was faced with the very real possibility that she would now throw up on Ross's feet. How had she ever run for all those miles and miles when she and Jason had been together? Perhaps it was because he used to nag her. It was true that since he hadn't been around she hadn't been out for one solitary jog but, judging by today's performance, it wouldn't be a bad idea to start training again. Because all she felt fit for now was a quick and merciful death.

'She's shaking like a leaf,' he continued as Trixie cowered in his arms, her little ribcage pumping like a piston. She looked as exhausted as Hannah felt, and there was something unsavoury but rather satisfying in feeling glad that she wasn't suffering alone. It was Trixie's fault after all that they were both knackered and she felt like hurling on Ross's boots.

'Car… backfired…' Hannah managed to pant as she made an almighty effort to push herself upright.

'Oh… no wonder she was haring off like that. Want me to walk back to George's with you? She seems quiet enough with me now.'

Hannah gave a grateful nod, and began her shaky walk beside Ross, who continued to rub Trixie's head as he cradled her in his arms.

'Car trouble then?' he asked cheerfully. Hannah nodded.

'It cut out by George's house. He was having a look when the engine went bang and Trixie shot out of the gate like a prize whippet.'

'Lucky you were there to run after her; there's no telling where she might have ended up.'

'Lucky *you* were there,' Hannah corrected. 'There's no telling where the two of us might have ended up if I'd had to chase her much further. Probably Millrise General – for me at least.'

Ross chuckled. 'I'm usually knocking about here on a weekday; there's always something to be done on the farm.'

Hannah wondered why, if he was always knocking around in the week, she hadn't run into him more often in the past. It was just another strange coincidence in a week of them, starting with her very odd Christmas Day. 'Don't you ever take holidays?' Hannah gave him a sideways look. 'You were working on Boxing Day and it was only New Year yesterday but you're back at work again.'

'I'm not one for sitting around,' he said simply. 'And anyway, the animals need feeding and looking after every day of every week.'

'Did you have a day off yesterday?'

'A bit of one,' he said. 'I was done by midday so I took the evening off.'

'God, what time did you have to start to be done by midday?'

'About four-thirty.'

'You started at four-thirty even with a hangover?'

He laughed. 'I wasn't on the lash on New Year's Eve. To tell the truth, I'm not the partying sort… nightclubs – I can take them or leave them. They're mostly full of the wrong sort of people anyway.'

Hannah wondered who the wrong sort of people were. Did it include her? After all, she'd spent enough evenings in nightclubs during her wayward youth. Not now, of course; these days she'd rather curl up with a book than rave.

'We didn't do much either,' Hannah said. 'It was nice but quiet. We did get through enough drink to keep Nelson's navy afloat, though.'

There was a heartbeat's pause.

'So… your sister is still staying with you?' Ross asked.

Hannah looked at him. His gaze was trained on the road ahead, and his expression was neutral enough, but there was no mistaking the sound of hope in his voice.

'Yes… although I'm supposed to be taking her to the station to catch her train home. She'll probably miss it now, with the car out of action, so I don't know whether she'll try for a later one or stay on another day.'

'It's a shame she has to miss it,' he said, but Hannah wondered how genuine the sentiment was. She didn't think he really thought it was a shame at all.

The small talk continued as they made their way back. A light, freezing rain began to fall, but Ross didn't seem to notice at all. As he chatted, she gleaned snippets and hints dropped between the lines, and from what she could tell he was as interested in Gina as she was in him. Was this a good thing? He was a sweet bloke – there was no doubting it – but he was also very young and Gina was fresh from a damaging marriage, not to mention the teenage daughter who was probably closer in age to Ross than Gina was.

As they approached George's cottage, they could see the old man sitting on a garden chair by his gate, searching the road. As soon as he saw them, he leapt to his feet with surprising agility, and his face lit up as they drew closer and he could see Trixie in Ross's arms. Gina's face lit up too, though George and Gina obviously had very different reasons for their shared reaction to Ross striding down the lane towards them.

'Thank goodness!' George cried. Trixie gave a little yap, and her tail began to wag furiously as George took her from Ross's arms. 'Oh, you little devil,' George said, 'I thought I'd lost you for good.'

'Sorry...' Hannah gave him a pained smile.

George blinked at her. 'My dear Hannah; it wasn't your fault.'

'But if I hadn't come to you for help...'

'Nonsense,' George cut in. He laughed as Trixie licked his chin. 'The main thing is I have her back. Next time I'll be sure to close the garden gate.'

Gina and Jess were standing by Hannah's car and up until now they'd both been silent. But now Gina grinned at Hannah. 'You go chasing after a little doggie and come back with an extra surprise.'

Ross shot her a wide and rather soppy smile. It was all Hannah could do not to roll her eyes.

'You weren't exactly breaking your neck to catch Trixie.'

'I didn't think it was a very good idea, us all charging after her; it would have scared her half to death.'

'Hmmm,' Hannah said. 'Whatever. It was just lucky I met Ross; I don't think I would have caught Trixie at all without his help.'

Gina shot him a flirtatious look. 'You are making rather a habit of being in the right place at the right time.'

'I try,' Ross smiled. He dug his hands in his pockets and looked over at the car. 'Is it still not running?'

'I don't know,' Hannah said, glancing at George. 'We were all too busy worrying about Trixie.'

George scratched his head. 'I'm blown if I know what's wrong with it.'

'Would you like me to have a look?' Ross asked. 'I'm pretty good with engines, even if I do say it myself.'

'I bet you are,' Gina said, with such obvious lust in her voice that even Jess did a double take this time. She exchanged a glance with Hannah that conveyed barely disguised disgust. Hannah had to stifle an inappropriate grin and at least pretend to be disgusted too. She supposed that the idea of her mother as a sexual being would be a shock to any teenage girl.

Ross turned back to Hannah. 'May I?' he asked, inclining his head at the car.

'Be my guest. Some kind man offers to get my little Citroen going; who am I to argue?'

'I'll make us all a nice cup of tea while Ross looks at the car then,' George said. 'Unless you all want to come in and get out of the rain?'

Gina glanced up at the sky and held a hand out. 'I think it's stopping now. I expect we'll be alright.'

George nodded. He pottered back into his garden, carefully shutting the gate before setting Trixie down. She scuttled off indoors, George watching her with a fond smile. 'I bet she's gone for a nap after all her adventures today,' he said.

'Sounds like a good idea,' Hannah said approvingly as she wiped a film of cold perspiration from her brow. She was still sweating from her run in her duffle coat, and what she really wanted was a nice warm shower and a change of clothes, but that would have to wait for a while.

Ross disappeared under the bonnet of Hannah's car with a look of boyish glee at the prospect, leaving Gina with a look of equal glee as she appraised his denim-clad rear. George clapped his hands together. 'Right… I'll make myself useful and get that tea. Are you sure you ladies wouldn't like to come in to the warm?'

'I'd better stay outside in case I'm needed,' Hannah said.

'I'll stay outside too,' Gina added, 'in case I'm needed for… well, you never know.'

Jess shook her head but didn't say a word.

'That's fine,' said George, 'teas all round. I'll be back in a tick.'

Jess hoisted herself onto George's garden wall, her legs dangling as she stuck a pair of earphones in and turned her iPod on. Gina folded her arms as she watched Ross work.

'You'll probably miss your train,' Hannah said.

'Probably,' Gina replied, her gaze still trained on Ross's bum.

'Will there be a later one?' Hannah asked.

Gina shrugged. 'I expect so.'

'You don't seem too worried.'

'No point now, is there?'

Hannah sighed. 'I'm sorry this hasn't been the Christmas I hoped it would be for you. Everything keeps going wrong, even today when I'm trying to get you home. I think I'm jinxed or something.'

Gina turned to her now, eyebrows raised in vague disbelief. 'Are you kidding? It's been the best Christmas I've had in ages!'

'Really?'

'Compared to the dull round of cooking, eating too much and then falling asleep in front of the telly…'

'We did quite a lot of that,' Hannah cut in.

'We did,' Gina laughed, 'but I couldn't have asked for better company. Not to mention the added bits of excitement that I definitely never had with Howard at Christmas.' She gave an impish grin as her gaze returned to Ross. 'And we've met some very interesting new people too.'

Hannah smiled. Her mind also went back to an interesting new acquaintance, but it wasn't Ross. Hers was a man whose real name she didn't know, and whose whereabouts now were just as much of a mystery. And yet, she couldn't get him out of her thoughts.

'Could you turn the engine over for me?' Ross called, breaking in on her reverie. Hannah gave silent thanks for the distraction; one place she really didn't need to go right now was Tom – or whatever his name was. He was out of reach and out of her life and dwelling on anything other than that was not healthy.

She took herself behind the steering wheel and turned the key. The engine wheezed and clunked but it didn't start.

'Again?' Hannah called.

'Not yet,' Ross shouted back. 'I think I'll need to get some more tools.' He appeared at the driver's window and leaned in. 'You might want to take it easy for a minute or two, take George up on his offer of a warm kitchen.'

'I hate to sound ungrateful, but do you have any idea how long you might be? Only I'm worried about Gina and Jess getting home.'

Ross mussed his hair before clamping his cap back on. 'I could take them to the station and then come back to look at your car.'

'Oh, no!' Hannah said quickly, 'I didn't mean it like that! You've already done far too much for us, I don't want to turn you into a taxi service as well.'

'I don't mind at all. In fact, it would be my pleasure.'

Gina spoke up from behind him. 'I think it sounds like a great idea. I'd be ever so grateful and I'd really rather not wait for the next train home.'

Hannah raised her eyebrows as they both turned to look at Gina. She hadn't been that bothered about missing her train only moments before.

'Great,' Ross said. 'You'll be pleased to know that we can go in the Land Rover this time, so you won't have to rattle around in the cab of a tractor.'

'Oh, I would have quite liked the tractor again,' Gina smiled.

George returned with a tray of tea. Risking third degree burns, they gulped it down as quickly as they could while explaining that they had now decided to try and catch Gina's train, and so had to rush off. George had looked disappointed at first when they said they were going, but rallied at the idea that Ross and Hannah would be back to finish fixing her car later.

*

Even Jess managed to look impressed as Ross opened the door of his swish Land Rover Discovery for them some moments later.

'Just got it last month,' he said, and he looked almost as proud as he did whenever he mentioned Bess, his tractor. 'It's brand new too, the first time I've ever been able to afford that.'

'What's this one called?' Gina asked as she climbed in.

Ross coloured and gave her a sheepish grin. 'Sally.'

Jess burst out laughing, quickly followed by everyone else, even Ross.

'I have to ask,' Gina said as the laughter died down, 'why Sally?'

'Sally Cinnamon…' Gina looked at him blankly. 'Like the song?' Ross added, trying but failing to enlighten her.

'*Sally Cinnamon you're my world…*' Jess cut in. 'The Stone Roses?'

Ross turned to her, looking pleased that at least someone could place his reference. 'You know it?'

Jess shrugged. 'A bit before my time but, yeah, I've heard it.'

'Not that I'm an expert, but I'd say that's before your time too, isn't it Ross?' Hannah asked.

'A little,' he grinned. 'But only just.'

'Right… so now we've got that sorted, shall we go?' Jess suggested, looking rather bored with the proceedings already.

'Yes milady,' Gina said, throwing Hannah a knowing smile. 'Right away.'

*

Ross took back roads and shortcuts that Hannah had no idea even existed, and got them to the station in half the time it would have taken her. Not that her little car would have made it down most of the dirt tracks that counted as roads for Ross and his Land Rover, even if she had known about them.

As they said goodbye in the carpark, Hannah couldn't help but notice the spark between Gina and Ross, with a look so loaded passing between them that had Hannah not known Gina's whereabouts at all times during the last week, she would have sworn they were already embroiled in an affair. They left him waiting for Hannah in the car, while she accompanied Gina and Jess to wait on the platform for the train. It wasn't long before it arrived, and although they said the same goodbyes they had said a hundred times before, Hannah was still left bereft as she watched the train pull away. They were hardly a world away from her, but tears stung her eyes like they never had before at their departure, and she felt properly lonely in her little universe for the first time since Jason had left. She was all too glad to see Ross's broad smile as she hurriedly rubbed away the tears.

'Did they get off alright?' he asked cheerfully as he opened the passenger door for her.

'Yes. Thank you so much for coming to our rescue again.'

'It's really nothing. Hopefully I'll be able to get your car running when we get back. Do you mind if I pick up my tools on the way through?'

'Of course not,' Hannah said as they pulled out of the carpark.

'You could pop in and say hello to my mum if you like,' he said. 'Only the other day she mentioned that she hadn't seen you around in ages.'

Hannah wondered how she had become the topic of conversation between Ross and his mum, and for reasons she couldn't explain hoped it had nothing to do with the last time Ross had literally dug her out of a hole and taken her to the hospital to look for a man she barely knew. She wondered what else Ross's mum would have said about that particular scenario; she felt more than a little daft when she thought about it now. Not for the first time, she also wished that Gina hadn't been quite as chatty with Ross about it. She had no issue being involved in the Holly Way community, she just didn't want to be their entertainment.

'That'd be nice,' she said vaguely as these ideas, quickly followed by unwanted thoughts of Tom, raced around her head.

'That reminds me,' Ross added as he navigated a tight bend with such ease that Hannah wouldn't have been surprised to learn that he drove rally cars in his spare time. 'Did you lose a watch?'

'No. But I might know someone who has.'

'It was in the snow the other day when I ploughed the lane. An expensive looking beast, actually, and it's lucky I didn't crush it underneath Bess's wheels.'

'That is a bit of luck,' Hannah agreed. 'I think it might belong to one of the paramedics who came to our house on Christmas day. He came back later saying he'd lost one and left his phone number in case we found it. I'll call him.'

'I'll dig it out when we stop off at the farm and you can take a photo to text him.'

'Brilliant idea!' Hannah smiled. It certainly was a stroke of luck that Ross had come across the lost watch, if it was the right one, of course. Some would call it a coincidence; just another one in a set of coincidences that seemed to get stranger and stranger.

Ross pulled up on the wide gravel drive of a ramshackle farmhouse. Despite its chaotic appearance, Holly Farm was well maintained and obviously loved. The full majesty of the summer gardens weren't in evidence, but the grounds were still vibrant with evergreens; brightly coloured furniture and ornaments cheering the winter scene. Neat outbuildings flanked the main house. The farm building itself was sixteenth century, but over the years there had been many additions and much rebuilding, so that some parts were higgledy piggledy, and others had the straight, clean lines of modern buildings. At the far left was an annexe that looked to be the newest bit of all. Ross was quick to announce that this was his alone, built by his parents when he turned twenty-five in exchange for a promise that he'd stay with them rather than move out, and that he'd take on the farm when they'd both gone. It was a promise he had been only too happy to make, he said, as he wouldn't have moved very far even if he'd gone, and he loved the farm and his life on it so much that he couldn't imagine doing anything else for a living anyway. In preparation, he now had his own flock of sheep and sections of the business that his dad had parcelled up and gifted to him so that he could make some money of his own. It was

a scheme that made everyone happy and, from what Hannah could
see of Ross, she had to conclude that he was doing a pretty good job
with his dad's gift.

Hannah followed Ross into what looked like the oldest part of
the building, and found herself in a low-ceilinged kitchen. The floor
was flagged in ancient stones, worn with centuries of footfall, and
the wooden beams that supported the ceiling, though varnished, told
the tale of an age-old battle with woodworm. Nowadays, the ceiling
also sported modern spotlights, and the kitchen was well-equipped
with gadgets and labour-saving devices that the original inhabitants
of the house could never have dreamt of. A brick red Aga filled the
room with welcome warmth and made a handsome focal point. The
room was currently deserted, though Hannah could smell something
sweet baking.

'Take a seat,' Ross said. 'Mum must be in the house somewhere.'

Hannah hovered at the vast wooden table. She didn't really want to
make herself at home in a house when the owners didn't know she was
there. But Ross didn't seem concerned about whether Hannah accepted
his invitation or not, and merely strode towards a connecting door that
led to the rest of the house. He stuck his head through the doorway
and bellowed into the space beyond.

'MUM! Where are you? I've got one of those visitors you're always
moaning you don't get!' He turned back and gave Hannah a broad grin.
'Don't worry; if she had a houseful every day she'd still moan. She loves
visitors, does Mum. Before you know it she'll have you promising to
make jam for the next WI meeting.'

Hannah prayed to the gods of anything she could think of that
Briony Hunter did no such thing. It sounded pretty close to Hannah's
idea of hell.

A moment later there was a series of thuds from the floor above, and then Ross's mother hurried into the kitchen. She was slightly out of breath, and smoothed down a bob that would have been the exact shade of blonde as Ross's had it not been generously threaded with silver. 'Oooh!' she squeaked as she set eyes on Hannah, 'how lovely to see you! I'm so sorry about the mess, I've been cleaning upstairs. If I'd known I was going to get a visitor I'd have cleaned downstairs first.'

Hannah smiled. She couldn't help but notice that downstairs was already spotless – at least the kitchen was – and a lot cleaner than her own place right now. 'Ross is very kindly helping me with my car. I hope I won't be in your way for long.'

Briony shook her head at her son, but she wore a fond smile. 'Any excuse to tinker with an engine, eh?' She turned to Hannah. 'You'll stay for a cup of tea and a slice of cake, won't you? I have a lovely sponge just out of the oven, or some fruit cake left from Christmas. Ross can manage by himself, can't you?'

'I thought you'd say that,' Ross said. 'But I've only come to get some tools; the car is at George Maynard's place.'

'Take your time so we can have a little gossip,' Briony said. 'There's no rush.'

Hannah couldn't decide if she felt pleased or aggrieved that she wasn't being offered a choice about whether she stayed for tea or not. She half wondered how many other 'visitors' were still being held, perhaps in a cellar or under-stairs cupboard, dressed in rags and being force-fed sponge cake and WI jam every day.

As Ross let himself out of the back door with a chuckle, a brief blast of cold air swirled through the warm kitchen, until the door closed behind him again. Hannah had been abandoned and now took a seat and surrendered to Briony's well-meaning but endless chatter.

Before the tea had even brewed in the pot Hannah heard all about Nicola Robinson's IVF (she'd never met Nicola but already knew the intimate workings of her ovaries), the vicar's pulled hamstring during the Millrise half marathon, Jean Johnson's hysterectomy and how much the average lamb would fetch at auction. Briony was a lovely woman, and Hannah could see where Ross got his warmth and generosity from, but she wasn't half exhausting to listen to.

'So…' Briony said as she poured Hannah's tea. 'Ross tells me you found a stray man on Christmas Day. Have you heard any more from him since he went off to hospital?'

Hannah almost dropped the slice of fruit cake she was holding. She had thought that Briony not mentioning it until now meant that she didn't know, but it seemed she'd simply had a lot of gossip to get off her chest before the interrogation on a new victim could begin. Having heard how much she was happy to reveal about other people's affairs, Hannah decided that a policy of information economy might be wise. Before this week, she and Ross had only exchanged a few words in passing – a comment on the weather or the state of the potholes on Holly Way – so sitting here like this with Briony was new territory for her. She was sure they were a lovely family to be friends with, and would always be there to help out in a crisis, but Hannah wasn't sure she was ready to be that fully integrated into their life; she had the feeling, however, that after today, there wouldn't be a lot of choice in the matter.

'No, I haven't seen him,' Hannah replied. 'I don't expect I will now.'

'Oooh, that's a shame. It would have been nice to find out how things turned out for him. I bet you've been wondering.'

Hannah took another bite of cake, though it was more to stifle the need for a reply than because she wanted it. She'd thought of little else, and as the days went by she became more convinced that Tom had found one set of memories and lost another – the ones that contained her. She kept telling herself that it was only to be expected, but perhaps some recognition of their Christmas day together would have been nice. She supposed there would be lots of reasons why not, though, and it was silly to get worked up over it.

'I've just had a marvellous idea!' Briony said. 'We're looking for ladies to feature on next year's calendar for the church fund. I don't suppose you'd like to take part?'

'A calendar?' Though Hannah was relieved that the subject of Tom had been dropped, she felt even more uncomfortable at this new one. She had visions of topless women draped in vegetables, like that film she'd watched with Gina, and it was the last thing she fancied... She fancied the idea of offending her host even less though.

'We've done this year's of course, and I'm just waiting for the vicar to bring my copy so I can't show it to you, I'm afraid. It's all very tasteful though, and you'd make a lovely October.'

Hannah wondered what it was about her that said October. Perhaps it was something to do with Halloween and the fact that she was looking particularly scary today. 'I'm not sure it's really me...' she began, but Briony cut her off.

'Do say yes! It's the same old faces every year and it would be lovely to have a new one.'

'I'm not very photogenic...'

'Everyone is photogenic by the time Rainbow gets hold of them.'

'Rainbow?'

'Our photographer. She's absolutely brilliant.'

'I'm sure she is but...'

'You'd be great…' Ross stood in the doorway holding a metal tool box, and with a huge grin on his face. He turned to his mum. 'I can't leave you alone for ten minutes without you trying to recruit.'

'When you bring a lovely young lady over, what else am I going to do?'

'I wouldn't exactly say young…' Hannah gave a self-conscious laugh. She really wanted this conversation to be over.

'Come on, Hannah…' Ross angled his head at the back door. 'Let me rescue you.'

'Back to the glamorous world of broken-down cars – yes please,' Hannah smiled.

Briony looked rather put out and made Hannah solemnly promise to at least consider the calendar and to make sure she called for tea at the farmhouse again whenever she had time. She grumbled good-naturedly that Ross's dad was always out and she was forever alone, and that Ross was becoming almost as much of a workaholic as his father, and then Hannah finally managed to say goodbye before following Ross out to his Land Rover.

'They're not nudie calendars,' Ross laughed as he opened the door for her. 'More likely you'll be suffocating under pumpkins and apples, so we'd hardly see that much of you at all.'

'Oh… well, it's very nice of your mum to offer but I don't think it's really me.'

'That's a shame actually. I think you'd look pretty good buried under an artfully arranged mound of marrows.'

Hannah giggled. 'I bet my sister would be up for it, and she'd look a hundred times better.'

Ross was silent. Hannah glanced across and saw he had a faraway look, as if he was visualising just how good Gina might look under a mound of marrows. He was probably wishing that it *was* a nudie calendar. Then he seemed to shake himself, and his usual boyish grin was back. He started the engine. 'I'll do my best to persuade you while we drive back to George's. Mum would never forgive me if I don't. Perhaps your sister could join in too… might make you feel a bit less self-conscious?'

'Maybe…' Hannah replied. The truth was she did feel obliged to say yes, if only to repay the kindness Ross had shown her. But the thought of it made her feel sick, and it was going to take a hell of a lot of persuading, no matter how many cars Ross fixed for her.

*

After much discussion, Ross persuaded Hannah to let him drop her off at home while he went back to get her car going. Hannah wasn't crazy about the idea, especially as she felt like such a burden on his time; but the little jobs she had neglected at home over the previous week were beginning to nag at her, and the thought of getting back and starting on them was too tempting. If the truth be told, she was also a little tired and cold, and home seemed like a nice place to be right now.

'If I manage to get it going I'll bring it back, and if I don't then I can tow it over with Sally,' he said as he dropped her at her gate. His cheeky grin was back as he added, 'But I've never met an engine I couldn't get purring again.'

Unable to prevent the giggle that erupted from her, Hannah bade him goodbye and let herself in, alone again in her cottage for what felt like the first time in years.

The silence enveloped her as Hannah slipped off her coat and hung it up. It was chilly, but the central heating would kick in soon and if she cracked on with the tidying up she wouldn't get cold. She needed to keep busy, because she missed Gina and Jess already. It was almost enough to make her wish she'd enjoyed Briony's hospitality a little longer after all.

It was hard to believe that three women could make so much mess but Hannah was glad of the distraction. Her phone sat on the mantelpiece as she worked. Even though she'd set the volume as high as it would go so that she'd know as soon as Gina was back safe, and even though she was expecting it to go off, she still jumped when it bleeped the arrival of a text. When she checked, however, it wasn't Gina, but the paramedic who had lost his watch. As Ross had suggested, they'd taken a photo of it earlier and sent it to the number the man had left, and the text he sent back now confirmed that it was indeed his watch and that he was delighted they'd found it. Hannah replied that he could come whenever he wanted to pick it up. It was nice to have done a good deed for him when he was always doing them for other people.

It was later, as she was beating the crumbs from her living room rug and wondering just how they kept ending up there when she rarely ate anything in that room, that the car pulled up outside her gate. Not her own sunny little Citroen or Ross's sleek Range Rover, not a car belonging to anyone she knew for that matter. It was a sexy looking black Audi with personalised plates bearing initials that she didn't recognise either. The windows were tinted to a degree that made Hannah wonder whether they were entirely legal, so she had no way of preparing herself for who might emerge from the car. As hers was the only cottage in the immediate vicinity, she had to assume that whoever it was had come specifically to visit her.

The engine stopped, and there was a moment of suspense before the driver's door opened. Out stepped a slim blonde woman, immaculately turned out in a calf-length navy woollen coat, her hair pinned into a neat chignon. Hannah gave an involuntary gasp as she recognised the figure, and before she had time to fully process the information, another, more familiar figure, got out of the passenger side to join her. Physically, he looked a lot healthier than he had the last time she'd seen him – certainly a lot less bedraggled – but there was something somber in his expression, a strain that made Hannah want to run and hug him. He looked like a man whose mind was still not altogether as it should be. He looked very unhappy. And considering what circumstances she had encountered him in on Christmas Day that must mean he was very strained indeed.

The woman extended a hand as Hannah opened the gate for them. 'Hannah, I presume?'

'Hello…' Hannah glanced at Tom as she shook the woman's hand. What did she call him now? She gave him the brightest smile she had in her reserves, and the one he returned was like the sun breaking through clouds on a stormy day – bright and glorious. But as fast as it had appeared, it was swallowed up again by greyness. He seemed to be tussling with some inner turmoil, and looked extremely uncomfortable, as if he'd rather be anywhere else. There was no reason for either of them to feel awkward, really, so why did it feel like that? She wondered if her face told the same story. 'I'm Martine,' the woman continued. 'I'm so pleased to finally meet you. Mitchell has told me so much about you.'

Hannah forced another smile. 'Mitchell… so at least I have a proper name now. We had to make do with Tom on Christmas day, at the whim of my niece, I might add.'

'So I hear!' Martine laughed. Even her laughter was elegant and musical, though Hannah couldn't help but feel it lacked warmth. She shook away the thought. Jealousy was an ugly emotion, and she was feeling it in buckets right now, even though she knew she had no right to. This woman was so impeccable, so together, so obviously successful that Hannah would challenge any other woman she knew not to feel a little bit of envy. She and Mitchell made a handsome couple. 'It sounds as though it was quite an adventure.'

Hannah looked at Tom, who was now Mitchell, as she answered. His name was awkward and alien to her when she tried to attach it to him. She liked him better as Tom. 'It was. How's the head now?'

'It's on the mend,' he said.

'So...'

'Oh, his memory is still away with the fairies,' Martine answered for him. 'I'm sure a bit more time will sort things, though.'

'Oh...' Hannah replied. 'Nothing has come back at all yet?'

'Bits,' Mitchell replied. 'Annoyingly it's little things that don't seem important, like I'll recognise a coat I own and remember where I last wore it, but I don't recall important things...' He glanced at Martine, 'like my wife.'

'I know, it's a shocking state of affairs,' Martine said. 'A lesser woman could be very offended by that.'

Surely every other woman was a lesser woman, Hannah thought. There it was again, that little worm of jealousy. 'Um... would you like to come inside for a drink or something?' she asked. She prayed they would say no, because Martine looked like the sort of woman who might break out in hives at the sight of an unwashed cup, and her house still looked like a bombsite from Gina and Jess's visit.

'That's very kind but we really don't have a lot of time today,' Martine said. 'We were actually on a drive out to see if we could jog Mitchell's memory and then we're going to visit a few old friends to see if that will help too. But as we were passing here Mitchell insisted that we pick up some flowers to bring over for you. There's a petrol station not far from here and we got some rather decent ones from there.' She added the final sentence gleefully, implying that she herself would never receive petrol station flowers, thereby reinforcing Hannah's transient and inferior status as a part of Mitchell's life. Hannah was wondering where the flowers were, when Mitchell went to the boot of the car and produced a bouquet of white and yellow roses and carnations.

'They're lovely, but you needn't have,' Hannah said as he handed them over.

'We wanted to thank you,' Martine said. 'Both of us wanted to thank you for your kindness on Christmas day. Goodness only knows what might have happened to Mitchell had you not found him.'

'It was more a case of him finding me,' Hannah smiled. 'I really didn't do anything at all.'

'That's not what I heard,' Martine said. 'You certainly did more than a lot of people would have done.'

Hannah glanced at Mitchell. Why was Martine the only one talking? She didn't like this new, miserable, henpecked version of Tom-who-was-now-Mitchell, standing before her as though he wished a giant bird would swoop from the sky and carry him off. Did he feel at sea in the company of his wife, a woman he should have been intimately acquainted with but couldn't remember at all? Or was he simply finding her as irritating as Hannah was? Martine was perfectly courteous – as perfect in her manners as in every other aspect of her being – but there was something about her that Hannah simply couldn't warm to. Not that it mattered, of course, they were hardly going to be best friends; and she supposed it was nice of her to want to call and meet Hannah and thank her in person.

'So… you live nearby?' Hannah asked, grasping for some neutral conversation, anything that would stop her being a monumental bitch, which was what her thoughts were making her feel like right now.

'Chapeldown,' Martine replied, with obvious pride. There was a suitable pause to give Hannah time to be impressed. Chapeldown was the next village along Holly Way – more of a hamlet really – inhabited by stockbrokers and surgeons. It was way beyond Hannah's (and most other people's) budget.

'Very nice,' was all that Hannah could find to say.

'Close enough for you to pop over and see us sometime,' Martine added, which Hannah translated as *please never pop over to see us*. Hannah simply smiled.

'We should probably let you get on,' Mitchell cut in. Hannah could see that the meeting wasn't getting any easier for him. Perhaps he wasn't feeling as well as he looked after all. If he still hadn't regained his memory, then who knew what deeper injuries lay beneath the surface wound that was now barely visible beneath his hair. Maybe it would take him years to get right. Hannah couldn't imagine how horrible that would be, but she felt for him with every ounce of her being. She wanted to hug him, to tell him everything would be alright. Impossible, of course, or at least highly inappropriate.

'The flowers really are lovely,' she said. 'I appreciate you stopping by and I'm happy to see you both looking so well.'

'Flowers are the least we could do,' Martine said. 'As Mitchell said, we should let you get on.'

There were a million questions Hannah wanted to ask, but she had the distinct feeling that she wouldn't get straight answers to any of them – at least, not from Martine. Perhaps it was none of her business anyway, but they still fired around her head, desperate to be aired. Neither of them had even hinted at what had sent Mitchell out into the snow that day, to be injured and lost. Had the police been involved when he had turned up at the hospital? It must have been something bad, something traumatic; people didn't just take off like that for nothing. How were they dealing with it now he was home?

Martine shook Hannah's hand again, and this time, so did Mitchell. Her grip was cold and strong, whereas his warm hand lingered in hers for a fraction of a second too long, and he held her gaze as if trying to tell her something. 'Take care,' he said, and it seemed as if he had never meant anything so sincerely in his life.

'You too,' Hannah replied, 'and if you ever need anything you know where to find me.'

'Gracious!' Martine laughed, 'I hope he's not going to go wandering off and need rescuing again or I'll have to get a chip inserted.'

Hannah stared at her. She couldn't help it, when Martine's words were so cold and thoughtless. Mitchell was clearly distressed enough, without his wife belittling him. Martine didn't seem to notice Hannah's reaction, however, and Mitchell didn't seem to notice Martine's cutting remark. After another brief goodbye, the Audi was gone, and Hannah was left holding her flowers and more intrigued by Mitchell than ever before. She knew more about him now than she had done a week ago, but that only deepened the mystery.

*

Her flowers sat in a glass vase on the mantelpiece as Hannah finally cradled a glass of wine and curled up on the sofa with a book now that the evening was hers alone. She glanced up at them again as she had many times over the day. Petrol station or not, she liked them. Ross had left her an hour before, having been true to his promise that he would get her car running again. She'd also had a very interesting visit from her paramedic friend, who had picked up his watch and then, it seemed, was so grateful that he gave her far more information than he probably ought to concerning Mitchell, including his surname and why his wife was well-known to the doctors at the hospital. Hannah was sure he was breaking many rules of confidentiality so she simply took it in, feeling all at once wild with curiosity but sneaky and underhand too. If Martine and Mitchell had wanted her to have any of this information, surely they would have told her themselves? The more she thought about it, the more she was convinced that they had been hiding an awful lot earlier that day. Mitchell didn't seem happy to be back where he belonged. Even if he couldn't remember his wife, there would surely have been some residual spark of attraction, some sense of belonging. After all, he must have loved her when he married her and love was a powerful enough emotion to survive every assault on it, wasn't it? Hannah didn't really know enough about amnesia, but her logic told her this ought to be so. And Martine was just as puzzling. She didn't strike Hannah as someone who had been out of her mind with worry when Mitchell had wandered off. In fact, she seemed rather unconcerned by the whole affair. People made jokes about traumatic events, they made light of them to deal with the real hurt, but Martine wasn't even doing that – God knows Hannah had done enough of it over the years to recognise it. Martine really didn't seem to care.

Around eight, Hannah's phone rang and Gina's name flashed up on the screen.

'Hello you, did you make it home okay?'

'No drama, more's the pity. A bit of drama makes it all so much more interesting. Unless you count Jess's phone battery running out of course, which she definitely seemed to do.' Gina sounded cheerful and rested, despite the two-hour journey home. Hannah hoped some of that was down to her visit. Her sister had been subjected to a pretty awful year and she'd gladly do anything to help make it better. 'How's your car?' Gina added. 'Still a heap of shit?'

'No,' Hannah laughed, 'Ross managed to get it going with his magic touch.'

'Hmmm... I have an idea he could get anything going with his magic touch.'

'Even ladies who are a teeny bit too old for him?'

'Particularly ladies who are a teeny bit too old for him.'

'Know any?'

'I think I'm supposed to say no to that, aren't I?'

'Well done.'

'So, did you see a lot of him today?'

'I suppose I did really.'

'Lucky cow.'

'You say that but I also had to have tea with his mum.'

'Oh, how horrible. I'd definitely feel like a dirty old pervert if I had to do that. I bet she's hardly older than me.'

'You were the one insisting there wasn't much of an age gap between you and Ross.'

'I said there wasn't enough to put me off – there's a difference.'

Hannah giggled. 'You're terrible. It's lucky I didn't turn out to be a big floozy like you or Jess would have had no decent role model in the family.'

'She hasn't got one now. Why else do you think she's turned out to be such a little shit?'

'You don't mean that.'

'I've just arrived home and opened last month's phone bill. I bloody do!'

'Oh dear. Is she going to pay you back?'

'I don't know what with. And when you consider that I'm the one who gives her money in the first place it would just be me paying myself back. Anyway, enough of that. What did Ross say about me?'

'Nothing really.'

'Nothing? I clearly didn't make enough of an impression then. Ah well, I suppose there'll be other fish in the sea. He was rather yummy, though.'

'Actually I think he does find you attractive, but in all seriousness, he probably wants a girlfriend his own age.'

'Oooh, you can be heartless, can't you?' Gina laughed. 'Fancy crushing my dreams like that.'

'Sorry…'

'What else? You want to tell me something.'

'I do?'

'I always know.'

'Well… Tom came to see me. Except, obviously, he's not named Tom, and his wife was with him.'

'That's good. You wanted to know what had happened. Is he well? Are things back the way they should be? Did they come to let you know?'

'He looked alright, but he still doesn't have his memory back. Only bits, he says.'

'So what's his actual name?'

'Mitchell. Mitchell Bond.'

'Mitchell Bond?' Gina snorted. 'Are you serious? That's got to be a made up name!'

'I'm serious.'

'Did he arrive in an Aston Martin with a particularly suspect black umbrella?'

'Very funny.'

'What's his wife like?'

'She seems nice.'

'You hate her.'

'That obvious?'

'Of course. What else did you find out?'

'She's a GP. Loaded, so I'm told. He's a property developer. No kids.'

'They told you all this?'

'Not exactly... our paramedic friend called around to pick up his watch.'

'You found his watch? Now I'm confused.'

'Ross found it, actually.'

'Is there anything that boy can't do?'

'I don't know. I'll ask him when I see him next.'

'So your paramedic says they've got pots of money. How does he know all this?'

'One of the consultants at the hospital knows her. I think she's quite well respected but...'

'But what?'

'She's apparently a bit of a bitch to work with.'

'Hmmm... that figures.'

'Why?'

'She's in a competitive field. It needs a bit of mega bitch from time to time to make it.'

'You're not and you work in a competitive field.'

'I'm a sales manager. It's hardly the same.'

'Don't run yourself down.'

'It's just the way it is. So how did he end up bashing the memory from his head?'

'They didn't say.'

'No explanation at all?'

'They probably didn't think it was any of my business.'

'It's not, but I bet you still want to know. I certainly do.'

'Of course I do. I can't help feeling weird about the whole thing.'

'What? Like she was trying to bump him off or something and failed?'

'God, of course not! I'd never even thought of that. I just meant they seemed as if they were keeping some nasty secrets.'

'I bet she *was* trying to bump him off.'

'She's a GP.' Hannah wrinkled her nose. 'She wouldn't need to thump him on the head, she could subtly poison him or overdose or something. She must know enough about drugs.'

'Oh, right… do you think we should phone an anonymous tip off to the police?'

'No…' Hannah laughed. 'I'm sure there's been no foul play. But I do get the impression their marriage isn't very solid. He doesn't seem to want to be there at all. Maybe that's what it was all about: they were having a row and he stormed out?'

Gina was silent for a moment. 'You've been on your own too long,' she announced.

'That's a bit random.'

'I just think you're taking too much of an interest in this. You felt connected or whatever on Christmas Day, and you got close because he needed you, and now you feel like there's something special there, some bond that means you can't let him go and you keep beating yourself up about whether he's alright or not. It's twisting your logic.'

'You were the one who just suggested his wife was trying to murder him!'

'I was kidding. You're not. Walk away, Han. He's got his wife back, they're happy and rich in their big house, end of story.'

'But they're not happy, are they?'

'They might be on the rocks but stay away. It's a train wreck waiting to happen, and if things are as you say they are, then you don't want to be on the tracks when it does, no matter how much you like him.'

'I'm not going to be; I'm just discussing it with you, that's all.'

'I know. But you have to ask yourself why you're bothered about any of it. You don't know him… you don't know either of them. What do you care if their marriage is shit?'

'Because I'm a human being.'

'Because you're interested in him.'

Hannah sighed. 'This is a silly conversation. I've got no intention of breaking his marriage up.'

'I never said that.'

'But you implied it.'

'If you think that then you have a guilty conscience and that's down to no-one but you. I only meant that you shouldn't get involved. At best it would be a messy affair, at worst you'd be a rebound relationship; either way it wouldn't be pretty. Han… I hate to see you alone, and I do wish you'd find someone nice, but not him. You understand what I'm trying to say, don't you?'

'I suppose I do. But you're wrong if you think this is about me pining for a man. I'm perfectly happy alone and I wouldn't settle for any man just for the sake of having one. I'm certainly not going to go out looking for one.'

'You could go out a bit though, and maybe you'd meet one.'

'That's rich coming from you. Perhaps you should take your own advice.'

'I haven't been alone as long as you, and I still have a husband to get rid of.'

'That's not it.'

'It is soooo it. When my divorce comes through and I've cleaned the cheating bastard out of every penny I can, I'm taking myself off to Spain to find a hot waiter.'

'Howard really did a number on you, didn't he?' Hannah said with a faint smile.

'He hurt me, Hannah, I can't deny it. He might as well have cut my heart out with a blunt knife. But he'll be sorry. I'm going to have so much sex it'll make my eyes water and I might even film it to send to him.'

'Oh Gina… Please tell me Jess isn't there right now.'

'She went out almost as soon as we dropped our bags on the floor. She doesn't need me anymore, and when all the joking is done, I'm going to be on my own soon. That's why I don't want to see you lonely, because I know how it feels.'

'Well…' Hannah said, sensing her sister's mood darkening, 'you'll be back here soon, close to me for good, and we can keep each other company.'

'Like two mad cat ladies? Fabulous.'

'I'll bring the cats and you can provide the incoherent rambling.'

'I see you save the best job for me.'

'Of course. When will you hear from the solicitors?'

'Soon I hope. I just want it all sorted, to get my money and come and find a place back in Millrise. I want to come home now.'

'I can't wait,' Hannah said.

'Neither can I. Though I'm not sure Jess is as happy about it.'

'She'll adjust; kids always do.'

'She's leaving a pretty good social life behind.'

'It's only a couple of hours away from Birmingham. She'll make friends here and then she'll have two really good social lives.'

'I'll let you tell her that when she kicks off as I hand my house keys back,' Gina laughed. 'For now I think she's pretending it won't happen.'

'Want me to talk to her?'

'There's no point yet. It could be months before I'm in a position to go anywhere – there's just no way of knowing with legal stuff. When the time comes I'm thinking I might just get a sack and some strong rope so I can tie her up and throw her into the removal van.'

'Good luck with that,' Hannah laughed.

'Thanks. I'm going to need it.'

*

Hannah clicked *submit*. A message popped up on the screen to congratulate her for registering on *Starcrossed.com*. She chewed a fingernail and sat back in her seat waiting for something to happen. She didn't know why she was doing this. Perhaps something Gina said had sparked off a realisation. She was nervous as hell now, worried about what sort of nutters she might get replies from, but it was done. And you never knew… didn't lots of people meet their true love on dating sites, every day? So they couldn't be a complete waste of time, could they? There were biometric testing and glossy photos and profiles and scientific formulae of all kinds helping to match couples, not like in the old days where you turned up wearing a pink carnation and hoping he still had his own teeth. What she had said to Gina, about not needing a man – she felt sure that was all true; but there was no harm in seeing what was out there. She might even have fun in the process, meet some nice people, make some good friends. And maybe, just maybe, she'd find that elusive soulmate she had given up on.

She refreshed her inbox once, cursed herself for being stupid enough to think that anyone was going to respond that quickly, and then minimised the screen so she could get some work done. It had piled up during Gina and Jess's visit, and there was more than enough now to keep her working until midnight for the next couple of weeks.

Three days had passed since Gina had gone home, and the house had become Hannah's again. The peace had been welcome at first, but now it felt almost too quiet. Hannah had tidied away the Christmas mess, and then she had gone to the antique wardrobe in the spare room, bundled Jason's clothes into a bin bag and dropped them off at the church for their monthly jumble sale. It was a simple act of decluttering, but it had meant so much more. Everything had gone, even the clothes Mitchell had borrowed; it was Hannah's way of putting all that behind her, a promise to turn over a fresh page and start a brand new chapter in her life. It would be nice to date, have a few nights out, enjoy some frivolous sex once in a while, but never again would she get hung up on a man and let him take over her life. That was the intention, anyway. She'd heard no more from Mitchell or Martine, and while she was still intrigued by the mystery that surrounded them, she decided that it was probably for the best if she didn't see them again. It was even something of a relief, if she was honest, because Gina was right: it could only lead to trouble. She hadn't told anyone about signing up to the dating agency either; she'd just see what happened. Probably nothing, so until something did, there was really no need to tell anyone. Despite this, it would have been nice to share it with Gina. She had wondered a few times about telling her, but then decided against it for reasons she couldn't quite put her finger on. For now she was just quietly getting on with the rest of her life.

*

An hour later Hannah checked her inbox again. No messages so she went back to work. Usually she found the process of designing soothing, but her mind wouldn't stay on anything today. With a sigh, she grabbed her duffle coat. A breath of air might be just the thing to clear her head.

The morning was bright and clear, and if it hadn't been for the bitter wind, Hannah could almost imagine it was spring. She wandered in the direction of Holly Farm, for no other reason than her feet seemed to take her that way. Perhaps it was the subconscious need to see a friendly face, and when she found Ross digging a hole for a new fencepost on the farm's boundaries, she couldn't help a broad smile.

'If it isn't my favourite knight in shining armour.'

'Oh aye…' He turned to her and leaned on his spade with a sweaty grin, 'you know a lot of them do you?'

'Ooooh, tons. None as good as you, though.'

'What brings you this way? Come to see my mum? Please say you've come to see my mum because she's been going on about you ever since your last visit.'

'Has she?' Hannah smiled.

'Yup. Determined to get you involved in the WI.'

Hannah's face fell again. She had hoped to have dropped off Briony's WI radar by now.

'I thought that would wipe the smile off your mush,' Ross laughed. 'Actually she'd just love to see you again, says she really enjoyed your chat last time and I shouldn't have stolen you away.'

Hannah recalled that it had been less of a chat in the traditional sense and more of a barrage of gossip from Briony at Hannah. Still, it had obviously made her happy and Hannah couldn't grumble about that. 'I'll call tomorrow if she's going to be around. I'd love to see her today but I have a ton of work to do.'

'Looks like it…' Ross raised his eyebrows.

'Oh…' Hannah laughed, 'I just needed a walk before I exploded. Sometimes I have to clear my head and then I can concentrate, you know?'

'Not really. I've never been one for computer screens, that's why I work outdoors. I've got a laptop, but I rarely use it.'

'You must need to concentrate when you fix engines.'

'I suppose I do but I enjoy it so much I hardly notice.'

'It's the same with me. I love my work. It certainly beats what I used to do before.'

'What was that?'

'Territory manager for an art supply company. I liked visiting the clients and driving around but I couldn't stand the pressure of sales targets. Gina does a similar job, quite by coincidence, but she doesn't let it get to her like I did. When you don't give a stuff you seem to earn higher bonuses for some reason and she does well. Perhaps the customers can smell desperation on you.'

'Perhaps…' Ross chuckled. 'Well, it's all Greek to me. Give me an engine or a shovel any day and I'm happy as a pig in muck.'

'Which is lucky as you're a farmer.'

'So I am!' Ross laughed. 'So your sister got home okay?'

'Yes, no problems. Not that it would bother her if there were, she'd just rise above it like some serene and chilled disco queen.'

'I can imagine,' Ross smiled. 'Not that I know her that well, of course…'

They fell into an awkward pause, where Hannah wondered if he was thinking about what it might be like to know Gina well. He fiddled with the handle of his spade. It was an uncharacteristically doubtful gesture and showed a hint of vulnerability that Hannah hadn't seen in him before.

'So I can tell Mum you'll call in?' he asked, finally breaking the silence.

'Yes, most definitely. And I'll tell Gina that you were asking about her.' Hannah didn't quite know why she felt the need to reassure him of this, but it seemed like something he'd want to hear.

'Great…' Ross looked down at his boots as he dug his toe into a pile of upturned soil.

'Well,' Hannah said, 'I'll let you get on in peace.'

He looked up and smiled, more like his usual self. 'Enjoy the rest of your walk. Just be careful further down the lane – it's muddier than it looks down there and I don't want to have to winch you out with the tractor.'

'I'm going straight home now. I think I've wasted enough time for one day; I need to get some work of my own done.'

Ross tipped his forehead in a little salute. 'Don't forget my mum, will you?'

'I won't,' she smiled. 'What sort of cake does she like?'

'You're going to bake?'

'Not likely! I'm not in the habit of poisoning my neighbours! I was going to pick one up from the bakery.'

'Don't do that,' Ross said amiably, 'she'd be heartbroken if she wasn't able to make you a cake. She's always finding excuses to bake – me and Dad will be wobbling around the farm if we don't get more help eating them.'

'Really? I feel a bit weird turning up empty handed at anyone's house.'

'What will really make her happy is just that – you turning up. She loves company and sometimes I think the farm is a bit remote. That's why she gets involved in everything going.'

'Well I can definitely do that then. Maybe I'll see you when I pop in?'

'Maybe… if I'm allowed anywhere near the kitchen when the girlie conversation is in full swing.' Ross grinned.

*

After a few days had passed, Hannah had collected a healthier pile of enquiries from prospective suitors on the dating site. Most of them were entirely unsuitable, however, and she didn't need to read more than a few lines of their message to figure this out. They either talked about themselves with an alarming degree of narcissism, or described their male appendages in an equally worrying manner. The ones who didn't sounded like mummy's boys or the sort who would furtively steal your knickers to add to their private collection. Only one stood out as half human, someone calling himself Chris P. It was a normal name for a start, but that was probably all Hannah was going to get without meeting him. As she considered her options, Hannah asked herself, yet again, what the hell she was thinking of.

She read the message again. And then she re-read Chris P's profile. He looked okay. But only okay. Was that good enough? Was there any point in putting herself through this for only okay? *He's probably much nicer in real life*, she told herself, *most people find it hard to sell themselves without looking like a twat.* She was sure she probably looked like a twat from her profile too. And you couldn't get any sort of chemistry through a computer screen. There might be an instant physical attraction that she just wouldn't know about until they met. But, then again… he could be a twat.

In the end, it had seemed a much safer bet to let Briony Hunter cajole her into going to her charity salsa night. Nice and safe, as usual, Hannah thought. Not that the idea of a room full of virtual strangers wasn't a daunting prospect, but at least she had enlisted the support of her sister, who was even now on her way from Birmingham. Gina hadn't taken much persuading, stating that January was shit and anything to break the tedium was fine by her. Hannah suspected it was a welcome distraction from messy divorce proceedings but, either way, she was glad of the company. Everyone else would doubtless be there with dates and spouses and as long as she and Gina weren't expected to dance together they could get legless at the bar and have a pretty good night watching everyone else, not to mention helping various local charities in the process.

*

Later that evening, Gina and Hannah jostled for space at the bathroom mirror.

'Hey, this is my house!' Hannah giggled. She was already succumbing to the pleasant effects of a glass or two of gin and tonic, and Gina was similarly well-oiled on the mojitos she'd mixed for herself.

'But I'm your guest. You're supposed to go out of your way to make sure I'm happy.'

'You should be happy I let you come anywhere with me at all.' She gave Gina a playful shove. 'So shift it.'

'You should be honoured I'm allowing myself to be seen out with a social embarrassment like you,' Gina laughed as she shoved her back. 'Now, out of the way, munchkin. I've got beautifying to get on with.'

'You don't need it, you look gorgeous already.'

'Are you kidding? I've got a couple of years on you; it's hard enough as it is without keeping up with a younger model.'

'Only a tiny bit younger,' Hannah laughed. 'I think at this point in our lives it doesn't really make all that much difference.'

'You'd be surprised.'

'I don't know why you're worrying anyway – you got all the good genes.'

'That's not saying much from our parents, is it?'

Hannah's smile slipped.

'Still,' Gina continued quickly, 'who wants to think about all that crap now? We've got serious things to sort out. Like do I go in a classy black dress or a slutty red one?'

'Red. If it's the dress I'm thinking of it will shake things up a bit.'

'What are you wearing?'

Hannah frowned. 'I have absolutely no idea. Every dress I had thought about wearing looks horrible tonight and I didn't buy anything new because I didn't think it was worth spending the money. I wish I'd splashed out now, though.'

'Want to borrow?'

Hannah shook her head. 'They won't look the same on me. I haven't got the gravity defying boobies for a start.'

'It's all in the bra, my dear, I keep telling you that. Try one of my dresses, please. I've brought far too many with me so it seems a shame to drag them all over and not use them.'

'You could leave them here for when you come back.'

'You mean come over and get pissed in public with you more often? Hannah Meadows – what on earth has got into you? You hate clubbing!'

'I don't hate it; I just don't see the point of it most of the time. Right now, though, I feel like letting my hair down and having a little fun.'

Gina turned back to the mirror and dabbed at her foundation. 'Is that why Jason's clothes have gone?'

'You little sneak. Nothing escapes your notice, does it?' Hannah laughed. 'I thought it was about time. Besides, I need the wardrobe space if you're going to keep your clothes in there.'

'You know the minute I leave a dress here I'm going to want it in Birmingham?'

'You don't go out that much, surely?'

'I might start… I've registered on a dating site.'

Hannah blinked at her. And then she let out a peal of laughter. 'Oh my God! So have I!'

'Aren't they all just absolute wankers, though?' Gina said as she dusted some blusher over her cheeks. 'This one guy sent me a photo of his boat in the Med instead of a photo of himself. I mean, what's that about? *I don't have a personality but will my boat do instead?* It's doubtful he even has a boat, so either way he's a loser.'

'To be honest, in most cases I'd rather date the boat,' Hannah laughed. 'You can have a lot of fun in one of them.'

'And they don't shag their secretaries the minute your back is turned.'

'Too true,' Hannah agreed.

'So… have you had any decent offers?'

Hannah shrugged. 'One half-decent one, but in the end I couldn't be bothered. Half-decent isn't really decent enough, is it? I'll keep my membership for a while and see what else comes in but I'm not holding my breath.'

'I've had one or two interesting ones. I don't know about all these computer matches these sites run. Perhaps they'd work if the men they were trying to match me with weren't mostly lying bastards to begin with. They say they like kittens and shopping but turn up to the date with matching his'n'hers gimp suits and a penchant for shagging in custard.'

'Blimey, they're a bit more extreme in Brum, aren't they?' Hannah giggled.

'And that's just Howard.' Gina applied a last slick of mascara and dropped the tube into her make-up bag. 'The mirror's all yours – make yourself gorgeous.'

'How long have we got?' Hannah asked. 'I might have had enough time if I'd started last week.'

'Silly,' Gina smiled. 'You know I was always envious of you when we were teenagers?'

Hannah stared. 'Seriously? What on earth for? You were always the beautiful one and I was envious of you!'

'I was the tall, willowy one with what turned out to be pretty decent breasts but you were the one with the rosy little cheeks that everyone wanted to squish. You had the sparkle in your eyes and the huggable little bod. People wanted to love you, where they wanted to admire me. I only wanted to be loved.'

'I love you, more than any sister loved another,' Hannah said. 'And don't expect me to repeat that ever again because it's the gin talking.'

Gina pulled her into a hug. 'Come here, sis. Now, let's get ready for this… whatever it is you've dragged me here for. And there had better be some fit guys to compensate for my horrible train journey next to fried chicken armpit man.'

'You know Ross is picking us up. There's one straight away.'

'Ah… Ross…' Gina said in a deliberately dreamy voice. 'Such a pity he's not interested in an old lady. If the ball was for Help the Aged I might be able to persuade him to do me for charity.'

'I probably shouldn't say this… but I think he might be a bit interested.'

'In me? What makes you say that?'

'I don't know. Just the way he looks when your name is mentioned.'

'You say his mum is organising this event?'

'She's one of the organisers – yes.'

'Well, I don't suppose she'd approve of Mrs Robinson homing in on her son, then.'

'Perhaps not,' Hannah laughed. 'But at least he'll be pleasant company in the very likely event that the remaining male guests are rubbish.'

'There is that,' Gina agreed. 'In that case I'd better go for the classy black number to get mummy's approval, just in case Ross and I do get to… well, you know…'

*

The little black dress Gina had opted for was a fitted shift dress with lace sleeves and a deep V cut out lace panel that trailed the length of her back. It was simple and elegant and Hannah couldn't help but feel that she looked stunning enough to outshine every other woman at the party. Hannah herself had gone for an old favourite in the end – an emerald green tea dress which everyone had always said flattered her slightly curvier figure and brought out the auburn highlights in her hair. It wasn't perhaps very gala evening, but Hannah felt comfortable in it and figured nobody would really be looking at her anyway.

'You look lovely,' Gina said as Hannah slipped on her shoes. 'I don't know what you were worrying about.'

'So do you. That dress is amazing.'

Gina gave herself the once over with a small smile. 'Howard bought it for me. One of the last ones he did buy. Cost an arm and a leg and, with hindsight, I suppose it was a guilt purchase. Still…' she sniffed, 'who am I to look a guilty gift horse in the mouth?'

'Wreak havoc in it tonight, and think of it as revenge when you do.'

Gina's smile broadened. 'My thoughts precisely!'

*

When Ross had called to pick them up, a little after seven, Hannah couldn't miss his ravenous glances at Gina. She knew he wasn't that sort of a letch, and his reaction was genuine, involuntary lust, but she felt reassured that Ross was too much of a gentleman to act on his desires. Gina, however… she was a different matter entirely. She was out for a good time, and Hannah could only hope that whatever tryst she got involved in (and whoever the lucky man was) it would be for the right reasons.

As Ross pulled up at the venue, Hannah was surprised to see how upmarket it was. She had expected somewhere like the dusty old village hall she'd once gone to looking for second hand furniture at a bring-and-buy sale, and she hadn't really concerned herself with more details about where they were heading tonight, knowing that Ross had offered to drive. The building they were outside now was a sweet little hotel that boasted its own ballroom – not the swish luxury she had encountered at far too many wedding receptions than she had the energy to recall – but smaller and more intimate, with a charming, shell-pink art deco façade, and set in modest but pleasant grounds. The trees were strung with fairy lights, the lawns bordered by solar lanterns, gravel paths running alongside neatly trimmed shrubs and hedges. She'd driven past often, but never with an excuse to look inside. Now she was glad to be at the charity night, if only to visit this lovely building, and made a mental note that if she ever needed a party venue, this one would be perfect.

Inside, the ballroom was decorated for the occasion with all things Latin American – or, at least, the closest the organisers could find in the heart of England – with lights that looked like chilli peppers, paper fans pinned to the walls; red and black streamers and balloons festooned the ceiling.

'This looks fabulous!' Hannah said as Briony greeted them, looking suitably Latino herself in a corseted dress with waterfall skirt and a tropical flower pinned into her hair. 'And you look absolutely lovely. I feel I should have made more of an effort now.'

'Nonsense; you look as pretty as a picture. Besides, you could have come in a bin bag for me; I'm just glad you're here.'

Hannah laughed. 'Thank you for being so kind.' She gestured at Gina. 'This is my sister, Gina. She's come all the way from Birmingham to chaperone me.'

Gina smiled. 'It's lovely to meet you.'

'I'm so happy you could both come and support the event,' Briony replied, beaming at the sisters in turn.

'Has your husband come tonight?' Hannah asked. 'I haven't seen him in ages and I'd like to say hello.'

'He has, but I have no idea where he is now,' Briony said as her gaze swept the room. 'I expect he'll make an appearance when the band starts playing. Paul never misses an opportunity to dance and the passionate ones are his favourite.'

Somehow Hannah couldn't equate the no-nonsense farmer with a passionate ballroom dancer, but she supposed it just went to show that people concealed all sorts of surprises. 'I look forward to seeing him in action later,' she said. 'Will you be giving us a demonstration of your prowess on the dance-floor too?'

'Just try and stop me!' Briony said cheerfully. 'And I suppose somebody has got to put their feet out for Paul to tread on, haven't they? It might as well be me as some other poor woman.' She looked at Ross, who had been watching the exchange with an expression of faint amusement. 'Why don't you be a gentleman and hang coats up for these lovely ladies?'

Ross grinned. 'If I must.'

As Hannah and Gina removed theirs to hand to him, Ross shrugged off the battered old donkey jacket he had been wearing to reveal an unexpectedly sharp suit beneath it. The ensemble fitted him so perfectly and so flatteringly that it could have been cut especially for him. Hannah mused that it probably had been. He looked handsome, and Hannah chanced a peek at Gina, who seemed to be admiring the view too, though she probably wasn't thinking about the tailoring of his jacket. As Briony directed them to the bar to get drinks, Gina leaned in to Hannah and whispered, 'Bloody hell, he looks gorgeous! This is cruel! Don't blame me if I end up taking him home tonight.'

'I don't know how you're going to do that when you're staying at my house tonight.'

'You don't mind if I borrow the spare room for an illicit shag, do you?'

'Yes I bloody well do!' Hannah laughed. 'You'll have to take your illicit shag elsewhere. And please, please do not let Briony find out.'

Gina slipped her arm through Hannah's. 'Don't worry little sis, I won't embarrass you. For once I'll be a very good girl.'

Hannah shot her a sideways look. 'Thank you! Don't forget I have to live here.'

'Seriously, though,' Gina continued, 'do you think he dances? If his mum and dad are into dancing do you think Ross is?'

'I don't know,' Hannah said, 'but I expect we'll find out soon enough.'

'If he does, and he's good, I'm not sure my self-control will hold. It's only fair I warn you now.'

'I'll be there to keep you sane, so don't panic.' Hannah gave her a wry smile. 'Maybe if I ply you with enough drinks you'll have collapsed by that point and I won't have to worry about you getting into trouble then.'

Ross's dad, Paul, was at the bar. He looked every inch the farmer, no matter what he wore. He greeted them both with a warm smile and a brief enquiry after Hannah's health before returning to a rather intense conversation he'd been having about the state of the nation's economy.

It was early, and many of the invited guests were still to arrive, which made it easy for Hannah and Gina to get drinks.

'Do you think we should get a couple each?' Gina asked as she brandished a twenty pound note to let the barman know that they were waiting for service.

Hannah raised her eyebrows. 'Are you kidding?'

'In case it gets really busy later and we can't get served.'

'If you get a reputation as a lush it won't matter, but I don't want to be the subject of feverish gossip on Holly Way with people who think I have a drink problem.'

Gina giggled. 'Alright Miss Prissy Knickers – it was just a suggestion.'

'Hmmm…' Hannah turned her attention to the main doors where more guests were starting to trickle in. 'Do you think I'm underdressed?' she mused out loud as she noted some rather spectacular ball gowns.

Gina looked around and then caught sight of what Hannah was looking at. 'God, no!' She lowered her voice. 'I'd say they were a bit overdone if anything… I mean, look at those two…' She angled her head as discreetly as she could in the direction of a couple of elderly ladies, 'they look like Hinge and Brackett.'

It was Hannah's turn to let out a loud giggle. 'I didn't like to say it, so I'm glad I could count on you. I probably should have checked the dress code with Briony though.'

'So should they,' Gina grimaced. 'Unless they're the drag act.'

'Gina!' Hannah squeaked, trying to put on a shocked voice but laughing through it just the same. 'You're terrible! I'm not taking you anywhere again.'

'Yes you are, because you have more fun with me than anyone else.'

'Oh…' Hannah grinned, 'annoyingly, you might have a point there.' She felt a light tap on her shoulder and turned to find Ross behind her.

'Can I get you ladies anything?' he asked.

'I think Gina is ordering now, but thanks. In fact, we should be buying you drinks for all the favours you've done for us lately.'

'In that case I'll have a pint of Stella,' Ross replied with an impish look.

Hannah smiled, only too pleased to make some small gesture of gratitude. It was the first time he'd agreed to take anything from her. She nudged Gina. 'Can you get Ross a pint of Stella?'

Gina grinned. 'For Ross... anything.' As she turned back to add the order to the barman, Hannah felt herself blush on Gina's behalf. Her sister might not know how outrageous her flirting was, but Hannah did, and she suspected Ross did too. He didn't seem to mind, though.

'I'd better make this the only one,' he said, 'seeing as I'm driving you home later.'

'I did say we could get a taxi. It's good of you but we don't expect you to abstain on our account.'

'It's okay. I have to be up pretty early anyway and I don't really want to leave Sally all alone in that great big scary car park all night now that I've brought her out.'

'Oh my God, that car is your actual girlfriend, isn't it?' Hannah laughed.

'She'll do just fine in the absence of a real one,' he replied cheerfully.

Once Gina had collected their drinks they found a table where they could sit together and chat until the party really got started. Hannah wondered from time to time why it was that Ross chose to stay at the table with them for as long as he did. There were lots of people he knew arriving, as he pointed out on many occasions – indeed, quite a few walked over to say hello. But none could prise him away from Hannah and Gina's company, not even his mum. There was no shortage of conversation either, and he happily chatted about life on the farm and his hopes for the future, interspersed with enquiries about both Hannah and Gina's plans for the coming year. Three more rounds of drinks quickly followed the first, and by the time the band had started to play, Hannah was so pleasantly tipsy that she had quite forgotten she didn't actually know how to salsa and was itching to have a go.

Paul Hunter started the ball rolling, enticing Hannah up from the table while Gina watched and clapped her encouragement.

'I don't know how!' Hannah protested, but laughing all the same, and he was only too happy to lead the way, showing her simple steps that she soon got the hang of until she was loving the feel of the music vibrating through her and the swaying of her body to the rhythm. It might have been the gin, but salsa dancing was intoxicating. She looked around to see that Gina was now on her feet too, being whirled around by Ross, who was also surprisingly light on his feet. Hannah wanted to ask him later how he'd learned to dance so well. It was yet another surprising thing she'd discovered about him. Briony was dancing with the vicar, and then the song ended and everyone swapped partners, Hannah now found herself with Ross, and Gina danced off with a tall, balding man, who was apparently the hotel owner. Was that regret, longing – perhaps both – on Ross's face? Hannah wanted to ask him about that too, but realised it was probably the booze making her think of something so inappropriate. And right now, she wanted to get drunker, dance faster, laugh harder, and forget herself in the moment, just for once. As she began to dance again with Ross, she felt wonderfully free, all her worries falling away as she twirled and skipped to the beat, Ross's sure footwork making it easy for her to follow his lead.

'I thought you said you couldn't dance,' he shouted over the music.

'I thought you said you couldn't either,' Hannah shouted back, 'you're brilliant, a regular little Fred Astaire!'

'Did I say that?' Ross grinned. 'I might have been trying to preserve my street cred.'

'I never had any to preserve,' Hannah laughed, 'which is why I totally meant it when I said I couldn't dance.'

'You're not bad for a novice. You've got natural rhythm.'

'Have I?' Hannah smiled.

'Absolutely. And you're light on your feet.'

'Oooooh… Flatter me more you lovely man,' Hannah giggled.

Gina twirled past them and called over. 'Still standing, sis?'

'Cheeky cow!' Hannah shouted back. 'You're the one with two left feet.' But she couldn't help but admire the grace with which Gina spun and sashayed, not a step out of place or a beat missed. She caught Ross looking again and wondered how many other men were having similar thoughts about the newcomer in their midst. It was possible that Gina might cause a riot if she moved onto Holly Way, so it was probably a good thing that she was planning to head into Millrise itself when she finally left Birmingham.

The tempo of the music moved up a gear, and Hannah soon found herself struggling, even with Ross's help.

'I'll have to sit this one out,' she panted.

'I suppose I'll have to go and steal your sister from the vicar then,' Ross laughed.

Hannah wobbled on her heels as she made her way back to their table.

It was disappointingly empty of drinks – although there were plenty of empty glasses – and Hannah was gasping, not to mention sobering up rather quicker than she was happy about. Grabbing her purse from where she had stowed it underneath the table, she tottered over to the bar. The balls of her feet were throbbing, but the music still had her itching to dance and she drummed her fingers to the rhythm on the bar as she waited to be served. Maybe she'd grab a quick drink and throw herself back in, difficult steps or not.

It took a good ten minutes for any of the bar staff to get to her and she watched the dance-floor while she waited. Ross's dad, Paul was now dancing with Briony, and they looked so happy. Briony giggled like a schoolgirl as Paul swept her around and dipped her low to the ground in his arms as if she was weightless.

Gina had somehow managed to end up dancing with one of the Hinge and Brackett women, but she was laughing at something the woman had said. Hannah guessed that her sister might well be drunker than she was, but she'd lost count of Gina's shots after the first five.

Once she'd finally got her drink, and an extra one for the road (clearly now too drunk to remember what she'd said to Gina earlier about looking like a lush), she flopped into a chair at their table and sipped happily. Then Gina spotted her from the dancefloor, made a time-out sign and bounced over to join her.

'Give us that spare one,' she said as she sat down.

'No chance! Do you have any idea how long I just queued for that?' Hannah swiped it out of her reach.

'Oh, come on… you have two and I'm parched. Stop being so mean!'

'Get your own, lazy cow.'

Gina pointed across the room theatrically. 'Oh look! Johnny Depp just walked in with his widger out!'

'Nice try,' Hannah laughed, 'but you're not getting this drink.'

Gina pouted. 'Fine… I'll just have to get Ross to buy me one.'

'You do that.' Hannah gave her a tipsy smile. 'I'll just sit here and love my spare.'

Gina grinned and seemed to pirouette out of her chair, taking a strange, lopsided route across the dance-floor in search of Ross. Hannah's smile was wide as she watched her try to walk straight, doing her best to look sober. She was so glad they'd decided to come tonight. There'd been so many moments when she'd decided against it but now she couldn't remember the last time they'd had so much fun together out of the confines of her cottage.

Hannah should have known that whenever she let such a smug thought creep into her head, fate would make certain that it backfired spectacularly. She'd been minding her own business, just her and her hard-won Bacardi (at least she thought it was Bacardi but she couldn't quite remember what she'd ordered now) when the doors to the ballroom opened and two newcomers walked in.

'Bloody hell!' Hannah groaned. She watched as Briony glided over to greet the couple, and the man turned to scan the room until his gaze fell upon Hannah. Mitchell didn't smile, but looked as shocked to see her as she was to see him. Hannah quickly looked away, but not before she clocked that Martine had seen her too. Had Hannah been closer, she might have seen how cold her smile was.

Shit! There was no escape now. Hannah had been having a perfectly brilliant night, and now this. It wasn't fair. *Please, God, don't let them come over here…*

God was obviously washing his hair or checking his lottery numbers or something, because even as she uttered the prayer, Mitchell and his perfect wife began to make their way over to Hannah's table. In a life that now seemed to consist entirely of coincidences, Hannah shouldn't have been surprised that Martine and Mitchell would know Ross's mum. It was so obvious – Briony was a tireless fundraiser and local busybody with a reach into the surrounding area, and Martine was the glamorous GP with an equally attractive and successful husband, the sort of people who would be invited to everything. Why wouldn't they be here? Hannah was only surprised that it hadn't occurred to her before.

She looked up as they stopped at her table and tried her best to smile.

'Hannah…' Martine said, 'what a pleasant surprise to see you here.'

'I was thinking just the same thing when I saw you,' Hannah replied, hoping that they couldn't see through her thin veneer of courtesy.

'Do you know the organisers?' Mitchell asked.

'Briony's a sort of neighbour. I mean, in the sense that she lives on Holly Way, though I can't see her house from mine. Do you know her?'

'Not terribly well,' Martine said. 'We're friends with the Olivettis though.'

Hannah looked blank.

'The hotel owners,' Martine clarified. 'Mitchell worked on the hotel renovations… at least his men did.'

'It seems I did a good job too,' Mitchell said with a faint smile, 'although I can't actually remember doing it.'

'You still can't remember?' Hannah asked. Her tone was incredulous, perhaps even a little accusing, but she couldn't help it. It was as if he didn't want to remember. Was this normal? It had been three weeks since his accident on Christmas Day. 'Sorry…' she added and blushed as she realised just how rude her comment probably sounded. 'I've had a bit too much to drink…'

Martine's gaze swept the table full of empty glasses. 'It certainly looks as though it's been a good party so far.'

'They're not all mine,' Hannah said, her blush deepening as she arranged them into a neat cluster at the centre of the table, as though collecting them up would somehow make them look less incriminating.

'I'm sure they're not,' Martine said. 'It just makes me cross that we've arrived so late.'

Hannah tried to smile again, but as she looked at Martine, she was suddenly and acutely aware of what a drunken sweaty mess she must look right now. Before Mitchell's gorgeous wife had arrived, with her floor-length black evening gown, her hair cascading down her back in perfect blonde curls, her lashes supernaturally long over sapphire-blue eyes, Hannah hadn't cared that her own lashes were now sliding down her face from bloodshot, tipsy eyes, because she was having too much fun. Suddenly, it was all such hard work again. Her attention turned to Mitchell. In his black tie and crisp white shirt he looked incredible. Her treacherous heart skipped a beat. Damn it, now she felt even more of a mess.

'Mind if we sit with you?' he asked.

'Of course not,' Hannah lied with as much grace as she could muster. She would rather wrestle an angry porcupine, but there wasn't a lot she could do without being downright rude, and that wasn't in her nature no matter how drunk she was.

Martine didn't look much happier about the situation than Hannah, but she perched herself on the seat that had previously been occupied by Ross. Hannah glanced across the dance-floor. Ross had taken a breather too, and was standing on the other side of the room, clutching a glass of what looked like Coke and deep in conversation with his dad.

Martine smiled sweetly at Mitchell. 'Be a love and get me something to drink, would you?'

He nodded. 'What do you want?'

'Oh, anything… you know the sort of thing I like.' She waved her hand vaguely like a lord dismissing his servant. Mitchell frowned.

'I don't think I do.'

Martine's smile slipped. 'I'll have a spritzer. Make sure it's a good wine, I hate that house rubbish.'

'Would you like a drink?' Mitchell turned to Hannah. She shook her head. Actually, she really did want another. Perhaps another three or four in quick succession would blur the edges of this prickly situation, but she didn't feel right accepting his offer.

'I'm okay, thank you; I've got one here.' Hannah gestured to the almost empty glass.

'What is it?'

'I think it's Bacardi, only to be honest I've forgotten. But please don't worry.'

'You seem to have another one lined up anyway,' Martine cut in. 'Did you forget that too?'

'So I did.' Hannah emptied the contents of the almost finished glass into the new drink before taking a large gulp.

Mitchell threw one last uneasy glance at the two women before making his way to the bar.

'He's finding all this very difficult,' Martine said in a low voice as she watched him go.

'The memory loss?' Hannah asked, a little taken aback by Martine's sudden candour.

'Amongst other things, yes. He's not himself at all. In the old days he'd bury his problems in work and I'd never even know about them. Now he just mopes.'

'I suppose that's understandable,' Hannah said, wondering what else she was supposed to say. What had made Martine tell her that? And was her idea of moping everyone else's version of normal? It didn't seem very charitable coming from a doctor who, perhaps, ought to understand Mitchell's situation better than most.

'Do you know, you made quite an impression on him at Christmas?' Martine continued.

'Did I? I don't know why. I mean, I do, but it was nothing really. I just happened to be in the nearest house to the road.' Drink always loosened Hannah's tongue, and all the questions she had wanted to ask the last time they'd met were in danger of tumbling out if Mitchell didn't come back soon. She chewed her lip as she searched the dancers for Gina.

'You're enjoying the evening?' Martine asked, breaking in on her thoughts.

'It's been lovely,' Hannah replied. *Where are you Gina?* She scanned the dance-floor again, looking for anyone to save her. If Ross was still free, perhaps he would dance with her. Even his dad would do right now. If only she hadn't stopped dancing in the first place she wouldn't be stuck having this excruciating conversation.

Hannah had to endure another ten minutes of ever more stilted small talk in which she found it harder and harder to hold back the questions that jostled noisily inside her brain. More than anything, she couldn't believe that Mitchell's memory was still so fractured that he had no recollection of his wife's favourite drink. What did that mean? This was his wife, supposedly the most important person in the world and, since they had no children, the centre of his universe. If he still couldn't remember her, what did that say about their marriage? Or perhaps it was merely as simple as forgetting a favourite drink, just like Jason often had with Hannah. More importantly, the fact that Hannah was even contemplating this revealed more than she wanted to know about her own emotions and her attraction to Mitchell.

Thankfully, his return with a spritzer for his wife and a glass of water for himself ended further rumination.

'Are you driving?' Hannah asked, nodding at the water.

'Yes, but I'm not all that bothered about alcohol anyway.'

'You never have been,' said Martine, with such irritation in her voice that Hannah found herself staring in shock.

Mitchell was thoughtful for a moment. 'I think I was abstaining though recently... for a good reason... before the accident.'

'Don't let's talk about that now,' Martine cut in. She had been happy enough to discuss it with Hannah in his absence, so why the sudden change of heart?

'You weren't drinking either...' Mitchell added slowly, as if piecing together a puzzle.

'Of course I was,' Martine replied impatiently. 'I like a nice drink and I don't see why I shouldn't have one after a hard day. Do you?'

Mitchell stared at her. Then he seemed to blink and shake himself. 'I suppose not. I must still be mixing things up.'

'Have you gone back to work?' Hannah asked him, scrabbling around for a topic that wouldn't supercharge the already tense atmosphere.

'I went into the office... but I didn't really know what to do once I was there. It was sort of familiar and yet I didn't have a clue. Like a name on the tip of your tongue... you know?'

'He has this fantastic right hand man, though,' Martine added. 'Graham. He's running the ship until Mitchell is well again.'

'I *am* well,' Mitchell said. 'There's nothing wrong with me.'

'Physically, no, there isn't,' Martine stated.

Hannah quickly took a gulp of her drink to stop herself from commenting. Physically he was very, very alright... and that was why she found it so hard to be around him – at least when he was with his wife, although God only knew how much more dangerous the situation might be without her there.

'Mentally…' Martine continued, 'well, all I can say is that I'm a GP and I still don't know what's going on in your head. I've never come across anything like it.'

'Is this rare then?' Hannah asked, before she could stop herself.

'I'd say,' Martine replied. 'A lot rarer than films and books would have you believe, especially almost total memory loss like this. It's more common for short-term memory to suffer than established memories, and even then it will generally only last for hours – days at most – in a lot of cases.'

Hannah nodded. She wanted to ask so much more but she didn't think her questions would be welcome. She also wanted Martine to disappear in a puff of smoke so that she could throw herself at Mitchell and ravish him… but that was just because she was drunk.

Martine stood up, and Hannah was filled with panic as she realised that, in a roundabout way, she was about to get her wish. She knew that being left alone with Mitchell would be a lot more awkward than the erotic daydream that kept plaguing her suggested.

'I'm just popping to the ladies,' Martine announced. Mitchell looked at Hannah.

'Don't you normally go in pairs?'

It took a great deal of restraint not to tell him how that particular phenomenon only applied to women who liked each other. Martine offered him a withering look.

'I suppose it was a bit of a lame joke,' Mitchell said as she stalked off.

'Why do you let her talk to you like that?' Hannah asked, and the sharpness of her tone shocked even her. 'Was it always that way?'

Mitchell frowned. 'I don't have the vaguest idea. But I don't think the Mitchell Bond who ran his own property development company would let his wife boss him around.'

In spite of his certainty, he looked lost and vulnerable and Hannah regretted her question. She had to keep reminding herself what he must be going through, and what a strange and terrifying experience it must be to lose all sense of oneself. And perhaps Martine only spoke to him that way because she was tired, and it must be very hard for her – his not remembering anything about her… It was hard to imagine what that must be like.

'I think about Christmas day a lot,' he said.

Hannah's head flicked around to see that he had a peculiar look on his face as he gazed at her.

'In what way?'

'I can't explain it – I wish I could. It makes me feel…well, it gives me a nice feeling to think of it. Your little house… it was such a happy place.'

'That might be down to all the brandy we downed that day,' Hannah smiled. 'You're confusing happiness with drunkenness!'

'Maybe, but I liked it. And you… you were so sweet and kind… like a guardian angel or something.' He gave an awkward laugh. 'I sound like a nutter, I know, but I can't help feeling that some higher power meant me to fall onto your doorstep that day – I mean yours and no one else's.'

'Perhaps you were there to save my life. You did jump in front of a car for me, after all.'

'Or perhaps you were meant to save mine,' he said softly.

'Anyone would have done the same.'

'I'm not talking about the injury,' he said, holding her in a gaze that suddenly made her feel as if she might combust. She tore her eyes away from his. Was this a joke? What was he trying to say?

'I… I don't know what you mean,' Hannah said.

He paused. 'I'm not sure I do either. Everything is confused and muddy all the time, but then I think of you and it's all clear. You're the only part of the last few weeks that makes any sense.'

'I suppose it's because I'm the first person you met after the accident. I'm like the first new memory that you've saved on a blank slate.'

Mitchell smiled. 'Like I've imprinted on you or something? I sound like a duckling.'

'I suppose you do,' Hannah smiled.

'But I almost wish I could have that day back,' Mitchell continued. 'I mean, I know it was horrible and stressful, but in a weird way it was nice too. Everything was simpler because you were there. I wish you were around now too.'

Hannah's glass stopped halfway to her lips. 'I um… I have to find Gina… excuse me…' She stumbled as she shot up from her chair. This conversation was getting dangerous and it couldn't continue. Frantically she searched the dance-floor for a sign of her sister. There was no Gina, but there was Briony, chatting to the vicar beside a table of nibbles. They both turned at her approach.

'I'm so sorry to interrupt,' Hannah began, 'but have you seen my sister anywhere?'

'Not for a little while now,' Briony replied. She peered more closely at Hannah. 'Are you alright?'

'Yes… I'm not sure. Probably overdone the gin.'

'Is there anything I can do to help?'

'No… thank you. I just need Gina.'

'Have you checked the ladies'?' Briony added helpfully.

'Oh, right, good idea… of course.' Hannah rushed off in the direction of the loos, but a quick inspection revealed an absence of Gina. Hannah dashed back out onto the dance-floor. She glanced across at her table to see that Martine had returned and was now in animated conversation with her husband. They both looked at her, and then continued their discussion in earnest, Mitchell not shifting his gaze. Martine's hands flapped as she talked and she was obviously agitated about something. Hannah didn't care; she just needed to get out. As she scanned the crowd on the dance-floor again, Briony tapped her on the arm.

'You're worrying me, Hannah. Do you need to go home? Ross hasn't been drinking so he could drive you.'

'I know,' Hannah replied. 'He was taking us home anyway but I don't want to drag him away early. I just need Gina, that's all.'

'She wasn't in the loos?'

Hannah shook her head.

'Maybe she went out for a bit of air?'

It was then that Hannah realised she couldn't see Ross either. This fact obviously hadn't occurred to Briony, but then, why would it? *Your timing is bloody perfect, Gina.*

'I'll check outside. I expect you're right – she probably just needed to cool down.' Hannah made her way to the ballroom doors, sobering up at a rate of knots now that she felt the evening unravelling around her. What had Mitchell been talking about? Why was he saying things like that to her, just when she was beginning to get him out of her head? Why had he turned up tonight at all? It was like fate was trying to throw them together. But that was stupid – she didn't believe in all that crap anyway. And yet it seemed that wherever she was he was there too or, at least, some reminder of him. God only knew what he'd meant by the things he'd said, and Hannah could only hope that he wouldn't repeat any of it to Martine. Hannah didn't like her but nobody deserved that kind of betrayal.

Out in the lobby there was still no sign of Gina or Ross. Hannah considered going to reception to see if they'd booked a room but stopped herself. The drink had pickled her brain – even Gina wouldn't be that blatant.

Paul Hunter came back into the lobby through a set of French doors that led out to a veranda. Hannah could smell cigarette smoke as she met him.

'Was Ross outside with you?' she asked.

'No, I haven't seen him for a while now,' he replied, looking slightly puzzled by the question. 'He did go out to his car though, and I haven't seen him since then.'

Hannah thought back, trying to remember where they'd parked earlier in the evening.

'Do you want him for anything in particular?' Paul asked. 'Anything I can help you with?'

Hannah forced a smile. 'No, thanks. There was just something I needed to ask him … I don't suppose my sister was with him?'

'No. I thought she was with you.'

'She isn't… but I expect I'll find her shortly. Thanks.'

Paul went back to the party, and Hannah made her way to the front doors. It looked as though Gina was behaving herself after all and she felt more than a little guilty that she had doubted her. Either that or Gina had given up on Ross and acquired a new target… If she could only find him, Ross might know either way. And if not then perhaps he'd be kind enough to take her home. She did need to find Gina to let her know, though.

Outside, the cold air hit her, making her shiver. Apart from a cluster of smokers on the veranda, also shivering as they chatted, their laughter ringing through the frosty air, the grounds were deserted. Hannah followed the path that led around the hotel to the carpark at the back. Hannah wandered between the cars, arms clamped around her trying to keep warm and wishing she'd grabbed her coat before she'd rushed out.

Finally she spotted Ross's car but he was nowhere to be seen. Then, through the gloom she realised that the bright blob she could see through the windows was his blonde hair. So he was in his car and… *oh hell*! Gina was in there with him and whatever they were up to, had nothing at all to do with fundraising.

'Shit!' Hannah muttered. On a different night in a different mood she might have been mildly amused by her discovery. Tonight, she was just mightily pissed off. There was nothing else for it – she was going to have to make her own way home somehow.

Back inside, Hannah collected her coat from the cloakroom before realising that her handbag was still underneath the table in the ballroom where she'd stowed it. That meant she was going to have to face Mitchell and Martine again if she was going to get it, but without it she wouldn't have her front door keys. *Shit, shit, shit.* They'd probably want to know why she was leaving so early. There would be awkward questions. But it wasn't like she had to answer them, was it? Stuff them, if Hannah wanted to go and collect her bag it was her business. Still, she folded her coat up as small as it would go and stuffed it under her arm as she headed back into the ballroom.

'Is everything okay?' Mitchell asked as Hannah arrived back.

'Of course… why wouldn't it be?' Hannah ducked under the table. Shit… where was that handbag? Scooting underneath, she felt around, until her hand touched leather and she grabbed it, tucking it under her arm and bumping her head on the table on the way back out. As she emerged she saw Martine reach for her drink to steady it as the table gave a precarious wobble.

'Are you sure you're alright?' Martine asked, smoothing away an annoyed frown.

'Yes... I um... I just need... it was lovely to see you both, really, but...' Why did she think it was necessary to give them a reason for leaving? She had no idea whether Mitchell had meant what she thought he had, and if he had, what on earth could she say with Martine sitting there? It was far easier simply to leave. One thing was certain; her life would have been easier had Mitchell not ended up on her doorstep that day. Perhaps, had she known then what she knew now, she might have slammed it shut in his face. *Something was leading me to you...* that was what he'd said, wasn't it? Well that *something* could bloody well piss off because she didn't need that sort of complication in her life.

Without another word, she hurried out into the night.

*

The temperature seemed to have dropped by degrees in a matter of minutes as Hannah huddled into her coat, wishing she'd opted for a thicker one. Frost glinted on the grass that lined the roadside and her breath curled into the air. The road leading directly away from the hotel was well lit, but as she walked further on, the gaps between streetlamps became longer and longer, until she found herself in eerie pockets of blackness, thankful for the meagre light from her phone that she had now resorted to using in order to prevent her breaking an ankle on the road. Sobriety had hit too, and she was beginning to wonder if this was the stupidest thing she'd ever done. Gina would be furious, despite the brief text to let her know that she was heading home and would sleep on the sofa to let Gina in when she arrived back (if, indeed, she did arrive back that night). Hannah couldn't help but feel vexed about that situation, if the truth was told. She had no right to be angry about

Gina and Ross getting together – they were both consenting adults, of course – but she couldn't help but feel that they might have been a bit more discreet, bearing in mind that the party was full of people Ross and Hannah knew, including his doting parents. She expected Gina to know better, but then, wasn't she acting just as stupidly right now? Drink and betrayal did funny things to a person.

She was pulled from her thoughts by a faint rhythmic tapping from behind her. Were they footsteps? Footsteps on this dark and lonely road, miles away from her house – from any house for that matter… *Way to go, Meadows, hacked to death by a mad axe murderer, all because you can't handle a grown-up conversation with a member of the opposite sex.* She quickened her pace, trying to swallow the panic that bubbled up through her chest. But the footsteps behind seemed to quicken too, matching her own. The barely controlled panic was now turning into abject fear, and Hannah broke into a run. Where the hell she thought she was running to she had no idea. Not only would she end up dead in a field, her feet would be covered in blisters, her heels broken and her hair a streaming mess.

Whoever was behind her broke into a run too, and it took her a whole five seconds to register that her name was being called. She stopped and spun around. Mitchell was charging towards her.

'What are you doing?' Hannah panted.

'What am *I* doing?' he shouted back. 'What the hell are *you* doing?'

'Going home.'

'Like this?' He slowed to a stop as he caught up with her. 'On your own in the middle of the night? Anything could happen to you!'

Hannah couldn't help a wry smile. 'I thought it was just about to. You scared me half to death. Why are you following me? Where's Martine?'

'At the party.'

'I bet she's thrilled that you've left her sitting like a lemon while you chase after me.'

'She's alright…' he said, though he didn't look convinced of that. 'She's safe in a room full of people.'

'Unlike me?'

'Exactly.'

'I can handle myself. Besides, these roads are always deserted so it's not very likely I'd meet anyone, even if I walked all night.'

'That's why you shouldn't be out alone. What if you fell? Or if someone did choose this moment to attack you? There'd be no way of getting any help.'

Hannah didn't have a reply. She started to walk again.

'You're determined to walk home?' Mitchell asked as he fell into step beside her.

'I don't see how else I'm going to get there.'

'We could have given you a lift if you'd asked.'

'I don't think Martine would have been happy; you'd only just arrived.'

'She wouldn't have minded.'

'Hmmmm. Well, I don't like to take advantage.'

'Where's your sister?'

'Busy.'

'How's she getting home? Wouldn't she have come with you?'

'Like I said, she's busy. But I think she had the whole getting home thing covered.'

'Does she know you've left?'

'Yes,' Hannah replied, although that did depend on whether she'd looked at her phone or not. Hannah thought it better not to mention that bit.

'And she didn't try to stop you?'

'No… though… I didn't exactly tell her to her face.' She turned to him. 'What are you doing?'

'What?'

'You're walking with me.'

'Yes. Well spotted.'

'Why?'

'Because I can't let you go home alone.'

'Does Martine know this is your plan? And how will you get back to the party? It's miles away from my house, and Martine has been drinking so you can't call her to fetch you.'

'I'll get a taxi.'

'That'll cost you a small fortune out here at this time of night!'

'Then you'll just have to turn around and come back to the party with me until someone can take you safely.'

'You might have saved my life once, but that doesn't mean I owe you,' Hannah replied tartly. 'I can do what I like and I want to go home.'

'You don't owe me, but I owe you. Hannah…' He laid a hand on her arm and pulled her to a halt. His voice was softer now. 'I couldn't bear the thought of anything happening to you…'

'Nothing will happen to me –'

Before she could finish her sentence his lips were on hers. She could pull away… she *should* pull away… but she didn't want to. His lips were frozen from the chill of the night, but soft and yielding. They kissed as if it was the most natural thing in the world, and there was none of the awkwardness of first date kisses she'd known before, it was as if they'd always known how to kiss each other. It was so, so wrong, and yet it felt so right and so wonderful that she never wanted it to end. Her arms slid around his waist, travelling across his back beneath his jacket, exploring the firm contours of his muscles. He pulled her closer, his kisses more urgent, his hands now at the nape of her neck and in her hair. This was… this was…

Hannah yanked herself away, all at once burning for him and appalled at her lack of control. 'What are you doing?'

'I'm sorry… I thought…'

'You thought wrong.'

'But I… we… I sensed a connection…'

'You're married!' Hannah cried, choosing to ignore the question in his statement. Of course there was a connection, and she couldn't deny it, the only thing she could do was ignore it.

'I know… don't remind me.'

'Don't remind you? She's your wife!'

'I don't know her!' Mitchell said. 'I'm married to a woman I don't know!'

'That will come back in time.' Hannah's voice was softer now.

'It might, but I don't think it will change anything. I don't feel like I know her because I get the feeling things were already wrong between us, even before the accident. But I know you. And I can't get you out of my head. I sit down to eat with Martine and I want it to be you, I go to bed with Martine and I want to go to bed with you, I come home from work and Martine kisses me but I want it to be you…'

'This is ridiculous! You don't know me either.'

'Maybe. But I know you more than I know her right now. I feel like I can trust you more too. There's something she's not telling me…'

'You and Martine have a past together. You married her for a reason, in sickness and in health. You're sick right now, and she's doing her best for you. That has to be enough, doesn't it?'

'But it isn't. Why do I have to accept that, make the best of a bad job? Where's the rule that says I have to do that?'

'You might think you want me now,' Hannah said, her voice shaking with the emotion she was trying to hold back, 'but what happens when your memory comes back and you remember why you were in love with Martine? What happens when you want her again? Do I just step aside?'

'It won't happen.'

'You can't know that for sure!'

'So... what we just did... you didn't want to...'

'Of course I wanted it, you stupid git! I want to shag your brains out right here on the side of the road... but that doesn't make it right. And it doesn't make for a happy ending, does it, not when you're already spoken for.'

Mitchell ran a hand through his hair and let out a huge sigh. 'I don't know what to think. All I can tell you is what I feel right now. My head is a mess, but my heart is telling me that I need you, not Martine, in my life. The only time anything feels right is when I'm with you.'

'Stop it, please. You don't know what you're saying.'

'But I do. That's just it, I really do. How can I be mistaken when I feel it so strongly?'

'What about Martine?'

'I'll leave her.'

'Now you are talking rubbish. You can't leave her for a woman you've just met.'

'*She's* a woman I've just met.'

'This is ridiculous.'

Mitchell took her by the arms and searched her face. 'Tell me you don't want me and I'll go.'

'I'm not playing this game.'

'Who said I was playing? I've never been more serious.'

'Mitchell, I...'

They both spun around at the sound of a car roaring in their direction.

'Martine…' Mitchell breathed as the Audi sped down the road towards them. Hannah felt sick. A minute or two earlier and Martine would have seen everything. Was this who Hannah was now – the other woman, who snuck around with husbands who didn't belong to her? It certainly wasn't who she wanted to be.

The car pulled up beside them and Martine wound the window down.

'I told you to wait,' Mitchell frowned. 'I said I'd be back.'

'I got sick of waiting,' Martine snapped back. 'That's all I seem to do these days – wait around for you…' She threw an irritated glance in Hannah's direction.

'You've been drinking,' Mitchell added.

'Yes, I have. Is that a shock to you?'

'Don't be so facetious. I just can't believe you've been stupid enough to drive.'

'I'm stupid?' Martine squeaked. '*I'm* stupid? I'm not the one wandering about on deserted country roads on the coldest night of the year.' She pressed her lips together so hard that Hannah thought they might disappear. 'Another habit you seem to have picked up.'

'I told you I was coming to look for Hannah and then I'd be back.'

'Yes, and I can see that you've found her so can we please all get in the car and take her to wherever it is she needs to be so desperately?'

'Swap seats,' Mitchell said curtly, 'I'll drive.' He started walking towards the car.

'I don't need to be taken home,' Hannah said, suddenly feeling belligerent about the whole thing. She didn't particularly want to walk home but she certainly didn't want to be stuck in a car with them like this. 'I'm perfectly capable of making my own way.'

Martine raised her eyebrows as she got out of the car. 'There you go,' she said to Mitchell, 'I told you as much.'

'Just because she says it, doesn't make it true. I'm sure in normal circumstances it's alright but I can't allow it tonight.' He looked at Hannah, who was now standing at the roadside with her arms folded tight across her chest. 'Get in the car, Hannah.'

'Er… excuse me but you can't talk to me like that – I'm not married to you.'

'What's that supposed to mean?' Martine cried. 'He doesn't get to talk to me like that either!'

'She doesn't mean anything,' Mitchell sighed. 'Give the suffragette bit a rest, will you? The pair of you are drunk.'

'Yes, but you're sober so you think everything through before you say it,' Hannah fired back, giving him a meaningful look. It seemed to stop him in his tracks for a moment, before he recovered, and for the first time, Hannah wondered if she was seeing something of the real Mitchell Bond as he issued his command again.

'Get in the car.'

'No.'

'Hannah… please get in the car. I can't leave you out here, so if you don't it means we'll all stay out on this road arguing about it until the sun comes up.'

'Or we'll all get hypothermia and die,' Martine added, in a voice that suggested she rather hoped Hannah would.

Hannah folded her arms tighter. She didn't want to get in the car. Right now she'd rather climb into a vat of Ross's sheeps' poo, but she could see by the look on Mitchell's face that he meant what he said and she didn't fancy a standoff either.

'For God's sake, please get in,' Mitchell sighed.

'Fine,' Hannah muttered. 'But for the record I'm not happy about it.'

'You're not happy about us saving you a long and freezing walk home?' Martine scoffed. 'Who on earth would rather do that than get into our nice warm car and be chauffeured the rest of the way? You must be properly crazy…'

'Enough, Martine, please…' Mitchell replied as he held the door open for Hannah. She slid onto the back seat and could feel her hackles rising. If what he had said to her only moments before was true… and that incredible kiss meant something… then what was happening now? Why not tell Martine right this moment how he felt? If he wanted Hannah that badly, why not end it with Martine? She knew it probably wasn't fair, and the timing was hardly right, but his silence felt incriminating somehow – as though he was trying to have his cake and eat it. It wasn't as though Hannah would immediately fall into his arms but at least there would be a chance in the future for them. As things were now there was no chance at all. The fact that he did nothing only strengthened Hannah's conviction that he may have believed he meant what he said, but even he couldn't be certain of the truth. Perhaps he was suffering from some kind of guardian angel/ Florence Nightingale effect, some psychological syndrome that led him to believe he was in love with the woman who had happened to be there during his hour of need. But this was not a situation to build true love on, and Hannah had been in enough flawed relationships to know that getting involved was a bad idea… if only her heart would listen to her head's very sound advice.

*

The journey home was almost silent. Any pleasant tipsiness that Hannah had enjoyed earlier had now been replaced by nausea and a feeling of utter misery. She'd been having such a good night until Mr and Mrs Perfect turned up to ruin it. It was as though the moment in the lane had never happened, and Hannah and Mitchell had reverted to the strangers they really were.

When they eventually pulled up outside her house, the silence was broken by Hannah.

'Thanks,' she said, not even sure what she was thanking them for. It certainly wasn't for the lift home, which she'd wanted like a pocket full of cold jelly, and it wasn't for ruining her night either. It definitely wasn't for Mitchell helping to screw her up good and proper. She almost longed for the days when Jason had been around to screw her up instead. At least him having a good old fashioned affair was something normal that she'd known how to deal with. 'I don't suppose you could let Gina know I've come home if you see her,' Hannah added.

'Oh, I doubt we'll be going back to the party now,' Martine said icily. 'What's the point?'

Mitchell threw her a tired look. 'I didn't want to go to the party in the first place so it suits me.'

'You never want to go anywhere these days,' Martine shot back.

'Well, in case you hadn't noticed there's a very good reason for that.'

'Right…' Hannah interrupted. The last thing she needed now was to witness a domestic. 'I'm sure she's seen my text anyway. I just didn't want her to miss me and wonder where I was.'

'I don't think that will happen,' Martine said. 'If she's the woman Mitchell pointed out to me, she looked very happy last time I saw her on her way out of the ballroom with a bit of fluff.'

Hannah wanted to ask what she meant by this loaded comment, but instead, she left them without another word, aware of Mitchell's eyes on her as she made her way up the garden path, fishing for her keys as she went. It wasn't until she slammed the front door shut and was safe inside that she heard the engine finally rev up to signal they were leaving.

Kicking off her shoes on the way through to the kitchen, Hannah sent another text to Gina to let her know she was back. She was slightly cross that Gina hadn't replied to the last one, but realised she was going to have to wait to vent her frustrations. Instead, she busied herself changing into fluffy pyjamas and getting the fire going while she mused on her night. Mitchell's face kept popping up, his words swimming around in her head, and the awful truth was beginning to dawn on her. He didn't know his own mind, and his confession of how he felt was most probably flawed and not real at all – but Hannah's mind was sound, and that made it worse. She could deny it all she wanted but the ache in her heart every time she thought of that kiss, when she recalled his arms around her, told a different story. Through guilt, or a sense of duty, or for whatever reason, Hannah had to accept that she was not going to break them up. Mitchell and Martine had to work out their issues without her muddying the water. So where did that leave her? Even if she gave in to her desires, there could be no future with him.

*

Hannah bolted up on the sofa. She shivered, noting that the fire had burned down in the grate while she slept. It probably hadn't been very good to start with, as she'd been far too drunk to do a decent job of building it. The blanket she'd tucked over herself had slid off too, and now lay in a heap on the floor next to the cold cup of strong tea she'd made and then forgotten to drink. She grabbed it and took a swig anyway, her mouth as dry as sand. It took a few moments to focus, and then she realised that it was a knock at the front door that had woken her.

It came again, more like impatient hammering this time.

'Alright, alright…' Hannah muttered as she toppled off the sofa and got to her feet. As soon as she was upright the room began to spin and her head felt as though fireworks were going off in her brain. She hadn't cared too much about a New Year's resolution this year, but she made a belated one now: *stop drinking*! Anything that made you feel like this must be knocking decades off your life expectancy.

Gina and Ross were standing on the front-door-step. It looked as though Ross was trying to calm her, but it wasn't working – Gina looked furious.

'What the hell were you thinking?' she screeched as Hannah appeared. 'You just walked out! Nobody knew where you were; Briony and Paul were panicking… then I found out you were at home!'

'Sorry…' Hannah mumbled. She might have given Gina as good as she got, but her brain wasn't quite firing yet.

Gina pushed past her and into the house. 'I've been worried sick!'

Ross gave Hannah an apologetic shrug. This conversation wouldn't be happening if he and Gina had both shown a bit more restraint. But seeing how relaxed and natural they already were in each other's company, Hannah couldn't really be mad about that either.

'I should probably go,' he said, sticking his hands in his pockets.

'Maybe that's a good idea,' Hannah said. 'Thank you for bringing Gina back.'

'It's no problem. I would have brought you both back, even if you'd wanted to come away early; all you had to do was ask.'

'I know, and it's really sweet of you.' Now was not the time to explain that it had been a teensy bit difficult to ask. 'Goodnight, Ross.'

He gave her a strained smile, and looked over her shoulder where Gina had just disappeared into the depths of the house. 'Say goodnight to Gina for me.'

'I will.' Hannah felt bad for him. Gina shouldn't have shook him off like that, no matter how annoyed she was with Hannah. 'I'm sure she'll call you or something,' Hannah added, not sure if it was what he wanted to hear but feeling as though she ought to offer him something.

Ross gave her a brief nod, and then walked out into the night. Hannah closed the front door with a heavy sigh. Gina was in one of those moods where it was impossible to make her see anyone's viewpoint but her own. She shuffled along to the living room.

'Thanks a lot.' Gina had flopped onto the sofa in Hannah's spot. 'Thanks for worrying me to death.'

'I didn't mean to. Didn't you check your phone?'

'Yes, but only after I'd had the whole bloody ballroom searching for you. Briony and Paul told me you looked a bit off and then I had visions of you collapsed under a bush or something freezing to death. It wasn't until I checked my phone that I realised where you were and by then I looked a right chump.'

'I don't think you needed any help with that,' Hannah replied. She sat down in a chair opposite Gina and curled her feet beneath her. 'You should have checked your phone earlier, but I suppose you were too busy for that.'

'What does that mean?'

'You know what it means.'

Gina sniffed. 'I don't but if you're going to be cryptic about it then I'm not going to give you the satisfaction of asking. It's obvious you want to have a pop at me about something. But *I'm* the aggrieved party here.'

'Of course you are. That's why I was forced to leave by myself when you were nowhere to be found.'

'I didn't know you were going to go loco on me and want to run off, did I? If you'd waited for ten minutes then Ross could have taken you home.'

'Ten minutes? Is that how long it takes these days? I don't think much of your technique.'

Gina frowned. 'What the hell are you talking about?'

'You and Ross re-enacting the steamy car windows scene from *Titanic*.'

'Nope, you're still not making sense.'

'I saw you… at least I saw the car windows and that was enough. Very classy. You could have booked a room, but no, you chose the really discreet route and messed around in the carpark for everyone to see.'

Gina's mouth fell open. Then closed again. Then opened again but nothing came out. Finally, she clamped it shut. 'I'm going to bed,' she announced, and left Hannah alone by the fire.

*

Hannah was up hours before Gina. The events of the evening, followed by her argument with Gina in the early hours, weren't exactly conducive to peaceful sleep. Finally, she had to give up and took herself down to the kitchen as the grey morning greeted her through the slats of the window blinds. Dropping a couple of soluble paracetamol tablets into a glass of water and downing it to ease her hangover, made her brain a little clearer. She'd overreacted last night – over Gina and Ross, over Mitchell and Martine, over everything – and she'd made herself look an idiot. If Briony ever tried to persuade her to go to a charity dance again, Hannah would make damned sure she booked herself onto the next flight out of the country to be as far away from it as possible.

There were footsteps on the floor above, and a few minutes later, Gina sloped into the kitchen.

'Well, that wasn't the best idea we've ever had, was it?' Gina fixed a hand to her head as she sat at the dining table. 'That's the last time I let you talk me into going to a charity dance.'

'I was thinking just the same thing,' Hannah said from her station by the toaster as she waited for her breakfast.

'Ugh… I feel like shit. Why don't I learn to say no?'

'We had fun, though… at least for most of it… well, you did…' Hannah raised her eyebrows and turned to look at her. She whizzed back around as her toast popped up and she dropped the slices onto a plate.

'You're seriously eating this morning?' Gina said, grimacing as Hannah brought the plate to the table and reached for the butter dish.

'Soaks up the alcohol. You should really have something too.'

'Not likely. At least not yet.'

'I could make you some sausage… oh, no, hang on, you already had some last night.'

'You know you're not funny, don't you?'

Hannah grinned. Then she was serious. 'Look, I'm sorry about last night. I didn't mean to snipe at you and none of it was your fault.'

'I'm sorry too. I'm not sorry for not being joined at the hip to you, but I am sorry for snapping when I got home. I suppose we were both a bit the worse for wear.'

'I know I was…' Hannah looked up from the marmalade she was spreading generously over her toast. 'So… spill the beans about Ross. Was he worth it?'

'Was he worth what?'

'What was he like? Does the reality deliver what the package suggests or are there trade description issues?'

'I wish you'd just ask a straight question. I didn't have sex with him, if that's what you're hinting at.'

'You didn't?'

'No.'

Hannah took a sip of her coffee. 'Blimey.'

Gina frowned. 'You always assume the worst of me, don't you?'

'Of course not. Anyway, would you care if I did?'

'A little bit, yeah. I know I was joking about having sex with Ross before we went out but that didn't mean I was going to. I work fast but I do have some scruples you know.'

'So... what did happen?'

'I really have to spell it out for you?'

'You were just having a chat?'

A slow smile spread over Gina's face. 'Honestly? I probably would have had sex with him in the car last night if he'd let me – I was that drunk. But he was the sweetest thing. He said he didn't want to, not like that, and he said he didn't want a one night stand with me because he liked me too much for that and he didn't want anything that might start between us to be ruined by a drunken fumble.'

'So there wasn't even drunken fumbling?'

'Well, there was a little bit of that, but... you know... not a little bit of *that*.'

'And do you think something might start between you?'

Gina gave a slight shrug. 'Who knows?'

'But you like him?'

'Of course I do; he's gorgeous and funny and very sweet. But he's also a lot younger than me. We could fool around, but where is it going really?'

Hannah was thoughtful for a moment as she poured Gina a cup of coffee from the pot. It seemed that Gina's situation almost echoed her own. She and Mitchell liked each other – more than that – but with so much stacked against them, where could it go?

'Maybe I'd rather like the fooling around bit, though,' Gina added.

'I think he wants more than that.'

'Possibly. So, what do you think?'

Hannah blew out a long breath. 'I think I'm the last person on earth who should be giving out relationship advice.'

'You think it's a non-starter?'

'I don't know. What does your heart tell you?'

Gina threw her a withering look. 'Trust you. Since when did my heart ever steer me right? Look at what happened with Howard…'

Hannah pushed the empty plate away and reached for her coffee mug. She was still so hungry she could eat it all over again. 'You might have a point there. Sometimes life doesn't give a shit about what your heart wants.'

Gina folded her arms. 'So… what happened to you last night? Why the dramatic exit?'

Hannah sipped her coffee. In the cold light of day she felt such an idiot for her behaviour the previous evening, but Gina had been honest with her, and perhaps she owed it to Gina to be honest in return. Besides, she needed to talk it through with someone and there was no one else she could trust.

'Did you see Mitchell and Martine come in?' she asked.

Gina stared at her. 'No way! They came to the party?'

Hannah nodded. 'They know the hotel owners apparently. They decided to come and sit at our table. I don't know where you'd got to at that point but I guess you'd already gone out with Ross, or at least you were too preoccupied to notice. Mitchell saw you, though, or so Martine told me.'

'I never saw them at all.'

'They had probably come after me by the time you went back into the ballroom.'

'I'm not really firing on all cylinders this morning, so you might have to go at remedial speed for me.'

'Mitchell said some things… it all got a bit weird.'

'What sort of things?'

Hannah wrinkled her nose. 'Odd things. I wasn't even sure what he meant. But I had a feeling that what he meant was trouble, and I needed to get away from him, because it just wasn't right. Suddenly I was having a shit time and I really didn't want to be around him – around anyone, and certainly not in the middle of a crowded ballroom. I came to look for you to tell you and… well, you know. Anyway, when I left, Mitchell must have followed me straight out and he caught up with me on the road. Without Martine. And he told me all this stuff again… about how he didn't want to be with Martine and how he wanted to be with me.'

'He told you that!'

'Sort of. And then he kissed me. I mean, *kissed* me.'

'Bloody hell!'

'Yeah, my thoughts exactly.'

'What else? What did he say about Martine? Is he going to leave her?'

'He said he didn't want to be with her but he never said he was leaving her. We didn't really have time to discuss it further than that because she turned up in the car to find him and she was pissed as a fart as well.'

'Bloody hell!' Gina repeated.

'Quite. What the fudge do I do?'

'I take it Martine doesn't know about any of this.'

'No. That bugs me too. If he feels like that, don't you think he should tell her?'

'Well I'm sure last night wasn't the right moment for that sort of news. She had just broken about fifty laws driving out to find him and she was probably in a less rational state than she would normally be.'

'Maybe, but I'm sure there must have been plenty of right moments over the past few weeks. He says he hasn't been feeling right since the accident.'

'There's your answer. He must have needed her. Think about it.'

'I am, and I still think he needs to be honest with her.'

Gina shrugged. 'So you're blowing him off?'

'Yes.'

'Harsh.'

'How can I trust him? I barely know him and this… I don't know what to make of it.'

'What does your heart tell you?' Gina smiled, echoing Hannah's own words.

'My heart is a moron,' Hannah replied as she plonked her mug on the table. 'I think my track record is proof of that.'

Gina leaned back in her chair and stretched. 'So I guess neither of us is any the wiser. I think the only thing to do in this situation is head back to bed for a nap.'

Hannah smiled. 'God; that does sound good. I've had the crappiest night's sleep ever.'

'And I've had about four hours, so I reckon I'll see you in another four or so.'

Hannah laughed. 'You've had way more than four hours!'

'Really? It only feels like four.'

'That's called a hangover.'

Gina gave her a weak grin before pushing herself out of the chair. 'I don't know about that, but I do know that I really need to lie down again before I fall down.'

'Go on. I'll just clear up down here first,' Hannah replied, knowing that really, it was pointless going back to bed the way her thoughts were flirting around her head – there'd be no sleep for her no matter how tired she was or how much of a hangover she was still nursing.

Gina headed for the door. 'You're welcome to that little job.'

Hannah called her back and she stopped in her tracks.

'Yeah?' she asked, turning to face her.

'Thanks,' Hannah said. 'For listening to my dramas.'

'Hey... isn't that what sisters are for?'

'You mean they're not there to cut off your hair when your parents are out, steal your Barbie dolls and hide them in the neighbour's compost heap and generally make your childhood a living hell?'

'Oh yes, that too,' Gina grinned. 'See you later, sis.'

*

The rest of the weekend flew by and before either of them had time to think about it, Gina was packing. At least, that was what she told Hannah she was doing, but Hannah wasn't convinced that running around like a donkey with its tail on fire could be called packing.

'Have you seen my handbag?' she yelled down the stairs to where Hannah was shoving her smalls into the washing machine.

'No!' Hannah called back. 'Where did you last see it?'

'If I knew that I wouldn't be asking!' Gina shouted.

Hannah pursed her lips and flicked the dial on the machine. There was no point in getting involved; Gina would eventually remember what she'd done with it once she calmed down enough to think straight. She'd been in a state of agitation all morning, and it was probably something to do with Ross's visit the night before.

'Ross will be here any minute!' Gina called, confirming Hannah's suspicions.

'So?'

'I don't want to keep him waiting while I run around looking like an idiot.'

'You must be in love…' Hannah muttered, 'you never cared about keeping me waiting.'

Gina and Ross were an item. Not officially – which was a prickly situation that nobody wanted to tackle this early on – but he had been to see Gina as soon as she'd allowed him, and they'd disappeared out together for a walk to talk things over. Hannah didn't know where, or what they'd got up to other than talking (some things a sister really didn't want to know) but on their return, Hannah had to admit that it had been a long time since she'd seen Gina look so happy. Whether that would last once Ross's parents found out was a different matter entirely.

A series of thuds on the stairs reminded Hannah of what it had been like to live with Gina when they were kids, and with a speed that Hannah was shocked Gina still possessed, she appeared in the kitchen.

'Just popping out to the shed,' she panted.

'What for?'

'I think my handbag is in there.'

Hannah stared at her. She shook her head slowly. 'I don't even want to know why that could be possible.'

'Had to make a phone call,' Gina replied.

'And you had to do it from the shed?'

'It was kinda private, and it was too cold to stand in your garden.'

'Yes, because the shed is lovely and toasty warm…' Hannah's sarcasm was wasted on Gina, who was already on her way out of the back door. 'Weird…' she added to herself. It didn't take a genius to work out that Ross was the recipient of her private phone call, despite having seen him only hours before.

Gina returned a few moments later with her handbag and a triumphant grin.

'Why didn't you just take your phone out there, instead of the whole lot?' Hannah began, but then, 'never mind… I don't need to know.'

There was a knock at the front door. Hannah glanced up at the clock. 'Bang on time. I still don't know why I couldn't take you to the station.'

'We thought we'd save you a job, that's all,' Gina said as she followed Hannah through to the hall. 'Ross was free and it seemed like a good idea.'

'It's very nice of him to offer, but he must be sick of chauffeuring us around.'

'I don't think so,' Gina said brightly.

Of course not, Hannah thought. *At least not one of us anyway.* It was silly, but Hannah felt redundant and a little hurt that Gina had asked Ross to take her to the station instead of her. Hannah always did it (apart from when her car had been out of action and that was hardly her fault). But of course they wanted to grab another few moments alone together. Hannah could hardly blame them for that. Those moments would be few and far between, and fraught with difficulty if their relationship made it into serious territory. And the way they seemed besotted with each other already, that seemed like a pretty safe bet.

Ross stood with an awkward grin at the front door and an uncertain blush in his cheeks. He looked like an overgrown schoolboy getting ready to ask a sixth former out on a date. Which wasn't really far from the truth, Hannah reflected wryly.

'Morning!' he said, immediately glancing behind Hannah to where Gina stood with an equally soppy look on her face.

'Good morning, Ross,' Hannah said. 'She's right here…' *as it's obviously not me you're interested in…*

Gina kissed him as he stepped inside. 'Thanks for giving me a lift; you're a gem.'

'It's no problem. Are you ready?'

'The train's not for ages, is it?' Hannah asked. 'You don't have to go just yet, do you?'

'I wanted to get there early,' Gina replied, glancing furtively at Ross. But not so furtively that Hannah didn't see it and understand its meaning straightaway.

Right… so they wanted to pull over somewhere and have a chat… or whatever… Hannah couldn't blame them for that either, considering that they didn't know when Gina would next be here, or whether Ross was quite ready for a trip to Birmingham and all that represented in their budding new relationship. She supposed she'd feel the same way too, and she'd want to make the most of any stolen moments. Her thoughts strayed to Mitchell… but then she pushed them firmly out of her mind. Stolen moments anywhere with him were strictly off-limits from now on.

She reached for Gina and gave her a quick hug. 'Do you have all your stuff?'

'It's not like I can't get it back if I don't, is it?' Gina smiled. 'Unless you're planning a car boot sale?'

'I might,' Hannah grinned. 'You have some dresses that I'm sure would fetch a couple of quid.'

'Help yourself, then,' Gina winked. 'Thanks for a brilliant, if slightly surprising, weekend.'

'I should be thanking you for coming,' Hannah said. 'I'm going to miss you next week.'

'It won't be long until I'm back for good.'

'I hope so,' Hannah said, unexpected tears springing to her eyes. 'I really can't wait until you're down the road.'

'Me neither.' Gina turned to Ross. 'We'd better get going.'

He nodded.

'Look after her,' Hannah told him, and she hoped he understood that she meant so much more than just the trip to the station.

*

There was a time when Hannah would have found cleaning the house therapeutic, a chance to lose herself in the task and solve whatever problem was bothering her. But today, alone again after Gina's departure the day before, and with her head whirling from the sort of weekend that would try the easiest going person, housework wasn't having its usual effect on her nerves. Hannah switched off the hoover and wandered into the kitchen to put the kettle on. She didn't really want tea, but made it anyway. After raiding the biscuit tin for something to go with it, and then feeling guilty about the number of biscuits she'd eaten before she remembered to stop herself, Hannah decided to go and run a bath. She felt like an autumn leaf, spinning to the ground, buffeted by whatever winds decided to snatch it from its course and hurl it who knew where. Perhaps for the first time in her life, Hannah felt powerless to influence her own course.

The best thing about living and working alone was that if she wanted to stay in bed one morning and start work at noon, she could, as long as all deadlines were met. So when she finally sat down to her computer at three that afternoon, it wasn't anything out of the ordinary. She could always work on into the evening if it suited her and things would still get done. But today, it might have been wise if she'd started first thing after all. The laptop had barely booted up when there was a knock at the front door. Hannah let out a sigh. There were some days when she just had to accept that things weren't going to go her way, and some Januarys that should probably be scrapped and started over.

She made her way to the front door, expecting it to be George popping over to see her with Trixie, or her other neighbours, Brian and Cynthia, back from their holiday home in Greece and short of a bottle of milk or a cup of sugar. Either way, she wished she looked a little more presentable. She pulled her thick woollen cardigan around her and smoothed her hair, gathering together the rogue strands and retying her ponytail before opening the door.

'Ross?' she said, a faint note of surprise in her voice. 'I didn't expect to see you today. Everything okay?'

'Yes… I…' Ross shoved his hands in his pockets with an awkward smile.

'Would you like to come in?' Hannah asked, sensing him tussle with whatever subject he wanted to broach. She guessed it was probably something to do with Gina.

'It's okay… you're probably busy… I just wanted to ask… I should have phoned before I came over…'

'Ross, it's alright. You didn't interrupt anything. What's the matter?'

There was a pause. Then, 'You're okay with me and Gina, aren't you?' The words almost tumbled out. He looked so uncertain, so lost, so utterly dependent on her answer that Hannah couldn't help giving him a warm smile. He had asked for her approval when many wouldn't have cared either way, and she knew that it really mattered to him what she thought. He might be far too young, and there was probably more stacked against them than most, but looking at him right now, Hannah was left in no doubt about the honesty of his intentions. Ross was a lovely man, and if they made it, Gina could be very happy indeed. Was that a little tinge of envy scratching at her gut? Maybe, but if there was a happy ending for Gina, surely she deserved it after everything she'd been through, and how could Hannah deny her that?

'Of course I'm okay,' she said. 'But I'll warn you that she can be a handful.'

Ross broke into a more certain smile now, all traces of anxiety gone. 'I'll try to remember that.'

'Are you sure you don't want to come in?'

'No, I should be getting back… early start tomorrow and all that.' He stamped his feet in the cold, his breath curling into the air. Dusk was already creeping in, and new flakes of snow floated down from a lilac sky.

It was then that they both turned at the sound of a car engine out on the lane. They watched as a black Volvo pulled up outside Hannah's gate. And then Hannah caught her breath as Mitchell climbed out. He stopped when he saw Ross.

'I'm sorry… am I interrupting?' Mitchell asked, hovering at the gate.

Ross glanced at Hannah, asking a silent question.

'It's okay,' she said. 'I'll catch up with you tomorrow if you still want to talk.'

'Thank you,' Ross said, 'that sounds good.' He gave Mitchell a brief nod as he passed, and Mitchell made his way up the drive to Hannah. They both watched for a moment as Ross drove off.

'Are you okay?' Mitchell asked.

'I could ask you the same thing. I didn't think I'd see you again after the dance.'

'Why not? Didn't I make my feelings clear enough?'

Hannah sighed. 'More than, but I thought I had made my answer clear too. I'm not prepared to get involved in such a complicated situation…' In the cold light of day, Hannah's resolution was stronger than ever. How could she go down this road? It would only bring heartache.

'I was hoping…'

'I'm sorry if I let you think there was hope, because there is none. At least not while you're married.'

There was a pause. 'That's just it…' he said finally, holding Hannah's gaze. 'I've left Martine.'

Part Three:
Ways to Say Goodbye

Hannah stood in front of the mirror and applied another coat of lipstick. They weren't the worst pub toilets she'd ever been in, but they were draughty and there was a vague smell of damp in the air – not to mention the questionable blockage in one of the cubicles. But she had been at a loss for another pub within easy reach of them both. Even so, as she stood there staring at her reflection, she had to wonder why she had agreed to come on this stupid date in the first place. And then she had arrived so ridiculously early that she was forced to sit alone like a desperate old spinster. She clutched her stomach as it turned another somersault. Perhaps there was still time to run? She could get out before he arrived and never have to see him. She could email, make an excuse, tell him her cat was on fire. Anything had to be better than this torture.

With a last look in the mirror, she made up her mind. Blind dates – they just weren't for her and if she spent the rest of her evenings alone in front of the TV watching repeats of *Friends*, then that wouldn't be so bad, would it? Chandler Bing was pretty funny, and she could always pretend they were *her* friends.

As she walked back into the pub, she spotted a man come in through the entrance and search the room. She recognised him instantly from his profile photo. Hannah supposed that had to be worth something

– at least he had posted a real picture and not one of some random model he'd found online; although he did look older, so he'd obviously fallen victim to some sort of vanity. At a glance he was probably in his late forties. That wasn't too much of an age difference for her. He was dressed okay too; nothing embarrassing. Maybe it wouldn't be so bad. And she did need some distraction from thoughts of Mitchell, which still seemed to fill her head no matter what she did. She remained convinced that her decision to turn him away on the night he'd arrived on her doorstep telling her he had left Martine and professing his love had been the right one, but it didn't make it any easier to bear. She reminded herself sternly of Gina's warnings, and what a mess the whole situation was, and how Mitchell's confused emotions weren't the most stable and reliable barometer of his true feelings right now. God knew hers weren't much better when she thought about it. She wanted him, but that didn't make it right.

She took a deep breath, and then began to walk over to the newcomer at the pub doors. A broad smile lit up his face as she approached.

'Hannah?' he asked, in the sort of baritone usually the preserve of radio presenters.

Hannah stuck her hand out for him to shake, but instead he pulled her into a light kiss on both cheeks. It was a lot less formal, and not unwelcome. In fact, it was nice… warm and friendly. He was obviously confident and open too – no emotional baggage here, no lost memories, no existential crisis, just a normal bloke who might be fun if Hannah gave him a chance. Mitchell was in a hotel somewhere, sorting his head out, Hannah hoped, after she'd told him that was what he needed to do, and Hannah was fairly certain that once he did, he'd realise that he belonged in Martine's arms after all. And he'd probably get his memory back before then anyway, and Hannah would be gone from his thoughts once he'd remembered his old life and who he was supposed to be.

No, Hannah decided, *no more Mitchell Bond.*

'You must be Chris,' she smiled. 'It's lovely to meet you.'

'And you,' Chris said. 'You look fabulous – much lovelier than your photo and that knocked my socks off.'

Hannah blushed. 'Don't be silly…'

'I mean it. So lovely that I want to buy you a drink. You haven't been waiting long, have you?'

Hannah flicked a glance at the glass of wine she'd abandoned on the table before his arrival. 'No… I've only just got here… and I'd love a drink, thank you.'

'Great!'

She followed him to the bar where he ordered for them both, easily passing pleasantries about the cold snap with the barman. He turned to Hannah. 'Well, this is kind of weird, isn't it?'

'Yes.' Hannah smiled, feeling more awkward by the second. She had forgotten just what hard work first dates were. A blind date was ten times harder.

'Nice weird, though.'

'Yes.'

'Do you say yes to everything?' he asked. He had an amiable smile on his face, yet Hannah felt something else when she looked into his eyes. Okay, so, maybe not such a good start after all. God, it was so hard to read people.

'No,' she said.

'Oh!' he laughed. 'God, no… that came out all wrong; I didn't mean anything by it!'

Hannah relaxed and smiled. They were both nervous and people said and did odd things when they were put on the spot. Perhaps she ought to give him the benefit of the doubt. 'Would you like to eat?' he added. 'Let me buy you dinner.'

'That would be nice, thank you.'

They took a seat away from the bar in an area at the back set out for diners. As they perused the menu, they chatted about how bad the traffic had been on the ring road, the cost of filling his car with petrol, the mother's cat that had needed a visit to the vet that morning… well, it seemed that Chris chatted and Hannah mostly listened. At least it filled the space where there might be awkward silences instead. She was almost relieved when the food arrived and he had to take a breather to eat.

'I realise that I've talked your ears off and you've barely told me anything at all,' he said as he sprinkled salt over his food. 'That's very rude of me. My friends all say I have a gob on me.'

Hannah cut into a wedge of salmon. 'Oh, that's okay. There really isn't that much to tell.'

'There must be something. You haven't been living as a hermit, have you?'

'Almost,' Hannah smiled. 'Tell me about your job. What is it you do?'

'I'm a property developer,' Chris replied. Hannah's fork stopped in mid-air as she stared at him. 'Nothing big time,' he continued, 'I just buy one house at a time and do it up so I can sell it on and buy the next. They get a little bigger each time and the profit goes up a fraction but I'm basically a one-man band. I suppose the title of property developer is a bit grand really. More like DIY enthusiast.'

Hannah shook herself. The coincidences kept getting weirder. A property developer? Just like Mitchell… *No, brain!* Hannah thought, *we're not going there again!*

'What do you do?' Chris asked.

'Digital design… book covers, company logos, letterheads, blog headers… that sort of thing. I'm a bit of a one-man band too.'

'It sounds interesting.'

'I suppose it is if you love art and design like me, but it's not for everyone. It's a growth area, though, and it pays the bills.'

'That's the main thing, isn't it?' He swallowed a mouthful of his steak. 'So… dare I ask why you're on your own?'

'You mean how many crap relationships have I been through already? Well, it's no secret that I'm forty-two, so that's probably more than I care to count up over the years. I'm not a fruitcake just yet, though, and I haven't boiled anyone's pet rabbit, so there's hope for me yet.'

'God, no! I didn't mean that at all!'

Hannah took a sip of her wine. 'It's just how things have worked out for me, I suppose. Wrong places, wrong times, wrong men. I've been on my own for a while now, and I quite liked it that way. But lately I've been feeling it more – life passing me by and no one to share it with. I'm not sure I want to grow old alone.' She took a bigger gulp of her wine. Damn it, that was probably a little too candid. She always did give out more information than she ought to, especially when booze was involved. He would definitely think she was a fruitcake now.

'My wife ran off with another woman,' he said.

'Oh…'

'Turns out she only married me because she wanted her parents to think she was straight. But then it all got too much, living the lie, and now she's shacked up with a florist called Cindy.'

'Oh… my… I'm…' Hannah glanced around the restaurant. What the hell did she say to that? It certainly made her problems look simple. But when she looked back at him he was grinning.

'It does rather surprise people when I tell them,' he said. 'But I think I'm over it now, and at least past the point where I assume that all women are going to announce they're gay as soon as I get close to them… Well I hope not, anyway. That would be a bit damaging to the old ego.'

'I suppose it would,' Hannah replied, relieved that he did seem pretty okay with it after all. 'Did you never suspect anything?'

He shrugged. 'I don't know… I keep asking myself how I missed it. I suppose the possibility just never crossed my mind so I wasn't looking for it.'

'Well you wouldn't, would you!' Hannah looked up at him and suddenly they were both laughing, the ice well and truly broken.

*

As dates went it hadn't been too bad in the end. Hannah hadn't exactly been blown away, but Chris had been good company and the meal was nice – much nicer than the interior of the pub had suggested it might be. He had said he would call her again, and had even offered to let Gina have first refusal and a good price on a house he had just renovated in a suburb of Millrise that Hannah knew Gina really liked. All in all, a good result, Hannah felt, and she was glad she'd been prevented from escaping after all.

The following morning, the sun was bright, the day crisp with a dry frost, and after putting in a couple of hours of early work, Hannah decided it was about time she tidied the garden. There was the Christmas tree to pull up for a start, which wasn't a job that she looked forward to. She had potted it out in the hope it might take (as she did every year) and sadly, it hadn't (as was the case each year), and she couldn't leave it out there going brown and making her garden look like a tree graveyard. Despite this new defeat, she smiled to herself as she pulled on her gardening gloves. She could imagine the look of righteous glee on Gina's face: *I told you it wouldn't grow... I told you to bin it.*

By the time Hannah had got the offending tree to the composter, she was sweating in a most unglamorous fashion. Pulling off her fleece hoodie, she tied it around her waist, and spotted a hunched figure with a little dog on a lead, coming down the lane in the direction of her house.

'How are you, George?' Hannah called cheerfully. 'Out for a stroll?'

George waved back as he veered from the path towards her gate. 'I'm glad I've caught you; I wanted to have a word with you, actually.' He leaned over the gate as Trixie strained at her lead to carry on walking. Hannah pulled off her gardening gloves as she sauntered over to him.

'Is everything okay?'

'Oh, yes, everything's fine with me. It's just... Well, I don't want to worry you but when I went past your house yesterday evening I noticed a man hanging around in a car. He looked like he was watching your place.'

'Are you sure? What made you think that?'

'He was sitting there a long time, because I came back with Trixie an hour later and he hadn't moved... and he was definitely watching your house. I could tell you were out too – no lights on or anything. I hope he wasn't looking to break in.'

'Well, I haven't been broken into,' Hannah mused. 'I should have thought he'd have had plenty of opportunity yesterday if he wanted to; I was out until quite late.'

'It's a bit odd, though. You'll keep a lookout, won't you?'

'Of course. Did you see his face?'

'Not exactly. But I didn't know the car and I know most round here.'

Hannah was thoughtful for a moment. It could have been that George was mistaken, and there was a perfectly innocent explanation, but living alone always made her slightly more wary of news like this. 'Did you notice what sort of car it was?'

'I'm not very good on cars. Could have been something like a Volvo, I suppose.'

Hadn't Mitchell arrived in one of those when he came to tell her he'd left Martine (she presumed the sex-on-wheels Audi was Martine's). But Mitchell? Surely he wasn't stalking her like some weirdo? They'd talked things over for a long time after he had made his shock announcement, and much as she had longed to throw him into her bed and ravish him, she had made it quite clear that they had no future together – at least not yet and not until she could be sure he was in a fit state to make such a huge decision as leaving his wife. And anyway, didn't George know what Mitchell looked like from when they had met on Christmas day? He'd know him again, surely? So it couldn't be Mitchell… could it?

'Thanks for letting me know, George,' she said, trying to reassure him with her brightest smile. Should she contact Mitchell and let him know that if it was him he was causing a code red in her neighbourhood by hanging around like a second rate secret agent? And if he still had something to say to Hannah, then watching her house from his car wasn't exactly the way to go about it.

'Do you think it's worth contacting the police?' George asked.

'I have a feeling I know who it might be.'

George looked doubtful. 'As long as you're sure…'

'I'm sure. There's no point in getting the police involved if it's a false alarm – they wouldn't thank us.'

George tipped his cap. 'Righto then. Be careful, though, won't you.'

'Of course I will,' Hannah smiled. 'And thank you.'

She watched as he tootled off with Trixie panting and wagging her tail – far more energy in her than was right for a dog of her age. It was at times like these when she wished, just a little bit, that she didn't live alone in such a remote area. She could call someone… Ross, or his dad, Paul, perhaps? But what would she say? She couldn't have them patrolling the lane night and day in case George's possibly phantom stalker came back. Much as it vexed her to do it, Mitchell was the best phone call to make. She'd ask him straight out if it was him, and if it wasn't, well… he'd come over, wouldn't he? *And what then, Hannah?* They could have coffee… and she could ask him how he was… he'd have someone to talk to… there wouldn't have to be anything else in it…

Before her brain had been fully engaged, Hannah raced into the house and grabbed her phone from the mantelpiece. Mitchell had insisted on leaving his number when he last came to call, and now she was glad she hadn't deleted it from her phone, as she had almost done.

She dialled and held the phone up to her ear, waiting for him to pick up. A female voice answered.

'I might have known…' Martine's tone was sharp. 'I suppose you're the reason he's so messed up he thinks he wants to leave me.'

Hannah jabbed her finger on the screen to end the call. She dropped into the armchair. Why were her legs shaking?

She wondered why on earth she was shocked that Martine was with Mitchell, and why she was shocked that Martine was presumptuous enough to answer his phone. *Stupid, stupid, stupid…* Why had Hannah called him at all? *Stupid cow…*

Almost immediately, her phone began to buzz and Mitchell's name appeared on the screen. Hannah could only presume it was Martine trying to finish whatever tirade of abuse Hannah had just cut off. Hannah put the phone on the arm of the sofa and stared at it, as if it was a bomb that she could trigger just by breathing on it. After a few moments, the screen went black. And then another call – Mitchell's name lighting up again. Hannah watched it ring. A few moments more and her answering service flashed up a voicemail. She had no desire to listen to it.

Like a robot, she took herself back out into the garden. The patio needed pressure washing, and the moss needed scraping off the terracotta pots in the back, and the hedges needed a clip and… What was the point? The last thing she wanted to do now was garden – hell, she hadn't really wanted to garden in the first place. Pulling off her gloves again and dropping them into the empty wheelbarrow, she took herself back inside to get her phone.

'What do you want now?' Gina answered cheerfully.

'I don't really know,' Hannah said. It was true. She wasn't about to burden her sister with what was beginning to feel like something very silly and blown out of all proportion – she just wanted to hear a friendly voice. 'I fancied a chat, that's all.'

'Oh… well, I'm kind of in the middle of something. Can I phone you later?'

'Yeah… sure…'

'Hannah… are you alright? Do you need me? I can finish here if it's urgent –'

'No… no, don't do that… it's fine. I'll call you this evening.'

'Around eight. I've got to take Jess to martial arts class tonight.'

'Eight… Good…' Hannah murmured.

'Are you sure you're alright?' Gina asked.

'Yes. Eight. Speak to you later.' Hannah ended the call. Putting down the phone, she headed for the kitchen. Screw the New Year's resolution – the gin was coming out.

*

Hannah was half way down her second glass when there was a knock at the door. She was almost expecting it. Well, if Martine wanted a fight, Hannah wasn't going to give her the satisfaction. Ignoring the door, she filled up her glass.

But whoever it was didn't want to give up so easily. Hannah let out a sigh. She could pretend to be as rebellious as she wanted to, but when it came to it, she could no more ignore the front door than stop breathing. What if it was George, or Ross, or someone needing her help? As she walked through the house, she reflected wryly on the last time she had answered the door to someone needing help. *That had ended well...*

It wasn't Martine, but Mitchell who stood on the step, and a strange *déjà vu* swept over her as she recalled almost the same look on his face when she'd first opened the door on Christmas Day.

'Hannah... I am so sorry!' he began. She put up a hand to stop him.

'Forget it – you don't need to explain. It's only right you should give it another go with Martine; I just hope I didn't cock things up for you.'

'But that's just it... I wasn't there to patch things up; I was there to finalise moving out.'

'So why did Martine pick up the call?'

'Because that's what Martine does. She saw it ringing on the table and grabbed it before I had time to stop her.'

'She blames me for your split.'

'Yes...'

'And I don't blame her for that. I suppose I'd feel the same. So you're not getting back together?'

'I don't love her. Hannah... I know you don't want to hear this but...' Mitchell held her in a pained gaze. 'Oh... what the hell...'

Suddenly, Hannah was in his arms, his lips locked against hers. The moment of shock gave way to a wave of desire that crashed through her. She wanted him… she didn't care that he was married or screwed up or that she was out on the front doorstep in full view of the lane… she wanted him, and she wanted him right now. Wrapping her arms around him, she guided him into the house, her lips never leaving his, and she heard the sound of the front door slamming as he kicked it shut behind him. He had her up against the wall, passion she could feel burning through his skin, his hands all over her, driving her wild until her thoughts were filled only with the feel of him, the smell and taste of him. This was a bad, bad idea, and she'd live to regret it, but she couldn't think about that now. In his arms, Hannah was lost.

*

'I want you to know that I don't make a habit of turning up at women's houses and kissing them,' Mitchell said as he stroked a thumb gently over Hannah's shoulder.

'And I don't make a habit of falling into bed with the men who turn up at my house and kiss me,' Hannah smiled.

He chuckled softly and pulled her closer. God, he smelt so good; Hannah could lie next to him and breathe him in for the rest of her life and never need anything else. 'I'm glad you made an exception in this case. That was…'

'Very silly?' Hannah asked.

'I was going to say incredible. It was incredible. *You're* incredible.'

'You have to say that; you're in my bed.'

'So I am.' He kissed the top of her head.

Hannah rolled onto her elbow to face him. 'Mitchell… were you parked outside my house last night?'

'Me? No. Why do you ask?'

'It's just something George said. I was out last night and…' Oh God! She would have to call Chris and put things right. But he had promised to show Gina around his newest development, and when Hannah had returned home from her date and phoned Gina to tell her, she had been so excited about it… she couldn't let Gina down but she'd feel she was using Chris if she continued with the plan. As usual, Hannah had managed to make an almighty mess of things.

'What's the matter?' Mitchell asked.

'It's nothing. Just that George said he saw a Volvo parked outside my house last night while I was out, and it was there for a while. There was a man inside, but George couldn't tell who it was.'

'It wasn't me… but I don't like the sound of it. Maybe I should stay here with you tonight.'

'Seriously? That is the flimsiest excuse I've ever heard to spend the night in someone's bed,' Hannah laughed.

'It's not an excuse… well, a little bit. The spending the night bit would be nice. But I want you to be safe.'

'That's very sweet but you can't be here all the time. I'm sure it was nothing anyway.'

'I could be here all the time…' he said with a slow smile.

Her insides fizzed with anticipation and she leaned in to kiss him. It was a lovely idea. 'No you couldn't,' Hannah said. 'And just because you're about to seduce me again, don't think that this changes my stance on you and me. You have to sort things out with Martine and I have to be sure that you're clear in your own mind what you want before I commit to any sort of proper relationship.'

He frowned. 'Isn't this proof enough of that? I want you, Hannah, not her. That's why I'm here.'

'You think you do.'

'Please… don't let's start that again. My mind might not be what it should, but my heart… there's nothing wrong with what my heart is telling me. When I wake, yours is the face I want to see, and when I go to sleep, yours is the face I want beside me. Lying in that hotel room this week, it's all I can think about.'

'Yeah?' Hannah said, snuggling into him.

'Yeah. So give a poor hopeless, lovesick man a chance, why don't you?'

Hannah narrowed her eyes. 'Are you sure this isn't some elaborate ruse to get into my bed? You sit outside and pretend to stalk me so I ask you to stay here and protect me from… well, you, basically.'

Mitchell laughed. 'No, but I wish I had thought of that!' He pulled her close again and kissed her. God, it did strange and incredible things to her. Kissing him was like kissing for the first time in her life, all over again. She almost wondered if every other man had been doing it wrong. Flipping her onto her back, he leaned into her and began on her neck, raining tiny kisses all over and setting every nerve ending ablaze. She couldn't kick him out of her bed now, even if she wanted to.

*

'All I'm saying is don't tell him just yet,' Gina hissed.

'Seriously?' Hannah whispered back. 'Are you actually serious?'

'He's willing to do a brilliant price on this house and if I want it I don't want him changing his mind because you're shagging Mr Forgetful.'

'It's not fair to keep him in the dark…' Hannah chose to ignore Gina's jibe about Mitchell. She glanced across to where Chris was digging in his pocket at the front door of a neat terraced house. With a little grunt of triumph he produced a key with a numbered fob and rattled it around in the lock.

'It's always a bit tricky with an unfamiliar lock,' he said, smiling back at them.

'If you feel so bad for him you should date him,' Gina whispered as Chris turned back to his task.

'I should date him because I feel sorry for him, or so that you can get this house cheap? You're unbelievable!'

'No, because he seems nice.'

'Nice?'

'Yeah, nice.'

'Nice is a bit nondescript. Cupcakes are nice but I don't want to shag one.'

Gina stifled a giggle.

'What are you two whispering about?' Jess interrupted. Hannah turned to her, trying not to blush and hoping she hadn't heard any of the conversation. She was quite sure that Jess knew all about the birds and bees, but she was also sure she didn't need to know the details of her aunt's sex life.

The front door gave way, and Chris turned to them, clapping his hands together as if announcing a top-of-the-bill theatre act. 'Ladies…' He waved his hand for them to follow him into the house. They trouped in and stood in the entrance hall. 'This is it: number fifteen Susannah Street. Finished last week, and, if I'm honest, one of my favourite jobs so far. Lovely views of the park, and it was already quite well maintained before I got my hands on it – I think it might suit you and your daughter down to the ground.'

'If it was in Birmingham, yeah,' Jess muttered.

'It's lovely,' Gina said, gazing around in approval.

'You've only seen the hallway,' Jess said.

'Then let me show you the rest,' Chris replied. 'Unless you'd all rather take the tour alone? I can just as easily wait for you down here while you have a poke around.'

Hannah glanced at Gina, who nodded. 'I think that would be good, actually. You can take it all in better, can't you, when you have time to look properly.'

'Be my guest. I'll wait here for you. Let me know if there's anything you need.'

Hannah and Gina wandered into the living room, Jess sloping after them.

'Oooh, look at the fireplace!' Gina cooed. 'Inglenook. Gorgeous!'

'Nice,' Hannah agreed.

'So we're going to choose a new house on the basis of the fireplace?' Jess asked.

Gina ignored her. 'Lovely cornicing too,' she continued. 'He's kept all the period features… what a nice touch.'

'He just said most of it was done before he got it,' Jess cut in. 'So he hasn't done anything clever.'

They walked on to a kitchen that was small but well-equipped, painted in a cheerful primrose with dainty net curtains at the window to maximise the light as well as maintain privacy.

'You have to go down a step into the kitchen.' Jess looked at Gina. 'That's a disaster waiting to happen.'

'How do you mean?'

'When you're pissed carrying two bowls of spag bol… up the step you trip and smash your face in.'

'You make it sound like I need rehab or something!' Gina squeaked. 'I'm not constantly drunk!'

'Not constantly, no… just when you're awake.'

'Jess…' Hannah began in a warning tone.

'No…' Gina cut in. 'Leave it, Han. She's in a mood because we're even looking at this house.'

'I don't want to leave Birmingham,' Jess said. 'So, yeah, I'm in a mood. If you were being ripped away from all your friends and a place you loved you'd be in a mood too.'

'We've been over this. Besides, it's not like you're moving to the other side of the world. It's a two-hour journey. Before long you'll be able to drive it whenever you like.'

'I could live with Dad.'

'No, you can't. I don't know where this has suddenly come from. Don't forget the new woman will be there –'

'I don't have to talk to his slutty girlfriend… I can just keep out of the way when she's there –'

'Enough!' Gina walked over to one of the kitchen cupboards and peered inside. 'Nice units.'

Hannah gave Jess a sympathetic look. She could understand how Jess was feeling, but she could also see why Gina wanted to come home. It was something they would resolve in time, but they were both so stubborn that things would be fractious until they did.

'Let's look at the back garden.' A key already sat in the lock of the back door and Gina twisted it and stepped outside. 'It's a good size out here for a terraced house,' she called in. 'We could even do little barbecues in the summer.'

'Great…' Jess muttered. 'I'll be able to invite all my non-existent friends.'

'It all seems horrible now,' Hannah said, rubbing a soothing hand over Jess's back, 'but you'll soon get used to things. Your mum and I did when our parents moved us from Scotland.'

'You were little, though. It's easy to make friends when you're in primary school.'

'I was painfully shy back then – I had to rely on your mum to make my friends for me. You're fun and you're smart and a lot less shy than I ever was… you'll be surprised how quickly you get a new set of friends, and you're not too far away to keep the old ones either… so you get the best of both worlds. Like your mum says, when you're driving…'

Jess was silent as she studied Hannah. Then she offered her a withering look. 'Whatever…' she muttered as she walked out into the back garden.

Hannah let out a heavy sigh. She had hoped that Jess might be more receptive to her reasoning than to Gina's, but it looked as though it was going to take more than Hannah's encouragement to change her mind. As she wandered outside herself, Gina was peering into a compost bin at the bottom of the garden while Jess was standing, hunched into her coat pockets and glaring at her mother.

'It's a garden, Mum. It doesn't really matter.'

'Right then,' Gina said brightly, 'upstairs next. Is that more to your liking, Jess?'

'It won't make any difference what the bedroom looks like… as I have no plans to stay here.'

'You're wrong if you think your dad will take you,' Gina said stiffly as she made her way into the house. 'He's got a good thing going on with his floozy and he doesn't want a moody teenager pouring water on his fire.'

'Yeah?' Jess shot back. 'That all depends on what I tell him about you.' She folded her arms and waited for Gina to turn back and argue, but Gina simply continued on into the house.

*

By the time they left, Gina was in love with the house. It helped that Chris had promised to hold it for as long as he could while her divorce settlement went through (she assured him it was imminent) and he had also given them a good price, though Hannah couldn't help the burning shame that he was probably only being so generous because he thought that she was up for another date. All afternoon she had tussled with the problem of how to tell him that they weren't, because he seemed to really like her and, perhaps, under different circumstances she would like him well enough at least to date him a few times and see where that led them. It wasn't fair to string him along, but if she told him how things were now, Gina would probably lose all favours on the house.

'Mitchell could probably find you a place,' Hannah said as they sat with mugs of tea back at hers. Jess's drink sat on the coffee table going cold, its owner out in the hallway on her phone, having practically vaulted over the back of the sofa to leave the room the moment it rang.

'I thought his company was more into commercial properties?'

'Well… yes… but I suppose he has contacts who have houses.'

'You'd probably find Chris was one of them,' Gina said, arching an eyebrow. 'There can't be that many property developers in these parts. Besides, I like that house.'

'I knew it was a bad idea taking you to see it.' Hannah reached for another chocolate biscuit.

'You were being a good sister. I'd have done the same for you.'

'Would you have dated someone just so I could get a house?'

'You don't have to. I'm sure he'd be a grownup about it.'

'But I feel so bad.'

'Alright, date him a couple of times and be completely hideous – he'll soon dump you and you'll be guilt free. Just put Mitchell off for a bit until it's done.'

'You have a strange and twisted logic,' Hannah smiled.

'While you, on the other hand, have lots of very sensible ideas… like letting a man with serious psychological issues into your bed.'

'He's not a whack job. He's just got some memory problems.'

'He's also got baggage.'

'Lots of people have baggage.'

'Has he mentioned divorcing Martine?'

'Well… not exactly… we sort of haven't got that far.'

'That's what I mean: baggage.' Gina drained her cup and handed it to Hannah.

'Hmmmm,' Hannah replied as she stood up. 'Are you staying for something to eat before you head home?'

'What's on offer?'

'I was thinking chips from that new place in Chapeldown.'

Gina frowned. 'Isn't that where Mitchell and Martine live?'

'Just Martine now,' Hannah corrected.

'What if you bump into her?'

'I doubt she's a chippy sort of girl. Unless deep fried caviar's also on the menu.'

'Okay, it's a deal. I'm sure Jess won't complain about a nice bag of chips either.'

'Who's she on the phone to, anyway?' Hannah asked. 'She's been ages.'

'The new beau I expect.'

'Must be serious the way she leapt up when her phone went.'

'I bloody well hope so. He can look out for her from time to time; take the heat off me.'

'You don't mean that…' Hannah hovered at the door with the dirty mugs.

'Don't I? You don't live with her.'

'She's not taking the move too well, is she?'

'That's one thing she's making very obvious to anyone who will listen. She probably thought I wouldn't go through with it when I first mentioned it, so now she's realised it's an actual plan she's kicking off.'

'She'll come round.'

'I hope so. I've tried enough bribes on her.'

Hannah popped out to the kitchen. As she filled the sink with soapy water, she thought about Gina's predicament. She felt sorry for her sister, but couldn't see a way she could help – after all, she'd already tried talking to her niece and Jess had blanked her for her pains. Dumping the mugs in the water, she returned to the living room.

'What are you going to do about Ross?' she asked.

'What do you mean?'

'Well,' Hannah continued, 'if Jess is that upset about the move, how is she going to feel about Ross being on the scene?'

'Oh. I don't suppose I need to do anything at the moment. One problem at a time, that's what I say.'

'You'll have to do some sneaking around for a while then.'

'It looks like it. But sneaking around isn't so bad. We can pretend to be having a steamy, illicit affair and check into seedy hotels as Mr and Mrs Smith for debauched afternoon sex. It could be quite fun.'

'Sounds good,' Hannah smiled. 'Maybe I'll take a leaf out of your book.'

'So you and Mitchell… you're together now or what?'

'We've *been* together, but I don't know whether that means we *are* together. It's not that simple, is it?'

'Nothing ever is with you.'

'You can hardly talk! You and Ross aren't exactly a match made in heaven.'

'Oh, I don't know… age is only a number, isn't it? When I'm with him it feels pretty heavenly. It's strange, but I feel more right with him than I've ever done with anyone my age – even Howard – and yet we've been together for such a short time.'

'That's what great sex does for you.'

'It's more than that.'

'Really?'

Gina nodded. 'I know it's all brand new and everything is always shiny at this stage, but sometimes, I do think I can see it lasting.'

Hannah sat back in her seat and appraised her sister thoughtfully. 'Wow… I never saw that coming.'

'Me neither.' Gina grinned. 'It's exciting though.'

'Surprising is the word I'd use. If you do see it going the distance you're going to have to tell Jess sooner rather than later. It'll be far worse if you keep her in the dark – when it does eventually come out she'll be furious.'

'She doesn't need to know about every man I date and I doubt she wants to.'

'But we're not talking about a few dates, are we?'

'Han… with respect, you don't have kids. Nothing is ever as black and white as you make out when kids are involved. I'll choose my time and I'll tell her but it won't be just yet.'

Hannah chewed her lip as she looked away.

'Sorry…' Gina said.

Hannah turned back to her. 'It's okay. I shouldn't be sticking my nose in. I know you can handle it and my advice is probably not what you need right now.'

Gina was about to reply when Jess burst in, her expression thunderous. 'Is this *the* Ross? Weirdo Tractor Ross?'

Gina's head swizzed round, a furious blush to her cheeks. 'How long have you been earwigging? I thought you were on the phone in the other room.'

'He got called away.'

'So you thought you'd eavesdrop instead of coming back in?'

'I couldn't really help it, not when you were shouting!'

'We weren't shouting! You shouldn't have been listening like that – it's downright rude!'

'That's not the point!' Jess cried. 'How long would I have waited to find out you're cradle snatching?'

'As you have been listening, you'll know that I didn't think it mattered yet. And I hardly think it's cradle snatching.'

'Argh! It is; it's disgusting!'

'Jess…' Hannah warned, sensing the fireworks coming.

'Is he the reason we're moving?' Jess demanded, ignoring her aunt.

'Of course not!'

'I'll bet he's got something to do with it.'

'Jess…' Hannah pressed, 'I can vouch for your mum; Ross is nothing to do with this decision.'

'I suppose *Ross*…' Jess crooked her fingers into speech marks, 'will be moving in with us though. I bet he can't wait. Well, I'm never going to call him dad.'

Hannah glanced at Gina. Dad was one thing Ross would definitely never be to Jess. Perhaps a fun uncle or a big brother was more like it.

'Nobody will expect you to call him dad,' Gina replied tartly. 'Who on earth would want that dubious honour when the prize is a snarky little stepdaughter?'

'It's gross, I mean, he's almost the same age as me –'

Gina shot to her feet, her cheeks now blazing.

'ENOUGH!'

Jess clamped her mouth shut and stared at her mum.

'That's enough,' Gina repeated. 'Where's the rule that says I don't get a life after your dad? How come he gets to settle down with Miss Slapper and I get to be alone? How is that fair?'

'The difference is, he's not making me move to another town.' Jess was trying hard to remain sullen, but Hannah could hear the guilt in her voice.

'For the last time, it has nothing to do with Ross where we live. I'd already made that decision long before him – we talked about it, didn't we?'

'Yeah, but –'

'But you didn't think I meant it? Well, I did. You'd better get used to the idea.'

Hannah stared from one to the other. Was the argument over? A standoff between her sister and her niece wasn't her idea of a good night in.

Jess folded her arms tight across her chest and pressed her lips together. Gina held her gaze. Then Jess flopped onto the sofa, glaring at the fireplace.

'So… maybe I'll go and get those chips now…' Hannah said.

Gina turned to her with a taut smile. 'Sounds fine by me.'

*

Hannah stepped out into the night and breathed in a lungful of frosty air. The orange of the sky deepened into indigo as it stretched towards the first stars. For once, she relished the cold, glad to be out of the stifling atmosphere still hanging in the air of her little house. She had seen Jess and Gina have arguments before, but never with such menace.

She supposed it was bound to happen – Jess was becoming a young woman with firm ideas of what she wanted out of life, and she was increasingly unwilling to submit to Gina's rule. Gina had been through the same phase herself, and Hannah supposed that she probably had too, though she didn't recall being quite so belligerent. She was glad when they had both seemed content to let her go out for their tea alone. Perhaps they would talk things through while she was gone, or maybe they could tell that she wanted to get out of the way.

The windscreen of her car was already frosting over, and Hannah cranked the heaters up to full blast as she started the engine. It was then that she noticed another car, just visible in the shadows at the opposite side of the lane. She squinted through the clearing mist of her windscreen. As she looked closer, she was almost certain she could see a man sitting inside it. An involuntary shiver ran over her. Was this the man George had told her about? She couldn't see properly, but the car did look a little like a Volvo… and a lot like the one she had seen Mitchell pull up in the day he came to tell her he'd left Martine. But Mitchell had denied being parked outside her house and had, in fact, seemed deeply troubled by the idea that someone else was. What should she do? She could go and confront him, she supposed – not in an aggressive way, but just go over and see if there was a simple explanation. Perhaps she ought to get Gina for back up first? But would that in itself seem aggressive, the two of them going over together?

After a moment of procrastination, Hannah made her decision. But as she got out of the car and began to walk across the lane, the headlights came on, the engine roared into life, and the car did a swift three-point turn. Before she was even half-way across the road, it had driven off. Hannah watched it go for a moment. Was it her approach that had made the driver take off? If so, that didn't seem like a good thing. She had, however, seen enough to be fairly sure it wasn't Mitchell behind the wheel. So who was it? She half considered calling Mitchell and asking him to come over, but then dismissed the idea. She wasn't some damsel in distress. She had never relied on a man to keep her safe, and she wasn't about to start now.

*

Ten minutes later Hannah drove past the road sign that read: *Chapeldown, winner of Staffordshire's Tidiest Village Award*. Trust perfect Martine to live in a perfect village. She imagined the place on a Sunday, resembling a scene from *The Stepford Wives*, with every garden being mown in faultless synchronisation. Even the ducks on the pond were probably groomed every day and taught to waddle in formation. Personally, living in Chapeldown was her idea of hell. She'd much rather have the unruly garden and loose paving slabs of her own quirky cottage than anything Martine Bond could afford to buy. But the new fish and chip shop, which the residents had strongly protested against to no avail, was really good and well worth the trip. Her mouth watered at the thought of them and she realised then just how hungry she was.

It was lucky that there was only one other customer ahead of Hannah so that she was served quickly, because the smell was driving her mad. It would take all her self-control not to rip open the parcels on the way home and eat the lot. And this was the only thing on her mind as she thanked the proprietor and headed for the door… only to walk slap bang into a woman who was heading into the shop whilst talking and laughing with a man.

'Oh, God… I'm so sorry…' Hannah looked up and stared as recognition hit. Martine looked mortified to see her there, while Hannah was amazed to see her somewhere so obviously working class as a fish and chip shop.

'Hannah...' Martine said. She seemed to blush as she threw a furtive glance at the man who was with her, and then back at Hannah. Surely she wasn't embarrassed? Or was that a look of guilt on her face? Hannah took a quick look at her companion. He was in his mid- to late-forties, dark hair threaded with steel grey, well built and the sort of face that was probably more attractive now than it had been in his youth. 'I was just...' Martine began. 'We were just...'

'None of my business,' Hannah said curtly, recalling the last time they had spoken, when Martine had practically accused Hannah of being the sole reason for the failure of her marriage. But if this was what it looked like, it hadn't taken her very long to move on from Mitchell. She wondered if he knew. Without waiting for a reply, she marched out of the shop and hurried back to her car, her head spinning with questions. The biggest one of all was: did this mean it was okay for her and Mitchell to see each other now?

*

When Hannah arrived back, she could barely remember driving home at all. She'd been on autopilot while her brain dealt with the conundrums that seeing Martine and her companion had presented.

Of all the people she could have seen in that chip shop, it had to be Martine. Hannah would previously have put money on Martine being struck down with anaphylactic shock from even the thought of a chippy, but there she was – at exactly the same time as Hannah, who didn't really go there all that often herself. It was hard to shake the notion that some higher power was having a sick joke at Hannah's expense, especially when coincidences like this kept happening.

Who was the mystery man? A colleague? A friendly shoulder to cry on? The secret that Hannah was sure Martine had been hiding all along… the man who might hold the key to discovering why Mitchell had walked out of their home on Christmas Day with nothing but the clothes on his back? Hannah tried to tell herself that this explanation was wishful thinking on her part; she needed it to be true in order to quell the feelings of guilt she still had about her new relationship with Mitchell. When all was said and done, she knew she had probably influenced his decision to leave Martine, however innocently; if she wasn't the coin, she was at least the extra shove that had sent the penny into the falls.

As if fate hadn't had enough of screwing with her, Mitchell's car was parked in front of her gate when she arrived home. *What now?* Before she went in, however, she gave it a thorough appraisal. Was this the car she had seen earlier; the one that had driven off? Now that she looked closer, she didn't think it was. The idea put her mind at rest, although she wasn't quite sure enough to feel completely convinced. There was nothing else for it; she'd come straight out and ask him again tonight.

With the sharp tang of vinegar making her mouth water, Hannah juggled with the bag of food on her arm as she tried to find her house keys. With a groan, she realised that she had left them in the house, and hammered at the door instead.

Jess opened it a few moments later, dangling the wayward keys in front of Hannah's face.

'Did you forget something?'

'I was in a hurry to get out,' Hannah replied, without reiterating that it was Jess and Gina's argument that had sent her scuttling out in such a rush in the first place.

'You've got a visitor,' Jess added as Hannah followed her in.

'I noticed,' Hannah said. She wandered through to the living room to find Mitchell and Gina chatting. Mitchell looked rather less comfortable than Gina and it was possible that he was feeling slightly awkward about what Hannah might have told her sister regarding their relationship. At Hannah's arrival, however, his features instantly relaxed into a warm, sexy smile. 'Hey…'

Hannah's heart gave a jolt, although she was more than a little mortified at the realisation that she was about to stuff her face full of chips. If only she could have been planning to eat something a bit more erotic, like asparagus or okra, or whatever phallic vegetable they sucked in steamy films. Not that it would have been likely, even if she had she been warned of his arrival; she never ate any of those things, but perhaps she could have dusted off a tin of hot dog sausages.

'That smells good,' he said, nodding at the bag.

'They smell amazing,' Gina agreed. She jumped up from her spot on the sofa and grabbed the bag from Hannah. 'Sit down and I'll put them on plates.' She turned to Mitchell. 'Can we tempt you with some?'

Mitchell glanced at Hannah, who gave an encouraging smile. 'They do smell pretty good, if you're sure you have some to spare.'

'No problem. Jess needs to cut down on her carbohydrate intake anyway so you can have some of hers.'

'Oi!' Jess cried, and Gina left the room laughing, the glorious smell fading as she went. Jess stomped off after her.

'When did you get here?' Hannah took a seat next to him. God, that was a mistake. It was hard not to think of him naked right now – the scent of him and the taste of his skin in her mouth. She was doing a phenomenal job of maintaining her self-control.

'Only a few minutes before you.'

'Oh. So you didn't come round earlier… perhaps park outside thinking we weren't in or something?'

'No… why do you ask?'

'It was just… well, that car was outside again earlier, but when I went over to see what they wanted, it drove off. I was hoping I wouldn't have to deal with the possibility that it was some unknown weirdo.'

'Rather than a known weirdo, you mean?'

Hannah blushed. 'I didn't mean that!'

He flashed another smile hot enough to increase global sea levels by at least three feet. 'I know you didn't. But I'm sorry to tell you that it wasn't me. It is worrying me quite a lot now, though.'

'It's probably nothing.'

'I want you to tell me if he turns up again and I'll come right over.'

'That might be difficult. Don't you have work and stuff?'

'Not right now – Graham is still looking after things while I get well.'

'Your right hand man?'

'He prefers associate director.' Mitchell smiled. 'Or evil henchman number one.'

'I like evil henchman number one. Does that make you Blofeld?'

'I doubt I'm that clever. More like Doctor Evil.'

Hannah giggled. 'It's funny…'

'What, me as Doctor Evil?'

'No, the fact that I've just come from Chapeldown and when I get home, here you are on Holly Way.'

Should she mention Martine and the mystery man? Was it a slippery can of worms that she should leave well alone?

'I don't live in Chapeldown anymore,' he said.

'You used to.'

'I suppose technically I still do,' he conceded. 'The hotel off the motorway, as nice as it is, isn't really a proper address.'

'I'm pretty sure you can't register to vote from there,' Hannah agreed. 'Have you decided what you're going to do about your living arrangements yet? I don't imagine it would be hard for you to find a property in your line of work.'

He stared into the fire. 'Not really. I suppose it all becomes very final once I start looking for a place to live and perhaps I've been avoiding that.'

'But it is final, isn't it?' If it wasn't, then what had she got herself into? What did his being there now mean? He turned to her and smiled.

'Of course it is. That didn't come out the way it was in my brain. I mean that I've been putting off the inevitable because it's too painful to think about it, but I'm ready now… at least I hope I am. I know that I have to start building a new life. And I've been getting flashbacks too. I can't piece them together properly yet, but what I have is making me convinced that leaving Martine was the right thing to do.'

'Flashbacks?' Hannah repeated. She stared at him. What could they be? If they implicated Martine in something, was there a link with what Hannah had seen tonight in Chapeldown? She had opened her mouth to ask when Gina and Jess reappeared with four plates of chips and a plateful of buttered bread.

'Is that for chip butties?' Mitchell asked with a smile.

'You know it,' Gina said.

'I haven't had a chip butty in years.'

'You haven't?' Jess asked.

'And you remember that you haven't!' Gina said with a grin. 'Are you remembering lots more stuff now?'

Mitchell shrugged. 'Sometimes things come back to me unexpectedly. It must have been seeing all the bread and butter that triggered that particular memory.'

'You're doing a pretty good job of remembering where this house is too,' Jess said in a voice loaded with sarcasm. As she sat down and pulled a plate onto her lap, she reached for a slice of bread, doubled it over and began to stuff chips into the fold.

'That's none of your business.' Gina gave Jess a warning look.

'Of course it isn't,' Jess replied through a mouthful of food. 'Shall I go out of the room for a while so that the grownups can keep me in the dark about something else?'

Mitchell glanced between the two of them before throwing Hannah a questioning look.

'Mother-daughter domestics are such fun,' Hannah told him with a wry smile. 'That's one thing I don't miss by not having kids.'

'I wouldn't know either,' Mitchell said. 'Martine and I, we…' He stopped, his fork suspended in mid-air as he stared into space.

'Mitchell?' Hannah asked.

He turned to her but his eyes were vacant.

'Mitchell?' Hannah repeated.

His fork clattered onto the plate and he bolted for the door.

'What the hell…' Gina began, but Hannah dropped her fork too. Putting her plate to one side she leapt up after him.

In the garden, he was bent over Hannah's gate, gripping the wood as he pulled in great lungfuls of air.

'You're shivering,' Hannah said, a gentle hand on his arm. 'Come inside and tell me what's wrong.'

'I remember,' he said in a low voice, his gaze still on the ground. 'I remember it all.'

Hannah felt her heart thump inside her chest. She wanted to grab hold of the gate and hyperventilate too. She could feel her world falling away from her. He remembered… did that mean he would remember the life he was supposed to have – with Martine? Would he realise that Hannah was never meant to be part of the plan?

'What do you remember?' she asked.

'I... I don't know. It can't be right.'

Hannah was silent as she waited for more. The joints and tendons of his hands stood proud with the effort of gripping the gate harder still. She was mesmerised. Afterwards, that was the abiding image of the scene, weird as it was, and whenever she thought of that moment, she thought of Mitchell's hands displaying every emotion that was raging through his head. After a few moments, he took a deep breath and stood slowly to face her.

'It can't be right... she wouldn't do that to me...'

'What?' Hannah whispered.

Mitchell shook his head. 'No... she wouldn't... I have to talk to her...'

Hannah laid a hand on his arm, but she pulled it away at the reaction on his face. 'You should come inside,' she said less certainly, 'you need to calm down before you go anywhere. Please come and talk to me first.'

'I have to talk to Martine... I have to know that I'm mistaken...'

Hannah chewed her lip. In his current state, she'd bet that Martine could tell him anything and he'd believe it because he obviously needed to believe anything except what his new memory was telling him – whatever that was. Should she offer to go with him? No, that would only make things worse.

'Do you have to go now?' she asked.

He gave a brief nod, and then turned to go back into the house for his coat. Hannah followed miserably. No matter how much she tried to persuade herself that it was a minor hiccup in their relationship, she couldn't help feeling it was the death knell. Surely, now that he knew what the problem in his marriage was, they would work to fix it? Now he could remember everything, he would remember that he loved her.

But then Hannah had another thought: what about the man who was with Martine tonight? Would he have some bearing on it all? What if he was still there and Mitchell lost his temper? The way he was acting right now she thought that anything could happen. Should she warn him? But if it was all perfectly innocent then she'd be interfering in something that was none of her business.

Gina and Jess watched open-mouthed as he retrieved his coat and car keys from the arm of the sofa. It was clear that the expression on his face brooked no further discussion. He turned to Hannah.

'I'm sorry…' he said, and it was all she could do not to burst into tears. He was sorry. He was sorry because he knew that it was the end for them and because he should never have started it in the first place. That's why he was sorry, wasn't it?

She wanted to ask if there was anything she could do to help, what it was he had remembered and whether he would call – a million questions that clamoured inside her head. But she didn't ask any of these things, only stared after him as he headed for the door and out into the night.

*

Hannah checked her phone for the fourth time that hour. Gina plonked a cup of tea in front of her.

'Jess has gone to bed, though I don't doubt she'll have some complaint about wearing your pyjamas and having to get up at the crack of dawn for the train.'

Hannah forced a smile. 'She wasn't exactly in the best of moods to begin with and I've made it worse… sorry about that.'

Gina waved away the apology. 'There was no way I was going home and leaving you alone tonight.'

'I'd have been alright. It's not like we'd been together a long time or anything, was it?'

Gina cocked an eyebrow and Hannah couldn't help but laugh. 'We Meadows girls always did give our hearts too easily,' she said with a wry smile.

'We can blame our parents for that. We had to get love from somewhere and it certainly wasn't coming from either of them.'

'It's a miracle we've turned out so well-rounded.'

It was Hannah's turn to cock a disbelieving brow. 'Look at the state of us right now!'

'I can't argue with that,' Gina laughed. She paused. 'Ross messaged me earlier. I told him I was still on Holly Way with you.'

'Do you want to see him?' Hannah smiled. 'I'll be alright if you do.'

Gina shook her head. 'It's late. He's probably in bed now ready for his sheep shearing or whatever he does at stupid o'clock in the morning.'

'Text him,' Hannah insisted. 'I'm sure he'd put his bedtime off for an hour with you.'

'Maybe…' Gina replied. 'Are you sure you're okay?'

'I just wish I knew what was happening. I hope things haven't turned ugly.'

'Or that he's in bed with her right now?' Gina asked.

'I got the feeling bed was the last thing on his mind. What do you think it all means?'

'She was definitely having an affair,' Gina said sagely. It wasn't the first time she'd aired that opinion since Hannah had told her about the man Martine had been with in the chip shop. Hannah was inclined to agree, but she wanted to be more rational and less judgmental about it than that. Everyone deserved the benefit of the doubt, didn't they? Even Martine.

Hannah glanced at her phone yet again. 'Nothing,' she said. 'I don't suppose he will call.'

'Let him sort his head out. You never know. If he had strong feelings for you before he remembered, they came from somewhere, didn't they? He wouldn't just push those aside no matter what else came to light.'

'Neither would he push his marriage aside for a woman he hardly knows.'

'You don't know that. Give him time.'

From the corner of her eye, Hannah noticed Gina take another furtive look at her own phone. 'Go to Ross,' she said. 'One of us deserves some happiness and I'll take yours vicariously if I can't have my own.'

'You're not having the orgasms,' Gina grinned.

'Ugh! Too much information!'

'I'll message him and tell him I'm staying over tonight. He might not be up now, but if he is and he wants to come and fetch me he can, can't he? I know I just said I would stay with you –'

'Honestly,' Hannah said. 'I want you to go. There's no point in us both being miserable.'

'But…'

'Go!'

'It would only be for ten minutes.'

'I bloody hope not. If he only lasts for ten minutes at his age you've got no chance when he hits middle age.'

Gina grinned. 'You're sure you'll be okay?'

'Absolutely,' Hannah said. 'Jess will be fine with me.'

'She won't be asleep for hours, you know, even though she's in bed.'

'That's okay. She can entertain me with YouTube videos to take my mind off my misery.'

'I think it will probably be the opposite when she starts complaining about the fact I've gone off with Ross.'

'Does she need to know where you've gone?'

'Seriously? Where else am I going to be if I'm not here? Even Jess can work that out.'

'Okay, you might have a point there.'

Gina tapped out a message on her phone. Less than a minute later, it bleeped a return text. She gave a slow, broad smile.

'He says he'll be here as soon as he can.'

'He's keen,' Hannah said. 'I think it must be love.'

'Lust is probably more like it, but if it means I can have him I don't mind.'

'No…' Hannah sipped at her tea. 'Ross isn't like that. I think he's an all or nothing kind of guy.'

'That's what I thought about Howard.'

'Yeah, well… we were all fooled by him,' Hannah replied.

*

As promised, Ross's Land Rover was outside Hannah's gate less than ten minutes later. Gina had been waiting at the front door, ready for him. She turned to give Hannah a brief kiss on the cheek.

'Are you sure you'll be alright?' she asked.

'Yes!' Hannah said, forcing her reply to be as cheerful as possible. 'I have Jess to keep me company and I doubt I'll hear anything from Mitchell tonight. Go!'

Gina's expression was bright and full of expectation and Hannah couldn't help but absorb some of her excitement. Ross really was making her very happy and that made Hannah happy too. Jess had refused to come downstairs, and Hannah thought it was a pity; if she could see this look on Gina's face, perhaps she would find it hard to be so churlish about the relationship.

'Don't wait up!' Gina cried as she skipped down the path.

'I have to!' Hannah laughed. 'You don't have a key!'

She caught a snatch of Gina's answering giggle as the car door slammed shut. Ross leaned across and gave Hannah a brief wave before pulling out onto the lane.

But Hannah's broad smile faded. No sooner had Ross's car left, than headlights appeared across the lane. A car that had been hidden in the shadows now started its engine and pulled away in the same direction Gina had just taken. Hannah's heart almost stopped. She hadn't seen it – nobody had – but she was sure it was the same car she'd chased earlier. She craned for a look inside, but it was going too fast and there wasn't enough light for her to make out anything about the driver, other than that it was a dark-haired man. Mitchell had denied it being anything to do with him every time she had asked. But if it wasn't him, then who the hell was it?

*

The sofa wasn't exactly the comfiest bed. Hannah woke with a crick in her neck at the sound of a soft knock at the front door. Her phone lay on the floor next to her. She reached for it. One missed call from Gina. It looked as though she had tried to call ahead and warn her she was coming back and would need to be let in. That was at five-forty, twenty minutes ago.

She pushed herself from the sofa. It was amazing that she had been able to sleep at all, considering that added to her worries about Mitchell were new worries about Gina. Perhaps she had been seeing danger where there was none, her nerves already frayed and her senses on red-alert with everything else that had been going on, but she hadn't been able to stop thinking about the car in the shadows. Somehow, though, she'd drifted off, even though she had been trying to wait up for Gina's return. Looking at the time now it was a good job she hadn't managed to wait up – she'd have been exhausted and very crabby.

Gina, on the other hand, looked as fresh as the morning that came with her as Hannah opened the front door. Hannah was relieved to see her looking so well and carefree – obviously none of the disasters she had imagined befalling her had come to pass.

'Morning!' she exclaimed as Ross drove off. 'Time for a quick coffee and then I'd better get to the station. It's lucky I don't have my first meeting until midday today, isn't it?'

Hannah moved back to let her in before closing the door. 'So you had a good night?'

'That would be telling, wouldn't it? Is Jess okay? She didn't cause you too much aggro?'

'Actually, I went up to see if she wanted a hot chocolate and she was asleep, so I was pretty much left to my own devices,' Hannah said, recalling that she had felt so wretched and worried that she had almost woken Jess, just for the company to take her mind off things.

'No more word from Mitchell?' Gina asked, taking her coat off and draping it over the back of an armchair before plonking herself down.

'No,' Hannah replied. 'Everything was okay with you? Nothing weird happened… no strange incidents?'

'No.'

'Oh.'

Gina narrowed her eyes. 'That's a bit of an odd question. Should I have been involved in a strange incident?'

'No. It's nothing.'

'I know that look. That's not nothing. That's your something look. What's happened now?'

Hannah sighed. 'You'll probably say I'm paranoid, but you know how everyone keeps seeing a mystery car hanging around here?'

Gina gave a slow nod.

'Well,' Hannah continued, 'I think it was outside when you left with Ross. And I could have sworn it followed you.'

Gina shrugged. 'There might have been a car parked out there and it might have left when we did, but I never saw anyone follow us. I think you're probably over sensitive and worrying over nothing.'

'Yeah, you're probably right,' Hannah admitted. 'I'm so worked up over this Mitchell thing. I mean, who would be following us around? We're not that interesting.'

'Speak for yourself.' Gina let out a huge yawn, followed by a sheepish grin. 'Midday meeting… I just hope I can get through it without falling asleep.'

'You've only got yourself to blame. I hope he was worth it.'

'Boy… was he worth it! I don't know where he learned them, but the things that man can do with his hands…'

Hannah held up her own hands to halt Gina's flow. 'Enough… We share everything, but please not that.'

Gina pushed herself up from the chair. 'I'd better get some coffee and a slice of toast. I'm ravenous. Are you able to run us to the station early?'

'I've got nothing better to do,' Hannah said, following Gina through to the kitchen. 'So where did you go last night?'

'Ross sneaked me into his place. It was late anyway – too late for farming folk – and his parents were asleep in the main house so it wasn't that difficult. It was a lot more difficult to get away this morning, though. It's quite exciting; I feel like a teenager again.' Gina shook the kettle at Hannah. 'Want one?'

'I might as well.' Hannah pulled a loaf of bread from a crock and dropped a couple of slices into a candy pink toaster.

'So, what are you going to do about Mitchell?'

Hannah turned to her. 'Nothing.'

'You could call him. I'd say he's had enough space now.'

'Perhaps tonight,' Hannah agreed. 'But right now I'm more concerned about this guy who keeps parking outside the house. I'm going to take his registration down if I see it again.'

'Good idea. That way, when you've been murdered in your bed at least we'll have the reg of the man who did it.'

'Charming,' Hannah replied. 'Don't forget it was you he drove off after.'

'But he's always outside your house.'

'Actually…' Hannah was thoughtful for a moment. 'I can't honestly say that I've seen him outside at any other time except when you're here.'

'George did, though.'

'Oh yeah…' Hannah replied slowly, trying to place when it was George had seen the car. Then she remembered that it was while she'd been out on her date with Chris. Bloody hell… another problem she still had to sort. She'd almost forgotten Chris in all the drama.

'If it bothers you that much, why don't you set up a camera in your front window? Leave it running to see who comes and goes when you're not looking.'

The toast popped up and Hannah dropped it onto a plate to butter. 'That's not a bad idea. I don't have a video camera, though.'

'I'll ask Ross if he can get hold of one and pop it round for you. I'm sure he'd be happy to help, especially if I tell him you're worried. In fact, he'll probably want to stake your place out himself to catch them…'

'God, no! I can't have him doing that; he has enough to do already. It's probably nothing, but a video camera would be good. At least I'll have something to show the police if I need to.'

'Absolutely. So I'll text him later.'

'I can do it. I've been promising to see his mum for ages anyway, so today is as good a day as any. It'll take my mind off things.'

Gina gave a wry smile. 'I can't help thinking it should be me sitting with Briony and making the effort to get to know her.'

'Might be a bit awkward round about now, though.'

'Han... what if she hates me when she finds out? What if everyone thinks I'm some scheming cougar?'

'You like him, and I can tell he adores you. In the end, isn't that all that matters?'

'You've changed your tune. Before, you were telling me it was the most disastrous pairing since Romeo wolf-whistled Juliet.'

'That was before I saw how happy you both seem. If it helps, I'll do my best to talk you up to Briony, so that when she finally finds out she'll already like you. And Paul... well, I think he's a big pussycat. I reckon he'll be fine with it.'

'That would be good.'

'In fact...' Hannah said, the cogs beginning to creak in her sleep-deprived brain, 'I know that she's looking for recruits for next year's WI calendar. If you helped out she'd love you forever.'

'Me? On a calendar?'

'Why not? She asked me, but you're a lot more photogenic than I am. It'd be a great way to get into her good books and it would be fun too. Besides that, it would also be a good way to meet people here, especially if you're moving back to the area.'

The kettle clicked off, and Gina was thoughtful as she filled two mugs with hot water. 'Maybe. It depends on what they wanted me to do.'

'Oh, it's just posing with country props, I think. Hoes and sheaves of wheat and that sort of thing.'

'With clothes on?'

Hannah laughed. 'That's just what I said when she asked me.'

'Right… but if I do it you have to do it with me.'

'Gina –'

'No arguments. Both or none at all.'

'Well then, we might as well rope Jess in too.'

Gina handed Hannah a steaming mug. 'Yeah? Good luck with that – you're braver than I am.'

*

Hannah considered going back to bed for an hour once she had seen Gina and Jess off, but by the time she had arrived back home, she was well and truly awake – if a little groggy. There was too much going on in her head to sleep anyway. Gina's idea of getting a video camera had been a good one, and Ross had texted back almost immediately to say that they had one at the farm. He apologised that it was a little on the old side, probably a bit clunky, but they were welcome to borrow it for as long as they needed.

In the absence of sleep and the ability to concentrate on the ever-growing pile of work on her desk, Hannah decided to call in at Holly Farm instead. She could pick up the camera, keep that date she had been promising Briony for tea and cake, and do some gentle introductory work on the brilliance of her sister all at the same time – all in all a productive morning, and one that would put Mitchell and his baggage firmly out of her mind. She had to admit to being vexed that he hadn't at least sent her a text to let her know he was okay, but perhaps it was unreasonable to have any expectations of him.

Ross was clearing the guttering along the extension roof when Hannah's little Citroen pulled up in their vast driveway. He scampered down the ladders with surprising agility for a man who had been up all night, but Hannah couldn't help a knowing smile when he crossed the gravel to her car and she saw the dark circles beneath his eyes.

'Come for the camera?' he asked as Hannah clambered out of her car.

'I thought I'd pop in to see your mum too,' Hannah said. 'A promise is a promise.'

'Good thing too – keep her out of the way.'

'So you can have a crafty snooze?' Hannah grinned.

Ross shot back a soppy grin of his own. 'Not likely. I've got this guttering to clear out and then straight down to the big field. Lambing's come early this year and I've got to get to them before the cold does. Bloody nuisance.'

'How's it come early? Don't you control when they lamb?'

'Aye, as long as the randy old daddy doesn't get out of his pen and ravish the flock.'

Hannah giggled. 'You'll have to be more careful next time.'

'Too late for that now.' He pulled off his cap and mussed his hair before clamping it back onto his head. 'Mum's in the kitchen. Just go on and knock; she knows you're coming.'

Hannah nodded and began to make her way to the house, but Ross called her back.

'Is everything alright?' Hannah turned to him. 'It's just that… well… are you worried? About this car, I mean? That's why you want the camera, isn't it?'

'I'm not worried exactly; just concerned. If anything does happen – you know, damage to my house or something – I'd feel better if I had some evidence to take to the police. You see it all the time, don't you, on crime programmes? People have cameras set up in their windows and they catch the criminal easily.'

'So, I don't need to come to your place and keep an eye on things?'

'That's very sweet of you, but I think it will be alright. I have an alarm in the house and good locks on the doors and all he seems to be doing is sitting in his car at the moment. Perhaps there's an innocent explanation. That's what the camera will show us, I suppose.'

'Tell me if you change your mind.'

'I will.' Hannah smiled. 'Thank you.'

She made her way up to the house and knocked on the door, leaving Ross to get back to his guttering. Briony opened up with a broad smile.

'Come in, come in…' She stepped back and Hannah followed her into the kitchen. There was a wonderful cosiness in here – not the dry heat of radiators and gas fires, but the cocooning warmth of bricks constantly heated by the Aga. There was a sharp tang of stewed fruit, and Hannah glanced across to see a large pan on the boil.

'It smells wonderful in here,' Hannah said.

'I'm doing Paul's apple crumble,' Briony said. 'He gets crotchety if he doesn't have it at least once a month.'

'If it tastes as good as it smells I can see why.'

Briony waved away the compliment, though she was beaming. 'Sit down; let me get the kettle on.'

As Hannah did as she was bid, her phone bleeped in her coat pocket. She pulled it out, biting back the groan in her throat. Mitchell wanted to see her. He picked his bloody moments, and now she would be stuck with Briony for at least a couple of hours. Not that it should matter anyway – it wasn't her style to be at his beck and call – on the other hand, she was desperate to hear what news he had to tell her. She sent a reply, as short and discreet as she could, while Briony fussed at the stove, telling him that it would have to be later because she was tied up. She didn't tell him what with, and she half expected him to ask, but he simply said okay, and left it at that.

'Now then,' Briony began as she returned to the table with a plate of homemade cookies, 'are you going to tell me what happened to you at the salsa evening?'

Hannah had almost forgotten about that. She was going to have to tell Briony something, and it would have to be good to satisfy her razor-sharp curiosity. Not for the first time she was going to have to get creative with the truth.

*

On another day, Hannah would have arrived home pleasantly full of Briony's homemade cookies and Victoria sponge and content to have a quick nap. But today she was tense, despite enjoying her morning chat, and trying not think about what might be waiting for her when she met up with Mitchell.

When she saw the car outside, for a moment she was thrown, and felt her stomach drop away until she realised that it was Mitchell parked in front of her gate, and not the mysterious car that had been hogging the shadows every time she stepped out of her door lately. As she parked, he got out and ran towards her. Before she'd had time to speak, he'd taken her in his arms and was kissing her hard. It took her breath away – the need, the urgency, the fire in it. But whilst she felt his desire, this was a kiss of desperation, of a man who needed to be anchored. As their lips parted, he laid his forehead against hers and held her gaze as if he was trying to see into her soul. He pulled her closer, his embrace almost crushing.

'God,' he whispered, 'I can't tell you how good it is to see you.'

'You too,' Hannah replied, happy but taken aback by the force of his passion. 'You want to come in and talk properly?'

'That would be good.' He buried his face in her hair and pulled her closer still. 'I'm sorry... I must be such a burden to you.'

'Don't be silly.' Hannah pulled away to look up at him and smiled. 'I understand things must be hard for you.'

'I don't deserve you, Hannah. If only you'd come into my life years ago.'

'Then we'd have been two very different people. I do believe experience shapes you, year on year, it changes you. Maybe we just weren't ready to meet before now. If we had we might not have liked each other all that much.'

'I can't imagine that for a minute,' Mitchell smiled. 'How could anyone not like you?'

'Flattery will get you everywhere, you clearly know me better than I gave you credit for. So, how about we get in out of this cold?'

'Of course.' Mitchell took her hand and began to make his way up the path, but Hannah stopped him.

'Hang on, there's something I need to get out of the car. She dashed back to collect the camera from the passenger seat.

'What's that?' he asked.

'I've borrowed a video camera from Holly Farm. I'm going to set it up in the front window.'

He was silent for a moment. 'Are you sure you're not more frightened by all this than you're letting on? You seem to be taking it very seriously.'

'I'm not frightened, I'm just taking precautions; there's a difference.'

'Do you need some help setting it up?' he asked, sensing that Hannah was not going to admit to being scared even if she was. 'I could fit a bracket to the wall if you need me to.'

'No brackets, thank you. I'm hoping it won't be running for long and I don't want dirty great holes in my walls for the sake of some arsehole hanging around like bad aftershave.'

'I can fix the holes afterwards; you'd never even know they'd been there.'

'I'm sure you could but I'll just sit it on the sill and it should be fine.'

'Won't it be visible if you do that?'

'Perhaps, but it might work as a deterrent and get him to bugger off if he can see it, so, either way I'm happy. It's the buggering off bit that matters.' She handed him the case. 'Come on, you can help me set it up if it makes you feel better and you can tell me about last night while we sort it.'

'I wish I didn't have to,' he said as he followed her into the house. 'I wish we could be six months from now and all this pain would be gone.'

Hannah saw the hurt in his eyes. She wished the same for him too, but there was nothing she could do to make it better for him except be there. 'Do you want to tell me about it?'

He gave her a pained smile. 'I would if I knew where to start.'

Hannah shrugged off her coat and hung it across the back of a chair. She unzipped Ross's case and pulled out a bulky video camera. It was a bit on the old side, as Ross had warned her it would be, but it was well maintained. She handed it to Mitchell as she rifled in the case for the charger lead. 'How about you tell me what you remembered yesterday?' she said. 'Or at least the things that got you so upset. The other stuff, we have all the time in the world to talk about – at least, I hope we have.'

He gave a tense smile. 'I hope so too.' Despite his positive words, it looked as though he was finding it hard to keep things together right now. 'Martine and I…' He paused. 'Bloody hell, this is hard. Well, Martine and I weren't exactly love's young dream, I know that. But I thought she was content; I know I was. I thought that was enough. We had a good life, enough money to live well and enjoy ourselves. But things had got difficult between us over the past couple of years – petty bickering, frayed tempers over nothing – the sorts of things that don't come out as full-blown rows but creep in and fester and eat your love from the inside out. Eventually, we both recognised that something had to change. So we talked it through, and decided that we should try for a baby – at least, I thought we had both decided that.'

'A baby?' Hannah cut in. She had been listening carefully, trying to understand his past, and she thought she had until that point. She tried to damp down the incredulous tone in her voice but she was finding it hard. So much for not judging him and showing unconditional support. But this was so difficult to understand, especially in the light of her own childhood. She and Gina had been blessed with parents who took very little interest in their children and after a final and monumental family argument, they were both estranged from those parents now. Hannah could never wish a childhood like that on anyone else. She knew that it played a big part in the fact that she didn't have children herself; for her, having a baby was the most sacred act a woman could perform, and she would have to give her all to the life she was bringing into the world. Hannah's relationships, up until now, hadn't shown the sort of stability that made her confident she could give that to a baby. 'Your marriage was on the rocks so you decided a baby was a good idea?'

'In hindsight I see it wasn't the best,' he replied, looking suitably shamefaced, and Hannah could tell that he meant it. 'But I did really want a child – not just to fix the marriage. And I thought Martine did too. Over the years we'd discussed it – right from the start of our marriage, in fact – but she'd always been reluctant because she wanted to concentrate on her career. Well, now she has the practice she's always wanted and I thought, as she has partners in it too, she was happy to turn her thoughts to starting a family. Turns out I was wrong.'

'What happened?'

He shook his head slowly. 'We carried on, trying to get pregnant, or so I thought. I couldn't understand why it was taking so long but she kept telling me to be patient and that it would take a while for the contraceptive pill to leave her system. I did everything I could from my end to help – gave up drinking, ate the right foods, took supplements – but nothing worked. I began to notice that Martine had changed nothing about her lifestyle except for working longer hours than ever before. I started to wonder if she even wanted the baby at all.'

'She would have been entitled to that choice,' Hannah replied, aware that it sounded as though she was siding with Martine against Mitchell. She wasn't condoning what Martine might have done; she just felt strongly that every woman should have choices.

'Of course she would,' he said. 'I'm not some Victorian misogynist. But a bit of honesty might have been kinder than stringing me along. Just because I don't carry the baby, doesn't mean I don't get a say, does it?'

Hannah shook her head. 'So that's what you argued about on Christmas Day?'

He handed the camera back. 'That's only part of it. It's bad enough, but the other part... that's the bit I don't want to believe.'

Hannah placed the camera on the floor near to a socket and plugged it in to charge. 'You don't have to tell me if you don't want to.'

'It's not you. I don't want to tell this bit to anyone because I don't want to say it; I don't want it to be true.'

Hannah's mind went back to the previous night when she had seen Martine out with her mystery man. The words: *we were on a break* settled in her brain, and she had a feeling that she knew what was coming next. After all, she'd been there with Jason and she knew the signs well enough.

'I found a condom,' he said. 'A few weeks before Christmas. It must have fallen out of a pocket or something because it was in the bottom of our wardrobe.' Hannah gave him a questioning look. 'We never used them,' he explained, 'and Martine had stopped taking the pill to get pregnant. Not that there was much activity in that department at the end. Suddenly it all made sense: the longer hours at work, the bad moods, the reluctance to come near me or talk about the baby. I took the condom downstairs; I was fuming.'

'Maybe it had something to do with her work? Birth control education or something? Perhaps she'd had a teenager in the surgery and had been showing them one and it somehow got into her pocket and came home with her?'

'You know, once the dust had settled, that's exactly what she said and, gullible twat that I am, I believed her.' Mitchell grimaced. 'Such an obviously lame excuse and I swallowed it.'

'So you let it lie?'

'Yes. I wanted things to go back to what we once had. I wanted us to have a baby and be happy.'

'So what happened on Christmas Day?'

He paused, turned his gaze upwards as if steeling himself. 'Christmas Day. Where do I even begin? I suppose I'd been rooting around ever since the condom, trying to find something that would tell me I was right to be suspicious, but even more than that I wanted to prove to myself I was wrong. I shouldn't have looked, but her coat was just there on the bed and she was downstairs doing something else. It was weird, because she is always so careful to hang up her clothes. It was almost as though she was daring me to look. God, I wish I hadn't. Stuffed in the pocket was a letter…' Tears sprang to his eyes, and he sniffed hard.

'Jesus, Mitchell, what did you find?' Hannah asked, desperate to pull him into her arms and comfort him, but knowing that she needed to let him finish first, no matter how hard it was.

'A letter from a private clinic confirming an appointment…' He turned his gaze to her and his eyes were so empty, his expression was so hollow that it made her go cold. 'She'd been pregnant. The thing that we'd been desperate for. And she paid to get rid of it.'

Hannah's mouth fell open. 'Martine had an abortion?' she squeaked. 'You're kidding?'

He shook his head. 'Christ, I wish I was. It floored me. I couldn't get my head around it. I confronted her. I wanted her to tell me I was wrong, but she refused to give me anything. She can be so infuriating and so bloody self-righteous and I know that when she's like that it's because she's been caught out. I'll admit I lost it. I came this close to hitting her and…' His words faltered and Hannah could see that he was fighting to keep his emotions under control, even now, at the memory of it.

'It's okay,' she said gently, reaching for him, 'you didn't… did you? You know you can tell me anything.'

'I wanted to slap her; I've never felt that way before, no matter how infuriating she's been. I was afraid I'd lose control – I could feel reason slipping away from me. She could see it too, and she was goading me, like she wanted the confrontation; she was almost enjoying it. How could she do something that massive without telling me? I could have believed that there was a good reason, that maybe there was a problem with the baby or something, but the way she reacted to me when I confronted her told me everything I needed to know.'

'Which was what?'

'That she was having an affair. Either the baby was his or she didn't want it because it was mine and she couldn't have that tie to me. Either way, she'd been cruel in a way that even I had never thought she was capable of, and I know she can be a heartless bitch when the mood takes her. I had to get out before I did something I'd regret for the rest of my life. God, Hannah, I swear I could have killed her at that moment.'

'That's when you left?'

'I just walked out. I had to, I was too dangerous in that mood. I couldn't get my head straight and I didn't really notice the snow at all. It was like the outside world had been sucked away and I was left in this vacuum of hurt and anger and all I could think about was how Martine had betrayed me. I kept on walking, trying to calm down before I went back so that I wouldn't hurt her. I was so scared to go back in the state I was in, in case I couldn't help myself.'

'Didn't she come out after you?'

He shook his head. 'She'd never do that because that would mean her accepting some responsibility for what happened.'

'Do you remember how you injured your head?'

'I think I must have stumbled. I really wasn't equipped to be tramping about in the snow and before I knew it I was head-butting someone's gatepost. I must have blacked out… I don't know how long for. It was on the road between here and Chapeldown, and you know how deserted that stretch can be, especially on Christmas Day when everyone is inside celebrating – it's no wonder I wasn't found. When I came to

I was shivering and I felt dreadful. I couldn't understand what I was doing out there but I knew I had to get help. I tried the house of the people whose gatepost had done the damage, but there was no reply –'

'Where was the house?'

'I'm not sure… maybe the next one up the lane…'

'It could have been my neighbours; they were in Greece.'

'Lucky for me really…' His features softened. 'Because if they'd been at home, I wouldn't have found you.'

Hannah wondered what might have happened if Mitchell had never landed on her doorstep. How different would her life be now? It was strange how life turned on the tiniest twists of fate. She frowned. 'Last night… what happened with Martine? You were gone all night and I didn't hear anything from you; I was worried sick.'

'I'm sorry about that; it wasn't my intention to worry you. When I got home, Martine was there having tea with Graham. They said he'd come round so that she could ask him to talk to me, make me see there'd been a huge misunderstanding and that she wanted me back. When I told her I could remember everything that had happened on Christmas Day, I must have been in a state. Graham scarpered pretty quickly, just left his tea and went. I can't say I blame him. I needed time to get to grips with things and I needed Martine to give me answers. It was so late by the time we'd finished and you had your sister here so I didn't like to disturb you.'

'And did you get your answers?'

'We went round and round in circles as usual.'

'You left it then?'

'I didn't have a choice, did I? So I'm still none the wiser – at least not from the horse's mouth, anyway.'

Hannah was silent for a moment. 'Graham?' She asked finally. 'That's your business partner, isn't it?'

'Not yet. We've been talking about it, but at the moment he just manages the business for me. I think, with my brain as it is at the moment, and him doing such a good job of running things, I might as well let him have the whole damn thing.'

'Don't say that! You've worked hard to build that company up!'

'I know, but it doesn't seem important right now. I just want to get better...' He tapped his head, 'in here, you know?'

Hannah nodded, but she was still troubled by what she had seen of Martine. 'Were they eating chips when you arrived?'

Mitchell stared at her. 'Yes,' he said.

'I saw them together in the chip shop when I went to get ours. I saw Martine with a man, anyway.'

'It must have been Graham. He's a good bloke; I don't know what I'd do without him.'

Hannah recalled the scene from the previous evening. They might have been two friends seeking solace, but their body language said otherwise to Hannah. She was beginning to wonder if Graham was hiding secrets of his own. 'So you don't know who the other man is?' she asked.

Mitchell was thoughtful for a moment. 'It could be anyone, quite honestly. She's involved in a ton of committees and health groups and she's got plenty of opportunities for nights away. I might never know if she refuses to come clean. Anyway, she told me it's over and she wants me back.'

'So she's admitted the affair?'

'She didn't exactly admit it but she said I didn't have any more to worry about on that score and she wanted to make our marriage work.'

Hannah stared at him. 'Is she mental? What about the baby?'

'It's unforgivable, isn't it? How could I want her back after that?'

Hannah could understand his anger but she found it hard to be convinced. He was angry and hurt, but Martine was still his wife and she couldn't help feeling threatened by that bond, even though she knew it was an irrational fear. 'What do you want?' she asked. Her heart was thumping in her chest as she waited for his answer. If they wanted to save their marriage, did she have any right to interfere? But she was still troubled by Graham too. If there was something going on between him and Martine, now that Mitchell had left, why didn't they just come clean? What did they have to gain by keeping it secret now? And why was Martine still trying to get Mitchell back when she had treated him so appallingly? What could she possibly gain by it?

He held her gaze and her worries melted away in an instant. 'I want you.'

'But –'

'I knew you'd have a but,' he smiled, 'because you always do the right thing. You think we ought to put our feelings aside because a marriage is owed some loyalty, and you'd be right. There is nothing more sacred than marriage, and I would have been with Martine to the end, come hell or high water, no matter how strained things had got. But I don't love her anymore after what she did. And in all honesty, the love had died even before Christmas Day – so that's got to be real, hasn't it?'

Hannah blew out a long breath. 'It's a bit of a mess, isn't it?'

'You could say that. Do you still want me in your life now that you know everything? I'd understand if you decided it's too much and too complicated.'

'Of course I do!' Hannah threw herself into his arms. 'Of course I bloody do! I was worried that you were thinking the same!'

He kissed the top of her head. 'The only time I feel at peace is when I'm with you. Why would I want to give that up?'

She craned to look up at him. 'The heating hasn't clicked on yet, and I'm cold.'

He raised an eyebrow and she saw his mood turn like the tide on the seashore.

'So…' she continued, 'you'll just have to take me upstairs and warm me up, won't you?'

*

Hannah watched Chris's name flash up on the screen. *Shit*. Mitchell slept soundly beside her, despite the angry buzzing of her phone. Then again, after the activity of their previous night together, it was a miracle she'd woken either. She glanced across at the clock to see it had just gone ten. *Shit*. She hadn't wanted to sleep that late, not on a weekday. Should she wake Mitchell? Surely he had work he needed to do, no matter what he'd said about his business last night? Or was the blessed Saint Graham doing everything at the company now, making himself indispensable so that he'd be safe when he and Martine dropped their second bombshell?

She let Chris's call ring off. She would have to speak to him, but she wasn't ready and armed with enough white lies just now. She hated deceiving him like this – he was a decent bloke who deserved better but Gina wanted that house and what was Hannah supposed to do? She ran a hand through her hair as she rolled onto her back to stare at the ceiling. A slice of light from a gap in the curtains cut across it and blazed a trail down the wall. *Shit*. What a bloody mess everything was. Gina had warned her not to step in front of the train if she wanted to avoid getting caught in the wreck, and it looked like she'd been right. Why did Hannah never listen to her? She glanced across at Mitchell and couldn't help a slow smile. Some things were worth the risk, weren't they? If this was a train wreck then maybe it wasn't so bad.

She wriggled over to him and nestled under his outstretched arm, running a gentle hand down his bare chest towards the darkness of his groin. He stirred slightly, and hadn't even opened his eyes before he reacted, springing to attention beneath the sheets. Hannah let out a giggle. He slowly curled his arm around her and pulled her onto him. He opened one eye with a lazy grin.

'What are you trying to do to me?' he asked in a husky voice.

'I'm not doing anything. You're doing a pretty good job all by yourself.'

'That's because you're near me. I'm incapable of hiding any feelings when you're around.'

'I've heard of wearing your heart on your sleeve, but in your trousers?' Hannah laughed as she bent to kiss him. It didn't look like she was getting out of bed just yet.

*

Hannah rubbed her eyes and looked at the clock. Twelve-fifteen. She hadn't meant to fall asleep again. In fact, she hadn't meant to have sex again either, but with Mitchell naked beside her it was pretty hard not to.

The clatter of pans reached her from the kitchen downstairs, and she rolled over to see that the other side of the bed was empty. It was then that she also noticed the incredible smell seeping into the room.

Pulling her kimono around her, she padded downstairs to investigate.

Mitchell was in his boxers and Hannah's frilly apron and little else. He was standing at the stove frying a pan of bacon and whistling softly to himself. Hannah cleared her throat and he turned to face her with a broad smile.

'I didn't think you'd want to sleep all day so I thought I'd wake you with a nice treat,' he said.

'You already did that,' Hannah said, raising her eyebrows.

'Something a bit more edible and nutritious,' he laughed. 'Sit down, gorgeous, let me look after you for a change.'

Hannah pulled a seat from under the table and settled onto it. The floor was chilly under her bare feet so she tucked her legs up to rest them on the frame of the chair. Mitchell placed a coffeepot on the table with two mugs and the milk. 'You don't have sugar, do you?'

'No,' Hannah said, impressed that he had remembered. Jason had continued to ask for most of their relationship, and that was when he could be bothered to make coffee for her, which wasn't very often.

Flicking the stove off, Mitchell transferred the bacon onto waiting slices of bread arranged on the work surface. Hannah watched as he added this and that and finally turned with a flourish holding two plates aloft.

'*Voilà*! Bacon butties *à la* Bond.'

'Bacon butties?' Hannah giggled. 'Aren't they a bit working class for you?'

'I'm wounded by that comment,' he said, pretending (though not doing a very good job) to be hurt. 'I'll have you know I was raised on the roughest estate in Millrise. I might have a few bob in the bank now but I've never forgotten my roots.'

Hannah became thoughtful as he brought their plates to the table. It was the first time he'd mentioned money, and she couldn't help but wonder how much he had. Was his company worth a lot? He and Martine obviously had a lot of money together but Hannah had no idea whose income had contributed most to their joint pot. She now wondered whether Mitchell's company had some bearing on Martine's fight to keep him, despite her behaviour now coming to light. And recalling all this only brought her own fears for her relationship with

Mitchell back to the fore. Was any of this real? Were they strong enough together to weather this? Or would Martine eventually succeed in breaking him and bringing him back to the marital home? She certainly seemed determined, despite what he had remembered. If only Hannah could see all the pieces of the puzzle, she might be able to fit them together and find some answers.

'Are you okay?' Mitchell asked, peering at her.

Hannah shook herself. 'Of course.' She smiled. 'This breakfast looks lovely. I can't remember the last time a man cooked for me. Unless you count the guy who flips the burgers in McDonald's.' She bit into her sandwich, realising she was ravenous. 'Wow! This is incredible! How do you get the bacon to taste like this?'

He shrugged. 'I like cooking and I seem to be good at it. At least, they tell me so.'

'You must be, because it never tastes like this when I do it.'

'Perhaps you can taste the love in it too.'

Hannah felt the blush rise to her cheeks. Was that a declaration? Was that it – were they in love?

'I thought maybe we could take a walk later,' he said. 'You can show me around.'

'Show you around the fields and dirt track that passes for a road in these parts? That won't take long and I can't imagine it would be very inspiring.'

'I like fields.'

'Well that's good because there are a lot of them. But…' Hannah's mind went back to a pile of work on her desk in the office upstairs. It would be glorious to spend every second of every day with Mitchell, but if that meant running her business into the ground…? People said you could live on love but Hannah doubted you could pay your gas bill with it.

'Oh…' Mitchell said, reading her immediately. 'Of course; you must have loads to do. I forget.'

'Don't you have to go to the office at some point too – see what's going on?'

'Graham told me to take a week off and get straight. He'll take care of things while I'm missing.'

I bet he will, Hannah thought. She was beginning to develop a deep distrust of Graham the more she heard about him. She wondered if it ought to be Mitchell being paranoid and not her, but he didn't seem concerned at all. There was something not quite right here, and Graham was getting far too much control of Mitchell's company as far as Hannah could tell. Should she voice her concerns? Would Mitchell think it was none of her business? Would he think she was being silly? After all, what did she know about his company and how it was run?

Mitchell took a bite of his sandwich. He chewed slowly for a moment as he held Hannah in a thoughtful gaze. 'Have you checked your video camera this morning?'

Hannah blinked. 'To be honest, I'd forgotten all about setting it up last night. I blame you for that – you and your sex vibes leading me astray.'

'Guilty as charged. But please…' His expression became serious. 'Please set it up today. In fact, I'll do it myself before I go, then I'll know it's definitely done.'

'Are you saying I'm unreliable?'

'No, I'm not. But it would put my mind at rest if I could see for myself it was sorted. It's worrying me, knowing this weirdo is hanging around.'

'We don't yet know he's a weirdo. There could be a perfectly innocent explanation.'

'Hmmm…' Mitchell's noncommittal answer revealed that he didn't believe that for a minute, but he didn't want to argue with her. She couldn't blame him for that – she didn't really believe it was innocent either but she didn't want Mitchell to worry. She also had the strangest feeling that the mysterious driver wasn't necessarily hanging around her house to watch *her*. In fact, the more she thought about it the bigger the pool of suspects and reasons grew. Could it be something to do with Mitchell himself? Was Martine after a good angle to screw him out of a decent divorce settlement? Hannah had to be on her toes if she was going to be one step ahead and find out what was going on. She'd have a word with Gina and get her to talk to Howard. Gina wouldn't be happy about that but Howard was about the closest link to Mitchell's business world that Hannah could think of and he might hear some gossip in his day to day dealings that would give them some clues.

*

They'd had a lazy brunch, despite Hannah's assertions that she had work to do and was seriously behind schedule. The opportunity to spend time with Mitchell was just too tempting to resist. Eventually, Hannah had forced herself to make a move and had started to clear away while Mitchell went to get showered and dressed. She was elbow deep in suds at the sink when he returned and crept up behind her.

'Get off!' she giggled as he brushed her hair aside and began to kiss the back of her neck. 'You're not getting me back into bed again no matter how hard you try.'

'Who said anything about bed?' he breathed into her ear.

'Stop it,' she laughed.

'I can't help it,' he murmured. 'You do things to me.'

'I do believe I'm the innocent party…' She turned to him, wiping her hands on a tea towel. 'I'm going to get a shower and you are not to follow me.'

'I don't think I could if I tried,' he laughed, sinking into a kitchen chair. 'I think you've worn me out.'

'I keep telling you; that's your doing, not mine.' She kissed him lightly. 'Don't go anywhere – I won't be long.'

With a huge smile plastered to her face, Hannah left him in the kitchen. Passing her phone sitting on the mantelshelf, she noticed the missed calls on the screen. One was from Gina, and Hannah made a note to call her as soon as Mitchell had gone. Two more since the first that morning were from Chris. Hannah's good mood evaporated. She was going to have to put him straight no matter what Gina said; it wasn't fair to the poor man. Shower first, and then she'd wait for Mitchell to leave before she called Chris back.

But that stubborn, irritating, no-friend-of-Hannah's little cow called fate had other ideas. No sooner had Hannah made the decision than there was a knock at the front door. Mitchell appeared at the kitchen doorway.

'Want me to get it?' he asked.

'Better not. You never know who it is – it might be someone who shouldn't know you're here.'

'I don't care who knows I'm here,' he said, starting towards the hallway.

'No… it's fine. I'll get rid of them. It's probably George or Briony or someone.'

Hannah carefully closed the living room door behind her before she opened the front one, and she was glad that she had. She felt the blood leave her face as Chris stood grinning on the doorstep.

'I probably should have given you some warning,' he said, giving her kimono-clad form a swift and appreciative once-over, 'but you weren't answering your phone so I thought, as I was this way, I'd pop in.'

Shit! Why had Hannah let him bring her home that night? She should have realised that letting him see where she lived was a bad idea. What was it about her that made everyone feel they could turn up whenever they felt like it?

'It's um… It's kind of a bad time right now,' she said, wrapping her arms around herself against the cold now biting through the flimsy layer of silk that was her only protection. What was she thinking of, answering the door in that? It was lucky it hadn't been George; she'd probably have given him a heart attack. All she could think about now was how she could get rid of her unwanted caller.

'I won't stay long,' he said cheerfully. 'I just wanted to see how you were and find out how your sister is getting on with her settlement.'

'I'm sorry, but you can't come in.'

He looked crestfallen. 'But I came all the way out here…'

So much for just passing, Hannah thought. He'd obviously decided that it was okay to turn up regardless of whether she wanted it or not. The idea irritated her. 'Sorry,' she repeated, feeling more like a giant bitch by the second. 'Gina's still on track, as far as I know. If it helps, I'll speak to her later and let you know if there are any developments…' Even as she was finishing her sentence, Hannah was closing the door, leaving him out on the step. She leaned against it and blew out a long breath, waiting for the sound of footsteps that would signal Chris had gone.

'What was that about?' Mitchell asked as she returned.

'It's a long story. It was a guy I had one date with who now seems to think it's okay to turn up at my house at the drop of a hat like we're old friends. I mean, he's nice and everything but…' Hannah stopped mid-sentence. Mitchell looked… what was that look on his face? 'You're not jealous, are you?'

'Do I have anything to be jealous about?'

'God, no!' Hannah said. 'I had one date with him and he's helping Gina to buy a house – well, one of his houses actually.'

'One of his?' Mitchell frowned. 'He sells them? Builds them?'

'Renovates. One man band, he says. He does one up, sells it on and buys the next to do the same all over again.'

'I started out like that,' Mitchell said with a faint smile. 'Why didn't you ask me to get Gina a house? I could have sorted it.'

'Could you? I thought you dealt with large commercial properties – hotels and stuff.'

'I do, but I have plenty of contacts. I could have found her a place.'

'You'd probably have ended with Chris's name anyway; there can't be that many of you property developer types around these parts.'

Mitchell was thoughtful for a moment. 'Chris? Is that Chris Price?'

'Yes! Your memory is getting better by the hour! You know him then?'

'I know of him. I think Graham knows him, though. I'll ask him about it tomorrow; check he's kosher.'

'I don't think there's any need for that, he's…' Hannah checked herself. It obviously made Mitchell happy to try and look out for her so perhaps it was easier to let him.

'So… you're not going to see him again?'

'If it makes you feel better I'll wear a blindfold when I go with Gina next to discuss the house.'

'Very funny. You know what I mean.'

'Well, I didn't think you'd mind if I pencilled a threesome in the diary for next Tuesday afternoon.' Hannah held him in a steady gaze.

'Sorry.' Mitchell gave an awkward grin. 'Okay, so that was a stupid question.'

'And a little insulting too.'

'It's just…well, with what happened between Martine and me…'

Hannah crossed the floor and buried herself in his arms, the previous moment's vexation forgotten. 'There's one big difference you're missing here – I'm not Martine, am I?'

'I know; I'm sorry.'

'And I'll never, ever hurt you.'

*

The footage Hannah found on the camera was pretty useless. Mitchell had made her promise to take care of it before he would leave her the previous day, and she had dutifully done so. During daylight the lane had been as quiet as always, and when night fell the darkness was so dense that it was almost impossible to detect movement other than the occasional eerie reflection in a pair of nocturnal eyes staring unknowingly into the lens – foxes, badgers… but certainly no mystery Volvo drivers.

Hannah muttered to herself as she reset it. If what she had recorded so far was anything to go by, it seemed like a waste of time, but she'd promised Mitchell she'd keep it running and he'd probably want to test her on it or something. She was starting to feel a bit silly about the whole thing now. Who on earth would want to watch her dull little house?

Glancing at her watch, Hannah caught her breath. Once again, the morning had got away from her. She'd promised Briony she'd call at lunchtime with some posters she'd knocked up for a charity sewing bee. She was getting used to Briony, learning how to avoid making herself the subject of gossip, and was even beginning to enjoy their little meetings. The cakes alone made it worthwhile, although she wondered whether Mitchell would still love her when she looked like one of the Tellytubbies…

But if she didn't get her skates on it'd be more like bedtime when she arrived. The amendments she'd been asked to do on a set of promotional postcard designs for a local high school had taken longer than she'd planned and then there'd been the camera to check…

Restarting the camera, Hannah positioned it on the windowsill as before. Then she pulled her coat on and headed out to Holly Farm.

*

'These are brilliant!' Briony unrolled a poster and held it up to inspect. 'You're so clever!'

'Don't be daft,' Hannah said, 'I only just knocked them up. It is what I do for a living, after all.'

'Well, I wouldn't know where to start.'

'I'm sure I wouldn't know where to start connecting a cow up to a milking machine either,' Hannah smiled.

'Neither do I,' Briony laughed, 'as we don't have cows.'

Hannah giggled. 'Oh yes, I forgot about that. Well, I wouldn't know how to dip a sheep then.'

'You must let me give you some lunch to say thank you.'

'There's no need…' Hannah began, but Briony held up a hand to silence her protests.

'Yes there is. You must let me do something to repay you. Besides, I'm making a cottage pie and there's far too much, even for Ross and Paul with their gargantuan appetites.'

'That does sound lovely. You're very kind.'

'It's settled then. Make yourself at home and I'll put some veggies on.'

Hannah sat down at the table and shrugged off her jacket. 'Will Ross and Paul be back to eat with us?'

'I doubt it,' Briony said as she pulled a handful of carrots from the fridge. 'They usually take sandwiches and stay out on the fields all day. They'll eat late, but it'll be a huge meal to make up for it.'

'That seems like a long time to wait when they're doing all that manual work.'

'Ross pops in sometimes and steals a cake or two if he knows I'm baking.' She gave a fond smile. 'Little boys never really grow out of that, do they?'

Hannah couldn't imagine anyone still seeing Ross as a little boy, but then, she wasn't his mother. Briony would probably always see him as that cherubic little child who raced around her kitchen, stole her cakes and got under her feet. It also made her realise just how Gina had her work cut out persuading Briony, above everyone else, that she was the right woman to make that little boy happy. Hannah wanted to try and lend a helping hand – lay the groundwork however she could. She had promised Gina she would, but it was difficult to know how to introduce the topic.

'I was talking to my sister about your calendar,' she said.

Briony turned from where she was washing carrots at the sink. 'Were you?'

'She says she'd love to do it if you still need people. She's always happy to support a good cause.'

'She's certainly very pretty. I remember saying as much to Paul at the salsa evening. Even Ross agreed.'

Hannah wondered just what Ross had said, but knew better than to ask at this stage.

'She'd make a good November, I think,' Briony continued thoughtfully. She had allocated a month to Hannah off the top of her head when she had first mentioned it to her too, and Hannah wondered what bizarre criteria she used to do this.

'I could give you her number and you could have a chat with her about it some time.'

'Better still, bring her over one day. It'd be lovely to get to know her properly and if she's as lovely as you then I'm sure I'd enjoy the company. We didn't get that much chance to chat at the Salsa evening.'

Hannah beamed. It was the result she'd been hoping for and had been much easier to achieve than she had anticipated. Now, all Gina had to do was work her usual charm and Briony would love her – half the battle was won already. 'That would be really nice. I'll do that next time she's over from Birmingham.'

'Good. Now, would you like peas or green beans?'

'I really don't mind.'

'Then I'll do both.' Briony went over to her freezer and pulled out a bag of frozen peas. Hannah smiled to herself – even super domestic goddesses like Briony still fell back on convenience foods from time to time. The revelation made her feel slightly less incapable.

Briony hummed softly as she filled a pan with water, almost as if she'd forgotten Hannah was there. Depositing the pan on the stove, she turned around with a pensive expression.

'You chat to Ross quite often now, don't you?'

'Yes…' Hannah said, wondering where the conversation was headed. She had a slight sinking feeling though.

'He hasn't said anything to you about a lady friend?'

'No.'

Briony was silent again. 'Well,' she said finally, 'something is going on with him.'

'What makes you say that?'

'There's a lot of sneaking around for a start – phone calls that end when I walk into the room, he's missing early or goes off and doesn't say where he's been – that sort of thing.'

Hannah knew all about this, of course, but she wasn't so clear on how Briony knew so much. For the most part Ross inhabited his own little annexe away from the main house and, surely, if he was going to speak to Gina he'd do it from there. And grown men didn't have to tell their mothers about their every move. Either he was in the main house so often that he might as well not have an annexe of his own to live in, or Briony had been spying on him. Knowing Briony as she did now, it was probably the latter.

'You're not worried, are you?' Hannah asked.

'Oh no! He seems just like his normal self – perfectly happy. Happier, if anything. That's why I'm almost certain it's a lady.'

Hannah bit back a wry smile. 'Presumably it wouldn't be his first?'

'Oh, you couldn't keep them away from him at school, but at agricultural college he lost interest, he was so wrapped up in his studies. And over the last few years he's only been interested in the farm. Paul and I are glad that he takes it so seriously and that he wants to make it his future, but…' She shrugged slightly. 'Whoever she is, she must have really turned his head.'

'Have you asked him?'

'He says there's nothing to tell and the moment there is I'll be the first to know. He probably thinks I'm going to embarrass him or something if he brings her home.'

Or that you won't approve of her, Hannah thought.

'So he's told you nothing at all?'

'No, the little so and so. He knows it will drive me mad too. But I'll find out. I have my suspicions already.'

'You do?'

'I think it's someone he met at the auctions. He went out early last week and came back with a great big daft grin all over his face half the day later, then he was in an almighty rush because he hadn't seen to his sheep. The only place I can think he'd been to was the livestock auctions, and I happen to know that there is a sweet little thing who works in the office there – Lydia, I think her name is. Paul says she's always giving Ross the eye. Don't you worry,' she concluded cheerfully, 'I'll get to the bottom of it.'

'So you're not upset?'

'Why on earth would I be upset? I've been hoping he'd settle with a nice girl for the past couple of years now. It's not right for him to roam this place week after week and go nowhere else. Other men his age are already settling down or off out to pubs and clubs looking for a wife. Paul said I was overreacting, but I was almost ready to ask Ross if he was gay. I mean, it wouldn't have mattered to me one bit, but I just wanted to know whether I could ever expect any grandchildren.'

Hannah took a great slug of the tea Briony had just put in front of her. She silently wondered whether Briony would be quite so keen on grandchildren once she met Jess. Hannah loved her niece dearly, of course, and found her intelligent and witty company, but she could be something of an acquired taste, especially for someone as entrenched in the old country ways as Briony was.

'What are you going to do?'

'About Ross?'

Hannah nodded.

'Paul says I should leave him be. He says Ross will tell us in his own sweet time and I expect he's right.'

'I expect so too,' Hannah agreed.

'So he's never mentioned a thing to you?' Briony asked again.

'I don't think so,' she replied carefully, not wanting to lie but not being able to tell the truth. 'Nothing that I recall.'

'Pity…' Briony turned back to the stove and began to hum again. Hannah's gaze turned to the window. She was beginning to wish she hadn't agreed to stay for lunch, so it was almost a relief when Briony turned around again with a new question that didn't involve lying about Ross. 'I don't suppose you've seen anything more of your mystery car?'

'No, actually everything has been quiet. I hope it was all a silly false alarm and it stays that way. I played last night's footage on the camera and didn't see anything at all.'

'That's good. But you must keep it running a while longer. You can't be too careful these days.'

'I know, and I will. With a bit of luck it will all remain very boring.'

Briony smiled. She almost looked disappointed as she brought cutlery to the table. 'That's usually how it ends around here.'

*

The train pulled into New Street station, and Hannah gathered up her belongings. As she shrugged her jacket on, she almost slammed into a man who was trying get down the aisle.

'Oh, I am so sorry!' Hannah stammered.

The man turned and smiled. He was dark eyed, a sexy dimple in his chin. There was a startling resemblance to Mitchell. 'Bump into me any time you like.'

Hannah blushed furiously and he grinned as he continued on his way. She couldn't help a secret smile, though. A good-looking stranger casually flirting with her in passing – that hadn't happened for a long time and there was nothing like a bit of flattery to boost a tired ego. A year ago she might have been chasing him down the station to see where he went. But then, why did she need to, now that she had a good looking stranger of her own?

She stepped off the train and looked up the platform. She didn't have to search for long. There was Gina, a vision in her powder blue coat, hurrying towards Hannah's train. Hannah gave a broad smile and ran to hug her.

'It's about time you graced Brum with your presence,' Gina said.

'It does feel like ages since I was here. I'm looking forward to hitting the Bullring for some serious shopping.'

'There's a fab new shoe shop opened up in there. You'll just die when you see their stuff.' Gina slipped an arm through Hannah's as they began to walk.

'Will I die when I see the prices?'

'Probably. But at least you'll die wearing fabulous shoes.'

Hannah laughed. 'What a way to go.'

'Do you want to do lunch first or shopping? I'm easy either way.'

'Lunch, then you can tell me what's going on with Howard.'

Gina let out a groan. 'You haven't been worrying about it, have you? I knew I should have kept it until I saw you.'

'You can't send me half a tale by text and then not expect me to worry about it. You're not going to take him back, are you?'

Gina was silent for a moment.

'Gina... please tell me he hasn't got to you.'

'You didn't see him, Hannah. He looked so pathetic and sorry.'

'What about Ross!' Hannah squeaked. 'What about what Howard did to you?'

Gina glanced around. Nobody could possibly hear the subject of their conversation in the noise and hustle of Birmingham New Street Station on a Saturday, but she looked vaguely unsettled. 'This is not the time,' she said. 'Let's grab something to eat and I'll tell you about it properly. '

*

After negotiating a Bullring made even busier than usual by a demonstration about new government taxes, Hannah and Gina found themselves in a cosy restaurant on the main road down to the flea market and nestled in the shadow of the iconic Selfridges Building, its silver armour glinting in the winter sun. The air was fragrant with herbs and filled with the murmur of conversations all around them. Hannah sipped her glass of wine. It would be the only one, in order to avoid making rash, drunken purchases when she finally got out to do some shopping. She frowned at Gina.

'Who did the leaving?'

Gina paused. 'Howard says he left her. He realised that she was young and silly and that he still loved me after all; he'd had his head turned by a younger woman wanting him.'

'And you believe him?'

'I don't know.'

'You know what I think? I think she left him and he's turning it around to save face and to improve his chances of you taking him back so that he doesn't have to cook his own bacon on a Sunday morning.'

Gina snapped a breadstick in half. 'That had crossed my mind too.'

'Does Jess know?'

'Oh, he made sure he told her all about it before he told me. Extra pressure on me then, isn't it? I'm now the wicked witch who is keeping the family apart if I say no. Despite what Jess says about him and what he did with that slapper, I know that all she really wants is for all of us to be back together in our old house again, the way it used to be.'

'But you don't?'

'I'd be lying if I said I hadn't thought about it. But how can I? The trust has gone now, and I don't think we can ever get past that. Besides…' She gave a sly smile.

Hannah nudged her. 'Go on…'

'Why would I want a clapped-out old model – an unreliable one at that – when I can have a sexy young one who is as sweet and loyal as the day is long?'

'Why indeed?' Hannah mused, smiling to herself. 'Have you told Howard any of this?'

'I haven't told him about Ross, but I've a feeling Jess will have done, and if she hasn't already she will when I tell Howard that a reconciliation is not on the cards.'

'So you haven't straight out told him there's no reconciliation to be had?'

'I did. But he wouldn't accept my answer and said I should think about it. He said if I still felt the same way after a month he'd accept it and move on.'

'He won't, you know.'

'Of course he won't. But he'll have to start realising that he can't have everything he wants. A nice pay packet and lots of gifts will only take a man so far, but there are other things necessary to make a marriage work, like keeping your penis away from random passing women. He's had it all his own way too long now.'

Hannah smiled. 'Good for you. I'm glad to hear that you're sticking to your guns. You're far better off with someone like Ross.'

'With someone *exactly* like Ross.'

The waiter came over to their table and they quickly gave their order.

'I popped over to see Briony the other day,' Hannah said.

Gina was reaching for another breadstick, and her hand hovered over the glass as she stopped and gave her full attention to her sister. 'How was she?'

'She thinks Ross has a secret girlfriend.'

'Does she?'

'She thinks it might be a girl he's met at the livestock auctions.'

'Only slightly wide of the mark then – but she should be thinking mutton and not lamb.' Gina gave a wide grin, but it was too bright and too wide, and Hannah detected a hint of regret there. Gina was under no illusions about what she and Ross would be up against once their relationship was out in the open – if it even got that far.

'Don't talk yourself down like that. It doesn't matter if you are a little older; if you make him happy that's all they should care about.'

'I can't give him children, though.'

'You don't know that for sure. You haven't been sterilised, have you?'

'I'm too old.'

Hannah shook her head, though she couldn't help but recall Briony's comments about grandchildren. 'Lots of women still have babies in their forties. You might have to be more careful but it's not impossible.'

Gina took a gulp of her wine. 'We'd have to be bloody quick, that's for sure. I can just imagine what his parents would think about the possibility of no grandchildren. I know how I would feel in their place, and I think that's what makes it so hard.'

'You have to see past that.'

'To what? To the point some years down the line where Ross leaves me because he does want children and I can't give them to him?' She shrugged. 'Perhaps I am fighting for nothing.'

'Where the hell did this suddenly come from? A minute ago you were all loved up and now you've decided the relationship is doomed before it's begun!'

'A minute ago I hadn't thought about his parents and all the implications of his situation. I mean, I had, sort of, but I'd tried to ignore them. You mentioning a girl from the market just made it all real, I suppose. Do you honestly think this is folly?'

Hannah let out a long breath. 'You're asking the wrong person, I'm afraid. I can't talk about ropey relationships, can I?'

'I suppose not. But at least Mitchell is more suited to you. He only has a wife to get rid of and you're at the same point in life.'

'I think Mitchell does want children. You should have seen his face when he told me about the abortion. He was obviously devastated and I can't be sure I'm more capable than you in that regard; I'm only a couple of years younger.'

'But he's your age, at least. He can see it more sympathetically and he's probably accepted that he may never have any now. Martine would have been an older mother too so he was prepared for the risks of that.'

Hannah was quiet for a moment. Her gaze drifted to the window where shoppers rushed by, jostling for space, bumping into each other, squeezing past – tiny worlds colliding for a second and gone again. Was that her and Mitchell? Stolen moments that wouldn't last? Their worlds colliding – fantastic and explosive at first – but the fall-out eventually knocking their orbits off course and driving them apart?

'You've got a better chance than I have,' Gina said softly, reaching for her arm.

Hannah blinked as she looked back at her. 'Do you think? I'm not so sure. It's all passion now, but what about when that's gone? I'm not like Martine. I'm not strong and capable and independent.'

'Yes you are! Besides, he doesn't want another Martine. He wants you. Martine is a total bitch from hell.'

'Maybe he won't want me when he knows me better.'

'He'll want you more when he knows you better. You're a gorgeous human being and he'd be mad not to.'

Hannah turned back to the window. If only she could be as certain of that.

*

It didn't take long for Hannah's mood to lighten. It was impossible to spend time in Gina's company and not be affected by her quick humour. After lunch, they set about fitting as many shops as they could into their schedule before, finally, with aching feet and tired eyes, Hannah had to admit defeat and head back to the station for her train home.

Gina pulled her into a warm hug as they waited on the platform, the smell of diesel in their nostrils. 'I've had a wonderful day. Thank you so much for coming over.'

'I should be thanking you! It's always you who comes to Holly Way and I don't make this trip nearly as often as I should. I always have a brilliant time when I do.'

'Soon we'll be making the journey up from Millrise together for our shopping fix,' Gina said. 'Just think about that.'

'I can't wait…' Hannah began, but mentioning it brought Chris back to her mind.

Gina smiled. 'I can tell by the look on your face that you're worrying about your friend.'

'Chris? I would hardly call him my friend.'

'But I know you feel bad about him, and I was wrong to ask you to keep him in the dark. It's okay. Tell him about Mitchell and if he withdraws the offer of the house, then so be it. There'll be other houses.'

Hannah drew her back into another hug. 'You know you're brilliant, don't you? You always know what I'm thinking and you always say the right thing.'

'Not always, but I try. I don't want to see you worrying; you have enough to worry about already.'

The arrival of Hannah's train drowned out any more conversation, and Hannah turned to watch it pull into the station.

'Have a good trip home,' Gina said as it slowed to a halt.

Hannah hugged her again, and she put every ounce of her love into it. They may not always have seen eye to eye over the years, but these days Gina was her rock. Men might come and go, but her sister would always be there for her.

*

As usual, she'd made far too much stew. Sometimes, Hannah wondered if she was hardwired for family cooking. Nice as the stew had been, however, she didn't really fancy eating it for the rest of the week, and as the freezer was chock full of all the other dinners she'd made too much of, the only alternative to throwing it in the bin was giving it away. Her first thought was that George might appreciate a pot of something warm and wholesome.

Cutting a crusty loaf in half and wrapping it in cling film, Hannah scooped a large serving into an ovenproof dish and placed the whole lot in a rattan basket with a bottle of beer. George often joked that at his age it didn't matter to his liver if he drank too much or not.

Half an hour later she knocked at George's front door, watching her breath curl into the air as she stamped her feet to keep warm, wishing she'd worn her big duffle coat rather than throwing the nearest fleece on. Trixie's hoarse yap could be heard from within the house, so the chances were that George was definitely in – he rarely went out without taking her.

Finally, she heard the key rattle in the lock and George looked around the door, regarding her carefully through age-washed eyes before he realised who it was.

'Hannah!' he smiled. 'Have you been out here long?'

'Not too long,' she lied.

'Only you can't be too careful these days, can you?'

'Quite right. I've brought you some stew. I hope you haven't already had your tea.'

'Oh, that's grand!' George's face lit up as he spotted the basket on Hannah's arm. 'Just the ticket! That last one you brought round was delicious.' Hannah held the basket out and he uncovered it to peer inside. 'And beer too! You do look after me, young Hannah.'

'It's what neighbours do,' Hannah smiled, handing it over.

'Let me just unload and I'll give you the basket back…' George began, but Hannah interrupted.

'Don't worry about that. I'll call round for it on the way past tomorrow if that's alright.'

'That's no problem at all. Wouldn't you like to come in for a cup of tea, seeing as you've come all this way to feed me?'

'I've only bobbed down the road.' Hannah smiled. She was still weary from her packed schedule in Birmingham the day before but it was easier to make a different excuse. 'Thank you, but I've got a ton of work to do at home, so I won't, if that's okay. Another time, perhaps?'

'Oh aye, another time.' He patted the basket. 'I'll enjoy my tea tonight. I'd only got fish fingers and a little pan of chips planned, but this will be much nicer.'

'I expect Trixie will get a little bowl of it too…' Hannah asked, knowing full well that Trixie often got a plate of what George was eating, whether it was good for her or not.

'Oooh, she will. She loves a bit of braised beef.'

'I thought so,' Hannah said. 'Well, I'll see you tomorrow, George.' She turned to head back to her car.

'Mind how you go, won't you?' George called after her as she strode down the path.

'I will!' she shouted back. 'I always do.'

'Only with all this trouble around here lately, you can't be too careful… I mean, that car hanging around your house and that terrible business with young Ross –'

Hannah spun around. 'What's happened to Ross?'

'Haven't you heard? I thought you were thick with the Hunters.'

'No…' Hannah replied, cold dread creeping over her. 'I've been at home for most of the day. What's happened to Ross?' she repeated.

'Beaten to a pulp by all accounts. Not that I've spoken to anyone from Holly Farm myself. But I heard it from Brian up at the garage and he said the poor lad was in a right mess.'

'When did this happen? Where is he now? Is he alright? Are the police involved?' The questions tumbled out.

George held up a hand. 'I don't know all that. I can tell you that Brian says it was the early hours of this morning. He must have been on his way down to see his lambs. Paul found him on the lane in a ditch by the lower field. He was out cold from what I heard. Someone gave him a proper pasting.'

Hannah stared at him. She could see George speaking, and she could hear the words, but they weren't making any sense. 'Why would someone do that?' she murmured, almost to herself. Ross was the sweetest, friendliest man you could meet and everyone around Holly Lane loved him. Was this a random attack – wrong place, wrong time? It had to be. 'Was he mugged?'

'That I don't know. I expect so. Some druggie from a Millrise estate taking their chances as they passed through.'

Hannah considered this, but it didn't really add up. It was too far out of town for your average drug addict to bother with just for a bit of smack money, but Hannah simply nodded. She didn't want to alarm George with theories that might upset him even more than the one that he had seized on as the most obvious, the one that he could understand.

'So, you don't know where he is now?' Hannah asked.

'I don't. You could try at Holly Farm.'

Hannah paused. Then she pulled her phone from her coat pocket and phoned Ross. She stared at George as he watched her. She wasn't really sure what she expected to happen, but she didn't know what else to do. Her brain wouldn't compute the information it was being given. Nobody picked up, and Hannah frowned as she put her phone away. Perhaps he was okay, though. Ross wasn't surgically attached to his phone, unlike a lot of people she knew, so he wasn't likely to reply straight away, even if he was recovering at home.

'Thanks, George,' she said finally. 'Take care, eh? Get inside and lock the door so you're nice and safe when the sun goes down.'

'Don't you worry about me. Trixie will scare them off if anyone tries to cause trouble.'

Hannah doubted that very much, but she nodded.

'I could say the same to you,' George added. 'You'll be careful getting home, won't you?'

'Of course!' Hannah called, already hurrying down the path towards her car. First, she would call in at Holly Farm and see what she could find out there. George might have been muddled up, or the story could have been embellished, like so many other Chinese whispers. She would need to contact Gina too, because nobody else would if Ross himself was incapable. But it was pointless telling Gina anything until Hannah knew the facts.

*

When Hannah pulled up at Holly Farm, she found the main gates to their huge driveway closed. She couldn't remember ever seeing them closed before – Briony kept them open as an invitation to anyone passing because she loved the company. The house was in darkness too; at least, what she could see of it was. She got out of her car and rattled at the gates, but they were locked.

Hannah paced up and down in the gathering gloom. The temperature was dipping sharply now and she felt the early evening frost bite through her fleece. What should she do? Should she call Gina anyway and tell her what she knew? Which was what, exactly? She didn't really know anything except what George had told her and it wasn't the most reliable or complete information. Gina would dash over, or she would worry herself into a state, and she wouldn't be able to do a thing in either scenario that wouldn't involve coming clean to Briony and Paul about her relationship with Ross – probably not the best time to do that.

Pulling her phone from her coat pocket again, Hannah scrolled down the list of contacts as she mulled it over. Who could she call? Who might know what had happened? She didn't have a number for

Briony or Paul – she had never needed one before. In fact, she wasn't even sure they had mobile phones. Poring over the contact list once more, Hannah's attention was drawn to a recent entry. She had simply labelled it PARAMEDIC. The man who had come to help Mitchell at Christmas, and whose watch Ross had found. Hannah wasn't big on calling favours, but on this occasion she felt justified. He might know something – he might even have attended the scene himself. She had a strong feeling that he wasn't allowed to give out the sort of information that she was going to ask him for, but maybe he would bend the rules for her this once, and it wasn't like she would tell anyone.

Without further thought, Hannah dialled the number. It rang for what seemed like a lifetime, and Hannah was about to give up when he answered.

'Yes?' he said, sounding out of breath and slightly irritated.

'I'm sorry,' Hannah said, already regretting the call, 'you sound busy so… it doesn't matter. I'm sorry I disturbed you…'

'Who is this?' His voice was softer now. 'It's alright; you don't need to hang up.'

Hannah hesitated. 'I don't know if you remember me, but I'm Hannah Meadows. You came to my house on Christmas Day for a man who'd had a bump on his head. You lost your watch and I found it – or rather, my friend did –'

'Hannah!' he cut in. 'How the devil are you? Of course I remember you! I'm sorry if I was abrupt but I'm on shift right now.'

'Oh God, I am so sorry, I didn't think…' Hannah had a terrible vision of him trying to perform CPR on some desperate case and here she was, bothering him for information she really ought to be finding elsewhere.

'It's alright,' he chuckled, 'I'm just waiting around at the moment. You're lucky; it's an unusually slow day for the time of year.'

'How long have you been on shift?'

'Didn't start until lunchtime today so I've got a long stretch to look forward to before I can fall into my bed.'

'So you weren't on this morning?'

'No, not me. Is there something bothering you?'

'It's just… you might not be able to help, of course, but…'

'Come on, you might as well ask me now.'

Hannah smiled despite herself. 'I've been told by one of my neighbours that Ross – the man who actually found your watch – was beaten up in the early hours of this morning. My neighbour says it's bad but he heard the news second-hand. That's all I know, and I've come over to his place to find it all locked up and in darkness. I'm guessing they're at the hospital but I've no idea.'

The paramedic was silent for a moment and Hannah was beginning to wonder if she'd managed to cut him off. 'Early hours?' he asked finally.

'I don't know what time exactly, but I know he's out most mornings by five am. I don't know what time his dad found him but I imagine it would be before most people were up and about. He'd been left unconscious on Holly Way, apparently.'

'I could ask around, see if I can find out who brought him in – if they did bring him in. His dad could have driven him to A&E, of course.'

'I didn't think of that.'

'A lot of people do; they think they'll be quicker. They have no idea how much damage they can do by moving a patient like that… and then you get the other end of the spectrum who phone us out for a tummy ache, it drives you mad –'

'I'm sure,' Hannah cut in, sensing a rant that she really didn't have time for. 'His name's Ross Hunter, from Holly Farm.'

'Give me a few minutes to make some calls and I'll let you know if I find anything.'

'Thank you!' Hannah's gratitude wasn't empty words; she felt it with every fibre of her being. Ross had become a good friend and, more than that, Gina would be devastated if any serious harm had come to him.

'Don't thank me yet, I may not be able to tell you much.'

'Anything is better than nothing. I'll wait to hear from you.' Hannah ended the call. The cold was really getting into her bones now, and as there didn't seem much point hanging around the locked gates of Holly Farm, she climbed back into her car and started the engine to get the heaters going while she watched her phone and waited for news. Her thoughts turned to Gina again; what was she going to tell her? What if Ross really wasn't okay? She wasn't sure Gina could take any more heartache in her life, especially now when she was just pulling it together again. It seemed so cruel that the happy future she could see on the horizon might be snatched away from her.

She'd just made the decision to start driving home and wait for her call there when the phone rang. She'd been staring out at the dusky sky, where the first stars winked like points of ice, so wrapped up in her thoughts that the sound of it made her leap up, knocking her mobile to the floor of the car. Scrabbling desperately as it continued to ring, she finally managed to retrieve it from beneath the accelerator pedal.

'Hello?'

'I've got good news and bad news,' the paramedic began. 'The good news is that I know he was brought into Millrise Gen by ambulance, which, when you think about it, is also your bad news. They're keeping him in and, by all accounts, it's not pretty.'

'Do you know how bad the injuries are?'

'I've only got the triage info so I don't know the full extent. Almost certainly a fractured cheekbone, a couple of broken ribs and concussion. Anything they've found since he was admitted I'm afraid I can't tell you.'

'Do you know which ward I can find him on?'

'Surgical Assessment Unit as far as I know, which means they're planning to operate and you're probably not welcome to visit. I'd say the oral and max fax team –'

'The what team?!'

'Oral and maxillofacial. They deal with bone injuries on faces. I forget that not everyone understands the hospital lingo. Anyway, they'll probably be working to fix his cheekbone but that's only an educated guess. If it is that then he might be on an orthopaedic ward tomorrow at some point where you'd be more welcome.'

Hannah sat in the gloom of her car and shook her head slowly. Why Ross? No matter how many times she asked herself the question, it didn't make sense. 'I won't get you into trouble for all this, will I?'

'Not if you don't tell anyone it was me who gave you the heads up.'

'I won't, I promise. You're an absolute star for helping me.'

'My pleasure.'

'So, no real point in going there now?'

'Well if his parents are there you could sit with them. But if you want to see your friend it's a waste of time tonight.'

'That's okay; I just wanted to know…' Hannah stopped. The thing she had really wanted to know, but not dared to ask was whether Ross was in any mortal danger. 'I'll go down tomorrow,' she said. 'Thanks again.'

'No problem. Goodnight, Hannah.'

The screen went dark. Hannah locked it and slipped it back into her pocket. She stared into the darkness of the lane, gripping the steering wheel. Now she would have to deal with Gina. God, if only she didn't live so far away – this wasn't the sort of news you wanted to deliver by phone and Hannah wanted to be with her to provide the emotional support she knew Gina would need. She had no idea what she was going to say to her. There was a little information, but not nearly enough, and most of it only led to more questions. Perhaps it would be more sensible to wait until the morning and see for herself the full extent of Ross's situation before she called her sister. Even if she couldn't actually see him at hospital, Briony or Paul might come home and Hannah could find out from them. Maybe Ross would even be well enough to come home himself by then, and there would be nothing for Gina to be upset about. Punch ups outside any pub on any Saturday night in Millrise resulted in worse injuries than that, and people seemed to recover from them.

Hannah let out a sigh and reached for the handbrake. It was then that the twin beams of a pair of headlights flooded the road, and a black car that had been hidden in the shadows of the trees along the lane pulled out and drove away.

What the hell? The driver couldn't have been watching her with any ill-intent – she'd been out in the open for almost an hour and it would have been easy enough to do her harm. Nevertheless, they must have been watching her; there was nothing else to see on the near-deserted lane. Was it the same car she had seen outside her house on so many occasions now? An involuntary shudder ran through her, and Hannah suddenly felt vulnerable, despite what her common sense told her. She pulled out her phone. She wasn't the sort of woman who wanted to rely on a man for anything, but after the day she'd had, the only thing she wanted was a pair of strong arms to hold her and chase away the fear.

Part Four:
One Starry Night

'Gina!' Hannah jogged along the old hospital corridor, trying to keep up with her sister's leggy strides. 'There's no point in charging around like a nutter; you won't be able to do anything and all it will achieve is upsetting his parents.'

'I don't care about that, not now. I'd rather make a stink and get it all out in the open, no matter who I upset. I'm his girlfriend; why should I have to stay away?'

'Because upsetting his parents won't do anything for his recovery, that's why.'

Gina stopped dead, almost tripping up a porter who was wheeling a frail looking lady along in a wheelchair.

'Watch out, love!' he yelped, swerving to avoid running up the back of Gina's ankles.

Gina muttered an apology but he was out of earshot and off down the corridor before it had left her lips. She turned to Hannah. 'So I'm supposed to stay out of the way? To abandon him in his hour of need?'

'Nobody's talking about abandonment. All I'm saying is calm down. Think about this before you do anything. If you go bowling in and announce you're with Ross you're hardly going to endear yourself to his mum and dad, are you?'

'They'll find out sooner or later. Why not now?'

Hannah sighed. 'If you were in a less agitated mood you'd see why, and I get that. Just trust me. For now, we can visit, but keep a lid on things; pretend you've come to keep me company or something.' Hannah reached for Gina and squeezed her arm. 'Don't cry…'

'I'm not crying. Well, I am a bit but it's just frustration.'

'I know. I feel it for you too.'

'Do you think he'll be awake yet?' Gina began to walk again. She seemed calmer now as Hannah fell into step beside her.

'I don't know. The nurse on the ward said he came out of theatre a couple of hours ago so he should be. Maybe he'll be groggy with the painkillers, though.'

'So, what do we do?'

'Nothing. We're supporting Briony and Paul as far as they're concerned – and you get to see Ross in the process.'

'I'm not so sure I want to after all.'

'Make up your mind…'

'It's just that I don't know what to expect. I want to see him desperately but I also don't. I don't know what I want.'

'Don't be scared. The nurse said he was comfortable and I bet it will cheer him up no end to see you.'

Gina gave a stiff nod. 'God I hate all this sneaking around.'

'I know. But there are better times and places to set the record straight. Remember the plan – we get them to like you first, then you can tell them.'

'You're right. Just like you always are.'

'I don't know about that…' Hannah smiled wryly.

They found Ross in a private room off the main ward. They nudged the door open and let themselves in to find him asleep in bed, his face a patchwork of cuts and bruises, Briony and Paul pale and strained at his side. Hannah could see immediately that Ross's injuries were having a profound effect on Gina. They were having one on Hannah too, though she tried not to let it show; she could quite easily have burst into tears. God only knew how Gina was managing to hold hers back.

Briony turned with a tight smile. 'It's so kind of you to visit. Though, if you'll forgive me for saying so, I was also a little surprised when the nurse told us you wanted to.'

'It's like you said the other day,' Hannah replied, 'we've become good friends with Ross and he's helped us out of no end of tight spots. We just wanted to see that you were all okay.' She turned to her sister, 'Didn't we, Gina?'

Gina nodded vaguely, her gaze fixed on Ross as though it was magnetised. Hannah gave her a surreptitious nudge. 'Yes,' she said in a small voice, still staring at the sleeping figure in the bed.

'Has Ross been able to tell you anything?' Hannah asked.

'Not yet.' Paul said in a hoarse voice.

'But you've spoken to the police?'

'Yes.'

Hannah was thoughtful for a moment. 'Did you tell them about the car that's been hanging around lately?'

'Actually, we did mention it,' Briony said. 'But they didn't seem to think it was significant. They logged it, but we couldn't give them a registration or even a make or anything.'

'What kind of car did you say it was?' Gina had now shaken herself free of her fixation on Ross.

'I'm not great on cars,' Hannah said, 'but I think it was a Volvo. I only say that because it looks like Mitchell's... and before anyone asks, it's definitely not him.'

'I'm sure it's not,' Gina said. Her jaw seemed to tighten, but she kept any other thoughts she might have to herself.

'I um… I saw it again,' Hannah added. 'Last night.'

Gina spun to face her. 'Where?'

Hannah turned to Paul and Briony, 'I came to see you to find out what had happened after George told me Ross had been injured. Your gates were locked, but there was a car parked off the road for a while before it drove off. It was dark, but judging by the behaviour of the driver, I think it must be the same one I keep seeing.'

Paul shot to his feet. 'The car was at the farm?'

Briony grabbed his arm. 'Calm down. Are you sure, Hannah?'

Hannah shook her head. 'I can't be sure of anything these days. I've no idea what this driver wants. This is going to sound silly, but there's no chance someone has some sort of vendetta against you is there?'

'Don't forget it's been outside your house as much as anyone else's,' Gina cut in.

'We're assuming it's the same car,' Briony said.

Hannah glanced at her sister. She recognised that look on her face. Gina knew something about this. If she didn't know for sure she almost certainly had ideas. How could that be? Then Hannah was struck by a lightning flash of her own. Surely not? She would have to wait to compare it with Gina's hunch, but if she was right, then it was very serious indeed. 'So Ross didn't get a good look at his attacker?' she asked, turning back to Briony.

'No,' Paul cut in, his hands curling into fists at his sides. 'Ross says he was hit from behind and the first blow knocked him silly so he was in no state to defend himself. That coward knew Ross would be able to look after himself in a fair fight. I'd love to get my hands on the bastard.'

'Paul…' Briony said in a low voice, 'we've talked about this. We leave it to the authorities to dish out justice.'

There was a sigh from the bed. Every head snapped around as Ross's eyes flickered open. Briony shot over to his side.

'How are you?' she asked, stroking a hand over his forehead.

Hannah glanced at Gina, and she could feel the ache in her sister, how much she wanted to be the one to comfort him, how frustrated she must be to have to stand aside.

'I'm alright, Mum,' he replied in a thick voice. 'I could do with a drink, though.'

Briony reached for the water jug on his bedside cabinet, and Ross allowed his gaze to search the room. The instant it settled on Gina, the effect was like adrenaline in his system, and his heavy eyes lit up. Briony smiled back at Hannah and Gina as she put the glass to her son's lips for him to drink. 'These lovely ladies have come to see how you are. As soon as they heard what happened, they wanted to visit. There are still good, kind people in the world.'

Ross nudged the glass away. 'It's good to see you,' he said, but he wasn't looking at Hannah at all. For him, there was only Gina in the room.

'You look better for your sleep,' Briony said with real approval in her voice.

'I feel better.' Ross turned his gaze to her now. 'You look terrible though. When was the last time you and Dad went off to get a break and a bite to eat?'

Paul waved a vague hand. 'We're alright. We can get a coffee in a bit.'

'Get a coffee now, Dad. And don't tell me you don't need one. Besides, if you don't, Mum does, and you ought to be thinking about her.'

Briony opened her mouth to argue but Ross cut her off. 'I'm fine. Please go and get a break or I'll have to add worrying about you to my list of woes. I'll have company,' he said, turning to Hannah and Gina, 'if you don't mind staying for a while.'

Gina nodded mutely.

'Of course we don't,' Hannah said.

'We still have a farm to run,' Paul said, quietly. 'There's livestock that need tending and we can't keep relying on my cousin to do it.'

'You'd best drive over and check everything is alright there, Dad,' Ross said. 'And if you don't mind including my flock too, I'd be grateful.'

Briony rubbed her eyes. 'You're right. I just don't like to leave you.'

'Mum, you were here when it mattered. Look at me now – apart from a few scrapes and bruises I'm fine.'

'Much more than scrapes and bruises,' Briony replied stubbornly.

'And I'm in the best and safest place I could be,' Ross said. 'Please, go and have a break.'

'We don't mind staying until you come back,' Gina said.

Briony turned to her with a grateful smile. 'That's very kind of you.' She stood up. 'We'll just be an hour or two then. Thank you.'

Hannah watched as Briony fussed, searching for her bag beneath the chair, trying to get her coat on and getting tangled in the sleeves, losing her bag again, until, finally, Paul took her gently by the arm and led her away. She had always seemed so assured, so comfortable in her surroundings that it was horribly jarring to see her this way.

'That was the right thing to do,' Hannah said once the door to the room had swung closed. 'They looked dead on their feet.'

'I think Mum especially,' Ross agreed. He turned to Gina. 'Thank you.'

'For what?'

'For coming here.'

Gina frowned. 'As if I wouldn't.'

'So... I thought you were having surgery on your face?' Hannah asked. 'I expected you to be covered in bandages like the invisible man or something.'

'Oh, it was just minor... they wanted to stop my nose spreading across my face or something.'

Hannah took in the full extent of his injuries. He must have taken a fair few blows. He could have been attacked from behind, as he had claimed, but, as Paul had said, Ross could look after himself. 'There was only one attacker?'

Ross winced as he tried to push himself up on the pillow. 'Bloody nuisance, this...' he muttered.

'Anybody else would be resting, but look at you, trying to get up already.' Hannah smiled.

Ross didn't smile back. He turned to Gina, his expression suddenly full of pain.

'What?' Gina asked, seeing it too.

'Okay... When I told Mum and Dad that I didn't see my attacker, I lied.'

'I don't understand –' Gina began.

'Wait...' Ross grimaced as he rubbed a hand down his side. 'I have to tell you something before I go any further. Whatever it is he's accusing me of, I swear to you that I didn't do it... I would never do something like that and I would never hurt you or Jess –'

'Jess?' It was Gina's turn to interrupt. 'What on earth has Jess got to do with this?'

'It was your husband.'

'Howard?' Gina sat down on the chair just vacated by Briony. Hannah watched as the colour left her face.

'You thought it might be him, didn't you?' Hannah asked.

'I really didn't think he was capable of it, though.' She stared at Ross. 'Why?'

Ross glanced at Hannah and then back again. 'He said he was teaching me a lesson.'

'I didn't tell him about you…' Gina began and Ross held up a hand to stop her.

'I know. It wouldn't have mattered if you had. That wasn't what he was teaching me a lesson for. He said… he said that Jess had told him things, things I had done to her but I swear, I never –'

'You've only ever seen Jess when she's been with me!' Gina cried.

Ross had tears in his eyes, and Hannah was in no doubt that whatever horrible thing he'd been accused of had cut him deeply. 'What did he say?' she asked. She didn't want to ask, but it didn't look as if Gina would, and she could understand why.

'He said… He said that I'd been doing stuff… with Jess. And he said that he was going to kill me. You have to believe me; I don't have a clue what he was talking about or where he got that from. God, I've barely even laid eyes on her since we got together!'

Gina threw her arms around him and buried her face in his neck. 'I do believe you. I know you're a good man and I trust you.'

Ross gingerly wound his arms around her. He whispered in her ear, over and over, something that Hannah couldn't make out, though the emotion in it was unmistakable. What the hell was going on here? Where had Howard got this information? More to the point, why had he been so convinced that he felt compelled to attack Ross for what he had been told?

Hannah went over to the window and gazed out, partly to give Gina and Ross a moment of privacy, and partly to think about what she had just learned. She was reasonably certain that Ross wasn't telling the whole truth. Why had he not put up more of a fight? He was more than a match for Howard, so it could only have been to save Gina more pain. What a mess. When she turned back, Ross and Gina were kissing, gently, to avoid aggravating the injuries to his face.

'Do you forgive me?' he asked as they broke apart.

'What for?' Gina leant to kiss him tenderly again. 'You're the only person who hasn't done anything wrong.'

'But I've caused all this…'

'If anyone has caused all this, it's me,' Gina replied.

Hannah folded her arms. She needed to be practical now, because both Ross and Gina were too emotional to think further than this room.

'Have you told anyone else about Jess's accusations?' she asked Ross. He shook his head. 'And you haven't mentioned to the police that you know who your attacker was or the reasons why he attacked you?'

'Of course not. How could I?'

'I'd be happy to enlighten them right now,' Gina began, but Hannah interrupted.

'What would that achieve? I think Ross understands this better than you do.'

'I can't say I'm all that happy about letting it go,' Ross said, turning to Gina, 'but if you get the police involved and all this comes out, what do you think will happen? I don't give a toss what happens to your husband, but I do care what happens to Jess.'

'She won't get into trouble.'

'No, but her dad will, and whether or not she told Howard a lie, the effect on her will be the same. It will tear her and your family apart in a way that can never be mended, and I know that you care more for her than anyone else in the world –' Gina tried to interrupt him but he cut her off '– including me, and that is as it should be. I won't have that on my conscience, and I can't put you through it, which is why I haven't told anyone about this, apart from you. And if you ask me never to tell anyone, I won't.'

Gina nodded stiffly and rubbed her eyes.

'I'm not so sure it will be that simple,' Hannah said.

'I'll do my best to protect Gina and her family in any way I can,' Ross replied, 'so I'll make it simple.'

'What about your parents? Don't they have a right to know?'

'Perhaps, when I'm ready, and they'll know what I choose to tell them. I'm not a boy anymore, even if my mum wishes I was.'

Gina reached for his hand. She didn't speak, but she held it to her lips and kissed it gently. Ross pulled her in and kissed her forehead.

'I want to tell my parents about us,' he said.

Gina pulled away. 'You do?'

'Of course. It's not the time or place, but I'm sick of sneaking around and keeping secrets.'

'That's what I said,' Gina smiled. 'But I don't think they'll like it.'

'They'll love you,' he said. 'It might take a little time but they will. It's up to me who I choose to build my future with and they'll have to accept that.'

'You want to build a future with me?'

'Why the hell not? You're the most incredible woman I've ever met.'

Hannah was feeling very surplus to requirements, and started to shuffle towards the door.

'Apart from you, Hannah,' Ross grinned, wincing as the action pulled a cut at the corner of his mouth.

'Thank you.' Hannah bowed her head graciously before returning his grin. But hers faded just as quickly. 'I hate to be the killjoy here but we have a few things to sort out before I can choose my wedding outfit.'

'We certainly do,' Gina said, grimly.

*

Briony returned after a couple of hours. Ross was sitting up, looking better despite the discussions they'd been having. And although he was keen to announce his relationship with Gina, Hannah and Gina had persuaded him to hang fire – at least until he was back home and everyone was a little more relaxed.

The sisters bid their goodbyes and promised to call at Holly Farm over the next couple of days. Gina smiled and made a good job of looking at ease, but as they left, Hannah saw her features harden instantly.

'Wait until I get my hands on that bastard,' she hissed, the double doors of the ward swinging violently behind her as she burst through them.

'What are you going to do?'

'What I should have done a long time ago – cut his fucking balls off.'

'Gina!' Hannah squeaked.

'What? Can you blame me for being angry?'

'Of course not, but you need to calm down. First, we need to get to the bottom of what's really gone on here.'

'Oh, don't worry, I intend to.'

Hannah glanced across at her sister. Her jaw was tight, her walk stiff and purposeful and Hannah was in no doubt that she wasn't seeing things rationally. If she wasn't careful she could make the situation much worse. 'Let me talk to Jess.'

Gina's stride didn't break. She stared straight ahead. 'She's my responsibility and I need to deal with her.'

'You're too emotional to do that right now. And the truth is, you've no idea what she told Howard.'

Gina stopped at the glass doors of the hospital entrance. 'I thought I knew Howard. Beating people up, hanging around in cars, stalking, reacting to crazy accusations… it's just not him. If Howard is capable of those things then the world has gone mad and anyone is capable of anything.'

'He told you he wanted you back. People do desperate things when they're desperate.'

'He should have thought about that when he was shagging his secretary,' Gina fired back. 'This was his doing, not mine. He already had me, and I loved him; all he had to do was treat me properly.'

'What are you going to do?'

'I haven't decided.'

'So, you might tell the police the truth after all?'

'Ross might be sweet and forgiving and willing to sacrifice justice for my sake and I love him for that, but it's not right. Whatever Jess told Howard about Ross, he already knew I was seeing someone because he'd been stalking me, and that's unacceptable without any of the other stuff. He was looking for an excuse to wade in and if it hadn't been the one Jess apparently gave him, he would have found something else to hate Ross for.'

'He wanted you back that badly…'

'No, he just hates to lose.'

'But if you involve the police, what about Jess?'

'I don't know about that either yet. I don't even know where to start with all this.'

Negotiating their way through the rows of tightly packed vehicles in the car park, they finally arrived back at Hannah's little Citroën.

Hannah could see how angry and hurt Gina was, and how much she needed support right now.

'We won't bother with the train,' Hannah said, 'I'll drive you to Birmingham.'

'This is so you can come with me. I've already said you don't need to.'

'Yes I do. There's no way I'm letting you go alone the state you're in.'

'I'm fine.'

Hannah turned the key in the ignition. 'Of course you are.'

*

It had been a tense and silent journey. Gina had seemed calmer when they arrived back, but no sooner had Hannah yanked on the handbrake than Gina was out of the car and striding towards her front door.

'Wait!' Hannah cried, slamming the car door behind her as she gave chase. But Gina already had her key in the lock.

'Jessica!' Gina called as the front door flew open. But she needn't have bothered; Jess appeared from the next room immediately. The look on her face told Hannah that she already knew how much trouble she was in.

'Oh, Jess…' Gina began, 'do you have any idea of the shit you've caused?'

'What happened?' Jess asked. Her usual cockiness was replaced by a wide-eyed look of dread.

'What happened? What happened was that Ross got beaten to a pulp by your dad.'

Jess's eyes widened still. 'He got beat up? Dad said…'

'What did Dad say?' Gina asked.

'He said… we talked about moving in with Ross –'

'Nobody ever said we were moving in with Ross!'

'Gina…' Hannah cut in, 'calm down.'

'I am calm!' Gina said, drawing in a deep breath in an attempt to make it true. 'I'm just trying to understand what's going on.' She turned to Jess. 'So you told your dad we were moving in with Ross?'

'Not exactly,' Jess said awkwardly.

'But you told him we might?'

'I said I didn't want to…'

'What you really meant was that you didn't want to leave Birmingham and you were trying to persuade your dad that you should live with him, so you used Ross as your pawn.' Gina folded her arms. Jess looked at her shoes. 'Well?'

Hannah decided to intervene. She looked at Jess. 'Why don't you go and sit in the kitchen? I'll come and talk to you in a minute.'

Jess hovered uncertainly. 'Go on.' Without any argument, Jess dashed off.

Hannah crossed the room to close the door and turned to Gina. 'You're angry, and you're hurting. You're not in a state to deal with this now… I'll talk to Jess first.'

Gina looked as though she wanted to argue, but then she let out a sigh. 'You're right. Talk to her and see if you can make any sense of what's going on.'

'Give us an hour. Have a bath or something to relax you – you look as though you badly need it.'

As Gina disappeared, Hannah followed Jess through to the kitchen. She sat down opposite her niece and took a deep breath. 'Do you want to tell me what happened?'

'Has my dad really done that?' Jess asked.

'I'm afraid so.'

'I didn't tell him to do anything, I swear.'

'I believe you, Jess. But your dad went out to Holly Farm yesterday and beat Ross up and left him unconscious. There's no denying that this is all quite a mess.'

Tears began to well in Jess's eyes.

'Ross is so badly beaten,' Hannah continued, 'that he's in hospital. He's had to have surgery. He is devastated by the accusations your father is making – a lovely, sweet, kind man who doesn't deserve that sort of slur – and he may take a long time to recover from that. You may not care for Ross now, but if your mum stays with him long term, you need to build a proper, trusting relationship with him.'

Jess sniffed hard and rubbed the back of her hand under her nose.

'What, exactly, did you tell your dad?' Hannah asked.

Jess didn't look up, her gaze fixed firmly on the table. Hannah waited for a moment before trying again.

'You might not want to tell me but you'll have to tell the police if they ask. Ross is going to do his best to keep the police out of it, but there was a 999 call so it might not be that simple.'

Jess's head snapped up, a look of absolute alarm on her face. 'I didn't think Dad would go loco. I just wanted to move in with him.'

'Jess, it's really important that you tell me exactly what you did tell him.'

Jess started to cry in earnest now. 'I only said that Ross was really young – almost the same age as my boyfriend – and… I did say that I didn't want to live with him because it made me uncomfortable…

'Uncomfortable how?'

'…like I wouldn't be able relax when he was around and stuff.'

'Did you insinuate that there was anything… *weird* about Ross?'

'I… I don't think so…'

Hannah wondered if Jess had accidentally led Howard to the wrong conclusion but now was not the time to confront her with that possibility. And even if she had, the damage was already done and they simply had to find a way to undo it. 'Did you ask your dad if you could move in with him before?'

'He said my place was with Mum. He said she'd be the better parent because he worked such long hours. He said that I didn't need to worry about Ross being there because he would sort it.'

'All this because you don't want to move away from Birmingham?'

'All my friends are here. I don't know anyone in Millrise.'

'I know it's hard, but sometimes life is like that. Despite what you think now, you will adjust and you will be happy again. And you must be able to see how happy your mum has been since Ross came into her life.'

Jess's voice was barely more than a whisper as she asked her next question. 'Do you really think Ross would drop my dad in it?'

'Your dad has dropped himself in it.'

'But will he go to the police?'

'The police have already gone to him. And there may be other witnesses we don't yet know about,' she continued.

'Then dad's screwed!' Jess cried.

'We don't know that. We'll sort things as best we can, I promise.'

'What will happen to Dad?'

'I don't know. I guess the worst case scenario is that he could go to prison. What he did is very, very serious. But let's try not to think about that yet.'

'Ross will hate me forever.'

'He isn't like that,' Hannah said gently. She gave Jess an encouraging smile.

'So I have to tell the police everything?'

'If they ask, yes.'

'Will I get into trouble?'

'I don't know. It depends what they make of it.'

'Shit…'

'Shit indeed.' Hannah got up and filled the kettle. 'Do you think it's time to talk to your mum? You owe her an explanation, and you need to tell her how you feel – why you're so upset about moving away from here and how scared you are of things changing.'

Jess was silent as Hannah flicked on the kettle and pulled two mugs from the cupboard.

The door to the kitchen opened, and Gina put her head around it. Her eyes were puffy, and she showed no signs of having had a bath at all. Hannah wondered how much of the conversation she'd overheard behind the kitchen door.

'Cup of tea?' Hannah asked.

Gina gave a small nod, and then turned to Jess. 'We're in a mess, aren't we?'

Jess's eyes filled with tears again and Gina crossed the room to pull her into a hug. 'We'll sort it out, though, just like we always do,' Gina added, kissing the top of her head.

'I'm really, really sorry, Mum.'

'I'm sorry too.'

*

Hannah had finally left for her drive home, despite Gina's insistence that she wait and stay there until morning. Hannah wanted her own bed – more than that, she wanted warm arms to hold her in it and kiss away the stress. For once, she was glad she didn't have a misguided teenager trying to ruin her relationship with Mitchell, although Martine was quite enough trouble by herself.

It was gone ten p.m. when she sent the text to Mitchell to let him know she was safe and sound back on Holly Way. She hadn't really had time during the day to tell him a lot else, and there were parts of the story that she really didn't want to tell him, but half an hour after her text he was on the sofa with her and an open bottle of wine, and Hannah found herself pouring all her troubles into his willing ears.

When she had finished, he kissed her tenderly and wrapped her tighter in his embrace, and she lay there, content in his arms as she watched the flames of the open fire spit and dance. Before she knew it, she was asleep.

*

Although it was frosty, the day was bright and insects rose up from the long grass as Hannah, Gina and Trixie strode through it.

'It's getting warmer,' Hannah said. 'I think spring is just around the corner.'

Gina shot her a sideways look. 'You're kidding me? It's February and it's bloody freezing!'

'I didn't say it was warm, just warmer.' Hannah bit back a grin as her gaze went across the fields to where a familiar rooftop had just come into view. 'I don't know why you wanted to come out if you think it's cold.'

'I only think it's cold because I've just been somewhere really warm for a week,' Gina excused, 'I'm still acclimatising. And I thought the walk would do me good – work off all that food I ate last week while we were on holiday.'

'Oh, that's what it is!' Hannah smirked. 'So nothing to do with the fact that while you and Jess definitely needed a bit of bonding time together on a sunny Canary island – and I'm not a bit jealous, obviously – you've also been desperate to see a certain farmer all the time you've been away?'

'Of course not,' Gina said tartly.

'You don't generally go around begging people to walk their dogs.'

'I didn't beg, I offered. As a favour.'

'You know, if you'd wanted to see Ross you only had to ask. We could have just knocked on the door of Holly Farm instead of all this dog-based subterfuge.'

'This way seems less suspicious. We happen to be doing an elderly neighbour a favour.'

'So you do admit to an ulterior motive! I don't think Paul and Briony would have minded us calling anyway. Ross is a lot better now and they seem to be putting things behind them now that the chance of actually prosecuting someone seems very slim.'

'We won't tell Howard that. He's still shitting himself and it's no more than he deserves.'

'You're not going to tell him he's in the clear?'

'No chance. I'm not letting him think he can go around beating people up because he doesn't like them talking to me. As things stand now, he's keen to keep me onside which means the divorce will go through nice and quickly and I'll get what I want without a fuss.'

'Do you believe what he told you last week?'

'About what?'

'About only doing what he did because he loves you and Jess so much?'

Gina shrugged. 'I suppose I understand him being angry if he thought Ross was messing with Jess. It's natural for her dad to want to protect her and she admits she may have allowed him to think more than she actually told him. But the stalking – that was before Jess had said a word and there's no excuse for that. He ruined the marriage. He made the decision that has left him on his own, he shacked up with a woman who turned out to be a gold-digging airhead, but he can't see that. Typical Howard – everyone else is to blame for his woes but never him. He couldn't stand to see that I might be happy without him. That's mean and vindictive and petty. I honestly wonder now what I ever saw in him.'

Hannah shielded her eyes from the sun that now poured over the fields as they crested a gentle incline. George's dog was wandering off at a tangent. 'Trixie!' she called. 'Come on, girl!' The little dog's head snapped up and she came haring back towards them, tail going like a child's windmill. 'I don't like her wandering too far,' Hannah explained. 'She's not our dog.'

'I doubt she could get that far,' Gina said mildly. 'Her legs are so small she'd be knackered after a mile.'

'Don't forget I've had to chase her before and she's faster than she looks. I don't fancy another go.'

Gina grinned. 'Oh, yes, I remember that day particularly well.'

'Anything to do with a certain handsome farmer making an appearance?'

'It could be. He is so much more than handsome, though. I really can't wait to get things out in the open so we can be a proper couple.'

'Hopefully you won't have to wait for much longer.'

Gina glanced across as she kept step with Hannah. 'Do you think we're doing the right thing? Look how much trouble me being with Ross has caused already.'

'Don't be crazy! You love him and he loves you. Nothing else should matter.'

'Like you and Mitchell?' Gina raised an eyebrow.

'That's slightly more complicated, but I suppose so.'

'I don't think it's *more* complicated, just a different set of complications.'

Hannah was silent for a moment. When she couldn't think of a reply, she reached into her coat pocket and pulled out a bag of dog treats George had given her in case Trixie wandered off and refused to come back. The rustle of the pack caused the little dog to race over as Hannah produced a treat and held it out – just for the sake of watching her tail wag like crazy. 'Here you go, Miss,' she said as Trixie snapped it from her fingers and almost swallowed it whole. Hannah looked up at Gina with a smile. 'Now, there's a girl who sees what she wants and takes it.'

Hannah straightened up and they began to walk again, Trixie now a shadow at Hannah's side just in case the treat bag came out again. They walked for a couple of minutes in companionable silence, until the impressive vista of Holly Farm rose ahead of them. From this direction, the house was bordered by vast swathes of the hedge that gave the farm its name. The top floor was the only part visible above it, plus a corner window of the annexe that Ross lived in. Hannah caught Gina's broad smile, and when she followed the direction of her gaze, she could see Ross standing at the window, obviously watching them cross the field. Gina's hand went up in a little wave, and Ross mirrored it.

'Bloody hell, it's like Romeo and Juliet,' Hannah said, rolling her eyes but grinning just the same.

'Isn't it?' Gina returned.

'But, I suppose it must be frustrating, Ross being on his sickbed. I mean, you can't have any of your secret assignations while he's cooped up and has Briony clucking over him like a mother hen.'

'It is. We've had to make do with phone sex and it's just not the same.'

'Oh, God, please!' Hannah snorted. 'I did not need to know that!'

'He said that we needed to wait for the right time to tell his parents and he's right, even though I don't like it. It's best to tell them when he's well and this has all blown over. We were both highly emotional at the hospital and they were too, and it would have been a terrible move to do it then.' She reached for Hannah's hand and gave it a squeeze. 'Thanks for being the voice of reason when I didn't have an ounce.'

'That's me – Captain Sensible,' Hannah smiled. 'Boring and reasonable to the last.'

'Oh, I don't know about that. You've certainly livened up my life lately.'

'For all the wrong reasons,' Hannah replied with a wry smile.

Paul Hunter emerged from a side gate at the house's perimeter and made his way across the field. 'What brings you lovely ladies to these parts?' he called to them.

'We were just walking Trixie for George,' Hannah returned brightly. 'It's a nice day, we had a spare hour and George looked a bit peaky when we saw him getting ready to take her out, so we told him to take an hour in his armchair and we'd give her a good run.'

Paul bent down to tickle Trixie behind the ears, 'That's good of you. Proper little sisters of mercy, aren't you?'

Gina smiled at Paul. 'How's Ross?' she asked, not a flicker of anything but neighbourly concern on her face.

Paul stood up. 'Why don't you pop in and see for yourself if you've got ten minutes to spare? I'm sure he'd be glad of some company other than me and Briony.'

'Is Briony home?' Hannah asked.

'Oh, aye. Any other Sunday she'd be at church, but she wants to keep an eye on the lad. Not that he'd come to any harm now, but I think she finds it hard to let him be.'

Gina kept her face straight, but Hannah knew she was hiding her disappointment well. There had been texts flying back and forth between her and Ross all morning, and he had intimated that his mum might be out and that his dad almost certainly would be.

'We could pop in and say hello,' Hannah replied, shooting a glance at Gina for some sign that she was giving the right answer.

'Don't stay out too long; it'll be dark sooner than you know it,' Paul warned as he slung the spade he'd been carrying back across his shoulder. 'And mind you go back by the road,' he added as he began to trudge away in the direction they had just come from.

'We will,' Hannah called after him, vaguely wondering how he was going to dig anything when the earth must be frozen solid.

'Come on,' Gina said, her eyes still trained on his retreating figure. 'I suppose an hour with a chaperone is better than nothing.'

'He'll be happy to see you. And don't forget we're supposed to be winning Briony over too. If you think about it that way, then it's a good thing she's there.'

'Yes, yes... you're right, as always. So let's get it over with.'

'You could at least try to enjoy it a little. I know she's a bit full on at first, but she's actually lovely when you get to know her.'

'Easy for you to say. But when I'm sitting having tea with her all I can think about is ripping her son's clothes off and having him on the kitchen table.'

'My God!' Hannah giggled. 'You're obsessed!'

'Let me tell you, if the shoe was on the other foot you would be too. I don't know where he learned it, but in the bedroom, that boy is divine.'

Hannah could understand only too well. She tried not to think of Mitchell's hands all over her, the feel of his breath on her neck, the taste of him. She sighed and turned her mind instead to an hour of drinking tea and discussing the price of cattle feed.

*

As always, Briony was thrilled at the arrival of company and couldn't tell Gina enough times how beautiful the tan she had brought back from Lanzarote had made her look. Making a great deal of fuss, she put out a plate of chicken and a bowl of water for Trixie, and insisted Hannah and Gina cancel all plans to shoot off before dark, stating that Paul would drive them back. When Hannah tried to argue that George would wonder where they had got to with his dog, she assured them that Paul would call in at the old man's house and take care of that too. So they soon found themselves plied with tea and a plate of homemade scones the height of Everest that were so delicious Hannah decided she would eat them and nothing else for the rest of her life.

No sooner had they sat at the table than Ross joined them, professing as much surprise at their arrival as Briony had, and shooting furtive, longing glances in Gina's direction whenever Briony's back was turned. Loaded looks and mouthed messages passed between them at every opportunity, and Hannah decided that if it made them happy, then she was happy for them. Ross himself still looked to be in a great deal of pain – holding himself stiff and awkwardly – but it had only been just over a week since the attack and a lesser man wouldn't have been on his feet at all. He looked a lot brighter than he had the last time Hannah had seen him, though, and insisted on pushing himself up from his chair at every opportunity to help Briony with tea making and plate fetching and various other little jobs.

'He's going mad with boredom,' Briony said as she brought the full teapot to the table. 'Just look at him – can't keep his bum on that seat for more than a minute. But I suppose it's to be expected; he's just not used to sitting around.'

'I *am* going mad with boredom,' Ross agreed as he popped a jar of strawberry jam, thick with fruit, onto the table. 'I'm just not an indoors kind of guy. The doc has told me six weeks' rest, but there's no chance of that. I'll have to swap my bedroom for a padded cell if I stay there for that long.'

'But you can still go out walking, can't you?' Hannah asked. 'Around the farm, I mean, if you take it easy.'

'Walking would be alright,' Briony cut in, 'but it isn't enough for Ross.' She shot a disapproving glance at her son. 'So he's talking about going back to work next week.'

'You can take that look off your face,' Ross said with an easy grin. 'I told you it won't be anything too strenuous. It's hardly taxing, feeding a few sheep and wandering the fields.'

'I know you,' Briony replied, 'you won't stop at that. You'll be hauling bags of feed and hay bales, and probably pop a rib in the process. And that tractor's not exactly easy to drive but I know you're itching to get back in it.'

'You worry too much.' Ross crammed a hunk of scone into his mouth and chewed serenely.

'Someone's got to,' Briony said.

Hannah glanced at Gina, but there was not a flicker. She was doing a great job of looking neutral about a conversation she must have been desperate to get involved in. Briony turned to her visitors.

'Are you sure I can't persuade you to stay for dinner?' she asked, apparently deciding to let Ross off the hook for now. 'It's beef stroganoff and, though I say it myself, it's not half bad.'

'Ordinarily, I'd love to, but we should probably get back…' Hannah reached down to where Trixie lay next to her chair and scratched the little dog behind her ear. The lazy thump of her tail on the floor was as much effort as the exhausted pooch could make. 'For a start, George will be missing this one so I don't want to keep her out too late.'

'And I really need to get back to Birmingham tonight,' Gina added. 'Early morning meetings and all that. Another time I'd love to.'

'How about next Sunday?' Briony asked. 'What are you doing then?'

'I should probably do something with my daughter,' Gina said, glancing briefly at Ross, who was staring into his mug. 'I've been missing rather a lot lately and I'm afraid she hasn't been getting enough of my attention.'

'Why don't you bring her along?' Briony suggested, completely disregarding Gina's argument. 'I'd love to meet her and an extra mouth is no problem.'

'I don't know,' Gina began. 'It's a big chunk out of her day to travel up here and she has college work to get done on a Sunday night…'

'Please. I insist. If you're both moving back to the area I'd love to get to know you a little bit better, and it would be one more friendly face if she ever needed one. Besides, it'll be a change for Ross, a young person about the place.'

'I'm nearer to thirty than seventeen, Mum,' Ross put in. 'As far as Jess is concerned, I might as well be ninety. When you're a teenager eight or nine years is a lifetime away from cool.'

Hannah chewed her lip. Briony didn't know the half of it. She had a feeling that the reveal Ross and Gina had planned would have to be brought forward or Briony might take matters into her own hands and start playing cupid – maybe even with Jess herself (who was a very attractive and mature looking seventeen), and a more horrifying scenario than that she couldn't think of.

'It's lovely of you, but another time, maybe,' Gina smiled.

'Actually…' Ross put in, 'why don't you?'

Gina's cup stopped mid-way to her mouth and she stared at him. Hannah wondered if he was teasing, but she looked for a trace of humour or irony in his expression and found none. He was dead serious. Was he thinking it might be a good opportunity to get things out in the open after all?

'I… um…' Gina stuttered.

'I'd really like it,' Ross insisted.

'You've changed your tune,' Briony commented.

'Like you said, it'd be good to have some different company for a few hours.'

Hannah thought she was beginning to see his plan. It seemed that Gina finally got it too. 'Not next Sunday, but the one after might be okay. And you really want me to bring Jess?'

'Why not?' Ross said cheerfully. 'Like mum says, we should get to know you both better if you're moving to the area.'

Hannah took a great gulp of her tea so that she wouldn't have to add anything. This charade was getting out of hand, and it didn't seem very wise to Hannah. If Gina and Ross were planning to come clean at this lunch, things were about to get very interesting.

Briony turned to Hannah. 'You could bring your young man.'

It was Hannah's turn to choke. 'I could?' she croaked as a rush of hot tea stung her nasal cavity and tears sprang to her eyes.

'Mitchell, isn't it?'

'I… erm…' Hannah aimed a thinly disguised glare at Gina, who gave a confused shrug. Who had told Briony about Mitchell? Gossip always travelled fast, but Hannah was beginning to wonder why she was so worried about keeping it a secret, when Briony didn't seem to be too disapproving.

'I'll ask him if he's free,' Hannah said, quickly deciding that she'd have to discuss all this with Gina before she did anything.

'Well, let's call that settled then,' Briony announced to the room. She looked as though she'd just won fattest marrow in the parish veg contest. 'Now…' She shook the teapot. 'Who'd like a top up?'

Hannah glanced across at Gina. It didn't look as if they were going to wriggle out of this, and she could see by the look of thinly veiled despair on her face that Gina silently agreed.

*

The chair had been a steal from a car boot sale. It was shortly after Jason had left and she had probably been bored, or miserable, or lonely, or all three, and the sale was a place full of noise and bustle and life where she could forget herself for an hour and recall that there was still a huge world around her. She'd spotted the chair, standing in a sorry pile of junk, and her creative soul could see the beauty beneath the grime. In a funny way, now that she thought about it, perhaps she had fallen for it because it was a bit like her – the hope that she could be gorgeous and useful again with the right kind of love. She had brought the chair home, tied awkwardly to her car roof. Soon after, she had chosen paint to cover the flaking varnish, mottled with years of wear and damp storage, and picked out just the right fabric to reupholster the seat; but, somehow, life had got in the way, and everything was still sitting in her shed, gathering dust and waiting.

Now she had Mitchell, and perhaps it was time her chair got its happy ending too.

Rolling up her sleeves, Hannah began moving her other junk to pull it out. She set it in a specially cleared space where the paints and brushes sat on a dust sheet spread over the floor. This was time she had promised herself, where she could lose herself completely in a pursuit that was only about the pleasure she got from being creative.

Flicking the CD player on, she smiled as the first notes of *Mamma Mia* began to fill the shed. No sisters, no nieces, no men, no drama – nothing short of a giant comet hurtling to earth was going to disturb her until the chair was painted.

*

Two hours later, she was wiping her hands on a rag as she stood back to appraise her handiwork. The chair had gone from a sorry looking specimen, with scuffed varnish the colour and consistency of burnt treacle, to a beautiful chalky finish the shade of new parchment. Along with the blue and cream pastoral fabric she had chosen, and once the paintwork had been subtly distressed and waxed, it would be good enough to sit in any boutique in any town.

Just as she was clamping the lid back onto the unused paint in the pot, her mobile phone buzzed. Wandering over to the shelf she had left it on, she let out a groan as she caught sight of the display.

Chris.

She was going to have to talk to him sooner rather than later; her subtle tactic of ignoring him in the forlorn hope he would give up and go away wasn't working. If she didn't answer the phone now he'd probably turn up at her house anyway since he didn't seem to let a formality like an actual invitation get in the way. With a sigh, she swiped the screen to take the call.

'Hey, Chris,' she said in her brightest voice, 'How's it going?'

'Hannah… I hope you don't mind but you haven't called and well… I wondered if you still wanted that second date…'

Hannah grimaced. *Deep breath. Just tell him.* 'Chris. I'm sorry but I need to come clean about something. I'm afraid there isn't going to be a second date. You see, I didn't plan this but… I kind of met someone…'

There was silence at the other end of the line.

'Mitchell Bond?' he eventually asked in a quiet voice.

'How did you –?'

'News travels fast in these parts. And like you said yourself when we went out for that drink, there aren't that many property developers around Millrise. I had hoped the gossip was wrong, but I guess I'm to be disappointed.'

Hannah chewed her lip. They'd only been on one date and he really had no right to be upset that she had met someone else, but she still felt like a prize bitch. 'I'm so sorry you had to find out like that. I should have told you before. I wanted to but…' What could she say? There was no excuse for keeping him in the dark apart from one that didn't show her or Gina in a very good light.

'It's okay,' Chris said, 'I understand perfectly.'

'No you don't. I liked you and we got on well, and if things had been different… But Mitchell… well, I can't explain it, and I know that doesn't make you feel any happier about the situation but I have nothing else to offer. He was just sort of there at the right moment and we ended up together without really meaning to. You're a lovely guy and I'm so sorry to do this to you.' Hannah drew a deep breath. She had given him the best and only explanation she had and whatever he did or said now she probably deserved.

'I suppose it could be worse. You could have told me you've just discovered you're a lesbian.'

Hannah could hear the smile in his voice and suddenly and unexpectedly they were both laughing. She realised just how decent a guy

Chris was, and it made her wonder how different things might have been if she hadn't met Mitchell.

'I really am sorry...' Hannah felt she could never say that word enough. She wanted to say it again and again for the next week, just so he knew that she truly was.

'You don't need to be sorry. But just one thing... I don't want to rain on your parade but be careful with him.'

Hannah frowned. 'With Mitchell?'

'I don't know how he is with you but as a businessman he's a total bastard.'

Mitchell, a bastard? That didn't sound like the sweet, earnest, at times vulnerable man she knew. 'Are we talking about the same person here?'

'Bond Construction. That's him. He used to be alright, when he first got going, but since he's made a few bob and a name for himself, things have changed. Lately his company have pulled some pretty shitty stunts. Like greasing the palms of people who matter when chasing tender for the local authorities so that no one else is even in the running. That doesn't particularly affect me, but there are plenty of others unhappy about it. And now they've started moving in on the residential side of things.'

'They don't do houses,' Hannah said, more certain now that Chris must be mistaken.

'That's what he says. But the last few auctions I've been to the guy who works for him has been buying up all the best houses before anyone else has a chance and outbidding no matter how much it takes.'

'It's not illegal to outbid someone at auction.'

'No, it's not. But if Bond Construction don't do houses, why are they buying them so aggressively? It's almost like a deliberate tactic to drive out any competition that might threaten the future of the business in the area, no matter what the cost. If I can't buy properties at a reasonable rate, how can I turn a profit and keep expanding my own business?'

'It makes business sense to me.'

'Maybe, but that doesn't make it right. Competition and free trade – isn't that the basis of our entire economy? It's good for us, and what he's doing is wrong, whether it makes business sense or not. He doesn't even care about residential properties.'

Hannah was thoughtful for a moment. Even though she had defended Mitchell, she knew in her heart that Chris was right. It was a dirty trick to play if it were true. 'You didn't see Mitchell himself buying the houses?'

'No. It was that guy who runs the company with him.'

'Graham?'

'Yeah, that's him. But I don't see that it matters who did the bidding; it was still the same pot of money bankrolling it all, and that's Bond's.'

In a dark and dusty part of Hannah's brain, pieces of the puzzle were beginning to slot into place. Some were still missing, but the picture that was forming was far from pretty. What if Mitchell was bankrolling the purchase of all these houses but didn't know about it? He was barely in the office these days, and Hannah had never been comfortable with the amount of trust he was placing in Graham. Was this the reason Graham was so keen to make sure Mitchell did stay away from the office? Was he keeping Mitchell out of the picture so that he could siphon off company funds for his own private venture? How far was he going to go – until Mitchell had nothing left and Graham had a small empire of his own? And where did Martine fit in? Hannah was still convinced that the adulterer whose name she refused to give Mitchell was Graham, and if that was the case, did she know about Graham's dealings?

'Chris…' she began slowly, 'I know I have no right to ask you, but do you think you could find out more?'

'What do you mean?'

'About the houses. What's happening to them after they're bought at auction, are they sold straight on, developed first or rented out? Who officially owns them?'

'I can do better than that,' Chris replied. 'One of them happens to be on the same street as the house your sister is buying from me. There's a board up already. All you have to do is call up *Little Castles*, the estate agents, and pretend you want to buy it. You'll soon find out who the vendor is.'

'That's not a bad idea.' Graham would know her, of course, if it had anything to do with him, but he wouldn't know Gina. And if it turned out to be Mitchell himself then Gina had a perfectly valid excuse for looking at the house; although the idea of Mitchell being knowingly involved wasn't a happy thought. He had once offered to find Gina a house, but he certainly hadn't told her that he already owned some. If her theory was right – and it was an iceberg of an assumption – and Graham *was* fiddling the books to buy his own houses to sell on, it was a dangerous game to play by anyone's standards, even for the man she had never formally met but trusted less and less by the day.

Swiftly, Hannah pieced together the beginnings of a plan. She couldn't tell Mitchell any of what she had learned until she could be sure of the facts. If it turned out that Graham was acting alone, then she still didn't know enough about his intentions, and Mitchell trusted him too much to believe it without hard evidence. First, she'd subtly check with Mitchell that he hadn't actually decide to move into the housing market, and then, if the answer was what she suspected it would be, she'd get Gina to go and pretend she wanted to buy the house.

'Why do you need to know?' Chris asked, breaking into her thoughts.

'Something doesn't sit right with me, that's all. I can't tell you what it is because I might be wrong.'

'I think you probably should. This is my livelihood at stake and I'd appreciate the heads-up.'

'I don't want to get someone in trouble if what I think doesn't turn out to be true, though.'

'You have suspicions about Graham Bent?'

'Is that his name?' Hannah asked, almost snorting at its aptness.

'Yeah,' Chris laughed, in spite of the tone of the conversation. 'Imagine if he got control of half the company, they'd have to be called Bond and Bent Construction. Would you ask them to build a property for you?'

'Probably not,' Hannah smiled.

'So, am I right?' Chris insisted.

'I can't say. I'm sorry.'

'If I discover anything more, will you tell me then? After all, I'd probably have worked it out for myself anyway.'

'Of course. It's the least I can do.'

*

The warm air of the coffee shop was sweet with nutmeg and cinnamon and freshly ground coffee. Hannah kicked off her shoes and tucked her legs beneath her as she settled into the vast leather armchair across from Gina's. She cupped her mug in her hands as Gina shrugged off her jacket and flicked a business card onto the table between them. Hannah reached for it.

Nigel Santiago, estate agent
Little Castles

'Nice work.'

'I thought so. I told him I loved the house, and I felt rather sorry for him. He almost did a victory dance. We're going to really screw up his targets this month.'

Hannah shrugged as she put the card back onto the table.

'I've got another appointment tomorrow at the estate agent's office. I said I wanted more information. He probably wants to show me a ton more houses or make sure he pins me down to that one,' Gina continued.

'Don't forget this is only a front,' Hannah frowned. 'We told Chris you were buying that house and you absolutely can't back out now; he'd hate us forever.'

'It wouldn't hurt to look at a few more though, would it?'

'Why?'

'I like looking around other people's houses.'

'Hmmmm… So did you get any actual gen on our house – the one we're supposed to be checking out?'

'Of course!' Gina replied, looking slightly offended. 'Honestly, what do you take me for?'

'And?'

'The vendor is one Mr G. Bent.'

Hannah's face split into a huge grin. Not that Mitchell being ripped off was anything to smile about, but it was beginning to look like her hunch was right. 'I can't believe you got that so quickly.'

'I can be persuasive when I want to; don't forget I work in sales myself. But you still have to prove that he used Mitchell's money to buy the house in the first place. You're only guessing by what Chris has told you.'

'That bit can wait. We just need to find out how many of these houses he's bought at auction and then tell Mitchell everything. It's up to him then to talk to Graham and get to the bottom of it.'

'Do you still think the ice queen is in on it too?'

'I'm certain that's why they've been trying to manipulate Mitchell. It must have been a dream come true when he lost his memory. I think that's why she didn't want him to leave her too: while he was still living with her in Chapeldown she could keep an eye on him and keep him away from the office by filling his head full of shit. She's a GP and he'd trust her to give him good advice. It must have screwed things right up when he got his memory back.'

'You still don't know they are having an affair,' Gina reminded her as she took a sip of her divine smelling pumpkin spiced latte. 'I agree with your hunches but you're putting a lot of faith in them and we could be completely wrong.'

'I think we could remedy that. Are you up for a little private detective work?'

'Are you kidding? When have I not been up for anything?'

'I want to try and catch them in the act.'

'That's a tall order. Are you going to shove a ladder up to the bedroom window and try to film them shagging?'

'Not quite that, but I am going to go and watch her house, see if I can get some photos.'

'Ooooh, it sounds like a cheesy seventies cop drama – I like it. But I should go. Martine knows you too well and if she catches you she's likely to turn nasty, GP or not.'

'She knows you too.'

'She's only seen me for a minute or two in a dark room when we went to the salsa night. She won't remember me.'

'I don't know…'

'It'll be fine. I'll blend into the background like some human spy/ chameleon weird creature thing.'

Hannah laughed as she set her cup down. 'I'd like to see you blend into any background, but perhaps it is a better idea.'

'We could go tonight. Why don't we take Trixie, walk her around Chapeldown and keep swinging past Martine's house?'

'What about the long range camera lens and the dirty mac?' Hannah asked. 'Don't you need a battered old Ford Cortina too, full of chip wrappers?'

'Very funny. We'll have to make do with my iPhone and clean black quilted jacket. Maybe Ross will come too, it would do him good to get out for a walk.'

'Really? Do you think Ross would approve of all this?'

'I think he'd be on the side of what's right.'

'That's a bit of a grey area at the moment… Besides, it would mean whipping him out from under Briony's over-protective nose.'

Gina let out a frustrated sigh. 'Sunday. D-Day. It can't come soon enough as far as I'm concerned; then again, I don't want it to come at all. I wish it was all just out in the open and less complicated than it is now. It would be lovely to do a simple thing like go to the pub and hold hands over a pint without opening a whole can of nasty worms.'

'I know. I feel for you. Stick it out, though. You can tell his parents on Sunday.'

'They're not going to like it.'

'They might surprise you. They might not feel it's the best match at first, but they want what makes Ross happy, and if that's you then I'm sure they'll get used to the idea.'

'Do you really think that?'

'Yes,' Hannah lied.

Gina was silent for a moment. 'Okay,' she finally decided.

'So how are we going to catch Martine and Graham out? They're hardly going to shag on the lawn for us, are they?'

Gina sipped her latte as she stared into space. 'Maybe they don't need to,' she began slowly. 'Maybe we can find a way to get them to come out of the house *in flagrante*, as it were.'

Hannah raised her eyebrows. 'Go on then, Columbo. How?'

'Shhhh, I'm thinking about that bit.'

'Could you think a bit faster? The suspense is killing me.'

A slow smile spread over Gina's face. 'I think I've got it.'

*

Normal people didn't do things like this. Why had Hannah let Gina persuade her that this was a sensible idea? Not to mention that now the sun had gone down, the car was absolutely freezing.

'God, this is a boring place,' Gina said. 'Village of the well-heeled damned. Nobody is out doing anything remotely antisocial or unrespectable. It's all *good evenings* and smug smiles.'

'So you don't fancy living here?' Hannah grinned.

'What do you think?'

'And he hasn't been anywhere near yet,' Hannah said, diverting the subject back to what they had come to do. 'I don't think he's coming tonight.'

'Give him a bit more time, it's early yet.'

'I'm freezing.'

'You want to catch them, don't you?'

'Yes, but –'

'And it was your idea to do a little snooping.'

'I know but –'

'Stop moaning then.'

'All I'm saying is can't I run the engine and have the heaters on?'

'Draw more attention to your car?'

'My car isn't *that* bad.'

'Hannah, your car can be seen from space and that's not due to its size.'

'Rude!' She let out a sigh.

'Shhhh!' Gina hissed. 'I think someone's coming.'

Hannah watched, subconsciously sliding down the seat to make herself as invisible as possible, as a car pulled into Martine's drive. Moments later, Graham emerged from the driver's side of his black BMW and strode up to the house. He pulled a key from his pocket and let himself in. *So, Mr Bent...* Hannah thought... *pretty cosy for a casual visitor. None of my friends or acquaintances have their own front door key to my house.* But she still didn't know exactly what it signified.

The front door slammed behind him.

'That's him?' Gina asked.

'Yeah.'

'Well, I wouldn't go there but there's no accounting for taste.'

'Believe me, I think they're probably well suited.'

'So, what do you wanna do?'

'We might as well go with the original plan now he's here. She's definitely in there because we saw the lights on earlier. It'd be daft not to bother...' Hannah tried to ignore the vague sense of misgiving that was fluttering around in her stomach.

'Right. So we wait?'

'We wait. I've no idea how long for. I hadn't really thought about that bit.'

'I'm not sure we've really thought about any of it,' Gina retorted. 'But when did that ever stop us making tits of ourselves?'

'I suppose it is kind of funny.' Hannah smiled. 'Also extremely stupid. You know what, though, I could murder a bag of chips right now.'

'What about the stake out?' Gina asked.

'Hold on there, Cagney, I think you're getting a bit carried away with all this. Let's just pull my *cheese on wheels* up somewhere out of sight of the Hubble telescope and eat our box of police issue donuts while they get warmed up in the house.'

Gina laughed. 'No, we can't. What if either of them leaves and we miss it?'

'Ugh,' Hannah said, patting herself around the arms to try and get warm, 'next time I suggest something this daft, please slap me.'

'That's a very tempting offer. Can I slap you retrospectively now?'

'Shut up!' Hannah tried to frown but it turned into a grin. She looked back at the house. An amber glow was coming from the downstairs windows, but the upper floors were in darkness. Not that it meant anything for sure – there were no accepted rules about where intimacy took place and it might be that they had decided to get down and dirty on the sofa as soon as he'd walked in. But then she saw a shadow at the blinds and, sliding down the seat, ducked out of sight. As she peered over the edge of the car window again, she saw them closed, the light immediately muted to glimmering pencil stripes. She couldn't be sure, but it was as good idea as any to give them a bit of time. She turned to Gina. 'Do you think we can at least get that flask of hot chocolate out now, as you've insisted I wait until I'm almost frozen to death?'

*

An hour had passed and the windows of the car dripped with condensation from their breath and the steam from the hot chocolate. Hannah was warmed enough to feel human again. It was almost March, but winter still clung on so that it felt as cold as it had been in January. At least, it did when you'd spent an hour in a cold, damp car.

'I feel like a new woman.' Gina smacked her lips as she handed her empty cup to Hannah, who stuffed it with kitchen roll and wrapped it in a spare plastic bag until she could wash it at home.

Hannah blew out a long breath. 'Do you think we've given them enough time to get jiggy? Time to move on to phase two now?'

Gina shot her a look. 'You know we don't have to do this? We could go home now. You'd be lovely and warm and I'll buy you chips on the way.'

'But we wouldn't know the truth.'

'We know the truth. But Mitchell doesn't. He'll only have your word for it.'

Hannah chewed on her lip as she gazed into the blackness beyond the windscreen. 'That should be enough, though, shouldn't it? So why do I feel the need to go to all this trouble to prove it to him? I should tell him and that should be enough.'

'Because of your guilt complex.'

'My what now?'

'You feel you have something you're not entitled to – happiness with Mitchell. So you need to justify it somehow, by proving what an undeserving woman Martine is. Which is not really how you are because you would never do that deliberately, even though you'd want to. But you have to in order to make yourself okay with Mitchell.' Gina gave her a bright smile. 'It's quite simple.'

Hannah cocked an eyebrow at her. 'I know you had words coming out of your mouth just now but how they were supposed to fit together is anyone's guess.'

'Of course, you're far too close to the situation to see it objectively.'

'I'll take your word for that…' Hannah shook herself. 'So, are we going out there or not?'

'Yes.' Gina shoved the passenger door open. 'Not that we have a hope in hell of succeeding, but let's do it.'

Together they made their way to Martine's house, trying to look as inconspicuous as possible. As previously agreed, Hannah positioned herself behind a sprawling rhododendron bush at the outskirts of Martine's driveway and got her phone camera ready. She was hidden but could clearly see the front door. With a bit of luck, Gina would raise the alarm as they had planned, Martine or Graham (ideally both) would come dashing out in a state that would incriminate them, and in the chaos, Hannah would snap a quick photo and leg it with the evidence. They'd recognise her, of course, but if she got away fast enough she'd be able to show it to Mitchell before the consequences of her spying could catch up with her and the deed would be done.

With a brief and silent nod, Gina strode up the pathway to Martine's front door and swung into action. She hammered at Martine's door and started yelling, 'HEY, HEY! YOU INSIDE…GET OUT, QUICK!'

A strange, echoing silence followed, all the more eerie for the ripple it seemed to leave in the fabric of the night air. Gina thumped on the door again.

'FIRE! YOUR PLACE IS ON FIRE!'

This time, after another brief pause, the front door opened and an enraged Martine shouted back.

'What the bloody hell do you think you're playing at?'

'Are you deaf?' Gina cried. 'I'm telling you that your place is on fire and you're standing here demanding a written report or something!'

'I don't smell smoke,' Martine returned haughtily. 'I'm quite sure that if my house was on fire I'd know about it. Now go away!'

Most people would have given up at this point, but Gina had developed the sort of blind determination to succeed that athletes often cited for their gold medals. 'There are flames!' she insisted. 'Coming from the roof! If you don't believe me come out and see!'

She'll bloody well set the place on fire herself in a minute if Martine doesn't come out, Hannah thought.

'No!' Martine replied, not a bit rattled. 'If you don't get off my property right now I will call the police.'

'But your house is on fire!' Gina shouted.

Martine shouted back down her hallway. 'Graham! Call the police!'

Whether he had heard or not Hannah couldn't know, but Gina didn't miss a beat, delivering her *piece de resistance*, an Oscar winning performance if ever she'd heard one.

'My God!' she yelped. 'You have someone in there with you! You're just going to let him burn while you stand and argue with me!'

She pushed past Martine to shout at Graham in the house, 'Sir! You need to get out of the house right now, it's on fire!'

It could have been that Graham was more gullible than Martine, or that he had a shorter fuse. Either way, moments later he joined the fray.

'What the hell!' he boomed. 'What the fuck are you talking about?'

'Come and see, come and see,' Gina urged, moving towards Hannah.

'No!' he growled. 'Get away from here you mad cow!'

Gina shouted, 'IT'S NOW OR NEVER, HAN!' and Hannah took her cue.

Dashing from her hiding place, she took in Martine standing in a dressing gown, make up thick and vampish, hair that must have begun the evening in an elegant updo now dishevelled, and an expression on her face that bordered on psychopathic. Graham was still standing in the shadows of the doorway, so Hannah couldn't quite figure out what state of undress he was in. The way Martine looked would perhaps be evidence enough, so she took her chance, aimed her phone to get them both in shot as best she could and hit the camera button. The flash popped, blasting the gloom into daylight, just for a second.

'You little bitch!' Martine hissed and, forsaking any thought of Gina, charged down the path after Hannah, who was already running.

Hannah could only hope that Gina was following, and hoped her sister could run faster than Martine, because it might get very sticky if Martine made it back to Hannah's car before Gina did. She glanced back to see where Gina was, and clapped eyes on Graham instead, also thundering down the driveway in pursuit.

Around the corner Hannah fumbled with her car key before she finally managed to get the door open and throw herself in. Just as Martine arrived, close behind, she popped the lock down to stop her getting in. Martine hammered at the window as Hannah tried to catch her breath and calm her thundering heart. She looked past Martine for any sign of Gina, but her sister was nowhere to be seen. Graham, it seemed, had come to his senses and looped his arms around Martine to lead her back to the house so that they didn't make any more of a scene than they already had. Hannah turned the key and the engine roared into life. Never had she been so relieved to hear it start first time.

A few streets on and Hannah spotted Gina striding along the pavement, head down and making hasty progress. Hannah pulled alongside her and wound the window down.

'Need a lift?' She grinned.

Gina's face split into a grin too. She skipped around to the passenger side and slid in. 'That was brilliant!' she said. 'Best fun I've had in ages!'

Hannah was still shaking, but she was also buzzing, and she didn't really know why. She had never felt as alive as she did at that moment.

It was the adrenaline, perhaps, the sense of rebellion she had suppressed for so long that had suddenly been set free. Whatever it was, it made her feel like she could run a marathon, or cliff dive, or fight an army.

'I can't believe they ran out!' Gina laughed.

'Me neither. You must have really riled him. God, your performance was amazing. Even I was convinced the house was burning down!'

'Did you get a photo?'

'I think so. It wasn't as clear as I'd have liked but I think it's enough.'

'I'd call that a good night's work then.' Gina smiled, settling back into her seat and closing her eyes.

'You're tired,' Hannah said, the mood sobering a little now.

'Yeah. It's all this running backwards and forwards from Birmingham taking its toll. I don't think I can do it for much longer at this pace.'

'I can imagine. It will be easier once you're back here, and it looks as though that won't be too much longer. Both you and Jess can settle into a new routine and things will be back to normal.'

'At least Chris is still happy to sell me that house as we agreed. It's very sweet of him and a great load off my mind.'

'Yes, considering that he could have been a lot more upset about Mitchell, it is good of him. I still don't know exactly what I think about the things he told me about Mitchell, though.'

'I thought we'd decided that was all Graham's doing?'

'But what if Mitchell isn't quite the man I think he is? I haven't known him long and people show more of themselves over time.'

'What is your gut instinct telling you?'

'We're not relying on my unreliable heart again, are we?' Hannah gave a wry smile.

'Why can't you trust it?'

Hannah shrugged.

Gina opened her eyes and looked across at her. 'Trust it. If you feel he's a good man, then I don't think you'll be far wrong.'

Hannah was silent as she mulled over Gina's words. In her heart she felt it, but could she trust her heart? He was married to Martine, and she was about as horrible and ruthless as it got. Did birds of a feather flock together? Had he been drawn to Martine because he was really a little bit like her? Or had he been duped too? And Hannah had trusted Jason, but look where that had got her. She wanted to be comforted by Gina's assertion, but it wasn't as simple as that.

*

It wasn't easy, waiting. Not when she had so much to tell him. Hannah paced the floor of her living room, wandering into the front room to peer out of the window, and then back again. Checking her hair in the mirror for the fifth time, she let out a sigh. He had said twenty minutes, but that was half an hour ago. Where was he? Had Martine got there first? Had she told him her version of events? On reflection, Hannah realised that the incident at Martine's house that night wasn't going to show her in a very good light. So while it had been exhilarating at first, she was now filled with a sense of doubt and even dread over the outcome of her little shenanigan.

Gina had gone off to take Trixie out for George. To calm her down, she had said, denying that she intended to walk anywhere near Holly Farm. Hannah knew her better than that, but whatever plan she had concocted with Ross was none of Hannah's business. By Sunday, it would all be out in the open anyway, for better or worse. Once it was, it had to be less complicated and grubby than Hannah's situation felt right now. Although the intention behind it was good, what she was about to do wasn't very nice. At least, it didn't feel like the sort of thing that nice people did.

There was a knock and she ran for the door. Mitchell stood on the step, but there was no smile to greet her.

'Hey,' she said, but he looked at her as though he didn't know her. Martine had obviously wasted no time putting him in the picture – at least, the bits that suited her. Of course she had, because she had her back against the wall and she had to come out fighting whether she survived or not.

'Hannah…' he said, his voice low and urgent as he stepped in. 'What have you done?'

'Martine's called you.' It was a statement, because Hannah already knew the answer and he knew she did. She was beginning to wish that she'd told him what had happened, but it hadn't seemed like the sort of thing to share over the phone. It would have been more painful, but a ruthless text including a photo might have been safer. Now *she* had *her* back against the wall, already in the wrong before they had spoken a word to each other.

'She told me you and your sister have been dicking around her house like a couple of adolescents.'

'And did she tell you that Graham was in there with her?'

'He's often there. He's been a support for Martine as much as he has for me through all this.'

'Damn right there.'

'What does that mean?'

'Look, I don't know what Martine's told you, but don't you think it's odd that he's there so often? Hasn't it once struck you that something else might be going on?'

'What are you trying to say, Hannah? He's been a good friend to us both over the years.'

Hannah rolled her eyes. 'Jesus, Mitchell, open your bloody eyes! They came to the door tonight wearing dressing gowns and little else. Your good friend has been having sex with your wife!'

Mitchell clenched his jaw. Hannah's eyes flicked to his hands curling into fists at his sides. He stared at her.

'Say something,' she demanded. She'd gone too far and she knew it but she didn't care anymore. It was time he accepted what she knew he had been trying to deny. 'Say something,' she repeated. 'Try and defend them now.'

He took a deep breath and ran a hand through his hair. 'Why are you doing this?'

'Doing what?'

'This…' He wafted his arms up and down her length. 'You and Martine! Why are you so hung up about what she's doing?'

'Martine admitted to having an affair; don't you want to know who it's with?'

'No…' He shook his head, and his body suddenly seemed to sag. His tone was quieter now, less assured. 'It wouldn't be Graham.'

Hannah hated what she did next. She unlocked her phone and held it up. 'I'm sorry,' she said quietly. The picture of the man Mitchell had called friend, standing with his wife in the doorway of his marital home, must be cruelly painful.

'There could be an explanation for that,' Mitchell replied, but he sounded as unconvinced as Hannah was. He looked as though he'd had all the air punched out of him and then been kicked in the balls just to make sure he stayed down. He let out a huge sigh and looked up at her. 'Why?'

Hannah didn't know what to say. She felt like the worst person who'd ever lived. Why had she found this exhilarating, even for a second? 'I didn't mean to cause any harm; I just wanted –'

'I didn't mean you,' he cut in. 'Why did *they* do this to me? I never did anything but treat him as a friend and equal; I showed him respect,

taught him all I knew about the business, took him into my confidence…'
He raised his eyes to the ceiling, and Hannah wondered if the emotion
might just choke him. God knew she was barely keeping the tears at bay.
'God!' he groaned, 'I told him everything about me and Martine – our
problems, my fears… how they must have laughed. Mitchell Bond,
the stupid, trusting twat. They must have thought I was such a dick.'

The first tear slid down her cheek, and Hannah wiped it hastily
away. Mitchell was the one who'd been hurt here, and she had no right
to cry. 'I'm sorry you had to find out like this,' she said.

'I suppose a bit of me knew,' he said. 'I didn't want to believe it.
In a way his betrayal hurts more than Martine's and I didn't have the
strength to face it. I always knew that, deep down, she had the capacity
to be that cruel, even when we were first married, but I loved her and I
was enthralled by her – she was so glamorous, so driven, so intelligent
and beautiful – totally out of my league and yet she chose me and I
couldn't believe my luck. But Graham… I thought he was my friend.
I thought we were the same…'

He dropped into a seat. Hannah sat beside him and stared into
the fire. She wanted to reach for him, take him in her arms and kiss
him and tell him it would all be okay. But the void between them felt
vast and she couldn't reach across it. There was so much more of the
story to tell him, and he needed to hear it. But should it be now, hot
on the heels of this shock? And did he need to hear it from Hannah?
She felt sick at the thought of sharing the rest of Graham's betrayal,
but she knew that neither Graham nor Martine would come clean any
time soon. Mitchell had a right to know, and he needed to protect his
company, probably the only thing he had left now that meant anything
to him. Hannah had a duty to tell him, but also to choose carefully
how the story came out.

'There's something else, I'm afraid. Gina looked at a house today in Millrise. It was being sold by Graham.'

Mitchell looked at her but his eyes were vacant.

'I'm right in thinking that Bond Construction doesn't deal in residential properties, aren't I?'

'We never have and I doubt we ever will.'

'So it's not a new direction that the company's going in under Graham's leadership?'

Mitchell shook his head. 'I am still in charge, even if I'm not in the office; he would have had to run it past me and I'd have said no. I'm surprised Graham has got involved in anything like that; we always agreed that it was too much hassle for too little profit. That's why the company concentrated on bigger projects.'

'The vendor of this house was definitely Graham.'

Mitchell gave a vague shrug. 'I suppose he needs to make a little pocket money now to keep Martine in fur knickers,' he said in a dull voice. 'It's not really my concern what he does away from the company.'

'Only… he's selling more than one and I think he's buying them at auction *through* your company.'

Hannah waited. It was going to prise the wound open a little more, but she'd told him everything now and it was up to Mitchell to decide what to do next. It wasn't the way she had wanted to share this news and she'd have preferred to be certain she was right first, but her hand had been forced.

'Impossible,' he said. 'I'd know.'

'Not necessarily. You've trusted him to do so much that it's not such a stretch of the imagination, is it? He could easily be creaming off funds to buy places, and then sell on and pocket the profits before you'd even seen the money leave your account. I don't know whether the initial funds are going back into the pot each time, but even if it's not strictly illegal, or he's only borrowing it, it's still massively taking the piss.'

'Buying and selling houses is a lengthy process. He'd know that I'd find out before it all had time to go through.'

'Would you? Perhaps you wouldn't see anything going on unless you were looking for it? He's counting on your trust to play you.'

Mitchell was silent for a moment. Hannah could see his jaw working in the firelight; clenching and grinding as he mulled things over. 'It looks as if he's getting quite good at it,' he said finally.

'Do you believe me?'

'I don't know what to believe anymore. But I believe *in* you. I know that you wouldn't say any of this unless you had a damn good reason.'

'I hate being the one to tell you. It feels like I'm deliberately trying to screw you over and I swear I'm not.'

He reached for her and pulled her close, kissing the top of her head. 'Throughout all this you're the only person who hasn't been trying to screw me over. You're the only one who has truly cared for me.'

Hannah was moved by a rush of love for him, so strong, so fierce it burned. But her heart ached for his sadness. If she could have absorbed it all for him, taken it into her own heart and kept it there, she would have done without a second thought.

'What's next?' she asked.

'I need to go through the books to find out for sure what's going on.' He was quiet for a moment as he held her, breathing in the scent of her hair. Finally, he spoke again. 'Does he know that you know about the house? Does he know Gina? Who else knows? How on earth did you find out?'

'Whoa there. That's a lot of questions and none of them have simple answers. You might want me to open a bottle of something first.'

'I might. But right now I'd love it if you could just hold me. I think I could do with some of your healing power.'

'I doubt that. I seem to get people in a tizzy mostly, but not much else.'

'I don't think you realise the effect you have on people. You're the kindest, sweetest, most genuine soul I know. I'm just sorry that I didn't meet you years ago; we could have had a great life together.'

'You make it sound like you're about to croak,' Hannah smiled. 'We can still have a great life together. Why don't we start right now?'

*

The Sunday had arrived. Gina had taken to calling it this, although the way it dominated their thoughts, it hardly needed accentuating. Right now, Gina was in the passenger seat of Hannah's car, trying valiantly to listen to Hannah fill her in on the latest developments in the Martine/Graham/Mitchell saga, but Hannah had to wonder just how much of it was going in.

'Mitchell had his accountant go through everything and he found the discrepancies without much effort,' she continued. 'I think Mitchell was more amazed by Graham's arrogance than the actual crime; he didn't even try to hide the transactions, he just assumed that Mitchell was so out of the loop he wouldn't find out…' Hannah glanced across at her sister. 'Gina?'

'Yeah, I'm listening.'

'I'm sorry. I bet you're stressed enough without listening to me blab on.'

'It's fine. It's helping to take my mind off how much Briony is going to hate me by five o'clock.'

'She won't hate you.' Hannah gave her an encouraging smile. 'She's half in love with you already after our last visit. They might be a bit surprised at first but I think they'll be fine.'

'I hope you're right. So go on, tell me about the rest of what Mitchell found out.'

'That's it, really. He confronted Graham about it, who tried to deny it all, of course, but then shat himself when Mitchell told him he had evidence. Obviously Mitchell told him he knew about the affair with Martine too. Graham was a bit cockier about that, until Mitchell reminded him of the photo I took that night we caught them out. So I guess he's well and truly screwed.'

'Is Mitchell going to get the police involved? Graham has basically committed fraud.'

'I don't think he's worked it all out yet. I think he's still getting his head around how the two people he trusted most in the world could do this to him.'

'What now then?'

'He'll cite Graham in divorce proceedings and then he'll be free of them both for good.'

'Leaving you happy ever after,' Gina smiled.

'I don't know about that.'

'Why not?'

'Because this is me we're talking about.' She reached over and plucked her handbag from the back seat. 'Come on. Let's go in and get *your* happy ending. At least one of us deserves it.'

'I'd be more certain of that if Jess had come today,' Gina replied. 'It would have got all the introductions out of the way in one go.'

'She's probably too embarrassed to face Ross right now, and maybe it's for the best anyway, just until the dust settles.'

'No Mitchell either – Briony won't be impressed.'

'No,' Hannah laughed. 'But his head's not really in the zone either. It's not every day your business partner gets caught rogering your wife and then helping himself to your fortune. I think I feel more relaxed without him too, especially when this lunch is really about you and Ross, not me and Mitchell. I'd only be worrying about him, instead of concentrating on you.'

'You don't need to worry about me… I don't think, anyway… Is there anything to worry about?'

Hannah laughed. 'No, I don't think there is.'

They walked in step up the drive, arms linked, almost as if they were leaning on each other for support. Hannah reached for the door knocker but the door flew open and Briony stood beaming on the threshold.

'You're here! I'm so glad you could come!'

'We are,' Hannah said with a slightly bemused smile. 'We wouldn't have missed it for anything.' She never failed to be surprised by Briony's enthusiasm for company of any kind. If there were Oscars for sociability, she would undoubtedly have won at least a dozen.

'Come in, come in,' Briony urged them over the threshold and into the kitchen, warm with the smell of roast chicken and sweet baking vegetables. Paul and Ross were already at the table, Paul looking like a prisoner in his own clothes, wearing a stiff shirt that Briony had clearly bullied him into for the occasion. Ross looked rather more relaxed, despite the circumstances, and handsome in a soft blue and red checked shirt, his sleeves rolled up to expose forearms sculpted from years of outdoor work. He broke into a broad grin as Gina's gaze met his. Her return smile was slightly less assured, and she smoothed an uncertain hand over her dress as Briony took her coat and asked Paul to hang it up with Hannah's.

'Your train down was okay?' Ross asked Gina.

'I'm getting so used to taking it these days that I should have my own permanent seat,' Gina smiled.

'All the more reason for you to move back to Millrise,' Briony replied.

'It is. I can't wait to get back here.'

'It won't be long now, with a bit of luck,' Hannah cut in, accepting a small glass of white wine from Briony. 'Thank you. I'm driving, so I'll make this last,' she added as she took a sip.

'I said I would drive.' Gina took the glass Briony offered to her with a grateful smile.

'No, it takes a rare and special skill to drive my car.'

'Having been in the engine I can vouch for that,' Ross laughed.

Hannah gave him an impish look. 'Hey, cheeky!'

Ross chuckled as Hannah sat down at the table. Gina sat next to her with Ross on the other side, and Hannah caught the furtive look of encouragement he offered her. It looked as though they were going ahead with their plan – the question was, when.

'So…' Briony turned to Hannah, 'your Mitchell couldn't make it?'

'He sends his apologies. He's got so much to do right now that he's swamped.'

'And your daughter couldn't come either?' Briony continued, looking at Gina now.

'Sadly, it's her dad's turn to have her this weekend and I'd completely forgotten that when you invited us. It's very difficult to change the weekends he has her and she must go because it can cause all sorts of problems if she doesn't – legal involvement and that sort of thing. I find it's best to keep everything running as smoothly as I can. Divorce can be a messy enough business as it is.' Gina took a gulp of her wine. Hannah imagined she was tempted to grab the bottle from Briony's hand and swig it straight back from that.

'But it's not Gina's fault… the divorce, I mean,' Hannah added, instinctively feeling the need to make things clear to the Hunters. She didn't want Briony to think her sister was the sort of woman who cast men aside as soon as she was bored with them.

'Well… I did initiate it, so technically it is down to me,' Gina elaborated, blushing, 'but I wasn't the wrongdoer.'

'Oh, I see. I suppose it must be very difficult,' Briony agreed with a sage nod, although their world was so ordered and ruled by traditional values that it was hard to imagine she'd encountered a messy divorce like Gina's first-hand before.

'Dinner shouldn't be long now,' Briony announced. As she said this, she bustled off to the stove.

Hannah turned to Ross. 'How are you feeling?'

'Loads better. I'm going to get back to work this week. I feel well enough and I'm going mad sitting around doing nothing.'

Paul patted a great hand on his son's shoulder. 'I'll have your back so you'll come to no harm.'

'He'd better not,' Briony called from across the room.

Paul leaned in to the table and lowered his voice. 'I wouldn't dare let anything happen with the dragon in charge, would I?'

'I heard that!' Briony shot back and both Paul and Ross burst out laughing. Gina and Hannah gave polite smiles, not quite sure whether they were entitled to laugh too.

The next hour was a happy one. Like all Briony's cooking, the lunch she had made for them was fantastic. The chicken was crisp on the outside – the skin spiced with a delicate paprika marinade – the meat tender and succulent. She'd served it with a mix of roast potatoes, sweet potatoes and butternut squash, with carrots and green beans from their kitchen garden. It was finished off with the best gravy Hannah had ever tasted.

While she tucked in with gusto, she looked across at Gina to see that her sister was politely doing her best, but not making much of a dent in her plate. She was probably too nervous to eat, although Ross clearly handled his nerves differently as he was shovelling his lunch in as though the apocalypse was imminent.

Hannah pushed her plate away and sat back in her chair, nursing her stomach. 'Briony, that was the most incredible lunch – thank you.'

Briony's smile was almost wide enough to fill the room. 'Wonderful! I hope you've left room for pudding, though.'

Hannah pulled a comical face. 'I might explode! Or the suspension will probably collapse when I get in the car later.'

'Don't worry,' Ross cut in with a cheeky grin, 'the tractor will just about hold you so you won't be stuck.'

'Ross!' Briony chided, but Hannah let out a giggle.

'I'm sure I could manage a bit in a little while.'

'What have we got, Mother?' Paul asked.

'Morello lattice tart and *crème anglaise*.'

'You mean pie made from squished up cherries the birds spat out last autumn and a tin of Tesco custard?' Ross asked. 'Honestly, Mum, trying to make out we're posh or something.'

'You're not too old for a smack,' Briony said with a pretend frown.

'I am too big though.'

Briony let out a mock sigh of exasperation. 'I pity the poor woman who ends up with you.'

The mood suddenly shifted, emotional tectonic plates wrenching apart, and Hannah knew that the time had come. Ross looked at Gina, and she gave a tiny nod.

'Mum…' he began, 'there's something that I… *we*… really need to tell you.'

The moment's pause felt like a lifetime, and everything in the kitchen seemed to stop. Briony exchanged a puzzled glance with Paul. Hannah wondered if she ought to make an excuse and leave the room, but she was glued to her seat, and almost felt that if she moved, the moment would be shattered and gone forever.

Gina's hand rested on the table. Ross covered it with his own and gave it a squeeze. 'Gina and I…' he continued in a steady voice, 'we're together.'

For the first time in Hannah's experience, there was no sound from Briony's open mouth.

'Together?' Paul repeated.

'Yes,' Ross said. He was calm, as composed as Hannah had ever seen him. Gina, on the other hand, looked as though she'd stopped breathing.

'You're a couple?' Briony finally managed.

'I'm sorry we didn't tell you before,' Ross said. 'We wanted to but it never felt like the right time.'

'How long has this been going on?'

Gina and Ross looked at each other before facing Briony again. 'A couple of months,' Ross said. 'Since the salsa night, really.'

'And you couldn't even tell me? I'm your mother!' Briony squeaked. 'All that time and you couldn't tell me?'

Hannah suddenly felt sick for both of them. They had known this was going to be hard, but it looked as though it was going to be worse than anyone had anticipated.

'Please don't be angry with Ross,' Gina cut in. 'It's my fault we kept it quiet. I thought you'd be upset and I didn't want to be the cause of that.'

'Why would we be upset?' Paul asked, genuine confusion on his face.

'Well… because of the age gap…' Gina replied.

Another heavy pause held the room hostage. But nobody – not Hannah, Gina or even Ross – could have predicted what happened next. Briony leapt from her chair and rushed around the table. She grabbed Gina by the shoulders, yanking her to her feet. Hannah's blood froze, but her fear quickly turned to shock as Briony pulled Gina into a fierce hug.

'Oh, you silly girl!' she cried. 'I can't believe you were scared to tell us!'

'We didn't know what you'd say,' Gina replied. Although it sounded more like, 'Fmee thidnth fnow fwat youfd thay,' muffled as it was by Briony's shoulder. Only her sister's eyes were visible, and Hannah could see that Gina was as shocked by the turn of events as she was.

Briony finally let go of Gina, who had begun to turn a worrying shade of puce. She turned to Ross. 'I thought there was a woman… Didn't I say there was a woman, Paul?'

Ross's dad nodded.

'You're happy?' Briony asked, turning back to Ross.

'God, Mum, yes!' Ross replied, although Hannah thought it might be the daftest question ever when the answer was so obvious.

'Then I couldn't be happier,' Briony announced, beaming at Gina. 'All I want for my son is that he's lucky enough to find someone who makes him happy, and I've seen enough of a change in him recently to guess that it must be down to you.'

Gina smiled, but she still looked a little shell-shocked. They'd spent so long fearing the worst that they hadn't really considered the alternative – that Briony and Paul might be okay with it.

Briony kissed Ross on the head. And then, as quickly as she had sprung around the table, she was back at the stove, preparing pudding as though nothing had happened. She hummed to herself. Hannah and Gina waited to see if Paul would add anything, but he simply nodded at Ross and said, 'Next time, lad, just tell us, eh?'

There were lots of questions over pudding: how and when they had got together, what their plans were, what Jess thought of it, how

Hannah had found out. They answered each one as best they could and Briony seemed satisfied with their responses. All this while they waded through enormous portions of cherry pie until, after a while, when the most pressing questions had been dealt with, the conversation drifted to safer topics.

'The vicar says he called on George Maynard on Thursday,' Briony commented as she filled up Paul's wine glass, 'and he didn't look very well at all – grey as a bowl of old dishwater, he said.'

Hannah thought back to the last time she had seen George. Life had got so hectic lately she couldn't quite remember when it had been.

'He's got nobody looking after him and I don't think he looks after himself very well,' Paul said.

'Poor George,' Briony agreed as she cleared away the bowls – miraculously empty in spite of everyone's protestations that they were too full to eat another thing. 'He was never the same after Hilda passed on. Let's send him a little plate of something to cheer him up; there's plenty left.'

'He certainly did look a bit under the weather when I saw him yesterday,' Paul agreed. 'I bet a plate of your chicken and potatoes would perk him right up.'

'I'll put some out for him and you can drop it in later on.'

'Why don't I go and take it for him now?' Hannah cut in. 'It would put my mind at rest to know how he is.'

Briony and Paul had taken the news well, but Hannah sensed that there was still a lot left for them all to discuss. She felt it would be better if she went alone to see George and gave them time to do that without her.

Gina seemed to understand what Hannah was up to and nodded. 'I don't mind waiting around here for a while if it's alright with Briony and Paul.'

'And there's no need for you to come back – I can easily drop Gina off at yours later on,' Ross added.

'Paul will take her,' Briony said, frowning at her son. 'You might be driving again but you're not supposed to be.'

'Oh, Mum, no one takes that six weeks stuff seriously. That's just for doctors to cover themselves.'

'They don't just pluck a figure out of the air. It's six weeks for a reason.'

'Well, I'll be driving this week whether they like it or not.'

Hannah and Gina exchanged a faint smile. Briony had surprised them by her ready acceptance of Gina but that didn't mean it was going to be plain sailing by any stretch.

'Right then,' Hannah said brightly. 'Whenever you're ready, Briony, I'll take a plate over for George.'

*

The evening was chilly as Hannah left the warm cocoon of Briony's kitchen, but every night that week Hannah had seen it grow lighter by degrees. Spring was racing towards Holly Way and for Hannah it couldn't come quickly enough. While the winter had been an eventful one, she longed for warmer, longer days, with perhaps a little more calm too. And the way things seemed to be working out, the summer might just be one of the best she could remember for a very long time.

With great care, Hannah set the covered dish containing George's roast dinner on the passenger seat of her car and secured it with the dishcloths Briony had given her to keep it safe before she started the engine. The heaters were still up full from the journey to Holly Farm, and they blasted cold air into Hannah's face. She wrapped her arms around herself as she waited for it to warm up. As she sat with the engine idling, she took the opportunity to send a quick text to Mitchell to let him know that she was leaving Holly Farm and that things had gone well. His reply was immediate:

Does that mean I get to come over and see you?

Hannah smiled to herself as she sent a brief explanation that she had to run an errand first. Then she let go of the handbrake and pulled out of the Hunters' gravel driveway.

*

George's house was in darkness, apart from a dim glow edging the curtains of a downstairs room. As Hannah knocked at the door she heard Trixie's hoarse yap and the sound of her claws as she skidded up and down George's Minton-tiled hallway. Hannah waited, like she always did, to give George the extra bit of time he needed these days to get to the door. But when five minutes had passed and there was still no answer, she knocked again.

Her expectant smile had long since faded when George failed to respond a second time. She called through the letterbox, her own voice drifting eerily back to her through the still evening. There was no answering call, but Trixie's barking became more frantic. Hannah could see nothing through the letterbox and when she had clambered over George's borders to try and get a look into his front windows, one was in darkness and the other was obscured by curtains too thick to see anything through them at all.

She knew something was seriously wrong.

The first stars winked down from a frosted lilac sky as Hannah dialled Mitchell's number.

*

When Mitchell eventually drove up, Hannah was sitting on George's step, her knees pulled up tight and her arms wrapped around them as she gazed up at the sky. It was clear now, save for the thinnest ribbons of ochre cloud drifting across her vision and layers of stars scattered in every direction. It was strangely silent too. Trixie had stopped barking, though every so often Hannah could hear her snuffling on the other side of the door.

She jumped to her feet as Mitchell climbed out of his car.

'Are you okay?' he asked, his expression tense as he strode up the path towards her.

'God, yes, I'm absolutely fine. But I'm very worried about George.'

'So, what's happened?'

'Nothing. I mean, I've knocked on the door a ton of times. Trixie is going mad in there and I can see a light on but George isn't answering the door and I can't see any sign of him. He could be out, but he rarely leaves Trixie and since Ross got beaten up, George has been even more reluctant to be out after dark. I just have the horrible feeling he's in trouble.'

Mitchell angled his head at the roadside. 'Is that his car?'

Hannah followed his gaze and nodded.

'So, what do you want to do?' Mitchell asked.

'I think the only thing we can do is break in.'

Mitchell was thoughtful for a moment. Then he fished out his wallet and flipped it open. 'It would be better if we didn't have to break any windows.'

Hannah threw him a questioning look.

'You don't grow up on the roughest estate in Millrise without picking up a few tricks,' he said, pulling a credit card from his wallet and flexing it.

There were far too many questions behind this statement, but now was definitely not the moment. She gave a brisk nod. 'Okay, let's get it over with.'

It was an old Yale lock, and it didn't take Mitchell long to pop it. A wall of dry heat blasted out as they pushed open the front door, Trixie yapping and dancing around their ankles in the hallway. Hannah bent to give her a fuss.

'Hey, hey… now then, girl, what's going on here?'

'GEORGE!' Mitchell shouted.

Silence.

Mitchell felt along the wall for the switch and the hallway was flooded with light. Hannah followed as he began to walk towards the sitting room door, and she almost skidded on a wet patch. It took a moment for her to realise that Trixie must have been forced to pee in the hall. 'Oh, you poor thing,' she whispered as Trixie looked up at her and wagged her tail regretfully, as if she was waiting for a telling off.

Everything was neat and ordered in the living room. The television flickered in the corner, the sound down low, as if George had been trying to watch but his heart hadn't really been in it. And George was in his favourite armchair, facing it, eyes closed.

'George?' Hannah whispered. Instinctively, she scooped Trixie into her arms.

Mitchell crossed quickly to the armchair. He pressed his fingers gently onto George's wrist. Then he turned to Hannah.

'I'm so sorry,' he said.

Hannah's world was blurred by tears as she buried her face in Trixie's fur.

*

Spring had issued a reminder to winter that it was time to go, and a gentle sun skimmed the windowsills of the kitchen at Holly Farm. The vast wooden table had been pushed up against a wall and was piled with savoury snacks, and a kitchen unit was stocked with various bottles of alcohol and soft drinks, while Briony fussed at the kettle for those who wanted something hot. Hannah stood and sipped the wine Briony had just handed her and cast her gaze around the black-clad gathering that filled the room. As she spotted a forlorn looking Trixie lying in a basket under the table, it was all she could do not to cry again. George's little dog had been living at Holly Farm for the past two weeks, but she still looked as lost as she had when she first arrived. It seemed it was going to take a long time for her to get used to being without her old owner.

'Penny for them…' Mitchell's voice broke in on Hannah's thoughts. She looked up at him and gave a watery smile.

'They're not even worth that.'

'Oh, I don't know. I wouldn't mind a peek to see what goes on in there.'

'You'd be disappointed. It's mostly what I'm going to have for tea and whether I've set the recorder for Coronation Street.'

Mitchell rubbed her arm. 'Are you okay?'

She nodded. 'Yes. I can't help feeling that I could somehow have prevented it, though.'

'You need to stop that. You couldn't have been there all the time and he wouldn't have wanted you to either. Besides, you aren't his only neighbour.'

'I know. But I ought to have called more often than I did. Especially in his last week.'

'He was a good age, Hannah, and he had a wonderful life surrounded by good people. That's a lot more than many of us get and if he could tell us now I'm sure he'd say he was thankful for it.'

Hannah was thoughtful for a moment. 'I suppose he's with Hilda now. Perhaps he's happier after all.'

'He must have loved her very much.'

'He did. They were devoted to each other. I wish I'd known her, but she died before I arrived on Holly Way. He talked about her all the time; she must have been a lovely woman.'

'He was lucky to have had her then.'

'He was lonely for ten years without her after she died. That must have been very hard.'

Mitchell took Hannah's wine from her and placed it on the worktop beside her. He stroked a gentle hand over her cheek. 'If all this has done one thing, it's made me realise that I'm jealous of what George had, even if he was lonely for the last ten years without Hilda. At least he had her, no matter how long it was for. To find a true soulmate is so rare. And it's a lucky person who does. Han… I think I've found mine. If you'll have me.'

'If I'll have you?' Hannah gave a shaky laugh. 'Surely that should be the other way around.'

'Not a chance. I've been thinking. It's time I bought a new place to live. Would you like to come and look at some houses with me?'

'Well, of course, but I'm not sure how useful my opinion would be.'

'I think if you're going to live there too, then you do need to look.'

Hannah stared at him. 'Me?'

'I'd love it. What do you say?'

She hesitated. 'I don't know… this is all a bit sudden.'

'Oh… well you don't have to give me your answer now. Say you'll think about it?'

'I will, but I need time. You must understand that I love my house and independence, right? It's a lot to give up without being sure.'

Mitchell's face fell, the bright hope dulled in his eyes.

'I don't mean never,' Hannah said, pulling him into a kiss. 'I just need time. It doesn't mean that I don't want you.'

He nodded. 'I want to do something for you though. I want to show you just how important you are to me.'

'You have already. The fact that you're here today tells me that.'

'How about we go away? A long holiday – Mauritius, Barbados, Mexico… Wherever you like. And don't start arguing about the cost because it's my treat.'

'I don't really have time for a holiday and I couldn't have you pay for it all.'

'I have to do something! I want to treat you, to show you you're loved like mad.'

Hannah smiled. 'You still haven't got it, have you? I don't need big houses, fur coats and posh holidays. I just need you.'

He pulled her into his arms. 'I suppose I've got a lot to learn about real women.'

Hannah laughed. 'As opposed to the pot plant you put a wig on and talk to in the mornings?'

'As opposed to my so-called ex-wife who clearly only wanted to screw me for anything she could get.'

'It can't always have been like that.'

'I suppose not, but I'm struggling to remember the last time it wasn't.'

Hannah was about to reply, but perhaps now wasn't the time to go into all that. She glanced to her left to see Ross and Gina making their way over. Despite the sombre occasion, they both looked blissfully happy, Gina with her arm linked through his and her head leaning on his shoulder.

'Good service, wasn't it?' Ross said, extending his hand for Mitchell to shake.

'It was,' Mitchell replied. 'He sounded like a real character in his youth. Is there much in the way of family here? It seems like almost everyone is a neighbour.'

'There are a few old friends and some distant cousins. I don't think he had much family left. They lost their son, you know. He was only about five. They never had any more children and very rarely spoke about it.'

'I didn't know that,' Hannah said, fresh tears springing to her eyes. 'How sad.'

'Come on, now,' Gina said, sniffing herself, 'stop that crying and cheer up. George wouldn't want us all standing around sobbing into our drinks.' She turned to Ross. 'Although you had better cry when I go because I'll haunt you if you don't.'

Ross chuckled and pulled her close. 'I'll be inconsolable. Although you're a morbid sod, bringing that up already.'

'I'm just getting you used to the idea. I am a lot older than you.'

'I'm a man and we wear out quicker.'

Gina reached up to give him a peck on the cheek. 'True.'

Hannah gave an indulgent smile. 'My sister's weird sense of humour will take some getting used to, Ross.'

'Don't I know it,' he replied. 'But I think I'm going to have a lot of fun in the process.'

*

In the end, Hannah was earmarked for May and Gina was allotted November. Jess had been roped in to do January, much to her chagrin, although Gina reminded her that she owed Ross and his family big time and despite her complaints, there was no choice over whether she did it or not.

The day of the calendar shoot had arrived. All three were now standing next to Briony as the bright June sun slanted into the church hall. Tables at the far end were piled with props of all kinds, including pumpkins, sleigh bells, a large glittery heart and even a full-sized rowing boat. Costumes hung on racks along the opposite wall, giving off that strange musty smell of clothes that hadn't seen the light of day for a very long time, next to another table stacked with biscuits, cakes and a tea urn. Clusters of other women were dotted around the hall, greeting each other or already deep in juicy gossip or comparing outfits. Jess's eyes roved the room and settled on the hangers with a look of disdain. Gina caught Hannah's eye and grinned.

Briony nibbled a digestive biscuit as she balanced a tea cup and saucer in her other hand. 'Do you feel a bit more settled in the new house now?' she asked Gina.

'Oh, yes, it didn't take long. I think I just needed to give it a good clean. Once everything was spick and span and my stuff put away in its right place it felt much more like home.'

'I couldn't agree more. There's something quite unsavoury about living in someone else's dirt. A house never feels like yours until you've cleaned it to your own standards.'

Hannah wasn't entirely sure how Briony knew this, considering she had lived at Holly Farm since she married Paul, who had inherited it from his father. Perhaps she had moved around a bit in her youth. Hannah resolved to ask her about it next time they met up for an idle afternoon of chat. Briony turned to Jess.

'And how are you liking Millrise now that you're here?'

Jess gave a noncommittal shrug, but was then spurred into a reply by a sharp look from her mother. 'It's okay,' she said. 'It's just different to what I'm used to.'

'You'll be fine once you get settled in at college,' Gina said.

'I suppose,' Jess replied, though she didn't sound convinced.

'And you're enjoying covering your new sales territory?' Briony asked Gina.

'It's not that different from the old one, really. In fact, I managed to keep some of my old customers, which is good because although the new area is a little more relaxed and has a smaller client base, they spend less too. It means that the commissions from my lower spenders are evened out by the bigger commissions from my old customers – handy when you have a huge mortgage to pay.'

'We would have been happy for you to move in with Ross,' Briony said. 'He did speak to us about it.'

'I know, and it's so kind, but I really couldn't take advantage of you.' Gina exchanged the briefest glance with Hannah, who knew the real reason Gina had refused the offer. They had discussed it at length since Ross had put it to Gina, but she'd decided that it was just a little too close to Ross's parents, nice as they were. It was still early days for her and Ross, not to mention that Jess would have had to live there too, and Gina understood it would all be too much for her daughter on top of the other upheavals in her life. The three of them squished into an annexe with a family she barely knew wasn't going to help her adjust.

'Perhaps, when George's estate is settled and Ross can put in an offer on his place, you'll all be able to live there,' Briony said mildly.

'Perhaps…' Gina began, but her reply was cut short by a woman calling Briony's name from across the room.

'Oh, would you excuse me?' Briony said as she dashed off.

'She's not letting that house thing go, is she?' Hannah said with a wry smile. 'And there was you worrying that she wouldn't like you. I'm sure she'd have you and Jess living in the farmhouse with them if she could get away with it.'

'Imagine that. Exactly why there was no way we could move into that annexe, no matter how lovely and rent free it was.'

Hannah sipped her tea and grimaced. It was nice and stewed – the opposite to how she liked it. 'I suppose it would be ideal if Ross did buy George's old place. You could all live there and I'd have you as a neighbour.'

'That's still a big if. There's a lot to be done before we could even think about that. And I suspect others might try to get their hands on it.' Gina gave Hannah a knowing look.

'You mean Mitchell? He's already got a house.'

'You know he's desperate to find a place nearer to you since you refuse to move in with him and there's nowhere closer than George's house.'

'Hmmm, as much as I love Mitchell and I love being with him, that's just a bit too close right now.'

'You're so cruel!' Gina laughed. 'The man is obviously besotted with you.'

'I know. I suppose I'm just too used to pleasing myself and it's going to take some time to get used to the idea of sharing a home with someone else. We'll get there, eventually.'

Gina nodded. 'I get that.' She turned to Jess. 'Have you seen your costume yet?'

'Yes,' Jess pouted. 'It's ridiculous.'

'Awww, I bet you look lovely in it,' Hannah smiled.

'It's one of those shower things that you use on kids to stop shampoo getting in their eyes with a snowflake stuck to it. I don't think anyone could look lovely in that,' Jess replied.

'No, but there won't be any tears if anyone does decide to sneak up behind you and start washing your hair,' Gina quipped.

'You're soooo funny,' Jess said. 'You'll be laughing on the other side of your face when you see your outfit.'

'I've seen it,' Gina replied serenely. 'I'm going to be a firework.'

'In some knackered old Christmas tinsel.'

'I'll look majestic,' Gina grinned.

'At least neither of you have to be done up like a maypole,' Hannah cut in. 'I'm going to look utterly ridiculous.'

'Yes, but we can't let Briony down, can we?' Gina asked.

'You're only saying that because you have the best costume.'

'And because you have to stay in her good books,' Jess added.

'Yes, and you have to stay in mine,' Gina replied. 'So suck it up, snowflake girl.'

'Ha ha,' Jess said, and stuck her tongue out. Gina pulled her into a hug. 'You think I'm hilarious really.'

'That's the problem,' Jess said with a grin as Gina let go.

'You must admit that you might find it a teensy bit fun to dress up and have photos taken? You used to love it when you were little.' Gina gave a fond smile. 'Seems like only yesterday that you were demanding to be taken to the supermarket dressed as Snow White. I kinda miss those days.'

'I'm sure *I* could dress as Snow White for you next time you want to go to Sainsbury's,' Hannah laughed.

'It's not quite the same,' Gina said.

'Yeah,' Jess agreed, 'all that will do is get you going viral on YouTube.'

Hannah chuckled. 'Wouldn't you be proud of your aunt then?'

Rainbow, the photographer whose apparel was every bit as colourful as her name, came over and tapped Jess on the shoulder. 'You're my January, aren't you?'

Jess nodded.

'Fantastic. You're going to look divine. Why don't we go and get your costume sorted? We've got Beryl in from the market stall to do make up. She'll do a lovely job with cheekbones like yours to work with.'

'Great…' Jess said in a voice that suggested nothing had ever been less great, and as she followed Rainbow, she turned and mouthed to Gina, '*help me*,' but Gina only laughed.

'She's never going to forgive you,' Hannah said.

'I know. But being humiliated once in a while is a valuable life lesson, don't you think?'

The door to the church hall opened, and Ross sidled in, a sheepish grin on his face as he spotted Gina.

'I knew he wouldn't be able to stay away,' Gina said as she watched him walk across the hall. 'He's been threatening to come all week.'

'Have you been photographed yet?' he asked, kissing her.

'No. Why are you here?'

'Mum asked me to bring some cakes over…'

Gina raised her eyebrows. 'So where are they?'

'In the car.'

'A likely story.'

Ross made the sign of a cross over his heart with a huge grin. Hannah started laughing, but Gina nudged her and pointed to the entrance.

'I don't know what you're laughing about,' she said, 'look who else is here.'

Hannah flicked her head around to see Mitchell come in. She glanced at Ross. 'Have you cooked this up between you?'

Ross placed a hand to his chest. 'Of course not! I just happened to mention that I was coming over and he said he would give me a hand carrying the cakes.'

'Oh of course… those non-existent cakes!' Hannah said.

'Have you had your photos taken yet?' Mitchell asked as he kissed Hannah.

'No.'

'Great. I didn't want to miss it.'

'Bad luck then, because you're both leaving,' Gina said.

'What?' Ross and Mitchell cried in unison.

'If you think you're having a laugh at our expense, you're sadly mistaken.'

'We weren't going to laugh,' Mitchell said. 'We were just wanted to show our support.'

'Hmmmm…' Hannah replied. But her attention was distracted by Briony racing over.

'Ross!' she called, 'Thank goodness! You've timed it perfectly.'

'I have?' Ross asked, his face losing a shade. 'What for?'

'Our July has shingles!' she panted as she reached the group. 'Rainbow is desperate. You'll have to replace her.'

Ross held his hands in the air. 'No way!'

'You'll be perfect!' Briony insisted. 'With your lovely sunny blond hair. It's wonderful that you can help us out of a spot.'

'Mum, no –'

'Nonsense…' she replied, grabbing him by the wrist to guide him away to the costumes. 'You'll be so covered in flowers that nobody need know it's you anyway.' Ross looked horrified, and Mitchell burst out laughing. But then Briony turned to him. 'Our August hasn't turned up yet either. What size feet are you?'

Mitchell went almost as pale as Ross. 'I don't think…'

'Oh, come on. August is nautical, I'm sure we can find a big grey beard to cover your face.'

'But I thought it was women only,' Mitchell protested.

'Needs must,' Briony replied cheerfully. 'If we haven't got enough models we'll have to find volunteers from somewhere. Come on, chop chop.'

Gina and Hannah were almost doubled over with laughter. Even Mitchell knew better than to argue with Briony. As she led them away, Briony turned to the girls with a crafty wink.

'Oh that's so funny…' Hannah spluttered once they were out of earshot. 'She doesn't want them in the calendar at all.'

'Shall we let them sweat for a bit before we go and rescue them?'

'I vote we let them get dressed up and even get a few photos for future use, stop them getting cocky.'

Gina giggled. 'Whatever happened to my straight-laced little sister?'

'Life happened, that's what.'

'I suppose it does that. But things feel pretty good right now.'

'Yup. Things are as they should be and those who deserve it are getting their just desserts. Martine is stuck with penniless Graham, who is working in a builder's yard and lucky to have a job there at all since Mitchell exposed him for the conman he really is. Howard is giving you anything you ask for just to keep his little secret –'

'That makes it sound like blackmail,' Gina laughed.

'No, just some gentle coaxing, right?' Hannah grinned. 'We both have fabulous men who are now being tortured by your rather fabulous almost-mother-in-law, Jess is nearly human again, though we won't get too carried away there as I'm sure things will be back to normal in a week or so, and we have a wonderful new life to look forward to. I'd call that a good result.'

'And I think it will only get better.'

Hannah lifted her mug of stewed tea and Gina did the same.

'A toast,' Hannah smiled, 'to us.'

'To us!' Gina echoed, clinking her cup against Hannah's. 'Long may our new lives be awesome!'

Epilogue:
Under a Midsummer Moon

Hannah placed a tick next to 'birthday cake' on the list, then glanced up at Gina.

'That's one less thing to worry about. Briony will make an amazing cake too.'

'I bet it won't be posh enough for Jess, though,' Gina replied with a dark look that was so melodramatic Hannah laughed out loud.

'I don't think she'd dare to complain. Besides, she's going to be eighteen – all she'll be bothered about is how fast she can drink the bar dry. Remember my eighteenth birthday party?'

'How can I forget? I found you pissed as a fart in a cupboard and very close to having sex with Shanie Weston's boyfriend.'

'He was gorgeous.' Hannah grinned. 'I still haven't forgiven you for stopping me.'

'I stopped you from getting a beating from Shanie. I deserved a medal for my actions that night.'

'Still, Jess's will be different because there will be responsible adults there. Is she bringing this new boyfriend… what's his name again?'

'I'm finding it hard to keep track myself. I think it's still Archie – at least it was this morning.'

Hannah laughed. 'Now, who does that remind you of? Like mother, like daughter?'

'Oi! I'm perfectly constant and faithful to Ross. And I was to Howard too.'

'I'm talking about when you were eighteen.'

'Well…' Gina gave a sheepish smile. 'It's allowed at eighteen.'

'Which is exactly what Jess would say.'

Gina opened her mouth. Then closed it again before finally answering, 'I can't have this conversation – what else is on the list that we still haven't covered?'

Hannah bit back another grin as she read down her notes. 'Balloons are sorted, Paul has organised the booze, Briony the cake, Howard is paying the DJ, we're doing the sandwiches…' She looked up and the grin broke free. 'Male stripper? Do you know anyone who can do a strip for us?'

'Ha ha, very funny.'

'I thought so. In that case, I think we've covered most of it. No doubt we'll think of more as we go along. Have you decided what you're doing about Howard coming to the party?'

'He's Jess's dad…' Gina rested her elbows on the table. Her shoulders slumped and Hannah didn't need to ask any more. Gina was madly in love with Ross, and it seemed as though she'd moved on. But pain of the kind Howard had inflicted on her when he'd had the affair that broke up their marriage, and then later when he'd tried to snuff out her happiness with Ross – that sort took much longer to heal than others.

'You'll have Ross there for support.'

'I know. It's going to be awkward but, if anything, I almost feel it's Ross that I should un-invite if I have any doubts at all about having them in the same room.'

'Seriously? After everything his family have done to help?'

'Of course I'm not going to leave him out. I'm just saying, Howard probably has more right to be there than Ross. He's expecting to come, and Jess is expecting him to be there – I know who she'd be cutting from the guest list if the decision was left to her.'

'She wouldn't, no matter what she says. She knows how much Ross means to you.'

'Probably, but I don't want to put it to the test.'

'So you're not going to mention that George's old place is nearly done? And that Ross is keen for you to move in there with him?'

'Are you kidding? She's only just settled down to the idea that we've left Birmingham! I think I'll save that little nugget for a while longer – in fact, the longer the better.'

'You'll have to tell her sooner or later… unless you've changed your mind about it?'

Gina paused and stirred her coffee slowly as Hannah waited for a reply. 'It's not that I don't want to commit to Ross,' she said slowly.

'But?'

'You know I adore him – he's the best thing to happen to me in a very long time. That's why I'm hesitant. I don't want to tie him down; he's so much younger than me–'

'I don't think he cares about that.'

'He might one day.'

'He's not a teenager; he's a steady, reliable grown man who very much knows his own mind. I think he can decide for himself what he wants and as far as I can see that's you. Even his parents can see it and they're behind your relationship no matter whether the age gap bothers them or not.'

'I wish I could say the same for Jess.'

'She's coming round to the idea, even if it is slowly.'

'While we're just dating it's okay. But remember what happened last time she thought moving in together was on the cards.'

'Howard exacerbated that situation by twisting her fears into something he could use to get back at you and see Ross off.' Hannah folded her arms and leaned back in her chair, eyeing her sister. 'You know what I think? I think you're scared.'

'Wow, well done Sherlock! Of course I'm scared. Say we do move in together, maybe he'll want to get married next. And then have kids, but maybe it's already too late for me to have kids with him. He could get bitter about it –'

'He knows all this and he's chosen to accept it to be with you.'

'For now, yes. Who's to say what'll happen ten years down the line?'

'Who can predict that for any of us?'

Gina shook her head. 'Forget it, Han. You're trotting out arguments that make perfect sense on paper but in reality life doesn't work like that. Ross may know his own mind now but that could change.'

'Is that any reason not to take the risk? If we thought like that about everything no one would dare make a life with anyone.'

'Nothing is certain – that's true. But some things are more certain than others. Like you and Mitchell.'

Hannah raised her eyebrows. 'You think?'

'Not so convinced by your own argument now? He's besotted with you and why wouldn't he be?'

'I can think of a few reasons.' Hannah smiled.

'So can I…' Gina shot her a mischievous look. 'But sisterly ribbing aside, his *decree absolute* will be through any day now and then you'll have to make some decisions too.'

'How has this suddenly become about me?'

'Since you chose to lecture me. Do you think Mitchell is finally going to be free of Martine and not ask you to marry him?'

'I should think he'll have had enough of marriage by then.'

'No, you don't. You know I'm right. And if you turn him down you're a fool.'

'We're alright as we are; we're happy.'

'You could always be happier.'

'And we might not. Marriage doesn't always make things better – as you know.'

The sound of Gina's front door clattering shut echoed through the house, followed by footsteps and voices, and a moment later Jess appeared with a dark haired young man in tow.

'Hey, Mum… Hannah…' Jess greeted them.' Is it okay if me and Archie go upstairs? He wants to play me some stuff on Spotify and his iPod dock is broken.'

Hannah had heard some lame excuses to get a boy up to her room in her time – she'd probably invented quite a few herself – but this one was ready for the knacker's yard. She glanced at Gina, who was nodding slowly.

'I suppose so.'

Jess disappeared without another word, dragging a sheepish looking Archie with her.

'Don't you mind them being up there alone?' Hannah asked once they were out of earshot.

Gina shrugged. 'If I don't let them they'll just find somewhere else to be alone. At least this way I know where she is. She's practically an adult anyway, so I don't suppose I can do a lot about it.'

'I suppose not. I can't imagine having that sort of responsibility. I went into a cold sweat at the thought of having George's dog live with me.'

Gina laughed. 'I suppose it can be scary at times.'

Hannah smiled as she sipped her coffee. 'So,' she continued as she replaced the mug on the table, 'it looks as though we're both going to turn into sad old spinsters.'

'Speak for yourself. I've been married, don't forget. I'll be a mad old cat lady and you'll be the sad old spinster all by yourself.'

'What are you going to tell Ross when he's finished doing George's old place up and he wants you to move in there with him…'

Gina rolled her eyes. 'You don't give up, do you? I love Ross, but I don't know. Everything changes with a leap like that, doesn't it?'

'Yes, but sometimes change is a good thing.'

'I'm going to throw that back at you, then.'

Hannah smiled, and raised her hands above her head. 'Okay, I surrender. We're both being ridiculous.'

'When you've been hurt before like we both have, then it's hard not to be a little bit ridiculous from time to time. And it's perfectly excusable.'

Pulling the writing pad back towards her, Hannah tapped at it with her pen. 'Now that's sorted, don't you think we'd better get back to organising this party?'

*

Hannah walked the space, hand in hand with Mitchell. In preparation for the party, lights had already been strung around the wooden walls, cascading from beams and nailed into eaves, filling the place with an ambient glow. A temporary wooden floor had been installed over the straw that would normally cover the ground, and the place had been painstakingly scrubbed clean. Mitchell stood and frowned.

'It looks great but…'

'What?'

'I can't imagine Jess being pleased about a birthday party in a barn, not at her age. Don't you think it smacks of barn dance a bit – you know, something old people would do?'

'I think it's great,' Hannah insisted, but her smile faded. Perhaps she had misjudged it. Jess had said she didn't care about a party, that she'd rather go to the pubs in Birmingham with her old friends for her birthday. But Gina and Hannah had been so disappointed by this that Jess had, uncharacteristically for her, relented, and agreed that there would be two celebrations, one of which they had free rein to organise. It had been Ross's idea to use the barn on the Hunters' farm, and Hannah's creative mind had immediately jumped on his suggestion, her imagination flooded with ideas to make it the best and most memorable birthday party ever. It was a project that had very much occupied her mind these last few months, and she had loved every minute of it. But now she wasn't so sure. 'I wish you'd said something earlier.'

He squeezed her hand. 'I'm sorry, I didn't mean it to sound negative. I was just thinking aloud what probably should have stayed in my head.'

'If it's in your head, maybe it will be in Jess's too, though,' Hannah replied. 'Now I feel sick...'

'Don't worry!' Mitchell pulled her into a hug. 'It's going to be summer solstice, there will be a glorious strawberry moon, great music and food, and the wine will be flowing. Ignore me, I'm sure it will be impossible for anyone not to have a good time with all that on our side.'

'But what if Jess does think it's full of old people? I mean, it will be!'

'But fun old people,' Mitchell laughed. 'Her friends are invited too, right? So the old person/young person ratio will probably be quite respectable in the end. Besides, that's what you get at family parties, and even Jess knows that, which is why she's doing the two celebrations.

She might pretend she doesn't want to be seen in public with you, but I can tell she completely worships the ground you and Gina walk on and she's incredibly proud of you both.'

Hannah gave him a bemused smile. 'You think?'

'I know it. So stop your worrying and let's get these last bits finished off. I don't know about you but I'm about ready to have some dinner.'

*

The following day, when Martine pulled up at Hannah's gate, she looked as impossibly glamorous as ever, but Hannah couldn't help noticing that some of the light in her usually arrogant stare had faded. She looked tired, a woman defeated, and although Gina would have insisted it was no less than she deserved, Hannah couldn't help but feel sorry for her. Mitchell made it very difficult for his soon-to-be-ex-wife to get hold of him these days, and it wasn't the first time since their split that Martine had come to Hannah's house looking for him. She wondered whether it was in part a morbid curiosity to see how Mitchell's new life was panning out as well as trying to find him. Hannah wouldn't blame her – after all, Martine had not only lost Mitchell and the cosy life they'd had together, but since her infidelity and their split, she had also parted from the man she'd been having an affair with. Graham had gone to Scotland, working on some oil refinery in the highlands. It seemed that he had chosen a destination as far away from Millrise as he could without actually going to another continent and Hannah was sure that had to sting too.

'Is he here?' she asked, striding up the path as Hannah stopped weeding the window box and turned to face her.

'No.'

'Where is he?'

Hannah pulled off her gardening gloves and frowned. 'I'm not his nanny. I don't need to know where he is all the time. Now is one of those times.'

Martine stopped short of Hannah on the path. 'Oh…' she said. Hannah was expecting her to add something derogatory or sarcastic, but she didn't.

'Do you want me to give him a message?'

'No.' Martine turned to go. But then she turned back. 'Actually, yes. You can tell him the divorce is through.'

'Won't he get a letter telling him, as you have?'

'I suppose so.'

'Then why come all the way out here to tell him that?'

She shrugged. 'I suppose I just wanted to tell him… He won.'

'I don't think there are winners or losers here. It's just life.'

'I wanted him to know there're no hard feelings. I mean, we're hardly going to be best buddies but I don't lay any blame at his door for what happened.'

Hannah realised there was no point in telling Martine that what had happened was solely down to her, and that any forgiving could only come from Mitchell. She also knew that it must have taken some guts for Martine to admit she was wrong. Hannah forced herself to smile. 'Will you be alright?'

'I expect so. I don't have much choice, do I?'

Hannah didn't have a reply. There was a moment's silence, and then Martine turned and walked back down the path. As she drove away, Hannah stared thoughtfully after her. So that was it – Mitchell was free. What now? For so long she had been able to put him off pressuring for a decision about their future because he was still married, but now there was no excuse. What did she want? She loved him, of that there was no doubt, but the idea of moving in with Mitchell, possibly even marriage, was exciting and terrifying all at the same time. She had been on her own for so long it was hard to imagine what life would be like without that autonomy. Sure, they had been a couple for a while now, but the big decisions about how she ran her life were still only hers to consider. All that would change and she had to figure out how she felt about it before she could make any decisions.

Even as these thoughts ran through her mind, her mobile phone buzzed in her pocket. She pulled it out to see Mitchell's photo light up on the screen.

'Hey gorgeous!'

He sounded excited and adorable, and Hannah almost felt guilty for the doubts she'd had only a moment earlier.

'You'll never guess what,' he continued.

'You'd better tell me then.'

'Try and guess!'

'You just said I wouldn't be able to,' Hannah smiled.

'Spoilsport! I've only gone and got this amazing band to play at Jess's birthday party! They're called Spartan Down and they're literally just about to sign a massive record deal. They'll be huge in a few months' time. What do you think?'

Hannah paused, taken aback. They hadn't discussed this. 'That's…'

'You're angry?' Mitchell sounded less sure now.

'No… how could I be angry? I'm just surprised. I didn't know you were up to anything like that.'

'Well, it was a surprise because that was the idea.'

'How on earth did you manage it?'

'Friend of a friend – six degrees of separation and all that. Do you think she'll like it? I'm pretty sure they're her sort of music.'

'You know better than I do then, because I don't have a clue what she's into from one week to the next.'

'Yeah, well we had a chat about music a couple of weeks ago, me and Jess. I think I've got what she likes.'

'She'll probably just love the idea that they're going to be famous, even if she doesn't like them.' She smiled. 'It's brilliant. And very thoughtful. What did I do to deserve you?'

'I don't know. I am pretty awesome aren't I?'

'And sounding very smug right now.'

'Aww, let me have this one victory, eh?' he laughed. 'You're always right about everything, so for once let it be me.'

She smiled. But it didn't last long, because Martine's visit was still fresh in her mind. And she guessed that the fact he was so chirpy meant he hadn't picked up his post yet. 'Are you going home before you come over later?'

'Yes, is that okay? I won't be late as I'm packing up here soon.'

'That's great – see you soon then,' Hannah replied with forced jollity. There was a pause. 'Are you alright?' he asked. 'You sound a bit weird.'

'Never better. I'll see you later. Love you.'

'I love you too,' he replied before ending the call.

She stared across the gate and down the lane as she stuffed her phone back in her pocket. She could have told him about Martine's visit, and she'd half wanted to, but she didn't think it was her place to break the news that his divorce was final. If he was going home now, he'd find out for himself soon enough.

*

Briony slapped Ross's hand away from the plate of sandwiches. 'You're getting fat – you can have salad!'

Ross's eyes almost popped from his head. 'Fat!' he squeaked in an impossibly high voice.

'Oh, I don't blame you, Gina,' Briony added, turning to where she and Hannah were sitting across the table. 'He's all settled and content and he's never been one to turn his nose up at food – it was bound to happen.'

Ross stared at them all, apparently robbed of the gift of speech. Gina looked slightly uncomfortable but Paul Hunter let out a roar of laughter. 'That's you told, son.'

'I'm not getting fat, am I?' Ross asked Gina, pulling his shirt up to inspect his belly. 'You should have said.'

'I don't think so,' Gina replied, casting an uncertain glance at Briony who was busy removing the cling film from a plate of sausage rolls. 'I hadn't noticed.'

'You're just filling out,' Paul said, 'becoming a man.'

'A fat man,' Briony cut back in. 'All those takeaways and wine in front of the television every night.'

'We only have a takeaway once a week,' Ross protested, while Gina nodded agreement.

'Maybe you've put on a couple of pounds,' she said. 'But it's nothing bad and I'm sure if we both cut back together –'

'That's a good idea,' Briony said cheerfully, and it was Gina's turn to look shocked. Hannah shot her a little smile. Maybe they had both put on a few pounds but she would never tell her sister that – it was more than her life was worth. Besides, they both looked well on it; happiness and contentment suited them. 'So… is everyone clear about what they're doing tomorrow?' she added, changing the subject.

'All the decorations are up,' Paul said. 'We've got to finish screwing together that temporary stage Ross hired but we can do that after tea.'

'I've had RSVPs back from everyone now,' Gina said. 'And Mitchell has the band coming in after the DJ has finished his set, right Hannah?'

Hannah nodded. Jess had been thrilled with Mitchell's surprise, which was a huge relief. Her doubts about it being a deeply uncool barn dance had now been lifted, and with the addition of Spartan Down it looked more likely to become an extremely cool mini festival type celebration. If all went to plan, it was something Jess would carry fond memories of for the rest of her life. But all that depended on more than just the entertainment. Ross and Howard hadn't seen each other since the night Howard had beaten Ross to a pulp, and even though he had well and truly learned his lesson, it was difficult to see how they were going to be in the same room without some sort of trouble erupting. Ross had offered to step aside for one night and let Gina and Jess go to the party without him, but Gina had stubbornly insisted that he had as much right to be there as Howard did, perhaps more so when you considered that it was Ross's farm and family hosting the event.

'Let's hope the weather holds,' Briony said, pouring tea for everyone from a huge brown pot. 'The reports are saying it will be a fine solstice night but you never know in Britain what you're going to get.'

'At least we'll have some cover in the barn,' Ross offered.

'It'd be muddy though, people to and fro outside. And perhaps cold. I'd rather it didn't rain at all.'

'I think we'd all rather that, love,' Paul said cheerfully. 'It will do what it does and we'll just have to make the best of it.'

'So that's music, food, decorations and guests all sorted,' Briony said in a satisfied tone. 'I think we're all set to throw a party.'

'I can't tell you how grateful I am for all this help.' Gina said, her earnest gaze sweeping the table. 'You've all been brilliant and you didn't have to do any of it.'

'Of course we did,' Briony said. 'You and Jess are family now, and we always help family. You wouldn't have been able to keep us away.'

'Well, it's brilliant.' Gina smiled. 'Thank you.'

Paul helped himself to a pile of salmon sandwiches as Ross looked on with an expression so forlorn it was almost comical. Clearly Briony's remarks were still stinging. 'No need to thank us,' Paul said, 'like Briony says, family is family. We look after our own.'

Hannah watched as Gina's smile grew. All those fears about whether Ross's parents would accept her had been groundless. If anything, they had pulled her to the family bosom so quickly and with such force that it was hard to imagine a time when she hadn't been in their lives, and it was a far cry from the cold distance Howard's parents had always maintained. The Hunters were wonderful people, and Hannah was immensely happy for her sister's good fortune.

*

Saturday night had come around a lot quicker than everyone would have liked. Hannah was nervous. It was ridiculous to feel this way about an event where she would not even figure in the proceedings; all eyes would be on Jess and rightly so. But the feeling was there all the same and she suspected that Gina felt it too. Not only were they responsible for the success or failure of the evening (a fact Mitchell disputed, though it didn't make her feel any better) but there were so many uncertain variables that she couldn't control. Howard and Ross had both pledged they would keep it together for Jess's sake, but when the drink was flowing and promises became hazy, would that change? And Mitchell had been strangely quiet about the fact that his divorce from Martine was finally through. Hannah had expected some heartfelt conversation about his and Hannah's future, at least a mention, but there had been nothing. He had simply acknowledged the fact and then they had carried on as they always had. It made Hannah nervous. What was he up to?

Hannah was at Gina's house, helping her and Ross load up the last bits and pieces into his beloved car, Sally, while Jess hopped from foot to foot, almost bursting with excitement despite the cool act she had tried hard to maintain all day. Hannah hadn't seen her this wound up since her seventh birthday when Clappo the Clown had been invited as guest of honour. It just went to show that the girl you once were never really left you, no matter how old you got.

'Is that everything?' Ross asked, pushing his hair back and surveying the full boot space. There was so much at the barn already that Hannah couldn't believe they needed more, but you didn't argue with Briony, especially where entertaining was concerned. So when she'd given Ross the list of last-minute items, he and Gina had duly gathered them up.

'Extra tea towels,' Gina began, 'first aid kit–'

Jess let out a giggle. 'What's that for? Are we expecting a riot?'

'It's for all those dancing related injuries,' Hannah laughed. 'That or the mass hysteria when the band comes on stage.'

'Briony asked me to pick one up so I'm picking one up,' Gina said as Ross flashed her a sheepish grin. She continued, counting on her fingers as she went through the rest. 'Plastic tubs for leftovers, extra glasses… cleaning cloths and a sweeping brush, rubbish bags… I think that's all of it.'

Ross slammed the boot shut.

'I'll take Hannah and Jess in my car,' Gina said. 'You go on with the stuff for your mum and we'll see you there once I've finished getting ready.'

Ross frowned. 'Aren't you ready now?'

Gina turned a wry smile on him. 'You think this looks ready?'

'You look fine to me.'

'Typical man,' Hannah said.

'I just don't see why you women have to make such a fuss,' Ross said. 'You always look lovely to me.'

'Maybe you simply have low standards,' Gina laughed. 'Let me tell you, I would not be seen dead at any public function dressed in these leggings.' She reached up to give him a quick kiss. 'We won't be long… you can go ahead and entertain the band or something while you wait for us.'

'Isn't it their job to entertain us?' Ross asked.

'Go on!' Gina laughed, and Ross left them with a grin.

Shortly afterwards, Mitchell's car pulled up and he almost tumbled out, looking flustered and a little distracted. But he wore a huge smile despite the obvious imbalance in his usually calm demeanour.

'Sorry… I know I'm late.'

'Not quite, but I was beginning to wonder where you were,' Hannah said.

'Yeah, sorry about that.'

'No need,' Hannah replied. 'You're here now. We've probably got time for a quick drink while Gina finishes up and then we'll be off.'

'Get the party started early, eh?' Mitchell turned to Jess. 'Are you having one, as you're now officially old enough to drink?'

Jess offered him a withering look, and Hannah laughed. 'I think she might have had the odd drink before today,' she said in a stage whisper.

'Almost certainly,' Gina put in with an attempt at disapproval that nobody was really buying. 'Come on then, let's get you all on your way to tipsy, while the designated driver here keeps you all in line. Honestly, sometimes I feel like a nanny.'

Hannah smiled, though she suspected the real reason Gina had volunteered to drive that night was much simpler. If Ross and Howard were both drinking, somebody had to stay sober in case the worst happened, and Gina had obviously decided she was the best person to do that. Hannah didn't blame her – not one bit.

*

By seven o'clock the first guests had started to arrive. They were mostly the older members of the party, and the place had the refined air of a country club get together until the teenagers began to arrive shortly after eight. Their ranks were swelled by extra invites Jess had issued on the promise that they'd be among the first people to see a hot new band. Once the DJ began his set, the atmosphere changed into something far more frenetic – there was giggling, dancing, yelling across the room, huddles of girls throwing flirty looks at huddles of boys, the clink of beer bottles – and Hannah was feeling distinctly old and surplus to requirements. She stood by the makeshift bar next to Mitchell, with Briony behind serving drinks.

'I often say I want my youth back,' Hannah said, gazing across at Jess who was dancing with four other girls, 'but looking at this lot, I think being eighteen again would be the worst thing ever. It's all noise and chaos.'

Mitchell slung an arm around her. 'I know what you mean. I'd take twenty-five again, though. Perhaps twenty-five until twenty-seven. Things calm down but you're still young enough to feel like you rule the world.'

Hannah turned to him with a smile. 'Did you think that?' She pretended to write on an invisible notepad, 'delusions of grandeur…'

Mitchell threw back his head in a gale of laughter. 'Come on! You didn't ever feel invincible when you were young? Like the whole world was just there for you? Not even a bit?'

'If I did I certainly don't remember it. Must have been that one hour in 1995.'

He pulled her closer and she snuggled into him. Mitchell had built a huge business for himself and she supposed part of that self-belief he'd has as a youngster must have carried through and driven him later in life. She'd never felt that way about herself, and although her design business paid the way, it was far from the success Mitchell had achieved. But when she was with him, something strange happened. She felt like more than herself, and since he had arrived in her life, things had suddenly escalated. They had talked for hours about what her future might hold, as well as a future together, and Mitchell had almost subliminally begun to implant in her the conviction that she could succeed in whatever she wanted to do. And as his divorce to Martine had got closer and his memories of the pain she had inflicted faded, so had his confidence and belief in both himself and Hannah. It was one of the many things that made him so special and she loved it. He believed in *them*, as individuals as well as a couple, and no man had ever given her that before.

It was as these thoughts ran through her mind that her attention was diverted by someone new arriving. Jess let out a squeal as she raced across the dancefloor to greet him.

'Dad!'

Howard picked her up and swung her around. In any other circumstances it would have been heart-warming, the obvious love of a father for his daughter, but Hannah could think only of the trouble he'd caused. She looked at the far end of the bar to see that Gina and

Ross were deep in conversation, heads bowed together, and hadn't noticed Howard's arrival. She glanced at Mitchell, whose jaw seemed a little firmer as he clocked Howard too. Despite her promises to Gina, Hannah had eventually confided in Mitchell, telling him what had happened. She had been desperate to share it with someone, to make some sense of a situation that defied logic. Mitchell had listened and had never said a word to Gina, so the only person who knew that Mitchell knew was Hannah.

'I still can't believe that bastard has the nerve to show up,' Mitchell said in a low voice.

She grabbed his hand and gave it a squeeze. 'He is Jess's dad. She would have been devastated if he hadn't come.'

'I'll bet your sister is devastated that he *did* come.'

'She'll be grown up about it, like she's been about everything.'

'Ross is a better man than me; I'd want to punch his lights out.'

'You say that but you managed to keep a lid on it with Graham. We all do what we have to do, don't we?'

Mitchell gave her a tight smile. 'Always so wise. Now I know why you're good for me.'

'I was just thinking the same thing.'

She looked at Howard again. He was being introduced to Jess's friends, but now as she watched, she noted that Gina and Ross had both seen him. Ross watched silently, his expression giving nothing away, while Gina chewed on a nail, her gaze flicking from one man to the other. Then Howard saw them. He gave the tiniest nod of acknowledgement, and Hannah wondered who he was going to sit with. She had the awful sinking feeling that no matter what he had done wrong, she wouldn't be able to let him sit in a corner by himself. But just as she was gathering herself up to go and talk to him, a woman walked through the barn doors and Howard put his arm around her. It was a familiar, easy action and he looked relaxed in her company. Hannah had never seen her before – she wasn't the secretary he'd had an affair with – but as he introduced her to Jess, and Hannah wondered whether it was perhaps a little inappropriate to bring her to the party, she realised that at least he would have someone to talk to. She allowed herself to take a closer look. The woman was attractive, well-dressed, and definitely more Howard's age than the adulteress who had ended his marriage. She looked like someone who could stand her ground with him, and that had to be a good thing. Perhaps now he might not care so much about what Gina was up to either, which had to be good for her and Ross.

After a brief chat with Jess, Howard and his woman found an empty table in a corner furthest away from the bar. Hannah saw him look in her direction, and she tried to smile. There was no point in being anything but forgiving on a night like this, if only to keep the peace for Jess. Then he got up from the table and walked across. Hannah felt Mitchell's hand tighten around hers.

'Are you okay?' he asked in a low voice.

'Yes,' she managed back.

The trademark grey streaks in Howard's dark hair looked a little wider than when she had last seen him, and the lines on his face that had once made him look distinguished and Gina called rugged, now made him look plain old. If he had any inkling of what his divorce had done to him physically, it was no wonder he'd been insanely jealous of the youthful and frankly gorgeous Ross. Hannah almost felt sorry for the man. He gave Hannah and Mitchell a nod, and then put in his order at the bar.

'Oh, you must be Jess's dad!' Briony exclaimed brightly, and Hannah was suddenly struck by the absurdity of the situation as Howard did a double take. Briony and Paul had no idea that the man who had put their son in hospital was in the room, and Howard had no idea who Briony was. He probably thought he'd run into a psychic barmaid. In many ways it wouldn't be a bad thing for it to stay that way.

'I am,' he said.

'Oooh, she's such a lovely girl,' Briony cooed. 'So pretty and, although she doesn't like anyone to know it, very helpful and polite. Paul and I love having her visit.'

Howard stared. 'You do?'

Briony nodded cheerfully. 'She comes over most Sundays with Gina and Ross for dinner and I'm sure she gets better invites. Not many teens would do that.'

The penny finally dropped, and Howard shot a hate-filled glare in Ross's direction. But then he must have recalled his promise to behave, and smoothed his features. 'So you must be…'

'Ross's mum,' Briony said. 'Briony Hunter.' She laughed, a little self-consciously. 'I suppose it's a bit strange and awkward you being here and me chatting to you, all things considered, but I'm glad we could all get along for a special night and it is good to meet you. Now, what can I get you?'

'A rum and coke and a gin and tonic please,' he replied stiffly. Briony smiled broadly and busied herself getting his order and all the while Ross, Gina, Mitchell and Hannah watched him as he waited.

'I bet Ross is dying to get his hands around that guy's throat,' Mitchell whispered.

'It's a good job Paul doesn't know – Howard would be dead by now.'

'Let's hope it stays that way, if only for Jess's sake, because I don't know which side I'd pick if it came to stopping a fight. I'd be tempted to help Ross and Paul stick the boot in.'

'Which would get everyone precisely nowhere, and make you all as bad as him,' said Hannah, 'and you're better men than that.'

'What about the women?' Mitchell fired back, and Hannah couldn't help a smile.

'They say hell hath no fury like a woman scorned.'

Howard returned to his table with his drinks having said not a word to anyone but Briony. Hannah was impressed with Ross's tolerance, but could see by the set of his jaw and the worried expression on Gina's face that being in the same room as his attacker was proving rather more of a test than he had anticipated.

'I'm going to see if they're okay,' Hannah said. She crossed over to them.

'Well?' she asked, looking at Gina and Ross in turn. 'What do you think?'

'I think that's about as close as it's safe for him to get,' Gina said. 'With a bit of luck he'll finish his drink and sod off. We told him to come, and Jess has seen him so she's happy, but I think he knows that the invitation wouldn't extend to him staying all evening.'

'Jess will understand,' Hannah said. 'She's not silly and after all that happened she's probably just grateful he was allowed to come at all.'

'I suppose the car he bought for her has helped to make her a bit more forgiving too,' Gina returned with a faint smile.

'Well, I suppose it would,' Hannah said.

They were prevented from any further analysis by Paul and Mitchell, who had come armed with top-up drinks. Mitchell pointed to where the band were standing, already surrounded by admiring teenagers. 'This might be the last time you can get this close to a member of Spartan Down. Are you sure you don't want to get their autographs?'

Hannah smiled. 'I think I can live without it. I don't think I'd get a look in now, in any case. The way Jess is looking at that lead singer I think poor Archie might be a distant memory in a few hours.'

They turned to see a forlorn looking Archie watch as Jess joined the group of girls vying for attention from a lead singer who was undoubtedly sexy as hell.

'I'd better go and have a quick word with them before they start their set,' Mitchell said.

'Okay.' Hannah kissed him. 'Don't get any ideas about becoming their roadie, because I'm not going on a world tour, I'm too busy.'

'I won't,' he laughed, before wandering off into the throng.

Hannah turned to Gina and Ross.

'Are you two okay?'

'Yes,' Gina said, drawing a long breath and looking at Ross. 'We're okay, aren't we?'

'Of course. This is Jess's night and we're going to make sure it's a brilliant one. Your ex can glare all he wants but he's not getting a fight.'

'I couldn't have put it better myself,' Gina smiled.

*

For the next hour, Spartan Down mesmerised their young audience, who jumped and cheered and whooped while the older party guests looked on with indulgent smiles. Hannah's gaze was frequently drawn to Howard's table, but he and his date didn't move and kept their heads close together as they shared a private conversation, barely glancing up at anyone else. Whenever she looked at Ross, he was watching them too, although he tried very hard to make it seem as if he wasn't. Briony was relieved from bar duties by Rainbow, the calendar photographer every bit as colourful as her name, and Briony made her way over to Hannah with a frown.

'Rainbow just handed me this – she found it on the floor in the portaloo.' Opening her hand, she revealed a diamond ring.

'Oh, wow,' Hannah said. 'That's some rock. Someone's going to be very upset later when they realise it's missing.'

'The size of this I'm surprised there hasn't already been an announcement,' Briony said. 'You couldn't miss that falling off your finger, it would land with such a thud.'

'True,' Hannah said. 'What shall we do?'

'I'll keep it for now,' Briony decided. 'Maybe someone will make it known they're looking for it and then we can let them have it. Not that I don't trust any of the people here but I don't think it's wise to advertise the fact that we have an owner-less ring here for the taking.'

'Good idea,' Hannah agreed.

Briony slipped it into her apron pocket and went off to find Paul, while Mitchell returned from a rather earnest looking conversation with Ross. Mitchell looked stressed as he approached Hannah.

'What's the matter?'

'Nothing,' he said, trying to smile.

'Don't give me that. What is it? Has Howard done something?'

'No… honestly.'

'Then why did you and Ross look like the sky fell in just then?'

'Something and nothing. Mostly nothing, though, and not for you to worry about.'

'Right…' Hannah replied slowly, and waited for him to elaborate; but he didn't. Instead, Mitchell looked decidedly awkward for a moment before announcing that he had something to do and would be right back.

Hannah watched him go and he seemed preoccupied, head down, almost bumping into someone as he went.

When Hannah glanced over to Howard's table again neither he nor his date were there. Had they slipped out to get away with the least fuss? Then she saw them both, Jess hanging from her dad's arm, as they headed towards Ross and Gina.

Shit!

What should she do? Was this the moment to intervene? Would she be making things worse? But even as these thoughts ran through her head, an incredible thing happened. Howard appeared to offer a handshake to Ross. And Ross accepted it. It was a brief encounter, and in moments it was over. Hannah couldn't quite believe that it had happened at all. Then Howard looked across at her and nodded, before kissing Jess on the cheek and turning for the exit with his date. Hannah rushed over to where Gina, Jess and Ross watched them go.

'What was all that about?'

Gina gave a bemused smile. 'An olive branch, I think.'

'And you're okay? I mean, after all that happened?'

Ross nodded. 'It was always my intention to make sure it didn't affect the family, or Gina and me…' He gave a knowing look at Jess. 'And I think we know who persuaded Howard to bury the hatchet.'

Gina grabbed her daughter in a tight hug. 'I moan about you at times, but you really are the most brilliant daughter ever!'

'Yeah?' Jess laughed. 'I'll remember that next time you're nagging me about cleaning my room.'

'Not that brilliant.' Gina smiled as she let her go. But Jess looked happy – not the temporary excitement that a birthday party or a new car could bring, but a happiness that seemed to infuse her whole being, a true and fundamental contentment. Hannah hadn't seen her look like that for a long time. Maybe this was the beginning of a new chapter in everyone's lives, the sign of things to come for them all?

'I'm going to catch the last of the set before the band finishes; I just needed to bring Dad over before he left.'

'You're okay?' Hannah asked. 'That he didn't stay for the whole evening?'

Jess shrugged. 'I didn't expect him to and I don't blame him. It was pretty brave that he came at all.'

'I suppose it was,' Hannah mused. She had found a grain of new respect for Howard for facing what he knew would be a very difficult night, and even more so now that he had faced Ross and tried to make some amends for the damage his actions had caused. It must have been a huge thing for a man as proud and opinionated as Howard to admit that he was wrong.

*

Jess had returned to the dancefloor, and Ross seemed subdued considering the small personal victory that Howard's apology represented. And as Mitchell came back to Hannah's side, he didn't seem much better either. He shot Ross a quick, knowing look, one which Ross returned with the tiniest nod. The two of them had become good friends over the last few months, but Hannah had never seen them look this thick together before. What were they up to?

'We've just got to nip outside for a bit,' Ross announced. Gina looked up at him.

'But I'm watching the band.'

'No, Mitchell and me,' Ross said. 'Won't be long.'

Gina looked puzzled as she watched them go. She turned to Hannah.

'That's weird. They haven't started smoking, have they? Standing outside right now like naughty schoolboys with a crafty cigarette?'

'It would probably be more reassuring if they had; at least it would be a simple explanation,' Hannah replied.

*

The band finished their set to wild applause, the food had just about been hoovered up by the hungry guests, the drink had flowed, and most of the partygoers with the stamina still to be up had moved outside the stifling air of the barn to enjoy the mild midsummer night and the beautiful creamy moon that now hung above them. They sat on the ground in clusters, or leaned against the barn chatting, the mood still good but considerably calmer than it had been an hour before. Mitchell and Ross had been missing for a good hour but had returned to Gina and Hannah now, though Ross in particular didn't look happy. That was a thing to remark upon in itself, because for as long as Hannah had known him he almost always had a smile on his face. When Gina had asked him what was wrong, he had done his best to paint it back on, but nobody was fooled.

'I'm exhausted,' Gina announced, something like frustration on her face as she failed to get to the bottom of Ross's sombre mood. 'But I don't suppose Jess is ready to go home yet.'

'She could stay here,' said Briony, who had joined them, still clinging onto a black rubbish bag she'd been using to clear up. 'Paul and I will be up for a while yet; she could stay until everyone's gone and sleep in our spare bed.'

'That does sound tempting,' Gina said. 'That's the trouble with not drinking – everyone else is drunk and ready to party all night while I'm just ready for a Horlicks and my bed.' She turned to Ross, who stood listening with his hands sunk in his pockets. 'I bet you never imagined in a million years you'd end up with such a dynamo, eh?'

He gave a weak smile, and Briony laughed lightly. 'It's been a long day for everyone – I wouldn't blame you for being a bit tired.'

'I'm a bit pooped myself,' Hannah put in. 'And I have been drinking. Don't forget we've been up since six.'

'But Jess has had a good day, hasn't she?' Gina said. 'That's the only thing that matters, in the end.'

Hannah glanced across to where Jess was giggling with a group of friends, Archie's arm slung around her. 'I think she's had a very good day. How does it feel to be the mother of a brand new adult?'

Gina laughed. 'I think she's been an adult for a long time. I feel old, though.'

'Right…' Briony continued brightly. 'So, I'd better get cleaned up so we can do whatever we're going to do.'

'I'll help,' Gina said.

'But I thought you were going home?'

'It can wait. Jess is busy so I won't disturb her yet, and I can't very well leave you to do all the cleaning up alone.'

'Oh, Paul will help.'

'I will too, of course,' Hannah put in. 'By the way,' she added, 'did you find the owner of that ring?'

'Nobody said anything to me,' Briony said doubtfully. 'Do you think I should have made an announcement?'

Ross turned sharply. 'What ring?'

Briony fished in her apron pocket and produced it.

Ross sucked in his breath. 'Oh…' He looked up at Mitchell, and everyone seemed to reach a conclusion at the same time.

'Ross!' Briony squeaked. 'You weren't!'

Gina was beaming. '*You* lost it? That means…'

'Well, yes, but…' Ross began before trailing off.

'Is it…?' Gina asked, her own question unfinished.

'Well. . .' Ross looked helplessly at everyone.

'You were going to propose?' Briony asked.

Ross was blushing. 'I… you see…' Then he looked imploringly at Mitchell. 'Help me out, mate.'

Mitchell took the ring from Briony. 'Actually, it's mine. At least, it is until I give it to someone else.' He turned to Hannah. 'This isn't the way I had planned it at all, but it seems fate had other ideas for tonight… just like it's had all through the last few months.' He looked up at the sky, the lanterns strung around the barn throwing a warm glow over his features, and then back at Hannah. 'But the moon is high, and the air is warm, and my ring has turned up, so this seems as good a time as any to ask if you'll marry me.'

Hannah's eyes widened. She looked from him to Gina to Ross to Briony and then back again. 'But I don't understand, I thought…'

Ross shuffled and his gaze went to his feet as his blush deepened. Gina grabbed his arm and kissed him. 'I'm glad you weren't asking me,' she said in a low voice with a smile. 'We're not quite there yet.'

'Well?' Mitchell asked.

'This is…'

'A shock?' he said, his face falling. 'I'm sorry, I shouldn't have done it like this–'

'No.' Hannah stayed his hand as he started to retract the ring. 'I mean, yes, it is a shock. And if you'd asked me yesterday I would have said I didn't want this. But…' She looked up into his eyes. Something about tonight felt right. Now that he stood before her, offering her his whole self for the rest of their lives, she did want it. How could she have been so blind to all that it represented for her? The most perfect man she had ever met, who had gone through so much and had never once used it as a reason to be mean or cruel, who had been kind and patient and noble in the face of adversity, and he wanted her by his side. How could she say no to such an offer? She loved him, and if commitment was the issue, she needed to put that behind her because she had already made a commitment to love him, one that bound them in steel because she knew she would never stop.

'Yes,' she said.

'Yes?'

She nodded. 'Absolutely.'

Mitchell stared at her. 'You're saying yes?'

'It can't be that much of a shock,' she laughed. 'You must have asked with the fifty percent hope that I'd say yes.'

'I know, but…'

Gina rolled her eyes. 'For God's sake, kiss her and get that ring on her finger before she changes her mind!'

'Or before I lose it again,' Ross said sheepishly. Gina shot him a wry look. How he'd had the ring to lose in the first place was a mystery that would have to be explained later. She guessed that Mitchell had asked him to keep it with some elaborate proposal in mind, or perhaps just because he didn't trust himself to keep it safe all night, but Ross had scuppered that by dropping it on the floor of the portaloo.

'It's alright, Ross,' Hannah smiled. She turned to Mitchell and held her left hand out, fingers splayed. 'It's a yes.'

Mitchell grabbed her and pulled her into a kiss. She drew away a few moments later, breathless and laughing. 'And I still don't have that fabulous ring on my finger!'

'Oh, right…' Mitchell took her hand and slid the ring on. 'There. You can't change your mind now.'

'I don't want to.'

They stood smiling at each other while Gina watched, nuzzling into Ross, and Briony wiped a tear from her eye.

'What a night!' Briony said. 'What a wonderful midsummer's night! Reminds me of the night I met Paul.'

'You met Dad on midsummer's night?' Ross asked.

'At an eighteenth birthday celebration too,' Briony nodded. 'He walked into the room and I couldn't see anyone else after that. I knew I was going to marry him.'

'Did Dad know?' Ross laughed, but Briony simply gave him a soppy smile and batted away the quip.

'Be off with you. If it wasn't for my foresight you wouldn't be standing here today.'

'That's true,' Gina said, 'so behave yourself.'

Briony shook herself. 'I must go and find Paul and tell him the good news!'

And with that she took herself off. Mitchell took Hannah into his arms and kissed her again.

'Are you sure you don't mind?' Ross asked Gina in a worried voice as they turned away for a moment to give Hannah and Mitchell some privacy.

'Why would I mind? Mitchell is a lovely man and I can tell Hannah's so happy with him. She deserves it, after all she's been through – after what they've both been through.'

'No, not that,' he said. 'When you thought the ring was for you…'

Gina let out a musical little laugh. 'Of course I would have been flattered but…'

'Only flattered?' Ross asked, sounding defeated.

'More than flattered. Ross…' She grabbed his hand. 'You know that I love you, right? There needn't be doubts just because we're not quite at the stage Hannah and Mitchell are. Their relationship has far fewer complications than ours does, but that doesn't mean I care for you any less.'

'So…' he looked down at the ground and kicked the toe of his shoe in the grass. 'It won't always be a no.'

'You haven't asked me yet, so it's never been a no.'

'But if I asked you would it be a yes?'

'Are you asking me?'

He looked up at her. 'I don't know. I didn't think you'd say yes even if I was.'

She smiled. 'Maybe I would. Why don't you try me?'

'You mean that?'

'Not straightaway,' she said.

'But one day?'

She nodded.

'Gina… Will you marry me?'

'Yes, Ross. One day I will marry you.'

He grinned and planted a kiss on her lips. 'One day. That's good enough for me.'

Gina smiled as he pulled away. Hannah and Mitchell were still buried in each other's arms. 'Maybe we should leave the lovebirds to it,' she said in a low voice. 'They've probably got a lot to talk about.'

Ross nodded. 'Maybe we have too,' he said hopefully, and they went back to the barn leaving Hannah and Mitchell gazing out over the moonlit fields together.

A Letter from Tilly

Dear reader,

I want to say a huge thank you for choosing to read *Once Upon a Winter*. If you did enjoy it, and want to keep up to date with all my latest releases, just sign up at the following link. Your email address will never be shared and you can unsubscribe at any time.

www.bookouture.com/tilly-tennant

I'm so excited to share this new and extra-sparkly version of *Once Upon a Winter* with you. Having re-read the story to polish it up, I've been reminded of just why I'm so fond of these characters and I hope new readers become fond of them too.

I hope you loved *Once Upon a Winter* and if you did I would be very grateful if you could write a review. I'd love to hear what you think, and it makes such a difference helping new readers to discover one of my books for the first time.

I love hearing from my readers – you can get in touch on my Facebook page, through Twitter, Goodreads or my website.

Thank you!
Tilly x

tillytennant

@TillyTenWriter

www.tillytennant.com

Acknowledgements

Once Upon a Winter started life as a tiny germ of an idea that eventually became four novellas and then four novellas and a short story, because I couldn't leave these characters alone! The more I wrote about them the more I wanted to write about them. Eventually, my very good friend (back then she was also my agent and editor) Peta Nightingale persuaded me that there were also other stories to tell! The result is the book you've just read and I hope you enjoyed being a part of Hannah and Gina's world as much as I did.

There are some people I must thank, and I want to apologise in advance if I forget you – that doesn't make you less important, it just means I have a brain like a sieve! My heartfelt gratitude goes out to each and every one of you, whose involvement, whether small or large, has been invaluable and appreciated more than I can express.

My family, of course, are always first on any list of special mentions for the patience and tolerance they show when I'm working. I know I'm not easy to live with when I'm deep in story territory but they support me and love me nonetheless.

I also want to mention the many good friends I have made and since kept at Staffordshire University. It's been eleven years since I graduated with a degree in English and creative writing but hardly a day goes by when I don't think fondly of my time there. I'd also like to shout out to Storm Constantine of Immanion Press, who gave me the opportunity to see my very first book in print, and Philippa Milnes-Smith and the team at the Soho Agency, who did such a wonderful job of supporting me in the early days of my career and continue to do so where they can.

I have to thank the remarkable team at Bookouture for their continued support, patience, and amazing publishing flair, particularly my editors Cara Chimirri, Lydia Vassar-Smith and Jessie Botterill. I'd also like to shout out to Kim Nash, Noelle Holten and Sarah Hardy and the rest of our amazing publicity folks. Last but not least I want to mention Alexandra Holmes who keeps my schedules and my wandering attention on track, and the most wonderful Peta Nightingale – if not for a chance meeting with her I'm certain I would not be where I am today. I know I'll have forgotten someone at Bookouture who I ought to be thanking, but I hope they'll forgive me. I'll be giving them all a big hug at the next summer bash whether they want it or not! Their belief, able assistance and encouragement mean the world to me. I truly believe I have the best team an author could ask for and I'm so grateful every day for them.

My friend, Kath Hickton, always gets an honourable mention for putting up with me since primary school and Louise Coquio deserves a medal for getting me through university and suffering me ever since, likewise her lovely family. I also have to thank Mel Sherratt, who is as generous with her time and advice as she is talented, someone who is always there to cheer on her fellow authors. She did so much to help me in the early days of my career that I don't think I'll ever be able to thank her as much as she deserves. I'd also like to shout out to Holly Martin, Tracy Bloom, Emma Davies, Jack Croxall, Carol Wyer, Clare Davidson, Angie Marsons, Sue Watson and Jaimie Admans: not only brilliant authors in their own right but hugely supportive of others. My Bookouture colleagues are all incredible, of course, unfailing and generous in their support of fellow authors – life would be a lot duller without the gang! I have to thank all the brilliant and dedicated book bloggers (there are so many of you but you know who you are!) and readers, and anyone else who has championed my work, reviewed it, shared it, or simply told me that they liked it. Every one of those actions is priceless. Some of you I am even proud to call friends now – and I'm looking at you in particular Kerry Ann Parsons and Steph Lawrence!

Finally I'd like to give a special mention to my agent, Madeleine Milburn, and the team at the Madeleine Milburn Literary, TV & Film Agency, who work so hard on my behalf.

Printed in Great Britain
by Amazon